THE CROSSING AT CYPRESS CREEK

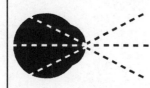

This Large Print Book carries the
Seal of Approval of N.A.V.H.

A NATCHEZ TRACE NOVEL

THE CROSSING AT CYPRESS CREEK

PAM HILLMAN

THORNDIKE PRESS
A part of Gale, a Cengage Company

Farmington Hills, Mich • San Francisco • New York • Waterville, Maine
Meriden, Conn • Mason, Ohio • Chicago

Copyright © 2019 by Pam Hillman.
Scripture quotations are taken or paraphrased from the *Holy Bible,* King James Version.
Thorndike Press, a part of Gale, a Cengage Company.

Thorndike Press® Large Print Christian Historical Fiction.
The text of this Large Print edition is unabridged.
Other aspects of the book may vary from the original edition.
Set in 16 pt. Plantin.

LIBRARY OF CONGRESS CIP DATA ON FILE.
CATALOGUING IN PUBLICATION FOR THIS BOOK
IS AVAILABLE FROM THE LIBRARY OF CONGRESS

ISBN-13: 978-1-4328-6867-3 (hardcover alk. paper)

Published in 2019 by arrangement with Tyndale House Publishers, Inc.

Printed in Mexico
1 2 3 4 5 6 7 23 22 21 20 19

The Crossing at Cypress Creek *is dedicated to my daughter-in-law, Savannah.*

When Savannah and my son were dating, Savannah became a certified nursing assistant (CNA) and worked at a nursing home. Let me tell you, she was amazing at her job, and all the residents as well as her coworkers loved her. It was obvious she'd found her calling in health care. It wasn't long until she decided to pursue her dream of becoming a nurse. And just as she'd excelled at being a CNA, she excels at nursing. She would have been right there with Alanah and Lydia saving the lives of everyone in Cypress Creek.

Savannah, I'm so proud to call you daughter-in-law.

CHAPTER 1

August 1792

Caleb O'Shea jerked awake to utter stillness.

Swinging his legs over the berth, he shook Reggie Caruthers. "Docked, we have."

Reggie's only response was a groan.

Caleb swept his palm across the younger man's brow and felt the heat that emanated from clammy skin. "Reggie, lad, did you hear?"

"O'Shea, is that you?" Caruthers stirred, his voice sounding weak and scratchy from disuse.

"Aye. We've docked."

"Where?"

Caleb frowned. The lad must be sicker than he'd thought. He'd told him twice already that the captain had said they were making land upriver from New Orleans at an inland port on the Mississippi River. "Natchez."

"Natchez?"

"Aye, that's the truth o' it. You're home, lad."

"I've got to get off this boat." Caruthers sat up, struggled to swing his legs over the edge of the cot. Even in the dim light cast from the open hatch, the landlubber looked like death warmed over. "Must . . . must see Bloomfield."

"You're no' in any shape t' go anywhere."

Caruthers stood, gripping the edge of the upper bunk. He reached for his jerkin, arms trembling as he tried to remain standing.

Caleb sat on his bunk, watching. The boy was nothing if not determined, but he'd proved that fact three months ago when he'd saved Caleb and half a dozen others after the British merchant ship they were serving on had capsized off the coast of Africa during a storm.

A clatter on the rung ladder caught Caleb's attention. Tiberius, the tall, broad-shouldered Moor who'd been one of those rescued, descended the ladder, a bowl of tepid broth in hand. Sweat glistened on the big man's ebony brow, and the early morning light from the open hatch glanced off the gold hoop in his left ear. "How goes he?"

8

"Out o' his head with the fever."

Caruthers lost his grip on the berth, then tipped sideways. Caleb caught the frail body before he slammed face-first into the berth on the opposite side. "Lad, why don't you lie down and take a bit o' broth? You need your strength if you do no' want the captain t' feed you t' the fishes."

Caruthers pushed him away, his pale-blue eyes blazing — from fever or fury 'twas hard to say. He jabbed a finger at the ladder. "I'm going topside, and I'm going to leave this ship if I have to crawl all the way to the wharf. Eight months at sea. Eight months of unlawful conscription when my family probably thinks I'm dead. I am going home." He enunciated each word carefully.

"Home? Why, you as much as told me your home is a week's travel north o' Natchez. You'll never make it."

"I'm going." Caruthers threw his jerkin, and Caleb caught it in midair. "Just get me off this ship. You owe me." His attention shifted from Caleb to Tiberius and back again. "You both do."

"Aye, that we do. We'll get you t' this Bloomfield. After that, you're on your own." Caleb's gaze met Tiberius's dark stare, and he jerked his chin toward the deck. "Find Duff. We're goin' ashore."

"Is the mortar to your liking, miss?"

Alanah Adams jerked her attention away from the marble mortar and pestle and focused on the apothecary.

Regretfully, she placed the mortar back on the shelf and picked up her basket, heavy with items she couldn't harvest from the deep, dark forests surrounding Cypress Creek. "Yes, very much, but alas, I haven't the means to purchase it."

Mr. Weaver hefted the leather pouch in his hands, his appraisal calculating, albeit in a fatherly manner. "I beg to differ. There's plenty of coin here. And you could use it, if you don't mind my saying so."

The temptation to take him up on the offer was almost more than she could stand, but Alanah shook her head. "No thank you, Mr. Weaver. The coins are needed elsewhere, I'm afraid."

"If you're sure . . ."

"Quite sure." Alanah held out her hand. "My payment, if you please."

"Of course."

The apothecary handed over the pouch, and Alanah tucked it safely away, then moved toward the door.

He followed. "Don't forget that I could use more cypress oil and bloodroot the next time you come to Natchez."

"You know bloodroot is hard to find."

"I'm depending on you, miss." Mr. Weaver spread his hands, indicating his shop filled with a mixture of medicinal cures. "If anyone can find it, I'm sure you can."

Alanah paused, her hand on the latch. "I'll do my best, but I don't know when I'll make it back to Natchez."

The trip had been fraught with danger. If her uncle found out she'd gone against his wishes in his absence, he'd be livid, but she'd needed more bottles and stoppers, muslin for bandages, as well as supplies to survive the coming months. And Mr. Weaver paid well for the herbs she delivered to his shop.

The door pushed open, and Lydia peered inside, a frown creasing her forehead. When she spotted the apothecary hovering nearby, the brown-skinned woman lowered her gaze, showing uncharacteristic deference. "We must go, mistress."

"Of course." Alanah turned to the apothecary and curtsied. "Good day, sir."

Outside the shop, Lydia jerked the basket from Alanah's arms, then glowered at her, all trace of the meek and obedient servant gone. "What took you so long? The morning's half-gone."

"I'm sorry, Lydia, but I had to wait on Mrs. Simson to open her shop for the muslin. You know how much she enjoys a bit of gossip over a cup of tea." Alanah stepped aside to allow a stevedore carrying an unwieldy trunk to pass.

"We'll be lucky if someone doesn't spirit away the horses." Lydia pushed ahead, her big-bodied frame making the way easier like the parting of the Red Sea. "And even luckier if your uncle hasn't returned."

"You didn't have to come with me." The glare Lydia tossed her way let Alanah know how the woman felt about allowing her to make the overnight journey alone. "And besides, I didn't have a choice."

Her uncle seemed to think they could live on the meager gleanings from the swamp, but some things couldn't be found in the wild. He'd been gone three weeks, preaching in every hamlet and hollow for miles around.

When they'd run out of salt five days ago, she knew she couldn't wait any longer to make the trip to Natchez. She and Lydia had hurried to Natchez as fast as they could. And they must make haste to return before he did. It wouldn't do for him to spot

12

the extra provisions she'd purchased to see them through the coming months.

Best to keep them stored in the root cellar, where he'd be none the wiser.

Alanah struggled to keep up as Lydia pushed her way through the crowded streets. To her left, a crowd had formed around an auction block as gentlemen farmers bid on the poor, unfortunate souls just off the ships. All around, the mass of humanity surged and buckled, some shackled and shuffling along, others scurrying about their business.

Shifty-eyed boys wove in and out of the crowd.

She kept her hand firmly on the money pouch, experience teaching her that the boys could filch her hard-earned coins with ease. After being bumped and pushed along the narrow thoroughfare, she had the sudden urge to get out of Natchez, to get back to the peace and quiet of the forest, to home. Home on the bluff above Cypress Creek wasn't much more than a dogtrot cabin and a barn, but it was theirs, hers and Lydia's, now that Betsy —

Suddenly Lydia sidestepped, and Alanah came face-to-face with three of the roughest-looking men she'd encountered in a long time, and she was no stranger to the vilest of sorts.

Of varying heights, the three clung together, the slight one in the middle slumped between his companions. An ebony-hued man with a gold hoop in one earlobe, tall and broad-shouldered enough to over-shadow even Lydia's statuesque height, supported the smaller man with ease.

Alanah wrinkled her nose. Drunk, if she didn't miss her guess.

And the sun had yet to climb past mid-morning.

She locked gazes with the third man. Dark, piercing midnight eyes rimmed with charcoal lashes captured and held hers. A quick glance at billowing shirtsleeves and worn breeches tucked into scuffed knee-high boots, along with a leather jerkin hanging loose at his trim waist, not to mention the red sash tied around his waist, matching those of his companions, led her to the conclusion that the men were fresh off one of the ships lining the wharf.

Much to her surprise, he shifted out of the way and waited for her to pass through the narrow space between the buildings and stacks of crates lining the cobblestone street.

The slight man centered between the two groaned, then buckled, his legs giving out. The black eyes flickered away as both he and the ebony giant struggled to hold their companion upright. A fourth man, duffels slung over his shoulders, stood behind the others. It was then that it dawned on Alanah the men were not drunk as she supposed, but that the frail young man was ill. From what, she could not tell. But the glazed look of his eyes spoke of fever.

Involuntarily, she made a motion toward the man, but Lydia stepped in front of her, blocking her view of the sick man and his companions. "Mistress Alanah, if you please?"

Reluctantly Alanah nodded. "Yes, of course."

As she passed by, the man with the dark eyes, square jaw, and windswept hair inclined his head ever so slightly, careful to acknowledge her presence without giving the unseemly appearance of accosting a lady. It was all she could do not to smile. Her finery was a ruse only worn as she flitted into Natchez and just as quickly quit the place for the dark, shadowy undergrowth of the cypress swamps.

Impulsively she reached into the basket over her arm and pulled out a pouch of ground magnolia bark. Pressing it into the man's hand, she whispered, "Steep for an hour. It will help the fever."

He clasped her hand, the pouch held fast between them, his dark gaze searching hers. "Bless you, lass."

Her stomach did a slow roll at the unexpected lilt of an Irish brogue.

Clutching the pouch, Caleb watched the golden goddess as she hurried away. What kind of woman paid attention to four pieces of flotsam adrift on the wharf?

He blinked, trying to pinpoint the exact color of the lass's eyes, but all he could think of was the majestic golden lion he'd come face-to-face with on the African savanna. The wide tawny eyes, the light-brown hair shot through with shades of red and gold reminiscent of the woman who'd paused long enough to feel compassion for Reggie's plight.

"Caleb?" Tiberius's heavily accented voice pulled him back to the task at hand.

"Sorry, mate." Caleb hoisted Reggie's limp form higher. "I was woolgathering."

"I should say so." The Moor's gaze shifted in the direction the women had gone. "A pity that we have been on board ship for three months and now we're honor bound to take this one on a fool's mission."

Caleb grunted, in full agreement with Tiberius.

"I heard that." Reggie roused, found his footing. "Go on with you all, then. Chase your skirts. I can find Bloomfield's office with my eyes closed."

"Your eyes *are* closed." Caleb chuckled. "But if you could be so kind as t' open them for a wee bit and point us in the right direction, we'd be much obliged."

Reggie squinted, then pointed toward the row of buildings tucked against the hillside. "It's around the bend there. James Bloomfield, Esquire. My father's lawyer."

They led Reggie in that direction. The boy had told them of how he'd come to Natchez to deliver a load of cotton for his father, of heading to an establishment called the Blue Heron, then waking up aboard ship, with no memory of how he'd gotten there.

It was a common enough tale, one that Caleb was all too familiar with himself. In his three and a half years crisscrossing the Atlantic, fighting in Africa, slashing his way through the jungles of South America, he'd been conscripted more than once. In the beginning, he'd embraced his lot with gusto, not caring whose flag he served under, which captain he answered to, nor even what kind of cargo the ship carried. If he signed on for a voyage willingly, he could jump ship whenever and however he pleased without fear of repercussion.

Until the next time he was hauled up the gangway with a knot on his head.

His was a hard life, with no guarantee he'd see the next sunrise, but it was better than working in the bowels of the earth back home in Ireland.

But young Caruthers's pining for his plantation home, his *mam* and *da,* and his younger brother had put a damper on Caleb's own wayfaring ways. To his shame, he hadn't thought much of his own brothers since he'd wiped the dust of Dublin off his boots.

Caleb pushed thoughts of his brothers to the back of his mind. Surely, after all this time they'd managed to better themselves and find their way in the world, or in Ireland at least. They weren't his responsibility. And he'd paid Caruthers back for saving his life. He'd gotten the lad to Natchez. He'd hand the landlubber off to the lawyer, then go back to living from day to day, port to port, going wherever the wind pushed him.

And maybe then the niggling sense of loss and guilt that bubbled up every time Caruthers spoke of hearth and home would go north with him and leave Caleb in peace.

Because there was no way he could go back home. Not after the things he'd done.

He scowled at the signs over the doorways. While he couldn't read worth spit, he could decipher a letter or two and could muddle his way through. And if all else failed, the type of clientele usually gave a strong indication of what kind of establishment he was entering.

But he'd never had need to find a lawyer's office. And Reggie wasn't much help. The lad was barely conscious.

A man staggered out of a nearby tavern and bumped into Caleb, too far gone to take offense or blame Caleb for his own clumsiness.

"Could you point us toward Bloomfield's?"

"That way, my good man." The drunk pointed. "Next to the Black Horse Inn."

Without further ado, he continued down the street. Caleb and Tiberius headed toward the inn, Duff following. Moments later, they passed the tavern. To the left was the burned-out shell of a warehouse, and to the right a small building tucked against the base of the cliff. A sign showed that the proprietor wore many hats, but the one that caught Caleb's eye was a pair of scales, the symbol of justice.

"Reggie, lad, we're here."

Caleb rapped on the door. A raspy voice

bade them enter.

An older, bald man with round spectacles glanced up as they entered, his eyebrows raised, assessing gaze going from one to the other in rapid succession. His attention ricocheted back to Reggie like shot from a cannon. Lunging to his feet, the portly gentleman rounded the desk.

"Young Master Caruthers. You've returned." He clasped Reggie by the shoulders, looking him up and down. "And not a minute too soon, from the looks of you."

Reggie gave the ghost of a smile. "Thank you, sir. Have you had news of my father? Is he well? My mother?"

Bloomfield's face clouded. "I'm afraid I have bad news. Please, won't you have a seat?"

A pall quickly descended over Reggie's homecoming as Bloomfield shared that both his father and his mother had passed from this life to another since he'd been gone. Reggie's shoulders slumped, and Bloomfield patted him awkwardly. "I'm sorry to be the bearer of such tidings, son. But, my dear boy, your parents would be pleased to know of your safe return."

"What of my brother? And the plantation?"

"Your brother is married and, with the

help of your uncle, running Caruthers Estates."

"Married? But Weston's hardly more than a child." Reggie struggled to his feet. "I must get home posthaste."

"You're in no shape to travel." The lawyer's shock mirrored Caleb's own thoughts on the matter. "Surely a few more days won't hurt."

"I've been away too long as it is. I must see how my father's holdings fare. I'll need horses, provisions. Could I impose on you to make the arrangements?"

"I cannot persuade you to delay?"

"No, you cannot."

"I see. In that case, I'll take care of everything." Bloomfield steepled his fingers. "And if you don't mind my saying so, you would be wise to join yourself to one of the parties heading north. The highwaymen are in fine form and any lone traveler is asking to have his head bashed in."

"Of course." Reggie winced. "I'm all too familiar with the tactics of the lawless sort without the benefit of friends to watch my back. That's how I woke up with a splitting headache in the hold of a ship eight months ago." His gaze swept over Caleb, then moved on to Tiberius and Duff in turn. "Will you accompany me? I'll make it worth

21

your while."

A week's worth of travel — make that two — would mean the ship would likely be gone by the time they returned. But none of them would even be alive if it hadn't been for Reggie. A landlubber he might be, but he'd risked his own life for theirs.

Caleb didn't hesitate. "You have me word. And no compensation will be necessary."

"Aye," Duff muttered from his spot by the door.

Tiberius didn't say a word, but he didn't have to. The four of them had formed a tight bond, odd as it seemed. They'd see Caruthers home, then make their way to the nearest port.

"Thank you." Reggie turned to the lawyer. "My apologies, Mr. Bloomfield. I should have introduced my companions. Without them, I would have expired these many weeks past. This mountain of a man is known simply as Tiberius. Not his given name, but none of us can wrap our tongues around his native dialect. The quiet one is Henry Duff, and the dark Irishman is Caleb O'Shea."

"My pleasure, gentlemen —" Bloomfield broke off mid-sentence, brow furrowed. "O'Shea? Would you be related to Connor and Quinn O'Shea?"

22

Caleb stilled. What did this man know of his brothers? The last he'd heard from Connor he'd been in the Carolinas, and Quinn and the little ones back home in Ireland.

"Aye. They're me brothers."

"Well, what do you know?" Bloomfield smiled. "Your brothers have settled in Natchez. Well, not here, exactly, but about a day's ride north along the trace."

"Me brothers are here? In Natchez?" Caleb swallowed. "All o' them?"

"Last I recall, there were four here in the colonies." Bloomfield smiled. "Are there more?"

"No. That is all." Caleb couldn't quite believe what he was hearing. He hadn't seen Connor in years, not since his eldest brother had left Ireland, his reputation in tatters. "But how?"

"It's a long story, but the governor granted your brother Connor a tract of land, and if that wasn't enough, the lucky fellow married a plantation owner's daughter. He lives on a plantation called Breeze Hill." Bloomfield laced his fingers across his chest, looking pleased with himself. "And he's partnered with Thomas and William Wainwright to start a logging enterprise floating logs down the river. As a matter of fact, Mr.

Wainwright tasked me with finding loggers to send to their logging camp. The caravan's leaving tomorrow. Perhaps you'd like to see your brothers while you're here?"

CHAPTER 2

"Lydia, are you ready?"

When Lydia didn't answer, Alanah turned from tightening the girth on her horse. Lydia stared into space, usually busy hands idle. And Lydia was never idle.

"Lydia?"

Guilty black eyes swept up to meet Alanah's before dropping to the task at hand. Quickly and efficiently, Lydia finished securing the last bundle on the packhorse. "Forgive me. I was daydreaming."

Alanah's lips twitched. Somber as the day was long, Lydia never indulged in such fancy. On occasion, though, when she heard a bit of African music or the beat of a Choctaw drum, Alanah caught her humming to the music that lay dormant in her breast.

"About what, pray tell?"

"Nothing, mistress." Lydia's mahogany skin flushed; then her broad lips flattened.

And suddenly she was back to the practical woman Alanah knew and loved. She jerked her head toward the north. "We must go if we're going to make it home in time to return Mr. Davies's horses before dark."

"I agree."

"Should we change clothes?"

Alanah shook her head. "No. It's best if no one knows that Addled Alanah and Looney Lydia made the trip to Natchez this day."

Muttering at the inconvenience of the layers and layers of petticoats she was obliged to wear while in Natchez, Alanah eventually managed to swing her leg over the saddle. A sidesaddle would have made her guise more believable, but Mr. Davies didn't own a sidesaddle, and she wouldn't know how to ride one if he did. Besides, once she was astride and her voluminous skirts arranged, one could hardly distinguish what kind of saddle was beneath the yards and yards of cloth.

Soon, they left Natchez behind, keeping off the main route. Riding single file, they traversed the narrow trails that only locals knew and used, avoiding the much more widely traveled Natchez Trace.

They didn't stop for the noon hour but continued on. Thankfully, they encountered

26

no one on the trail, not even the highway-men.

Alanah glanced over her shoulder at the packhorse. The small mountain of supplies might have to last for months. The fall months provided ample opportunity for forage, but she'd be hard-pressed to make another trip when her uncle returned home. She supposed it was too much to hope he remained on the preaching circuit until after the first frost.

Wincing, she glanced heavenward, silently asking God to forgive the thought as quickly as it formed. Her uncle might not be much of a provider, but he did care for her, and his presence would keep her safe from the riffraff that frequented Cypress Creek. If he'd been home when Micaiah Jones first came to Cypress Creek, things might have been different.

She swallowed, wishing she hadn't let her thoughts wander down the path that led to her sister's disappearance. Even her uncle's presence wouldn't have been any match against Micaiah and his band of river pirates.

Hours later, she breathed easier. Only a few more miles and they'd be home. They'd return the horses, store the supplies, and —

A faint yell brought her up short. As one,

she and Lydia pulled the horses to a halt. In the distance, she heard crashing, cracking limbs, followed by the thud of a massive tree slamming against the earth. Her mount shied at the sound, then stood quivering. She soothed the skittish animal with one hand even as the other reached for the bow slung over her back. "What was that?"

"Dead tree, perhaps?"

"Perhaps, but —" Alanah broke off as the sound of sawing reached them. "Listen. Someone's clearing land."

Lydia's eyes widened as a second shudder shook the ground. "More than one someone. No one man fells another tree that quickly."

Alanah dismounted, and Lydia shot her a glance. "What are you doing?"

"There's no creek here. No stream. Why would anyone build a cabin here?"

Lydia joined Alanah, and they crept forward, their attention on the sound of sawing. A third tree fell, then a fourth before they ended up prone atop a ridge overlooking the wagon road that snaked through the woods.

Three, four — no, six crews of men were strung out, each sawing a massive tree.

She watched as one after another, the trees toppled, each crash thundering through the quiet woods. The sawyers moved on, deeper into the forest, while more men led teams of horses forward, hitched the logs with massive hooks, and pulled them out of the way.

"It is true, then."

Alanah glanced at Lydia. "What's true?"

"Men — wealthy men — are cutting a path from the trace to the Mississippi River. There, they will cut more trees and float them downriver to Natchez to build bigger and bigger houses for other men who have more coin than they know what to do with." The scorn in Lydia's voice showed how she felt about such extravagances.

A knot clenched in Alanah's stomach as she eyed the freshly cut swath that widened the faint trail along the ridge toward home. "That means they'll come to Cypress Creek."

"Perhaps." Lydia's gaze met hers, the black depths filled with concern.

Darkness had fallen by the time Alanah and Lydia reached home. Thankfully, nothing had been disturbed, except that the goats ran amok. They'd managed to break through the wattle fencing — the third time in less than a week.

Working quickly, they unloaded the packs

and stored most of their supplies in the root cellar dug out of the hillside, where the outlaws who dotted the hills and hollows around Cypress Creek wouldn't find them. Not that Alanah really expected anyone to steal their food — they were too frightened of the two crazy healers to do that — but she didn't want to take the risk of storing everything in the cabin.

While Lydia rounded up the goats, Alanah shucked out of the fancy dress she'd worn to Natchez. Every time she wore the dress, she wondered about the woman it had belonged to. She ran her hand over the soft, satiny material, remembering the day Micaiah Jones and his men had landed at the dock, flush with their latest haul on the river.

She and her sister had stood by in rags, watching from behind the safety of a grove of trees overlooking the landing. Lydia had shooed them back up the path toward home, but not before Alanah had seen the pirates toss a trunk to the shore, where it burst open revealing a treasure trove of women's clothing.

The dresses had lain there in the dust and dirt until nightfall, the highwaymen, cutthroats, and river rats who spent their ill-gotten gain in the tavern not caring one whit about a few women's fripperies.

Alanah and Betsy had scuttled down to the docks after dark and scooped up the pretty clothes, stuffed them in the trunk, and lugged it all back to the cabin.

And that's when the trouble started.

Oh, not that very day, but later, the day Micaiah had seen Betsy in her finery.

Stomach churning as it always did when she thought of Betsy, Alanah thrust the dress in the trunk and slammed the lid. Then she donned her ragged brown dress and dug her fingers in the cold ashes heaped on the side of the fireplace, Betsy's plight all the more reason to keep up the guise Uncle Jude insisted on.

A rap at the door had her scrambling to finish transforming herself from a proper lady to a slightly deranged healer. Quickly she dumped the last of the ashes on her head, then took both hands and plunged them through her hair.

Ashes rained down all around her.

Satisfied that her unruly locks and soot-stained face would scare even the hardiest highwayman away, she flung open the door. The saddler's boy stood a few feet shy of the porch. "You've come for your father's horses?"

The boy shook his head and backed away,

his dirt-encrusted face no mask for the fear that rounded his eyes. Alanah softened her tone. "What is it, Billy? Speak up now."

"Papa sent me for Looney Lydia. There's . . . there's been a . . . a knifing at . . . at the tavern. There's a lot of blood."

A knifing? Blood? Alanah's head started buzzing. Turning off thoughts of the injury itself, she started making a mental list of all the supplies they'd need. Moss. Catgut. Bandages. And Lydia could use the new suturing needles they'd gotten from Mr. Weaver just today. Something for pain and fever.

Billy was still standing there, waiting. She waved him away. "Tell your father we'll be there directly. And take the horses with you."

The boy sidled to where the horses were ground-hitched next to the barn, took the reins, and led them away, giving Alanah and the cabin a wide berth. Alanah chuckled. She hadn't meant to frighten the child, but her disguise and unhinged behavior were the only things that kept her alive in a burg as dark and evil as Cypress Creek.

Alanah stepped to the edge of the porch. "Lydia —"

"I heard."

Hurriedly, they packed their supplies and

took the moonlit path along the ridge to the settlement. If it could be called that. There wasn't much in Cypress Creek that could be called a permanent dwelling of any kind, except the tavern. And the men who frequented the shacks and shanties along the waterfront weren't looking for permanence.

As they neared the tavern, they spotted the injured man sprawled on his back in a ditch. Even in the faint light, Alanah could see the sheen of greasy, worn buckskins, matted hair, and a long, scraggly beard. The prone form looked like any number of river pirates and riffraff that paraded through Cypress Creek day in and day out. Mr. Davies knelt beside him, Billy hovering close to the stable.

Lydia crouched down, examining the man. "He's bleeding bad."

Stomach churning at her first glimpse of a knifing, Alanah concentrated on Mr. Davies. "Do you know him?"

"No. But I didn't figure he needed to die just because nobody cared enough to see that he lived."

"You have a compassionate heart, sir."

He chuckled. "As do you. In spite of this ridiculous disguise you insist on wearing."

"You know why I look like I do." Alanah spoke softly, lest others were near.

"Aye. That I do, missy. That I do." He motioned to the stranger. "Billy, help us get this feller to the stables —"

"The stables?" Alanah asked. "Isn't there somewhere else better suited?"

"Perhaps. But I don't dare take him into my own home. He's liable to slit my throat and the wife and kids' as well." He wagged his finger under her nose. "Same with you and Lydia. Without your uncle around, you don't need the likes of this one up at your place either. If he has friends, they'll find him in the stable by and by."

Alanah knew he spoke the truth, so she didn't argue. The four of them hauled the man to the stables and laid him on a makeshift table. By the feeble light of a half-dozen candles and Mr. Davies's single lantern, Lydia went to work on the unconscious man, washing away the blood. Alanah leaned in, determined to learn everything she needed to know about taking care of injuries.

Alanah blinked as the red swam before her. The jagged edges of flesh came into focus, then blurred again.

So much blood.

"Sutures." Lydia's voice seemed to come from far away.

Alanah shook her head to clear it.

34

"Yes, of course." She rummaged through the pack, her fingers closing on the carefully hoarded box of curved needles. She selected one, threaded it, and handed it over.

Her mentor nodded at the patient. "Hold him."

Anxious to please Lydia, Alanah reached out and pressed the slick flesh together. Suddenly it was all she could do to keep her hands in place, and she couldn't bear to watch. She drew in a breath and locked gazes with a curious horse peering over the stall gate. But the animal did little to engage her attention. Desperate to take her mind off what was going on at her fingertips, she focused on Mr. Davies, standing close with the lantern held high. "We saw the loggers today," she blurted out.

He threw her a sharp glance. "Where?"

"Along Gridley Ridge, about five miles to the east."

"Well, I'll be. I heard they were cutting a path through the woods but didn't believe it." He shook his head. "It's gonna spell trouble."

Lydia kept silent, but her dark eyes flickered toward Alanah, the frown between her brows clearly telling Alanah that she agreed with him.

"The river pirates?"

"No. They went north. No one's seen them since —" Mr. Davies broke off, and an awkward silence filled the void.

"Since they took Betsy."

"Yes, miss." He cleared his throat. "There's been talk. People are afraid that an open road will bring more travelers this way, more purses for the river pirates to steal. And many are afraid they'll come back."

If Micaiah came back, would he bring — ?

"Alanah, pay attention." Lydia covered Alanah's hands with her own, pressed the flaps of skin together.

"Yes, Lydia. Sorry."

Without the distraction of the conversation, all she could think about was how Lydia's needle tugged against the man's flesh. She could feel the jerk and tug —

In. Out. In. Out. A tug. A pull.

Her breathing grew shallow. What was wrong with her? Spots flashed before her eyes, and with horror, she realized that if Lydia didn't hurry up, she was going to pass out right there in the middle of the stable, shaming them both.

In. Out. In. Out. A tug. A pull.

"There. It is finished."

Alanah dropped her hands, moved away without looking at the injured man. She felt clammy all over. She collapsed on the hard-packed dirt, leaned against the rough wall, the satchel next to her. She took a deep breath, wiped the needle with shaking hands, and carefully packed it away. Then she rummaged through the pack, hoping Lydia didn't notice how long it took her to organize the contents of the bag.

"Alanah, what do you recommend we give our patient for pain?"

Finally something she could manage without fainting. "Magnolia bark tea."

Lydia nodded, looking pleased. "Very well."

They'd just spooned the last of the warm tea down their patient when a commotion at the wharf drew Mr. Davies outside.

"Alanah —" he turned back, his face ghostly pale in the flickering candlelight — "it looks like Micaiah's men. They've returned."

Alanah surged to her feet and moved toward the barn door on unsteady legs. She hardly dared to hope . . . "Is Betsy with them?"

"I — I can't tell from here —"

Alanah heard no more as she lifted her skirts and ran toward the dock.

Her heart hitched as she spotted a slight figure huddled on the flatboat. There was no mistaking her sister's riot of golden-brown hair splayed against the rough timbers of the boat.

She came to a halt, searching for Micaiah. When she didn't see him, her attention settled on his cousin Elias. She forced words out of a mouth as dry as cotton. "I've come for my sister."

Elias's gaze raked over her, but he stepped back and waved her forward. "Take her."

Before she lost her nerve, Alanah clambered aboard. With blood on her hands, soot on her face, and wearing little more than rags, she looked like the crazy woman the river pirates believed her to be, and they parted ranks for her.

Quaking with fear, she hauled her sister off the flatboat.

When she'd put some distance between them and the gawking cutthroats, she hugged her sister, then held her at arm's length and ran her gaze over her frame — thinner than when she'd left — bone thin, as a matter of fact. But there was more. Betsy wouldn't look at her. "Are you all right?"

Her sister didn't respond.

Alanah tipped Betsy's chin, and fear roiled in her stomach. It wasn't the filthy, tattered shift she wore, and it wasn't her bare feet, or even that her hair hung tangled and matted down her back. It was her eyes. Flat, lifeless. She looked —

Alanah shook her head, refusing to dwell on whatever had happened to her sister in the last six months. Betsy was alive. Micaiah Jones could have killed her. But for whatever reason, he hadn't, and she'd come home. That was all that mattered. For now.

"Come. Let's go home."

"But — Micaiah." Betsy's panicked gaze whipped around. "Where's Micaiah?"

"I don't know. Let's get you home."

"No. I can't leave Micaiah."

Alanah gaped at her. "Betsy, Micaiah kidnapped you. He stole you away. Look at yourself. You're skin and bones. He —"

"No." Betsy jerked away. "I want Micaiah."

Alanah's heart squeezed into a tight, fear-filled ball. "Betsy . . ."

"Betsy, sugar, give Lydia a hug." Lydia pushed in front of Alanah, who stood frozen in shocked silence as Lydia gathered the frail form in her strong embrace.

Quietly and efficiently, Lydia calmed Betsy.

Gripping the hilt of the knife at her waist, Alanah faced Elias Jones. "Where's Micaiah?"

"French Camp." Elias looked her up and down, more bold than the rest. Behind her, Lydia shook the small gourd at her waist, and Elias's gaze darted toward her. The gourd meant nothing, but the pirate blinked, the ominous sound doing its job of instilling fear into the man. "He knifed a man and is to stand trial for murder."

"No!" Betsy's wail curdled Alanah's blood.

Lydia shushed her and turned to lead her away.

"She's been like that the whole way. Silent as a tomb for the most part, then screaming like a banshee the rest. Glad to be rid of her."

"Yet you brought her all the way from French Camp?"

"Aye. We brung her. And nary a one of us touched her." Elias spat a stream of tobacco juice that splattered into the dirt. "Micaiah would have our heads if we did. She's his woman."

As good as dead, Micaiah Jones still held sway over this lawless cutthroat.

CHAPTER 3

Before dawn, the Wainwright caravan was ready to go, and Reggie was determined that they not be left behind.

Caleb helped Reggie into his saddle, and the young plantation owner clung to the saddle horn with the same tenacity he'd clung to Caleb when the wind-whipped waves had threatened to tear their small boat apart off the coast of Africa.

"Should I tie you t' your mount, lad?"

"You might have to before the day is out."

"Aye." Caleb arched a brow. "It seems likely."

Arms folded, Tiberius glared at his own mount. "I will walk."

Scowling, Caleb looked from one to the other. "A wagon would make more sense for the lot o' us."

"Wagons are for women and children." Reggie adjusted his seat and grinned. "Climb aboard, Tiberius. I've never known you to back away from anything."

Tiberius approached the horse as if he were stalking a tiger. Caleb held the horse's head until the tall, muscular Moor climbed aboard, his ascent similar to scaling the rigging on a ship, but not nearly as graceful. Caleb tried not to laugh since he didn't relish the thought of Tiberius kicking him in the teeth. Adjusting the leathers, he grabbed the big man's boots and shoved them into the stirrups. Tiberius grabbed the horn in a death grip.

Caleb pried one of his ham-like hands loose and pressed the reins into his grasp. "It's like riding the rigging. Just keep your feet in the stirrups and hang on."

Hours later, Caleb grimaced and shifted in the saddle, the old wound in his thigh cramping. He rubbed the gnarl of scars, trying to ease the pain.

He'd made sport of Tiberius, but the truth was he'd only ridden a horse a few times himself. Even as he squirmed in the saddle, an older, distinguished man rode from the head of the caravan.

He turned his mount and fell into place beside them, his gaze landing first on Reggie, Tiberius, then Caleb. "Caleb O'Shea?"

Caleb nodded. "Aye."

"Thomas Wainwright. I own land north

and west of Breeze Hill."

"My brother's plantation?" Even speaking the words twisted Caleb's insides up. He could hardly fathom Connor owning a plantation. Surely everyone was mistaken, and either this Connor O'Shea was someone else entirely or the plot of land was so insignificant it wouldn't feed a pig in a poke, and the whole thing was Bloomfield's and now Wainwright's idea of some kind of cruel joke.

But they'd mentioned Quinn and the boys.

Nobody in the colonies would know that much about him and his brothers, unless they were telling the truth.

"Well, actually, Breeze Hill belongs to Connor's father-in-law, and my grandson will inherit it. Connor is simply managing the place for the foreseeable future."

Ah. The truth comes out. An O'Shea who'd risen in the ranks of the landed gentry would have been laughable. Connor was no more a landowner than —

"However, Breeze Hill is just a drop in the bucket to the much larger tract of land called Magnolia Glen, the plantation the governor granted to your brother. An amazingly fertile valley in the wilds beyond Breeze Hill. Your brother Quinn has taken over management and is doing a splendid job of it. Too late for much of a cotton crop this year, but next year should yield a bountiful harvest."

Caleb's head was spinning. So it was true. Still, he'd have to see it to believe it.

As the horses plodded along, Wainwright peppered him with questions about his travels. "So you've been to Africa, have you?"

"Aye, I have."

"Fascinating." Wainwright's attention strayed to the dark forests around them, to the swamp, then the bluff high above their heads on the right. "Was it very different to Ireland and to what you see here, then?"

"Some. The trees and undergrowth are different. Snakes this big." Caleb cupped his hands in a circle, then patted the scimitar strapped to his waist. "I learned t' keep a weapon handy. Good for snakes, both the slithering kind and the two-legged ones."

"Impressive." Wainwright eyed the deadly blade, the twin pistols tucked securely in his waistband, close at hand. "You'd do well to keep your weapons at the ready here as well. Highwaymen lie in wait for those who've sold their wares in Natchez and New Orleans."

"Bloomfield said as much."

"Earlier this year when their leader was

killed, the rudderless cutthroats disbanded, and we thought we'd eradicated them. But the attacks have become more frequent and even more savage in the last few weeks as travel along the trace has resumed."

"Then why no' chase them down, attack, and get rid o' them?"

"Things are never as simple as they appear." Wainwright motioned toward the head of the caravan. "My wife and daughters are in the carriage up ahead. Sometimes protecting what you have and those you love is the better choice than chasing off after a villain."

"And sometimes hiring others t' do the task is the solution."

He'd battled alongside Tiberius and his countrymen, fighting off marauding bands of Arabs and Turks whose sole purpose was in stealing, killing, and raping the country and its inhabitants.

At first Caleb had relished his role as protector, savior, and soldier of fortune, but eventually he'd had enough of the horrors of war and returned to the sea. At least at sea, men butchered men, not women and children.

But even there, he'd had his bellyful of unscrupulous captains, slave ships, and pirates, all trying to outdo, outlast, and outlive the next man.

He'd left Ireland to escape poverty, to escape oppression, but he had escaped nothing. He'd run straight into more of the same everywhere he turned: in Africa, in the Atlantic and the Arabian Sea, and now it seemed in the wilderness surrounding Natchez.

No matter the land, the evil in the hearts of men was the same.

"Yes, sometimes taking the fight to the enemy is the only solution." Wainwright rode along without saying anything more for another hour before motioning to the road ahead. "We'll be at Mount Locust soon. There's a road that leads to a small settlement on the river. We'll save time going that way, then cutting across to the logging camp."

"We are no' going to the plantation?"

"Not if you want to see your brothers. Unless I miss my guess, Connor and my son, William, are hard at work cutting a swath through the woods toward the river."

"I see."

"We'll need to look lively when we separate from the main party. We'll be considerably less in number and an easier target for attack."

They approached the cutoff, and the lead

buckboard carrying Mr. Wainwright's family pulled out of line. Four wagons loaded with supplies for the logging camp fell in behind the first. The indentured servants and freemen Bloomfield had secured for the logging operation rode the string of draft horses trailing the caravan.

Caleb itched to see the grand plantation his brother had married into, but more importantly, he wanted to see Connor, Rory, and Patrick.

As for Quinn? He'd just as soon take another tack around the Horn of Africa before seeing that one.

But first, it was time to say good-bye to Reggie and Duff.

The four friends pulled to the side and let the rest of the travelers pass them by. Reggie, looking like death warmed over, rode close and clasped Caleb's hand. "Godspeed, Caleb."

Caleb scowled. "You should have stayed in Natchez, lad. Or at the very least stay here until you gain your strength back."

A sad smile lifted Reggie's lips and he shook his head. "I could no more stay in Natchez knowing what I know about my family than you could fail to travel north with me after finding out your brothers are within a few hours of where we are right now. Besides, Duff will see that I make it home all right."

Caleb cleared his throat and turned to Duff. "Watch over the young whelp, will ya?"

Duff just grunted, which was his nature.

"Don't worry so, Caleb. We'll be with the party the entire way, and there are inns every fifteen to twenty miles. We'll be fine."

With nothing more to say, the four of them parted ways.

Caleb and Tiberius followed along behind the logging crew, both lost in their own thoughts. Tiberius shifted in the saddle. "How long will you stay?"

"Here with my brothers?" Caleb shrugged. "I don't know."

"It's good that you've found your family again."

Caleb sighed. He'd kept little from Tiberius and the others, but he hadn't told them of the bitter feelings he'd left behind in Ireland. The shock of discovering his brothers were here in the flesh had yet to wear off, and he was unsure of his welcome.

But he'd see Connor, try to make amends. As much as he was able.

Keeping low to the ground, Alanah crept forward.

She'd spotted the highwaymen as they flitted through the trees like ghosts. But they weren't apparitions; they were flesh-and-blood men, hot on the trail of those who risked their lives traveling the wilderness roads.

She knew what these men were up to. She knew what they were after, and it wasn't wild game to fill their empty bellies, but coin to fill their pockets and their lustful hearts. They stalked human prey on the trail a stone's throw from where she lay.

Pulling her tattered garments around her, she burrowed into the dirt and leaves, her brown skirt blending in with the debris-strewn forest floor. Digging her fingers into the dark, loamy earth, she smeared handfuls over her face and hair for good measure.

Within minutes, the cutthroats would attack. Blood would flow, women would scream, and men would shout obscenities. When it was over, some would be dead, and others would be dying.

She couldn't just let them be killed in cold blood.

When the stalkers melted into the shadows, she rose from her hiding place. Circling around, she eased along the ridge overlooking the trail, hoping to spot the travelers first. Soon, she heard the jingling of harnesses, the creak of wagon wheels, the steady *plop, plop, plop* of horses' hooves along the wilderness road less than a hundred paces away.

It was a small party, which wasn't surprising. What they were doing on the road to Cypress Creek was anyone's guess. Rarely did travelers come this way. Maybe they'd taken the wrong road instead of continuing north on the main trail. But for whatever reason, they'd put their lives at risk.

Heart thudding, she fell to one knee, reached for an arrow, and in one smooth motion, nocked it. She pulled back on the bow, found her target, let her breath out slowly, then released the arrow.

The missile shot between the trees, its whine swift and true, to embed itself in the side of the foremost wagon with a thwack.

The driver looked down, remained frozen for a moment; then realization dawned. He sawed back on the reins of the horses. "Fall back! We're under attack."

An unholy screech erupted from the vile highwaymen as they realized their surprise ambush had been foiled. En masse, they erupted from their hiding places along the trail and rushed toward the innocent party of travelers, intent on salvaging what they could of their plot to plunder and kill.

Fear spread through Alanah's chest as she crouched in the shadows.

Dear heavenly Father, let my warning be enough.

Shouts from ahead galvanized Caleb into action. But instead of reining away from danger, he plunged forward, Tiberius close behind.

As he raced his mount toward the head of the line, he dodged wagons attempting to turn on the narrow roadbed. Riderless horses milled about, braying in fear. Men dove for cover, and more than one ran in the opposite direction.

Only a few were armed and able to return fire. Mr. Wainwright urged his mount to-ward the head of the column, where his driver fought to hold back the horses on the narrow road. But his way was impeded by the chaos.

"Out of the way, you fools! My wife and daughters! They're in that carriage." Mr. Wainwright's horse reared, unseating him.

His horse raced away, and the man plunged into the melee, making more prog-ress on foot than mounted. Caleb looked at the carnage around him, hearing the screams as from a distance, the shouts as men scrambled beneath wagons seeking shelter from the shots fired from the bluffs overhead.

The normally docile draft horses broke free and raced down the trail, while those hitched to the wagons reared and screamed in fright.

"Enough o' this." Growling low in his throat, Caleb kicked his mount toward a swag in the high bank. The animal made it halfway up the incline before losing its footing on the loamy soil. But it was enough. Caleb kicked free, grabbed an exposed root, and scrambled up the bank like a cabin boy heading to the crow's nest.

"Caleb." His name was a whisper on the wind.

He glanced back, saw Tiberius clambering up behind him, hand outstretched. Clasping the man's huge paw, he grunted as he pulled his friend to the top of the bank.

Then the two of them crouched and moved forward. If there was one thing they were both good at, it was taking the fight to the enemy.

Alanah spotted movement and remained completely still, only allowing her eyes to follow the big black man as he crept along the bluff.

A head taller than most, a wicked-looking

curved blade in his right hand, and a dagger clenched between his teeth, he looked ferocious enough to send the most hardened criminal fleeing.

Even so, his size didn't stop him from moving through the wilderness as if he was born to it. His clothes weren't those of a backwoodsman or those of a slave. They were —

A glint in his left ear caught her attention, and she was immediately transported back to Natchez Under-the-Hill, to three men, one massive and ebony-skinned, one barely conscious, and one with piercing dark eyes, black brows, and a day-old scruff that did little to disguise a hard, chiseled square jaw. The sailors from Natchez.

Her heart pounded. If the giant of a man was one of the highwaymen, where were his companions?

She remained still, aware that the slightest movement might draw his attention.

As he disappeared over the ridge toward the rest of the highwaymen, she eased out of her hiding place. She needed to leave, to flee, before she was caught. Even the stigma of being known as Addled Alanah wouldn't save her if she was suspected of alerting the travelers to the danger they were in.

With one last glance over her shoulder,

she pulled her rags over her head and turned away. And that's when her gaze collided with *his*.

She froze, eyes locked. Even with the rest of him hidden by the underbrush, his hat pulled low, there was no question it was the man from the wharf.

Neither moved, neither blinked, and it seemed as if an ocean separated them, or simply a summer's breeze. The clash of fighting below — men yelling, horses screaming, highwaymen screeching as they attacked the travelers — faded into the background.

But those dark eyes never left hers. They narrowed slightly as if he was trying to place her.

She couldn't be caught. Not here. Not now.

A warlike roar unlike any she'd ever heard echoed through the forest, followed by a scream of rage. When the Irishman jerked his attention toward the sound, Alanah ducked out of sight.

CHAPTER 4

She was gone.

Caleb had shifted his attention away for a second, but that was all the time it took for her to disappear.

How could he even be sure the fleeting image had been a woman? Aye, he was sure. There was no question those eyes belonged to a woman. And they were the same golden-tawny eyes of the woman he'd seen at the wharf. But how could that be? That woman had been dressed in finery, her honeyed hair upswept. This one blended with the forest, all tan and brown and russet . . .

He blinked. All he'd seen had been wide eyes, the color of gold.

Perhaps she'd been with the travelers and, in a panic, had run into the woods to hide until the fighting was over. Yes, that had to be it.

Besides, now wasn't the time to worry

over her.

More shouts, then a rustling in the brush had him crouching, watching, listening. He spotted shadowy forms flitting through the forest away from the attack. Soon the wilderness swallowed them up as they fled, their surprise attack thwarted by the counterattack launched by Tiberius.

Silence reigned, broken only by the groans of the wounded on the blood-soaked roadbed.

He whistled, received an answering warble, and seconds later, Tiberius joined him.

"They're gone?" Caleb asked.

"They are gone." Tiberius crouched down. "I will keep watch should they decide to return."

Nodding, Caleb made his way back toward the roadbed. He joined Mr. Wainwright where one of the drivers attended him. "Are ya all right, sir?"

Mr. Wainwright waved him away. "I'm fine. Just a scratch. What happened to you? One minute you were here; the next you were gone."

Caleb jerked his head toward the bluffs. "We decided t' take the fight t' them."

"Well, it certainly worked. I've never known them to give up so easily."

"This happens regularly?" Caleb scowled.

"And the people just cower down and wait to be slaughtered?"

"What else can we do? Most of these men have families, responsibilities, and plantations to watch over." Without further ado, Wainwright batted the man's hands away and struggled to his feet. "No more. I must find my wife and daughters."

"Mr. Wainwright?"

The man glared at him, impatient to be on his way.

"I saw a woman in the woods. Perhaps one o' your daughters left the carriage."

Hope lit the man's features. "What did she look like? Fair? Blonde, blue eyes?"

Caleb shook his head. "The woman I saw did no' have blue eyes —"

"Then it was not my daughter. Gather the wounded and keep moving. We must make it to the logging camp before nightfall." He turned away. "Where's my horse?"

"Here, sir."

With some effort, Wainwright mounted and reined away, followed by half a dozen others. Caleb watched them go. He wasn't a praying man, but he prayed they'd find the man's family safe and sound, none the worse for wear.

By the time they rounded up the horses and

assessed the damage, it was far worse than originally thought. More than half the party had injuries and two men had been killed.

They made room in the wagons for the injured, loaded the dead onto the backs of the draft animals, and made haste to be on their way. Caleb didn't see the woman with golden eyes among the travelers. Maybe she was Wainwright's daughter after all. Maybe the lighting had played a trick on him.

Caleb and Tiberius rode at the end of the column, keeping a wary eye out. If they were attacked again, it would be a repeat of before, and they'd show the cutthroats who they were dealing with.

After a couple of miles, a ripple of good cheer came down the line. They'd located the Wainwright carriage. The women were unharmed, but unfortunately the driver had been injured in the melee and had been unable to hold the horses in check.

As they neared Wainwright's carriage, a middle-aged woman stepped out. With wispy blonde hair, pale skin, and blue eyes, she looked nothing like the woman he'd seen in the woods.

Two young girls, spitting images of their mother, leaned out of the carriage.

The woman he'd seen in the woods was definitely not one of Wainwright's daughters, and there were no other women in their party.

Then who was she?

The day was far gone when the logging camp, nestled in a wide-open meadow, came into view.

Caleb shifted in the saddle, his unease having little to do with being unused to riding. Any minute now, he'd see his brothers. Brothers he'd abandoned. He hadn't thought of it as abandonment when he'd left home. He hadn't thought of much of anything in his rage toward Quinn.

Later, after he'd cooled off, he'd planned to send money to help with caring for Rory and Patrick. But none of his labors had allowed for extra to send home. And he doubted the coin would have arrived if he had sent it.

The wagons rolled to a halt in front of a tent. A fair-haired man stepped outside, a smile wreathing his face when he spotted Mr. Wainwright. "Father, Mother, I wasn't expecting you."

"We were headed home from Natchez, so I took this opportunity to come see how things are progressing." Mr. Wainwright helped his wife and daughters to the ground. "Your mother was not happy about it after we were attacked —"

"Attacked?" The welcome on the younger Wainwright's face quickly turned to dismay. "Mother, are you and the girls all right?"

"Yes, dear, we're fine. A bit shook up. Your father twisted his knee —"

"It's nothing." The elder Wainwright waved away his wife's concern and limped toward the wagons. "These men need care immediately."

"Of course." His son motioned toward the tent. "Take them inside."

Caleb, Tiberius, and the other able-bodied men helped get the injured settled. Mrs. Wainwright and her daughters took on the task of tending them.

Mr. Wainwright's son frowned at the blanket-draped bodies of the dead. "These poor souls. Just off the boat good and proper, looking for a new life in a new land, only to meet an untimely death at the hands of a lawless bunch of cutthroats. It's a miracle the entire party wasn't slaughtered."

"Indeed. We have Caleb here and his friend Tiberius to thank for that." Mr. Wainwright motioned toward Caleb. "William, I'd like you to meet Caleb O'Shea. Connor's brother."

A look of surprise brightened the younger man's countenance. "Well, this is a pleasant development. I can't wait to see Connor's face when he realizes that the last of his brothers is here in the Natchez District." He pointed across the encampment. "As a matter of fact, here he comes now."

Caleb turned. On the far side of the camp, he spotted his brother heading toward them. Even after nine years, Caleb had no trouble recognizing his brother's tall, broad-shouldered stance. Whether Connor would recognize him was a different matter altogether. He'd been little more than a stripling when Connor left Ireland.

As he drew closer, Caleb found himself looking at the spitting image of his *da*. Instantly he was transported back to Ireland, back to the hovel he'd shared with *Da* and *Mam* and his brothers. Back when times were good, and *Da* would come home from the mines, grab him up, toss him in the air, and catch him even as Quinn danced around begging for his turn. Back before his father was injured, before Connor had been shipped off to the colonies. Before *Mam* had died birthing Patrick and then *Da* had passed on, leaving his sons to eke out a living in the coal mines.

Connor's steps faltered when his gaze landed on Caleb, but then he headed toward him. Caleb couldn't move. His feet were rooted to the ground, and something akin to fear rolled in his stomach.

Would his big brother accept him back into the fold? He'd abandoned them all. No matter that he'd had a good reason, that he'd planned to make his fortune, to send money back. All his dreams had gone up in smoke on the battlefields of Africa, had drowned in the roiling seas on both sides of the continent. He'd had enough trouble keeping body and soul together, let alone finding time, money, or energy to help his brothers.

Connor drew close enough that Caleb could see his eyes, green and so like *Da*'s that tears stung the backs of Caleb's eyes. He gritted his teeth and blinked them back. He'd fought off cannibals and pirates. He'd stormed Arabian strongholds. He wouldn't show weakness just because Connor reminded him of his *da,* with his furrowed brow and jaw clenched tight much like *Da*'s when he'd been angry.

Caleb braced for his brother's fist. He'd stand and take it like a man. He deserved it. He deserved a beating for leaving the others. He deserved —

Connor reached him, grabbed him by the shoulders, then pulled him close in a tight embrace.

"Caleb." His brother's voice trembled. "After all these years. I feared I'd never see ya again."

Caleb was relieved when the task of seeing to the dead and wounded kept Connor from asking too many questions.

But after they'd buried the dead, he found himself walking back toward camp beside his brother and the Wainwrights.

Connor glanced at Mr. Wainwright. "How do things fare in Natchez, sir?"

"They're going well. I've secured property along the river just past Natchez Under-the-Hill for the sawmill, and more than one contractor has expressed interest in purchasing every foot of lumber we can produce. Their appetite for quality building materials is insatiable."

"That's all well and good, but —" Connor scowled at the tent where the injured were — "we're almost t' the river and we're still shorthanded. I do no' know how we're going to meet the demand."

"I have faith in you, Connor." Mr. Wainwright slapped him on the shoulder. "I'd better go help Mrs. Wainwright. She's got her hands full."

William glanced at Caleb. "After you and Connor have a chance to catch up, come over and make your mark in the ledger. And bring Tiberius, too. We're glad to have two strong backs to make the work lighter."

"I'm no' sure —"

"William, I might need your assistance."

"Yes, Father."

When they were alone, Connor smiled. "It really is good t' see you, Brother. It's been a long time."

"Too long." Caleb glanced around. "Where's Quinn, Rory, and Patrick?"

"Rory's here somewhere. Patrick's back at Breeze Hill with me wife, Isabella, and Quinn and his wife, Kiera, are at Magnolia Glen."

Caleb shook his head. "Hard t' believe the two o' you are married men."

"Aye . . ." Connor swung his arm around Caleb's shoulders again. "You could no' have come at a better time."

"How so?"

Connor looked surprised. "The logging, o' course. I can use every man I can get my hands on."

"I do no' know a thing about logging."

"No' to worry. You're strong, and you'll learn. And that Tiberius." Shaking his head, Connor pointed across the camp toward a man who rivaled Tiberius in stature. "That's Moses. He's a sawyer, and I have yet t' find the man who can match him for strength and stamina. Do you know if your man has ever wielded a crosscut saw?"

"Tiberius is no' my man." Caleb crossed his arms. "He's my friend, and he's free t' come and go as he pleases."

"Pardon. I meant no offense."

"None taken. And as far as I know, Tiberius has never used a crosscut saw, but he's a fast learner."

"We'll scrounge up an extra tent for the two o' you and you can go t' work tomorrow."

And just like that, Connor was going to welcome him into the fold, put him to work in the logging camp, without so much as asking where he'd been and what he'd been doing the last three years.

"In the meantime, let's hunt up our little brother. He'll be glad t' see you."

Caleb and Connor strode through the camp, Connor introducing Caleb to the rest of the loggers, looking as proud as punch that his brother who'd been lost was found.

Which made Caleb feel lower than a snake's belly, as he had no intention of staying in Natchez indefinitely.

Unnerved by the events involving the highwaymen, Alanah stayed close to home all the next day. But a heavy overnight rain had her out early, searching for the medicinal herbs that were her livelihood.

Still, she made sure to stay far away from the roads and trails that crisscrossed the backwoods between the trace and the river. For where there were travelers with coin, there would surely be highwaymen.

As she foraged, her treacherous thoughts returned again and again to the dark-haired Irishman. Had he survived the attack? And if he had, would she ever see him again?

More than likely not if he was traveling farther north. And in the end, that was a good thing. He'd seen her in Natchez and now in the woods. If he put two and two together, her carefully constructed ruse could fall apart.

The noon hour was long past when she returned home, her bag bulging with the bounty of the forest. Lydia stirred a pot of hominy over an open fire, and a rabbit was roasting on a spit nearby, the savory aroma causing Alanah's stomach to rumble. She tossed her bag of roots and herbs on the table and gestured toward the rabbit. "Snare? In the blackberry patch?"

"Yes. You need to set another one."

Alanah chuckled. "Why didn't you?"

Lydia shrugged. "You're much better at it

than I am. And besides, I wanted to be here in case Betsy woke."

"Has she stirred at all?"

"No." Lydia bent over the spit, turned the rabbit.

Alanah bit her lip, then dumped her findings on the table. "Do you think she's sick?"

"Heartsick."

Alanah scowled. "Heartsick? Over Micaiah Jones? Surely you jest."

"Micaiah has a hold on her. She's afraid of him, but as long as she does exactly as he wants, he won't hurt her. And somehow she's got it all twisted up inside believing that's normal."

"It's crazy."

"Is it?" Lydia responded. "What would you do to survive?"

"But Micaiah took her against her will." Heart aching, hands shaking, Alanah sorted her findings. Bloodroot in one pile. Fresh mushrooms in another. Magnolia bark and cypress clippings in another. "For all I know, he defiled her —"

"We've known from the beginning that Betsy wouldn't come back the innocent girl she was when he took her away. If she came back at all."

Alanah swallowed. Lydia had cut open her darkest thoughts and laid them bare. She could no longer pretend that everything would return to the way it was before.

"I know, but she's so young. She's hardly a woman." She looked at Lydia, blinking back tears.

"She survived. That's all that matters right now." Lydia's voice was uncharacteristically soft, compassionate. "She'll heal with time. We have to give her that time."

Alanah moved to Lydia. Giving the older woman a hug, she smiled. "Have I told you how much I love you?"

"Not lately." Lydia's lips twitched. "Now, why don't you go see if you can get your sister to eat. The sooner she gets her strength back, the sooner she'll begin to heal. And bring some bowls. We'll eat outside and enjoy this breeze, such as it is."

Inside the cabin, Alanah rummaged through the cupboards, gathering bowls and utensils. She glanced over her shoulder toward the curtained-off room at the back of the cabin. "Betsy? Are you hungry? We have rabbit and hominy. You like that."

When she didn't get an answer, she placed the bowls on the table, then peeked through the curtain. "Betsy?"

The rope bed she shared with her sister was empty, save for a pile of blankets, her sister nowhere to be found.

"Lydia!" Alanah ran for the door. "Betsy's gone."

Her eyes scanned the area surrounding the cabin. A flicker of movement sent her running headlong into the forest. "Betsy! Stop. Please."

But her sister was having none of it. She threw a frightened look over her shoulder, hiked her tattered shift, and ran, barely heeding the limbs and briars that tore at her.

Alanah lost sight of her sister somewhere in the woods, but she kept going, coming out on the wagon road between Mount Locust and Cypress Creek. Heart pounding, she prayed that Betsy wouldn't take the road to Natchez. Walking, it would take hours to reach the town, but in Betsy's state of mind, she would just keep going until she arrived at her destination.

If some nefarious group of outlaws didn't run her down first.

Please, Lord, protect my sister. Show me the direction to take.

Alanah searched the pathway, the overnight rain making it easy to spot the two-pronged indentations of deer bounding across the trail, a raccoon that had meandered by. A squirrel — her heart lurched when she spotted Betsy's footprints, heading toward Mount Locust.

She didn't pretend to understand Betsy's mentality after what she'd been through. But she'd do anything to keep something equally horrible from happening again.

The only reason Micaiah's men hadn't had their way with her sister and left her floating lifeless in the Mississippi River was their fear of Micaiah. And the only reason Micaiah had threatened them was because he could.

Alanah didn't harbor any illusions that the vile outlaw cared for Betsy. He was too depraved for that. He'd used her for his own pleasure and as a means to keep his men in line. And if he hadn't been caught and imprisoned for his crimes, he would have done away with her if and when it suited him.

But she couldn't worry about Micaiah now. Her only concern was Betsy.

She ran another mile along the forested lane before, out of breath, she stopped to get her bearings. As she stood there in the middle of the lane, a cold finger of dread snaked down her spine.

The logging camp she and Lydia had spotted was just over the next ridge. Surely Betsy wouldn't —

CHAPTER 5

"You can handle Molly now. *Ja?*" Björn patted the large draft horse.

Caleb wasn't as confident as the big Swede, but he nodded. *"Ja."*

Laughing at Caleb's attempt to mimic his accent, Björn moved away, hitched his team of three to a massive log and, with little fanfare, pulled it out of the way. "We must clear all the logs from the road. Gimpy will be moving camp today."

Caleb turned to the one horse he'd been assigned. "I hope you know what t' do, Molly girl."

Surprisingly, the horse did know what to do as long as Caleb chose logs small enough for her to drag on her own. He left the large ones for Björn and the others. He lost track of how many logs he snaked to the side of the road, quickly learning how to get them out of the way so that teams of horses and wagons could pass through.

Some of the logs they left where they lay. Others they piled into bunches by the wayside or in small meadows. Once they broke through to the river and formed a permanent camp, they'd drag them to a staging ground and float them downriver. The idea of using the river intrigued Caleb, and he hoped to convince Connor and William to let him work with the rafting crews.

Late in the day, he spotted the supply wagons heading toward him. Gimpy, the cook, nodded, then passed on by, followed by two more wagons filled with bedrolls and cookware.

Connor brought up the rear. "How's it going?"

"Good." Caleb patted the draft animal. "Molly seems t' know what she's doing. What o' Tiberius? Is he learning how t' wield a saw?"

Connor grinned. "I paired him with Moses. Once he becomes accustomed t' the feel o' the two-man crosscut saw, they'll be an unstoppable team."

"He's a hard worker."

"That he is. Moses, too. I predict they'll see which one can hold out the longest, which will be fun for the rest o' us t' watch." Connor pointed to where the other wagons turned off the trail. "See that clearing up

72

ahead? That's where we'll make camp for the next few days."

"Aye. I'll be there when I finish up here."

"Those logs can wait till morning."

"I promised Björn I'd finish clearing this side."

"All right." Connor slapped the reins against his horses' withers. "See ya at supper."

When Connor was gone, Caleb hooked the chain to another log and pulled it off the trail. As he reached to unhook the chain, he spotted movement in the underbrush. Just a flicker, but enough to alert him that something was out there in the woods. Remaining still, he focused on the area.

There. Shades of brown and tan shifted, then blended with the forest, only to reappear again, moving stealthily. A deer? A wild hog foraging, perhaps?

Leaving Molly hitched to the log, he eased along the lower side of the ridge fifty feet beyond where he'd seen movement. Inching up the incline, he peered over the edge. With an open view beyond the ridge, he crouched in the underbrush and waited.

He froze in shocked surprise when a woman, not an animal, came into his line of sight.

With an impressive-looking bow strapped

to her back, she flitted through the forest like a woodland fairy, at one with the shadows. She paused, her tattered and patched clothing almost invisible against the bark of a massive pine. Quietly and carefully, she moved again, straight toward the clearing where Connor and the other men were setting up camp.

Caleb's jaw hardened.

Who was this woman and what was she doing stalking his brother's logging crew?

When she drew near, he stepped into the open. Their eyes met, hers surprised and wary. One minute she was staring at him with wide golden eyes, so out of place on her dirt-smudged face, and the next he found himself looking at the sharp end of an arrow, nocked, bow drawn. She backed away, her aim never wavering from a spot somewhere on his chest.

Caleb held up both hands, palms out. "I'm no' going t' hurt you, lass."

Her tawny eyes jerked to his face. Those eyes. It was the woman from Natchez, except —

Her foot caught on a root, a limb, something hidden in the leaves, and she lost her balance, letting the arrow fly. Caleb dove for cover as the missile passed within inches of his ear, the whine too close for comfort.

Then he rushed toward her before the fool girl could nock another arrow.

Alanah fell backward, the forest floor doing little to cushion her landing. Her bow went one way, and she went the other.

She rolled, scrambled to her feet, and grabbing her tattered skirts, ran. But she didn't get far.

A band of steel encircled her waist, sweeping her clear off her feet. She gasped; then pure terror kicked in, and she arched backward, kicking and scratching and clawing with everything within her.

Even as she fought, it dawned on her that her captor wasn't hitting back. He could have put a stop to her wild shenanigans right there on the spot, but he didn't. Suddenly her boot connected with his shin, and he let out a growl of rage.

"Enough." Faster than a striking adder, he twisted her around, and she caught a glimpse of his clenched jaw through the mass of hair that covered her face. Eyes flashing and chest heaving, he clasped her by the forearms and shook her. She glared at him, but he shoved his face within inches of hers and gritted out, "Enough, I say. I do no' know who you are, or what game you're playing, but you can stop it right now."

His narrowed gaze raked over her hair, her clothes. "You're the same lass from Natchez, or my name isn't Caleb O'Shea, so do no' bother denying it."

Fear shot through her. Not fear of this man. Not the kind of fear she felt when men like Micaiah Jones landed in Cypress Creek. But fear that he'd seen her in Natchez. Frozen in place, she tried to gather her wits enough to start fighting again, to claw and scrape and screech like the crazy woman she claimed to be, but all she could think of was that he knew she wasn't crazy.

He'd seen Addled Alanah when she wasn't the least bit addled or rattled.

Unlike at this moment, when he had her rattled to the core.

She tried to jerk out of his grasp, but he was having none of it.

"I'll let you go, lass, if you promise no' to start fighting again."

Alanah nodded. It was all she could manage. As soon as he let her go, she scooted away, put some distance between them, then surreptitiously started searching the ground for her bow. She'd grab it and go, run back home, hope Betsy had returned.

The man — he'd said his name was Caleb — took two long strides and scooped up her bow. "Is this what you're looking for?"

He ran his hands down the length of the bow, then arched a brow at her. "Are you any good with this?"

Alanah shrugged.

He cocked his head to one side, a quizzical look on his face as if he couldn't quite figure her out. Alanah didn't blame him. She couldn't figure herself out either.

"You can have it back —" he presented the bow, then held it fast when she clasped the other end — "if you promise t' no' shoot me and t' tell me your name."

Alanah tugged the bow and glared at him.

"I know you can talk. I heard you in Natchez." He shrugged. "It's none o' me business why you're dressed in rags, covered in soot, and your golden hair looks like a rat's nest. I suppose you have your reasons, and I will no' ask what they are. But I would ask your name."

He'd said she had golden hair. Alanah resisted the urge to smooth the tangled mess. She looked at the bow, then lowered her gaze.

"Alanah," she whispered. "Alanah Adams."

"Why are you — ?" Caleb checked himself. He'd promised not to ask any questions if she'd just give him her name. She'd upheld her end of the agreement. He gave a slight bow, the movement tugging against the weapon tethering them. "Pleased t' meet you, Mistress Alanah."

Her tawny eyes widened; then her lashes lowered, and she dipped in a curtsy.

A shaft of sunlight haloed around her, causing glints of gold to shine through the soot and wild disarray of her hair, and he got another glimpse of the woman he'd seen in Natchez. But still, he didn't let go of the bow. "Thank you for the tea."

She looked at him then and broke her silence. "How is your friend?"

"Much better. He's on his way home t' his family right now."

"I'm glad." She gave the bow another tug.

He let go and stepped back. "Do you live close by? Should I escort you home?"

Why he asked, he didn't know, but the thought of leaving her alone in the forest unnerved him. Even though she tried to hide beneath dirt and rags, any man with one eye and half sense could tell she was a bonny lass.

She shook her head and, the bow clutched to her, backed away.

A scream rent the air, and she whirled toward the sound. With one panicked glance in his direction, the woodland fairy took off at a dead run toward the logging camp. Caleb raced after her.

As he reached the edge of the clearing, he spotted a young woman — hardly more than a girl — huddled on the ground next to the cook's wagon. Skin and bones, her shift hardly decent, bare feet cracked and bleeding, and eyes wild and terrified, she shot fear — and compassion — through Caleb.

And from the looks of the other men standing in a circle around her, they weren't sure what to make of her either. Alanah rushed to her side, crouched in the dirt, and cradled the frail woman-child against her.

Caleb heard the whispers from the onlookers.

"That's Addled Alanah and her sister."

Sister? Yes, Caleb could see the resemblance in spite of the tangled hair, dirt-encrusted faces, and tattered clothes.

"Both of 'em are crazier than bess bugs."

"No wonder. Old Jude let Looney Lydia raise 'em after his wife passed on. What do you expect?"

Connor strode into their midst. "What's going on here?" he bellowed.

The simpleminded woman-child whimpered and buried her head in Alanah's shoulder. Alanah hugged the girl close, her expression wary.

Gimpy shook a slab of bacon. "She was sneaking around the wagon. Tried to steal this bacon right out from under my nose."

Brows lowered, Connor placed his hands on his hips. "I see."

Caleb pushed through the crowd of men. "I see no harm in letting them have the bacon. From the looks o' them, they could use it."

"River rats from the landing." Gimpy scowled. "Give 'em an inch, and they'll take a mile."

"That's enough, Gimpy." Connor took the meat from the crusty old cook, and just as his brother had welcomed Caleb back into the fold without so much as a question or concern over where he'd been or what he'd done these past three years, he hunkered down so that he was at eye level with the women huddled in the middle of the clearing. He held out the meat. "Take it."

Without a word, Alanah snatched the bacon out of Connor's hands, gathered her sister, then stood. Wrapping her tattered cloak around the younger woman, she urged her away. As they passed, her clear-eyed gaze lifted to Caleb's, pleading with him not to give her secret away.

And he wouldn't, but Alanah Adams was no more addled than he was.

As soon as they were well away from the logging camp, Alanah stopped, grabbed her sister by the arm, and gritted out, "What were you thinking? Stealing from those men?"

"I was hungry, and —" Betsy blinked up at her, looking confused — "Micaiah . . . Micaiah will be wanting dinner."

"Betsy, Micaiah isn't here. He's in French Camp." Alanah hesitated to remind her sister that the outlaw was in jail for murder, not after the last time she'd screeched like a banshee. "You remember, don't you?"

"I — yes, I remember." Betsy frowned, then moved closer to Alanah. "Don't let him take me again."

Alanah's heart twisted. One minute Betsy was willing to throw herself back into that vileness; the next, she was terrified of the monster who'd taken her. If Micaiah Jones wasn't set to be hanged one hundred and sixty miles to the north, she'd see him hang herself. "I won't, dearest."

Betsy slumped against her. "Alanah, I love you."

"I love you, too."

Not for the first time, Alanah hated pretending to be crazy, dressing in rags, and living in filth. But when she looked at Betsy, saw the consequences of looking pretty and normal and sane, how the men who frequented Cypress Creek had fought over her sister as soon as Betsy had defied Uncle Jude and started wearing the beautiful gowns in the trunk.

Uncle Jude had been right to worry, to insist they wear rags and steer clear of the landing any time the river pirates came ashore.

And then Betsy had put herself in danger once again. She cupped her sister's face. "Betsy, promise me you'll stay close to home. Those men back there. They could have hurt you like — like Micaiah did. Do you understand?"

Betsy nodded, one small jerk of acknowledgment.

Alanah searched her sister's face. Had her warning sunk in, or had Betsy pushed all memory of the past few months into a deep, dark hole for her own sanity?

"All right. Let's go."

They stumbled down an embankment, and Betsy slid into a heap at the base of a tree.

"I'm tired, Alanah."

"We'll rest for a moment." Alanah sat and

Betsy rested her head against her shoulder. Within seconds, her breathing slowed, and she dozed. Alanah took a deep breath and let it out in a long sigh.

How her sister had managed to walk all the way to the logging camp in her weakened state was a mystery. She'd let her sleep for a moment; then hopefully Betsy would be able to make it the rest of the way home.

After a few minutes, as long as she dared wait, she nudged her sister. "Betsy. We need to go. It'll be dark soon."

But her sister didn't stir.

"Betsy —"

A noise to her right had her nocking an arrow and swinging her bow up. She froze when she saw Caleb O'Shea and the huge dark-skinned man with the hoop earring. After a moment's hesitation, she centered the arrow on the big man. She'd shoot him first, then deal with O'Shea.

The men stopped at a respectable distance, the Irishman motioning to her sister. "I was afraid the lass could no' travel far."

Alanah found her voice. "So you followed us?"

"Aye." His black eyes shifted back to hers. "We mean you no harm. But we would see you home before nightfall if you'll allow."

The offer seemed sincere, but Alanah had

been around scoundrels of one sort or another all her life. Most weren't as smooth-talking as the Irishman named Caleb O'Shea, and most didn't politely ask to help. No, like Micaiah, they took what they wanted and discarded the rest.

Her gaze ricocheted between her sister, Caleb, and the broad-shouldered man who stood half a head taller than any man she'd ever seen. Could she trust them? These men and the ones back at the logging camp had been given ample opportunity to do with them as they wished, and they hadn't. Instead, the man in charge had given her the bacon that Betsy had tried to steal and sent them on their way.

Caleb motioned to him. "Tiberius won't hurt ya none, lass. He'll do as I tell 'im."

The African's broad nose flared, and he glared at Caleb. Then his gaze met Alanah's, and he all but rolled his eyes. The comical gesture swayed her in ways that the Irishman's words never could.

Alanah released the tension on her bow. "I'd be obliged."

Caleb moved aside, and the man called Tiberius lifted her sister in his arms as if she weighed no more than a newborn piglet.

"Lead the way, lass."

As she plowed into the woods toward

home, Caleb O'Shea by her side, the large, silent man carrying her sister, she prayed she hadn't made a mistake in accepting their charity.

Caleb couldn't believe the frail woman in Tiberius's arms had walked as far as she had, or that Alanah knew her way through the tangled wilderness as well as she did.

She skirted around a swamp, the game trail she followed almost nonexistent. He was surprised when she veered off the trail and struck out through the forest. But all became clear when woods gave way to a wilderness road.

Caleb eyed the road, not much more than a trail, but the faint ruts showed a few wagons had made the journey. "Is this the road that goes to Mount Locust?"

"Yes."

But instead of taking the road, she crossed over and plunged into the forest again. Caleb and Tiberius had no choice but to follow.

The afternoon shadows lengthened; then suddenly a clearing appeared, along with a small cluster of ramshackle buildings tucked at the base of a high bluff. Caleb took in the scene at a glance. A dogtrot cabin stood front and center. A barn and a small one-room cabin sat to the left along with an enclosure made of wattle fencing. A handful of hens pecked in the yard, and goats bleated a welcome from the enclosure. A rough-hewn table and a fire beneath a brush arbor caught his attention, and he eyed the two-room cabin again. No smoke wafted from the chimney protruding above the roofline. Whether because the fireplace was unsafe in some way or simply because it was cooler to cook outside during the summer months, he couldn't say. The entire place was as sorry a sight as he'd seen since he'd landed in the colonies.

The same African woman he'd seen in Natchez with Alanah hurried toward them. As she neared, Caleb realized her hair was long and sleek and braided down her back. Maybe not African after all, but of mixed race, perhaps?

But she had eyes only for the young woman in Tiberius's arms. "Betsy?"

"She's fine, Lydia. Just worn-out." Alanah turned back to Caleb. "This is Caleb, and — and Tiberius."

The woman's wary gaze met Caleb's before flitting to Tiberius. She motioned toward the house. "Bring her."

Without a word, Tiberius obeyed. Caleb

watched them go, then turned to Alanah. "Why?"

"Why what?"

"Why do they call you Addled Alanah?"

She shrugged. "It's who I am."

"We both know that is no' true."

"Tell me, Mr. O'Shea —"

"Caleb will do."

"Caleb, then." Her mouth twisted into a slight frown. "Have you been to Cypress Creek yet?"

"I'm afraid I have no' had the pleasure."

"Go visit the tavern, become acquainted with the men who frequent the settlement, and maybe you'll understand."

Out of the corner of his eye, he saw Tiberius storm out of the cabin, ducking to avoid hitting the low beam at the edge of the porch. The woman called Lydia followed, leaned against a post, arms crossed, glaring at his back.

Caleb straightened. It seemed as if it was a good time for them to take their leave.

"Good day, miss."

CHAPTER 6

"Here's yer slop."

Micaiah Jones scrabbled for the wooden charger before his cellmates could get their hands on it. Using two fingers, he shoved cornmeal mush into his mouth as fast as he could, angling his body to shield the charger from the others.

"Gimme some. I beg you." Morrill held out a trembling hand. Too weak to do more than ask, it was easy for Micaiah to push him away.

"Wait yer turn," he growled, feeling no remorse for the man starving at his feet. Cowed, Morrill could do little more than watch him eat. A third prisoner — the guards had called him Kemper — lay curled in a ball in the corner, watching them with fevered eyes, too weak to even beg for his share of the rations. Finally his eyes closed. Maybe in death for all Micaiah knew.

When he'd eaten his fill, Micaiah dropped

the charger. Morrill grabbed it, ate the remainder, and licked the wooden trencher clean.

The man in the corner never moved. No need in wasting food on him. He'd likely be dead by morning if he wasn't already.

Micaiah wiped his mouth on his filthy sleeve, then retreated to the corner on the east side of the cell, away from the afternoon sun that beat down on the thinly thatched roof. Nary a breeze stirred, but in some ways the heat was better than the rain. The rain turned the dirt floor to a sea of mud, and there was no relief to be found, not even in the corner on the high side.

But he'd survived worse.

He dozed, rousing some time later to the sound of horses arriving at the cabin on the bluff that served as a courthouse. Forehead pressed against the rough timber, he watched a youth help a black-clad woman down from a carriage. They went inside the courthouse. More men arrived, on horses and in wagons. Some in carriages. They all trooped inside. Micaiah eyed the horses. Given half a chance . . .

He closed his eyes, his thoughts scrambling for ways to get to those horses, even though there was no way out of the cage they called a jail.

A long time later, the chain rattled and the heavy door creaked open. "Jones."

Micaiah only obeyed because it gave him an excuse to get out of the hovel, maybe even a chance to escape. He shuffled to the opening and ducked through, but before he could form a plan of escape, one of the guards held a pistol to his head. "Hold out your arms."

There were three of them, all armed, all wary. He couldn't overpower them all and come away unscathed, so he decided to bide his time. They shackled his arms and his legs and led him toward the courthouse.

Once inside, Micaiah scanned the faces of those in attendance, stopping when his gaze landed on the smooth face of a lad who hadn't even started shaving. He shifted his attention to the woman. Dressed from head to toe in black, a veil covering her downcast face, it was impossible to tell who she was. But Micaiah knew. Knew who they both were.

The judge made eye contact with the boy, then nodded toward Micaiah. "Is this the man?"

"Yes, sir. That's the man who killed my pa."

"Mrs. MacKendrick?"

The veiled woman lifted her head, gave a

short nod.

The judge faced Micaiah. "Micaiah Jones, you've been accused of the murder of one Wilson MacKendrick. How do you plead?"

"Not guilty." Micaiah glared at his accusers.

"That's a lie, Your Honor. He killed my pa and stole his horse and his flintlock." The boy motioned to the gun on the judge's desk. "That's it right there."

"How did you come by this gun, Mr. Jones?" The judge hefted the weapon, eyeing Micaiah.

"I bought it and the horse." Micaiah didn't expect the judge to believe him, but he didn't have anything to lose by making the claim.

The judge sighed. "Mr. Jones, I knew Wilson MacKendrick for ten years or more. That mare was his pride and joy, and he would never part with this flintlock. His own pa gave it to him on his deathbed. By the order of this court, I find you guilty of murder. You are to be hanged by the neck until dead. Your sentence will be carried out two weeks from today."

For the next several days, Alanah kept Betsy busy and close to home. In spite of her sister's desire to lie abed, Alanah coaxed her out into the woods to gather herbs, nuts, greens. Anything to keep her occupied and bring her back to a semblance of normalcy.

They returned to find their uncle in the yard, his black frock coat dusty from travel. Lydia's jaw was clenched tight as she scrubbed a deer hide stretched over a frame.

Uncle Jude's gaze raked over Alanah, then moved to Betsy, his face mottled red with anger.

Alanah handed her sister the bag of greens. "Why don't you go out back and start washing these?"

Head down, Betsy scurried away.

As soon as she disappeared, Uncle Jude faced Alanah. "What is she doing here?"

"She lives here, Uncle Jude." The anger on her uncle's face twisted her stomach into knots. She'd hoped —

"She is no longer welcome here." Eyes blazing, he stabbed a finger in the direction Betsy had gone. "She disobeyed me —"

"Please, Uncle Jude, she meant no harm —"

"No harm?" he sputtered, his bushy white sideboards quivering with outrage. "She paraded herself in front of those men, intentionally bringing attention on herself."

Alanah bit back her own spate of temper. She wanted to tell him to be reasonable.

The only thing Betsy had done wrong was to put on a pretty dress. But all Uncle Jude could see was that she'd disobeyed him. He wouldn't listen to reason, so there was no point in trying to persuade him.

"It won't happen again. She learned her lesson." Alanah kept her voice low and calm, even as Lydia pressed her lips together and scrubbed the deer hide harder.

"And what of Micaiah Jones?"

"He's to be tried for murder. In French Camp."

"I see. An eye for an eye, a tooth for a tooth."

Alanah couldn't argue with him. Micaiah had done some horrible things, if all the rumors were true. "All the more reason to be thankful Betsy was spared."

"Spared? She got what she deserved, flaunting herself as she did."

"Uncle!" Alanah gasped. "Betsy didn't go with Micaiah willingly. He stole her away."

"Ha!" Her uncle shook his head. "I didn't believe that six months ago, and I don't believe it now. That girl got what was coming to her, and I want her gone. She's brought shame to this house."

Alanah clutched her hands in the folds of her skirt. Shame? The only shame was that which her uncle brought every time he returned from preaching abroad, his Christian charity not extending to his own family, this false piety ringing as hollow as the empty meal barrel tucked in the pantry inside.

"Do you hear me, girl?" he bellowed. "I want her gone by morning. I won't have the likes of her under my roof."

"Please, Uncle, show some compassion. She has nowhere else to go."

"All the more reason that she should have listened to me in the first place. Nothing good comes from mingling with the riffraff at Cypress Creek. Nothing at all."

"Yes, Uncle." Alanah held out a hand, hoping to persuade him. "Let her stay. For Aunt Rachel's sake."

The rage on her uncle's face diminished. "All right, but keep her out of my sight."

"Thank you, Uncle Jude."

"Now I will pray for her soul." Her uncle headed into the woods.

Alanah avoided Lydia's disapproving frown and hurried to find her sister. Uncle Jude would remain in the woods until dark, praying and reading his Bible. He'd return when the sun set, eat whatever was put before him before retiring for the night. Only to repeat the process at daybreak.

And suddenly — a day later, a week —

he'd leave again, the urge to take the gospel to a neighboring plantation or a far-flung settlement hard on him.

Not for the first time, Alanah wondered why God required her uncle to travel so far and so often, leaving his family to fend for themselves and those at Cypress Creek to wallow in their sin.

Caleb slapped the reins against Molly's withers, and the draft horse snaked the last log of the day to the side of the road. While it would be a long time before he was as proficient in the task as Björn and the rest, he could hold his own.

After he stripped the mare of her harness, rubbed her down, and picketed her, he rinsed off in the nearby creek and headed toward Gimpy's wagon.

He joined the others in line, his younger brother right ahead of him. Except Rory was hardly a boy anymore, in spite of his wiry frame that had yet to fill out. Three years didn't seem like any time at all, but Rory had become a young man while he'd been gone.

When he'd arrived last week and Connor led him through the camp, he'd been on the verge of telling his brother he wouldn't be staying. Even after finding out that the logging camp needed all hands on deck to meet the demand for lumber in Natchez.

And then they'd spotted Rory. When the youth ran toward him, lanky arms and legs flopping, his eyes filled with tears, Caleb could no more leave than he could cut off his arm.

He would stay; he'd help with the logging.

Someday he'd move on, but not this week. Not this day.

Grabbing his brother around the neck, Caleb scrubbed his fist across the boy's hair, digging knuckles into his scalp.

Rory yowled and twisted away, deftly avoiding the mock jabs Caleb threw at his midsection. It was good to tussle with his little brother. It had been a long time.

Before Rory could retaliate, they were at the front of the line. Gimpy grabbed a trencher and dished up a serving of greasy stew. But Caleb had no complaints. After eating salt pork and hardtack for months at a time on board ship, even the surprise dishes the cook served up tasted good. Grabbing a slice of corn bread, he straddled a log, one side chiseled flat, providing a serviceable place to eat. Rory sat, putting enough distance between them so that Caleb couldn't goad him. Rory didn't play around when it came time to eat.

Connor, William Wainwright, and the rest of the crew lounged about on logs, stumps, or on the ground. They made do with wherever they could find a spot to kick back after a hard day's work.

The conversation flowed as the men shoveled stew into their mouths.

"How much longer till we reach the river, Connor?"

"Three, four days, wouldn't you say?" Connor surmised, looking to William Wainwright for confirmation.

William, looking out of place in a spotless white shirt, shrugged. "Maybe a little longer. If I'm not mistaken, there's a swamp up ahead. We'll need to veer left and go around."

"I propose we keep going straight." Connor shook his head. "The lay o' the land doesn't lend itself t' a swamp."

Caleb opened his mouth to refute Connor's claims, but William beat him to it.

"The maps —"

"Maps?" Connor scowled. "More like childish scribblings that wander off toward nowhere."

"Those childish scribbles have gotten us this far, and I daresay they'll lead us straight to the river in due time."

"Straight t' the river. Not around imaginary swamps." Connor shoved a bite of stew in his mouth.

"There is a swamp. Mark my words." William continued to eat, looking smug and not the least bit cowed by Connor's insistence that the best path lay straight ahead.

"We'll scout it out on the morrow." Connor tossed his trencher to the side. "Then we'll see who's right."

"Quite right." William laughed. "We'll see."

Caleb chuckled to himself and decided to keep quiet about the best route to the river. It wouldn't hurt his brother to be taken down a peg or two.

He couldn't figure the friendship between his brother and the plantation owner. Except he kept forgetting that Connor owned a plantation too.

But the position didn't seem to have affected Connor's ability to get his hands dirty when the need arose. William, on the other hand, spent his days in the tent or riding up and down the fresh-cut trail, inventorying logs and giving orders while the rest of them toiled from sunup to sundown.

He'd met many men like Wainwright. Born with a silver spoon in their mouths, they never worked a day in their lives and wouldn't know a shovel from an ax. It had been the same back in Ireland with the English landlords and with the owners of the ships he'd sailed on. They made their livings on the backs of others, and no matter where he went, he didn't expect that to change.

"See here." William picked up a stick, drew a long, serpentine line in the sand. "We should come out near a small settlement right on the river called Cypress Creek. By my calculations, that puts the river and the settlement a mile or so up ahead."

Caleb's opinion of William ratcheted up a notch. If nothing else, the man knew how to read his maps, even vague ones that left a lot to the imagination. Caleb was willing to give credit where credit was due.

"I'd steer clear of Cypress Creek iffen I was you." Gimpy banged on his pots and pans. "Nothing but cutthroats and river pirates holed up there. And when winter sets in, with less travel on the river, the place will be crawling with them. Mark my words."

"And that's why we're heading that direction." William set his trencher to the side, then pulled a kerchief out of his pocket. Wiping his hands, he addressed the group.

"We're going to need raftsmen to navigate the river. I figure Cypress Creek is the perfect place to find them."

A ripple of surprise rose from the men seated around the campfire. Gimpy tossed a disgusted look over his shoulder. "You gonna turn these logs over to them river pirates? That's about the dumbest thing I ever heard. Iffen ya don't mind my sayin' so."

"How else are we going to get the logs downriver?" Wainwright pointed at the cook. "Gimpy, are you up for the task? Björn? Anybody else?"

All was quiet until a wiry, middle-aged man cleared his throat. "I'd be willing, Mr. William. I left my wife and family in Natchez, and it'd be nice to get to visit them every few days."

"Ah. Vickers. Do you have experience with rafting, with the river? That's what I want to know."

"I was born and raised upriver a ways, and I've floated my share of rafts and flatboats down the Mississippi."

"That's good enough. Anyone else?"

No one else volunteered. Clearly none was interested in taking on the job. They were woodsmen, not sailors or boatmen.

"I thought not. While it's not an ocean

voyage, navigating the river riding a bunch of bucking logs takes a skill none of us possess." William sat back. "But I've seen rafts of logs floating down the river, fifty, sixty feet wide and more, so it can be done. Cheaply and easily. We'll just need a pilot and a crew for each raft."

"Aye. That's the way o' it, lads. And the sooner we reach the river, the sooner we can send our first timber raft toward Natchez." Connor looked around at the crew. "But first thing in the morning, we'll find out about this swamp William has conjured up. Horne, I'll need you and Frank t' go with us."

Mr. Horne frowned. "But tomorrow's Sunday —"

"I haven't forgotten, Mr. Horne. We'll leave after your sermon. You men can spend the day sharpening your saws and repairing harnesses. Then you have the rest of the day off for your leisure."

As Caleb made his way to the tent he shared with Tiberius, his step was light.

Unlike the loggers who balked at guiding the logs downriver, the idea filled him with excitement.

CHAPTER 7

The sun was barely up when Mr. Horne began his sermon. As soon as the last *amen* was said, Caleb gulped down some leftover stew and went in search of his brother. He found Connor and William in the tent that served as the camp headquarters.

"Connor, I would have a word with you."

"Aye?"

Caleb twisted his hat in his hands, suddenly feeling unsure of himself. He had no right to ask to go along. He was the least of the men on his brother's crew, and he didn't plan on staying long. If anything, he knew even less than Rory about logging, and here he was asking for favors.

"You're going t' need a river pilot." His voice sounded gruff even to his own ears. "I'm the man for the job. I've spent most o' the last three years at sea."

"Are you sure you're up t' the task?" Connor frowned. "Sailing on the open sea is no' the same as navigating a river."

Caleb scowled. His brother must think he was an *eejit.* "I canna see how it'd be any harder. Without the sails t' worry with, I think I can handle drifting down a lazy river on the backs o' a pile o' logs."

"You heard Gimpy. Most o' the men who'll hire on will be little more than river pirates who'd as likely cut your throat as look at you."

"All the more reason you need me." Caleb narrowed his eyes. "I've spent my share o' time fighting off pirates."

What Caleb didn't say was that he'd ended up fighting *alongside* the pirates a few times in his life. Not from choice, but from necessity. He didn't like to think about what he'd done to stay alive, but the skills he'd learned would come in handy if needed.

"Connor, your brother has a point." Wainwright glanced from one to the other, then stuffed some papers into a bag. "We're going to need someone we can trust to oversee the river runs. Most of these river folk have been sailors at one time or another, and Caleb understands them better than either of us ever will. And as you heard last night, the men on the logging crew aren't interested in joining forces with the men who work the river."

Connor scowled. "I do no' like it, but if you're sure —"

"Aye, I'm sure." Caleb cleared his throat. "I'd like t' go along if you do no' mind."

"I have no objections if William is agreeable."

Wainwright's shrewd gaze assessed him, and Caleb decided in that instant that he'd misjudged the man. "I'm agreeable."

They joined Mr. Horne and Frank, and the five of them followed a game trail along a ridge heading west. Every so often, William would tie a strip of white cloth on a tree marking the route they planned to take, and they'd continue on.

More than once, they backtracked, pulled the markers, and changed the route, but overall, they followed the same game trail that Alanah had led Caleb on a few days before. They stopped in a clearing and William unrolled his maps. As they looked at the rough drawings, discussing the best route to take to get to the river, Caleb pointed to what looked like a road. "What's this?"

William's finger traced the winding path on the map. "There's a road — of sorts — that leads from Mount Locust to Cypress Creek."

"That's the road we took to get to the logging camp." Caleb studied the map. It was also the same road he and Tiberius had crossed when they'd helped Alanah and her sister get home. "Then why not use it for the logging trail?"

"For one thing, it's the edge of my father's holdings, and for another, we're going to be snaking logs to the river rain or shine. By the time we get through, that road would likely be impassable. No need in alienating the locals more than necessary."

Half an hour later, the men walked out of the woods atop a bluff overlooking the Mississippi River. At least a mile across at this point, slow-moving and lazy, the placid surface couldn't be more perfect for floating logs down the river.

Frowning, Connor eyed the narrow strip of sand along the riverbank. "This will no' do."

What? Caleb jerked his head toward his brother.

"We need a large sandbar at river's edge. Horne, you and Frank head south. Look for a cove, a stream, an inlet. Cypress Creek should flow into the river somewhere along here."

As the two men walked away, Caleb motioned to the river below. "Why no' build a flue here and shoot the logs into the river?"

"If we were going t' float them down individually, that would work. Instead, we're going t' lash the logs together, make rafts, and pilot them downriver to Natchez."

"And maybe even as far as New Orleans." William looked like the cat who ate the cream.

"New Orleans?" Connor started walking north along the bluff's rim. "What have you been up t'?"

"Nothing of import. Father will have the sawmill in Natchez up and running soon, but he's also talking to a business associate in New Orleans about a contract —"

A boom reverberated through the woods, cutting him off. Connor placed one hand on the pistol tucked into his waistband. "What — ?"

Another shot rang out, followed by a third, all from the direction Mr. Horne and Frank had gone. Caleb rushed forward as a fourth shot rang out, Connor and William following close behind. Depending on how many men there were, and how well they were armed, they might be too late to save Horne and Frank.

When they neared the sound of fighting, Caleb slowed, motioning for Connor and William to spread out. They had the element of surprise on their side. Connor took the left flank, William the right, each one with pistols drawn, moving stealthily toward the attackers.

The cutthroats never even saw them coming, they were so focused on the two men they had pinned down. Caleb cut a glance toward Connor, eyes narrowed in question. Jaw clenched, Connor gave a short nod, leveled his pistol at the attackers, and pulled off a shot. Concentrating on the shadowy form nearest him, Caleb took aim and fired. William's pistol boomed mere seconds later.

Caught in the middle, the attackers returned fire. As Caleb dove for cover, he felt a white-hot burn along his thigh. Glancing down, he saw a streak of red soaking into his breeches right above the knee. But there was no time to see how bad the injury was.

After one more volley of shots, the cutthroats took to the woods. Letting them go, Caleb hunkered down at the base of a pine and started reloading, watching the woods for another attack. Moments later, they heard the sound of pounding hooves as the outlaws fled.

"Zachariah? Frank?" Connor called out. "Are ya all right?"

"Frank's hit." Mr. Horne sounded scared. "He's hit bad."

"Hand me your pistol." Caleb held out his hand. "I'll keep watch while you see t' him."

Betsy sidled into the house and stood behind the door, looking pale. There was only one thing that frightened her sister like that.

Strangers.

Alanah hurried out the open door, pausing on the shadowy porch. Lydia joined her, dark eyes wary, the battered flintlock in her hands. Four men flitted through the trees, carrying a fifth on a makeshift litter.

They stopped at the edge of the clearing, lowering the litter to the ground. One man separated himself from the others and came forward. Alanah was relieved to recognize Caleb O'Shea.

He strode toward the porch. "We need your help. Someone's been shot."

Alanah's attention slid past Caleb to the three men hovering over their wounded companion. Unlike Micaiah and the river pirates, who pushed their way inside the cabin without regard to Alanah's or Lydia's wishes, these men asked for help instead of demanding it.

"Why did you come here?" Lydia's voice was cold and unwelcoming.

"It was the closest place we knew of, ma'am." Caleb squinted at her.

"Cypress Creek is just over the rise."

The man who'd given them the slab of bacon stood, walked toward the porch. His gaze swept over Lydia and the gun she held, before settling on Alanah. He gave a short nod of recognition. "Caleb, if they do no' want t' help, we will no' force them."

"This is me brother, Connor O'Shea." Caleb motioned to the other man.

Alanah nodded. She should have known. Both had the same square jaw, the same Irish brogue. "Lydia, please. They've been kind to us."

Lydia refused to let strangers in the house, not after what Micaiah had done to Betsy. She'd barely let Tiberius in long enough to put Betsy down. After a moment, she lowered the gun and stepped aside. The men carried the injured man up the steps, past her. Alanah's vision swam as she caught sight of the gaping hole in his side, his torn shirt trailing along the porch, leaving a smear of blood in its wake. She swallowed and averted her gaze.

Lydia glanced at her, then handed her the flintlock. "Fetch what we'll need and build up the fire."

Alanah took the gun and rushed to do

Lydia's bidding.

Caleb watched Alanah hurry toward a shack — smaller and more derelict than the two-room cabin with the breezeway — nestled in the woods beyond an equally rundown barn.

Her face had gone white as a sheet when she'd seen Frank's injury.

He wouldn't have thought the lass to be squeamish. In spite of the life-and-death situation, he chuckled, then ducked beneath the arbor and started feeding sticks into the fire.

His hair stood on end as a razor-sharp knife appeared in his line of sight. Cutting his gaze to the woman with eyes like charred coal, he arched a brow. With a flick of her wrist, she inverted the knife, holding it out, handle first. "Red-hot. To cauterize the wound."

Caleb took the knife. "Aye."

She reached for two more long, thin blades with sharp points and laid them on the flat rocks surrounding the fire pit. "Keep them ready."

"Lydia." Alanah rushed toward them, breathless, a large pack clasped against her. "I fetched plenty of dried moss to pack the wound. Do you need anything else?"

"Will you help with the injured man?"

If anything, Alanah paled even more, but she jutted out her chin. "If I must."

"Not today, little warrior." With a slight chuckle that belied her fierce glare, the woman called Lydia took the pack, rummaged through it, pulled out a handful of small packets, handed them to Alanah. "Tend this one's wounds. It will be great practice for you."

Lydia headed back inside, and Alanah eyed the strip of cloth he'd tied around his leg, the stain of red where his blood had soaked through. She swallowed. "You're injured."

Caleb shrugged. " 'Tis nothing. Just a scratch."

"But Lydia said —"

"Do you always do what Lydia says?"

"I'm her apprentice. It's expected."

It really was just a scratch, but if it made her feel better, he'd let her see to it. "All right. It will no' hurt to dress it properly, I suppose."

While Alanah fetched a bucket of water and fresh bandages, Caleb unwrapped the bandage he'd made out of his own kerchief and, knowing there was nothing for it, ripped his breeches to expose the injury. When she returned, he stretched his leg out.

She sucked in a breath. He wasn't sure what shocked her more, the tiny furrow the musket ball had gouged along his outer thigh or the vicious scar that ran parallel to it.

"See, 'tis no' so bad." He flicked the torn cloth of his britches over the old injury. No need in giving her reasons to ask questions. "Looks like the ball just grazed me. You can see where it plowed along my leg."

"Yes, I — I see."

Hands shaking, she dabbed something sticky and smelling to high heaven on his leg, the tips of her fingers smoothing on the salve. She sucked in another deep breath when his blood mixed with the salve.

Caleb glanced at her, saw that her golden complexion was now pasty white. "Are ya all right, lass?"

"I'll . . . I'll be fine." She grabbed a thin piece of gauze, draped it over his wound, then washed the blood from her fingers.

Aware that she was uncomfortable dressing his leg, Caleb pressed the gauze in place. "That'll do. I do no' need a bandage."

Her brows lowered. "No, we must bandage it properly."

Mr. Horne bounded down the steps and hurried toward them. "Lydia needs a knife. She dug the ball out, and now she's going to cauterize the wound."

As quickly as he'd come, Horne went back inside, hot blade in hand.

A scream of agony exploded from the cabin, and Alanah flinched. The next thing Caleb knew, her eyelids fluttered, and he barely caught her before she fell into a heap at his feet.

"Alanah?" He cradled her in his arms. "Miss? Are you all right?"

No response. Just deadweight against his chest, her head lolling over his arm, golden-brown lashes feathered against her cheeks, her hair trailing down. In a panic, Caleb turned toward the cabin, intent on calling Lydia, Connor, somebody, anybody —

A faint moan from the slight female in his arms drew his gaze downward, and he stopped in his tracks. She blinked up at him. "What . . . what happened?"

"You fainted."

"Fainted?" Her face still held too little color.

Caleb clutched her closer, lest she black out again. "Hold on, miss, I'll get Lydia —"

"No. Don't." Her voice came out high-pitched and panicky. "Don't tell her, please. Put me down."

Caleb stared at her. "If you're sure . . ."

"I'm sure. Put me down before —" red

suffused her cheeks — "before someone sees."

Caleb lowered her to her feet, keeping one hand on her elbow as she walked back to the fire, her gait unsteady. He was relieved when she sank onto a stump. He straddled one nearby, keeping an eye on her.

With trembling hands, she jerked up the small bags that Lydia had handed her and turned toward him, a fierce glint in her eyes. Jaw jutted out, she motioned for him to stretch out his leg. Caleb obeyed, expecting her to keel over again.

Instead, she took a deep breath and pulled a length of cloth from the bag, wrapped it around his wound. "I'd appreciate it if you didn't tell Lydia that I fainted."

"It is no' my place t' tell her, lass."

She searched his gaze, before returning her attention to the task at hand. "Thank you."

Her voice was little more than a whisper.

CHAPTER 8

Breathe in. Breathe out. Breathe in. Breathe out.

Alanah poked at the fire, trying to keep her mind off what was going on inside the cabin. Lydia needed her, but she couldn't bring herself to go inside.

She blinked back the hot sting of tears. What was wrong with her? She could set a snare, catch a rabbit, skin it, and cook it over a spit. She could butcher a chicken or quarter a deer, but when it came to the close, tedious work of cleaning a wound or extracting a bullet out of a man, she shut down.

What good would she be to Lydia if she couldn't be counted on to stay on her feet in a crisis?

Sure, she could identify every medicinal plant from here to Natchez and beyond, knew just how long to steep them to make them as potent as possible without losing the very nutrients that gave them their healing power. But to apply her knowledge to someone lying at death's door hollowed out her insides and turned her limbs to jelly.

"Miss?"

She jumped up and whirled around so fast that she thought she'd pass out again. Caleb's brother stood a few feet away. "Yes?"

"Your friend Lydia said to make some wild lettuce tea t' help Frank relax. Caleb, we need you t' help hold him down while she stitches him up."

"Aye." Caleb stood, joined his brother, and they both disappeared inside.

Alanah mixed the wild lettuce paste in with a healthy dollop of honey to sweeten the bitter concoction. All the time, her heart thudded against her rib cage. Would she shame Lydia by passing out when she saw the injured man laid out on the table?

Lord, give me strength. Lydia needs me. This man needs me. Please, Lord.

As soon as the tea cooled, she headed toward the cabin, but with each leaden step, she felt as if she were slogging through quicksand.

Breathe in. Breathe out. Breathe in. Out. In. Out.

Steps heavy, she crossed the porch and pushed open the door to see Lydia and the

116

four men hovering over the table. As one, the men's somber-eyed gazes followed her as she moved across the room. If she was going to pass out, there would be no hiding it in front of all these witnesses.

Breathe in. Breathe out. Breathe in. Out. In. Out.

Everyone except Lydia backed away as she approached. Frank's arm hung limp off the side of the table. Alanah focused on his face, trying not to look at —

She felt herself sway. Instantly someone slipped between her and the man's ripped torso. *Caleb.*

"Let me help."

With his back to the others, he reached for the cup of thick, syrupy tea. He held the tea as she spooned small amounts in the man's mouth, careful not to give him too much at once.

Barely conscious, the injured man grimaced at the bitter taste and spit it out.

Caleb's brother moved to his other side. "Frank, this is Connor. Can you hear me?"

Frank grimaced, then nodded.

"Drink the tea, man. It'll ease the pain."

Frank nodded again, and Alanah spooned a bit more in, repeating the process until he finished it all. As he drifted off, Alanah backed away. Her gaze met Lydia's. "He'll

117

sleep now."

She might not be able to stomach digging a musket ball out of the man, but she knew exactly how much wild lettuce tincture to give him to send him into a restful slumber. Lydia motioned to the men, and they gathered around Frank, leaving Alanah to flee before she passed out in front of the lot of them.

Outside, she came face-to-face with her uncle.

Caleb followed Alanah, just to make sure the girl didn't have another fainting spell.

Why a woman being groomed to be a healer would faint at the sight of blood was a mystery to him. Was she sickly? She didn't look it, but then he wasn't much of a judge of women's ailments.

He almost ran her over when she stopped dead in the middle of the porch. He reached out to steady her, but she didn't look to be wilting like a morning glory in the heat of the day. Instead, she stood ramrod straight, staring at a white-haired man, one hand on his flintlock, the other clasping a Bible.

Florid features screwed up in a frown, the man shifted his attention from Caleb to Alanah. "What's the meaning of this, girl?"

"It's nothing, Uncle Jude." Alanah's

118

cheeks bloomed with color. "This is Caleb O'Shea. He's —"

"O'Shea, you say? With the logging crew?"

"Aye." Caleb moved away from Alanah, not sure if the crusty old man was going to shoot him or try to convert him on the spot. "We were scouting out a permanent camp for the lumber crew along the river, and one o' our men got shot."

"Shot?" The bushy brows dove down. "Who would do such a thing?"

"I do no' know, sir, but your niece and Miss Lydia were kind enough t' patch him up."

"Is everything all right?" William, followed by Connor, stepped outside. "We heard voices."

"Alanah's uncle." Caleb motioned toward the old man.

"William Wainwright at your service, sir." William moved forward, hand held out in greeting. "Forgive us for barging in while you were away, but I'm afraid my man wouldn't have survived if it hadn't been for the skills of Lydia and your niece here."

"Reverend Jude Browning." Alanah's uncle shook hands. "I'm just glad that my niece had the good sense to assist you. And how is the unfortunate soul now?"

"He's resting comfortably. But I'm afraid

he can't be moved just yet." William pulled a wallet out of his waistcoat. "I'll be glad to pay for his care —"

The reverend shook his head. "Thank you, sir, but it truly isn't necessary."

"Please. I insist." William pressed the coins in his hands. "Medicine and upkeep cost money."

Alanah's uncle relented and pocketed the coins. "It will indeed serve us well. As you can see, we've fallen on hard times of late. The river pirates have sucked the very life out of Cypress Creek."

"I understand, sir. I suspect some of the same riffraff were the ones who shot at my own men."

"Most likely. I'd hoped they had left the area for good when Le Bonne and his gang of highwaymen were dispatched, but it seems I was mistaken." Alanah's uncle gave Connor and Caleb a shrewd look. "The river pirates who frequent Cypress Creek won't be pleased to learn of your presence here."

Connor shouldered forward, a wary look on his face. "Why is that, sir?"

"The highwaymen and the river pirates work hand in hand. The highwaymen pass stolen goods to the pirates to be sent downriver. Monsieur Le Bonne's men kept the road between the trace and Cypress Creek hot with travel. Eventually pilfered loot made its way back to Natchez to be fenced by Le Bonne and others like him."

"What makes you think they are back?"

"The attack on the party of travelers on the trace a few days ago. Your man lying there in the cabin, shot. And my niece —"

"Uncle, please." Alanah's voice was so soft that Caleb doubted Connor and William heard her interruption.

Caleb caught the look that passed between Alanah and her uncle. She shook her head, but he lowered his brows and plowed ahead, hands behind his back as if he were about to launch into a fiery sermon.

"It is obvious the river pirates have returned from farther north and are working their way down the river toward Natchez. Once there, they will sell everything, then join unwary travelers coming back up the trace. They come, they go." He scowled. "But they are always killing, stealing, and instilling fear wherever they go. That never changes."

"So Cypress Creek enjoyed a wee respite these past months as well?"

The reverend nodded. "Yes, Jones and his band of pirates haven't been seen since last spring. No one knew where they went. But we feared they would return. And they have."

Cry against them, for their wickedness is great.

William Wainwright and the O'Shea brothers were long gone and night had set in when Jude stopped fighting against the still, quiet, but insistent voice inside his head. He shoved away from his prayer stump and scowled at the heavens.

"All right, God. I'll go." He grabbed his Bible and stalked toward Cypress Creek, still grumbling to himself and to God. "But it will do no good. The inhabitants of Cypress Creek will not repent. This is a waste of my time and Yours. As it was the last time You sent me."

It didn't take long to make the trek to the river settlement. Without slacking his pace, Jude slammed through the tavern door, glaring at the thieving cowards who frequented the establishment.

The tavern owner glared right back, shook his finger. "You! I told you not to come back here."

"And why not, sir?" Jude held his Bible aloft. "If any a place needs to hear the Word of God, it's this one. You're nothing but a bunch of murdering, thieving cutthroats."

Elias Jones snickered, his guffaws quickly turning into a full-blown belly laugh. Slumping forward, he slapped the table with his open palm, laughing uproariously. Soon the entire place joined him in his merriment.

Jude's ire rose to a fevered pitch. He shook a finger in the man's face. "Laugh if you want, Elias Jones, but God will have His say. Vengeance is mine, saith the Lord!"

Just as quickly as Elias started laughing, he stopped, pulled out a long knife, and stuck it in the table in front of him. The place quieted instantly. "Reverend, if you know what's good for you, you'll turn around, head out that door, and go back to preaching where you're wanted, because you ain't wanted here."

"I go where God sends me." Jude stared Elias down.

"God?" Elias cut him off. "God has no place here. And neither do you, old man. And you have no say in how I run things around here. Now that Micaiah's gone, I'm in charge, and the men will do as I say."

"You are in charge?" Jude put his hands behind his back and rocked back on his heels. "All right. What do you have to say of the men who attacked those loggers this very day? I suppose they answer to you, do they not?"

"Any dandified plantation owner who thinks he can waltz in and line his pockets with the fat of the land has got what's coming to him."

"You tell 'em, Elias."

"Yeah. Hear! Hear!"

"I'll drink to that."

The men raised their tankards of ale in salute.

Jude growled low in his throat. If he weren't a man of God, he'd . . . "Mark my words. God won't stand for this. Repent of your wicked ways —"

"Enough," Elias bellowed. Standing so suddenly his chair fell backward to clatter against the floor, he grabbed the knife and wrenched it free from the table. He stalked toward Jude, bloodshot eyes blazing, and Jude tried not to flinch. In all his travels crisscrossing the Natchez District, he'd never encountered anyone who struck fear into him as much as cousins Elias and Micaiah Jones.

This is the last time, God. The last time, I tell You!

Elias stopped short of ramming the knife into his stomach. "To show the good reverend here that we're decent folk, would the men who attacked those poor helpless loggers step forward? We certainly wouldn't want to harbor such lawlessness in our midst, now, would we?"

Other than a few sniggers here and there, nobody said a word. Jude didn't expect anyone to admit to the attack. And what would it matter if they did? There were no courts within twenty miles of Cypress Creek and not enough law-abiding citizens to go up against the river pirates and expect to come away unscathed. Only Jude's standing as a preacher had given him leave to say as much as he had.

"See?" Elias spread his hands wide, knife gleaming in the lamplight. "We are all as innocent as lambs."

Jude snorted, turned his back on Elias, and scanned the rest of the men. He saw a few faces that weren't known to him. Some young and unshaven. Some who might be swayed to turn back to the straight and narrow. "There's a logging camp hardly a stone's throw away. I daresay they are in need of workers. It would behoove some of you to separate yourselves from men such as Elias Jones while you still can."

"You go too far, preacher," Elias snarled.

"As do you. God have mercy on your dark soul."

With those parting words, Jude shook the dust of the place off his feet.

■ ■ ■ ■

Two days after Frank had been shot, the loggers reached the Mississippi River.

Caleb, along with the others, stood on a steep bluff, the waters of the mighty river rolling past. The bluff overlooked a mile-long island separated from shore by a sixty- to seventy-foot side channel. And right below them, the river at high stage had cut an expansive sandbar along the water's edge.

"This could work." Connor nodded, looking pleased. "We can roll the logs off the bluff here, build the rafts on the sandbar, and launch them into the side channel and out into the river one at a time."

William eyed the setup, before turning to Vickers. "What say you, Vickers?"

Mr. Vickers pointed at the hillside to their right. "I would build a road around that knoll, for ease in getting men and tools to safety should the sandbar flood."

"You think the sandbar is likely t' flood?" A frown of concern wrinkled Connor's brow.

Vickers shrugged. "You know logging. I know the river. That island has very little vegetation. Makes me wonder how often it's submerged."

"So be it. We'll build the road. I do no' want t' lose men, horses, or tools t' the raging waters o' the Mississippi."

Caleb hunkered down, pulled a sprig of grass, and slid it through his fingers. "We're still going t' need sailors —"

"Raftsmen, not sailors," Connor corrected.

"Raftsmen, then." Caleb squinted at his brother. "Where will we get these raftsmen?"

Connor jerked his head downriver. "There's a tavern at Cypress Creek, so it shouldn't be too hard t' find somebody willing t' pick up a few days' pay. I'll put out the word."

"Good. Glad that's settled." William nodded toward the expansive plateau they'd picked for a permanent logging camp. "The first order of business is to build a cookhouse for Gimpy, an office, and living quarters for the men."

"Aye, this is the spot, then. Let's get started." Connor slapped Caleb on the back. "Then, tomorrow, we're going t' Breeze Hill. It's time the rest o' the family got a look at ya, Brother."

A midmorning shower cooled things off, but the afternoon sun beat down with a vengeance. Alanah took a deep breath as Lydia pulled back the sheet covering Mr. Abbott's wound. Would the sight of Lydia's sutures send her into a dead faint?

Over the last three days, she'd kept the man calm with a concoction of teas and tinctures, but she'd studiously avoided looking at his injury. Thankfully, Lydia had kept a close eye on the sutures and hadn't really noticed that Alanah had not.

Surfacing from the medicinal fog that had kept him blissfully unaware until today, Mr. Abbott glanced from Lydia to Alanah to Betsy, who stood next to the door, watching curiously but ready to flee at the slightest provocation.

The poor man looked scared out of his wits, and who could blame him? Caleb and the others had left him with three crazy women.

Lydia probed his side. He winced, and she glared at him. "Be still."

"Yes'm."

"Your side. It heals."

"Can I go back to camp now?"

"It is your choice." Lydia shrugged. "But you are not ready to use a saw or handle a team of horses. You'll rip those stitches out and your entrails will spill out onto the forest floor for the coyotes to fight over."

The man's horrified look just made Lydia cackle, and he frowned at her as if he realized she'd only been teasing. She turned away but paused as the sound of tiny hooves clattered across the front porch, followed by more clatter and the bleating of goats.

"Those goats. Betsy —"

"I'll get them." Alanah's sister giggled, before heading to round up the goats.

Moments later, she yelped. Heart in her throat, Alanah stepped into the breezeway just in time to see Betsy run into the one-room cabin across from where Mr. Abbott lay. The sound of the heavy bar falling in place meant Betsy wouldn't be emerging any time soon. There was only one thing that would make her sister bar the door.

A man.

Alanah grabbed the bow she kept handy and, with one quick motion, nocked an arrow. The flintlock might be a better option, but she had more experience with the bow. If she missed with the bow, she could have another arrow nocked before she could even think about reloading the old gun.

The goats stood at attention, watching something — or someone — at the edge of the cleanly swept yard. Keeping close to the log wall, her bow at the ready, Alanah peered at the spot, feeling relieved when

Tiberius showed himself. She released the pressure on the bow and moved out of the shadows onto the porch, waiting. Tiberius left the safety of the trees and approached the house. He gave a slight bow. "Miss Alanah."

For some reason, Alanah didn't feel the need to pretend to be crazy around Tiberius. She didn't even feel the need to pretend to be a fancy lady from Natchez. She could just be herself. A poor, plain girl scrounging a living from the earth.

"Good day, Tiberius." Alanah searched the woods for Caleb and the others but saw no one. "You're alone?"

"I am alone. Caleb and the others have gone to Breeze Hill for supplies." He cleared his throat and lifted a haunch of venison. "Mr. William asked me to check on Mr. Abbott and bring provisions."

Alanah's mouth watered. They hadn't had venison in months. "That's not necessary."

"It is in payment for Mr. Abbott's upkeep. Mr. William would be pleased if you would accept."

Put that way, she couldn't refuse. She took the offering. "Thank you."

"You are welcome." His attention shifted toward the cabin. "I would see Mr. Abbott?"

"Of course."

She stepped aside, and he mounted the steps, ducking his head to keep from slamming into the low beam. Suddenly he stopped, whipped off his hat. "Miss Lydia."

"Tiberius." Lydia blocked the door to the sickroom.

The three of them stood there without moving, but for some reason, Alanah felt as if the other two had forgotten her presence. Tiberius mangled his hat in his hands, gazing at Lydia like a moonstruck calf.

Alanah hefted the haunch of venison. "I'll just . . ."

Trailing off, she left the two of them standing there, doubting they even knew when she departed.

CHAPTER 9

Caleb bowed over his sister-in-law's hand.

"Pleased t' meet you, Isabella." He straightened. "Or should I call you Mistress O'Shea?"

She curtsied, a tiny smile playing over her lips, her dark eyes twinkling. His gaze narrowed. Was she laughing? At him?

"Oh, Isabella is fine. We don't stand on ceremony here at Breeze Hill." She took Connor by the arm, then reached up and kissed his cheek. "You didn't tell me that Caleb was so much like you, darling."

"Like me?" Connor scowled. "We look nothing alike. He looks like *Mam,* all black-eyed and dark-skinned. The rest o' us take after *Da.*"

She patted his arm. "Oh, he's more like you than you think."

A small whirlwind came flying around the corner, almost barreled Isabella over. Only Caleb's quick grab at the boy's collar saved her. Green eyes peered up at him. Eyes just like *Da*'s, just like Connor's. His heart squeezed.

Patrick.

Caleb bent to eye level, and the boy looked him over carefully. Gone was the pudgy five-year-old he'd left in Ireland. In his place was a strapping youngster whose tanned arms stuck out a good two inches past his shirtsleeves. Caleb grinned. "Do you know who I am, lad?"

"Aye. Ye're me other brother, Caleb." Patrick jutted out his chin. "Quinn says ya left us t' fend for ourselves back in Ireland. That ya cared more about sailing the high seas than ya cared about family. Is that true?"

"That's enough, Patrick." Connor's voice split the air like a shot. "You'll do well t' keep a civil tongue in your head —"

Caleb straightened. "The lad is only speaking the truth. I should no' have left."

Connor looked pained. "It was no' your place t' take care of them. It was mine. I should've been there —"

"Oh, hush, you two. All that's over and done with, and there's not a thing either of you can do about it. You're all here now, and that's what matters." Isabella plopped her hands on her hips and glared at them both. "And it calls for a celebration. Patrick, go find Martha and tell her to meet me in the kitchen. We need to have a special meal tonight to celebrate. All the O'Shea brothers are finally together at long last." She arched a brow at Connor. "You did bring Rory home with you, didn't you?"

"Aye, he's here, and so is William."

"William? Oh, that's wonderful."

"He's heading home, but I convinced him t' stay here tonight and get an early start in the morning."

"That was wise." Isabella threaded her arm through Connor's, then smiled at Caleb, eyes shining. "I'm so glad you're here. You don't know how devastated Connor was when he realized you weren't on the ship with the others. We've prayed you would find your way home."

"Thank you, ma'am." Maybe his sister-in-law wasn't quite as uppity as he'd first thought.

"Now, if you'll excuse me, I need to send Quinn and Kiera an invitation to dinner."

As she hurried up the steps and into the house, Connor motioned Caleb forward. "Would you care to see Breeze Hill?"

"Aye." Caleb followed his brother around the house to a shady courtyard and a grape arbor. A morning shower had dampened the fields, and there were puddles of water here and there. "Quinn's no' here, then?"

"No, he and his wife are at Magnolia Glen, the plantation I own."

"Aye. I remember now. Mr. Wainwright explained it all t' me." Caleb shook his head. "But I confess, the entire tale sounded as if he'd kissed the Blarney stone himself."

Connor stopped beneath the grape arbor, rested a hand on one of the sturdy posts. Beyond, long rows of cotton marched across the fields, dotted with a few spots of white, signaling that the bolls were almost ready for harvest. "I see. And what exactly did Thomas say?"

"He said that Breeze Hill belongs t' Isabella's father, and her nephew is the rightful heir, and that Magnolia Glen belongs t' you."

"Aye. That's the gist o' it."

"Then why are you no' there?"

"Isabella's father is no' well, so we've decided t' stay here for now. There's plenty o' room, and Quinn's rebuilding Magnolia Glen. He seems t' enjoy managing the place without my interference."

"He would."

Connor's brow furrowed. "What's that mean?"

"No' a thing." Caleb shrugged, thinking

135

of the times he and Quinn had gone head-to-head over some minor slight. "Quinn is no' the easiest man t' get along with. He used t' light into me at the slightest provocation."

Connor laughed, then clasped Caleb's shoulder. "The two o' you were just lads being lads. He's changed."

Caleb hoped so, because the last time he'd seen Quinn, they'd beaten each other to a pulp.

Alanah cut the venison into narrow strips and draped each piece over a drying rack, the smoke from the fire wafting up and over the meat to dissipate through the thatched roof of the outdoor summer kitchen. She dropped a few pieces into the stewpot, glad to have extra meat to supplement their diet in the coming weeks.

Out of the corner of her eye, she watched as Lydia shooed Tiberius out of the cabin and then stood on the porch blocking the entrance, arms folded. Tiberius towered over her, but she didn't back down. "He is in no shape to be moved to a tent in a logging camp."

"I wasn't going to take him away. He asked to sit on the porch." Tiberius edged closer to Lydia. "You will move, woman, or

I'll do the moving for you."

Alanah froze, watching the exchange. Would Tiberius show his true colors?

Lydia glared at him, her broad lips pressed into a tight line. Finally she shifted slightly, just enough to allow him to pass. "For a little while. In the sunlight. Out of the wind."

"There is no wind." Tiberius almost growled as he slipped by her.

"Fine, then. But if it starts raining again, he goes back inside."

Tiberius lifted his gaze to the cloudless sky and, without a word, went back inside. Lydia glanced at Alanah, and she bent her head to the task at hand, lest Lydia see her amusement. The light shower had come and gone hours ago, just wetting the ground enough to settle the dust.

Clearly exasperated, Lydia whirled, disappeared into the room behind Tiberius. Moments later, they emerged, Frank Abbott supported between them, Lydia barking orders faster than the warning shake of a rattler's tail.

Alanah stayed far away from the both of them as Lydia adjusted Frank's chair, then covered him with a blanket. Frank sighed. "It feels good to be outside. Thank you, Miss Lydia."

"Well, if you have a setback, don't blame me." Lydia jerked her chin toward Tiberius. "Blame him."

Frank laughed. In the days he'd been with them, he'd learned that Lydia was more bluster than bite. "Now, Tiberius, how are things back at camp?"

"Good. We have —"

Just then, one of the nanny goats jumped up on the porch. When she spotted the men, she shook her head.

"Shoo. Shoo!" Lydia flapped her apron and the goat jumped off the porch, her flight scattering the rest of the goats. "Betsy! Those pesky goats are out again."

But Betsy didn't emerge from hiding. They'd have to get the goats up without her. Alanah grabbed a bucket and tried to coax them back toward the pen with the promise of grain.

Instead, the animals scattered and, bleating, ran around the house. Alanah followed, hoping to shoo them into the pen. But they were onto her tricks. They made another dash around the house, trampling through what was left of the garden and generally wreaking havoc on everything they encountered. Lydia stood near the clothesline, flapping her apron at them.

As Alanah rounded the house behind the

goats a second time, Tiberius was standing in the middle of the yard next to Lydia. The goats, relishing their freedom, darted around the cabin, slipping and sliding on the thin layer of mud left by the early morning shower. Headed right toward Tiberius and Lydia.

Alanah skidded to a halt. "Watch out!"

The lead goat dodged Tiberius but couldn't avoid running into Lydia. She squealed and, arms flailing, tried to keep her balance. Tiberius's eyes went wide, and he grabbed for her.

But the slick ground, the rest of the goats almost running them over, caused him to slip. Both feet slipped out from under him, and he hit the ground with a thud, Lydia landing on top of him. Even from twenty feet away, Alanah heard the *oomph* as the breath was knocked out of him.

Alanah clapped a hand over her mouth to stifle the snort of laughter that bubbled up.

Tiberius rolled away, reached to pull Lydia up. She jerked out of his grasp, glared at him, then gave a pointed look at the goats that were now clustered at the edge of the yard, eyeing the scene as if they knew they were in deep trouble.

Without a word, Lydia lifted her muddy skirts and marched toward the porch.

■ ■ ■

Caleb stood in the middle of the sitting room that Patrick and Rory shared at Breeze Hill. It was bigger than their whole house back in Ireland, and certainly bigger than any cabin he'd ever encountered on a ship. And they didn't even *sleep* here.

They each had a bed of their own in separate bedrooms flanking the sitting room. Before Quinn had married and moved to Magnolia Glen, he'd shared the space with them, but even then, what was another body in rooms this size?

"Ya have t' wash up for dinner." Patrick scrubbed his hands, then passed the soap to Caleb.

Rory stepped through the doorway, wearing clean britches, a snowy-white shirt, and a green jerkin. Caleb had never seen such fine clothes on an O'Shea.

"Patrick, ya need t' do more than wash yer hands. Isabella has gone t' a lot o' trouble t' welcome Caleb." He jerked his head toward Patrick's room. "Ye're going t' bathe and put on yer Sunday best. Now off with yer clothes."

"Aw, Rory, do I have t'?"

"Ya do if ya want t' eat at Isabella's table

tonight."

Scowling, Patrick did as his brother asked, then howled as Caleb and Rory washed him from head to toe. It took a while, but finally Rory deemed him presentable, and he trudged to his room to get dressed.

Rory headed toward the other bedroom, and Caleb stripped to the waist, washed up as best he could in the dingy water left from Patrick's ablutions. He was reaching for his shirt when Rory stepped through the door. He tossed a clean shirt, butternut-hued breeches, and a supple leather jerkin at him. "Here ya go, Brother. These should fit ya."

Caleb held up the shirt, then eyed the youth standing in front of him. Rory was well on his way to becoming a man, but he wasn't full-grown yet. It'd take a while for him to fill out these clothes. He grabbed the breeches. "Whose are these?"

"Quinn's. They were in the wash when he and Kiera moved to Magnolia Glen. He has no' picked 'em up yet. 'Course that jerkin would probably be a little tight on him now."

"Tight on Quinn? Has my dear brother gone and gotten fat?"

"Not fat, just muscled." Rory pulled on his boots. "From working in the smithy."

"The smithy, eh?" Caleb tamped down the surge of resentment that bubbled up as he donned the vest and smoothed out the leather. A perfect fit. "So he ended up apprenticing with old Seamus, then?"

"Aye." Rory squinted at him, brow furrowed. "He started soon after ya left home."

Turning away, Caleb reached for a comb, slicked his damp hair back, trying to tame his temper and the unruly strands. "I'm sure the job provided a better living for all o' you."

"Aye, I suppose. But . . ." Rory frowned. "Caleb, why'd ya leave so suddenly?"

"Quinn did no' tell you?"

"No, he —"

"I'm ready." Patrick trudged in, shirt half-tucked in, hair sticking up.

Rory looked like he wanted to continue the conversation, but Caleb grabbed Patrick and ran the comb through the squirming boy's hair. "There, that's better. Now, tuck your shirt in."

As he looked over his brothers, Caleb's heart swelled with pride. "Well, we're a fine-looking lot, ain't we? Lead the way to the table, Patrick, me lad."

"Aye, aye, captain." Patrick grinned and wrenched open the door, then marched along the veranda toward the dining hall.

Caleb's smile faded as he followed his brothers. He'd covered his worry over seeing Quinn again with a joviality he didn't feel. But regardless of how his brother reacted to seeing him, Caleb determined not to fight.

Unless Quinn hit him first.

CHAPTER 10

After they rounded up the last of the goats, Alanah stared at the hole in the wattle fencing. Just one more thing that needed fixing in a never-ending list of repairs.

She heard a chopping sound and looked up. Tiberius stood at the edge of the forest hacking down a young sapling. He walked toward the fence, stripping the bark as he went.

Alanah waved a hand at the sapling. "You don't have to do that."

Tiberius didn't respond but measured the height of the fence before cutting the sapling into appropriate lengths.

Alanah cleared her throat. "Mr. Abbott's back in bed?"

"Aye. And I am banned from the house." He pounded one length into the ground, making the task look easy. "Lydia said Abbott almost busted his stitches laughing."

Alanah shook her head. "It wasn't your

fault that the goats got out or that you and Lydia fell."

He grunted, pounded another stake into the ground, then pointed toward the tree line. "I saw some vines over there."

Alanah took that as her cue that he didn't want to talk about it. She cut several lengths of the pliable vines and hauled them back to the fence. They worked in silence for a while, Tiberius hammering stakes into the ground to reinforce the fence, Alanah weaving in the vines to deter the goats.

She sneaked a glance at him. "Did Mr. Wainwright really send you out here to check on Mr. Abbott?"

He didn't answer, just kept working. That was answer enough for Alanah.

"She likes you, you know."

He lifted his dark eyes to hers but still didn't respond. They worked in silence for a time before Alanah spoke again. "Has the logging crew reached the river yet?"

"We made camp on a bluff a mile or so upriver."

"A bluff?" Alanah frowned. *Her bluff?* "Close to a slow-moving side channel?"

"Aye. We'll roll the logs off the bluff, then build timber rafts and float them down the river."

"I see. That's one way to get the logs to

Natchez. Does Natchez have a sawmill?"

"Mr. William's father is building one." He eyed her. "Are you done asking questions?"

"That depends." She smiled. "Are you done answering?"

His chest rumbled with laughter. "That depends, mistress."

"Why did you come to Cypress Creek, Tiberius?" She continued to reinforce the fence. "You're not a woodsman. You're a sailor."

"I came with Caleb."

"Caleb?"

"Aye."

She focused on pushing a particularly stiff length of vine between two saplings. "And Caleb? Does he plan to stay? I mean, here, with his brothers."

"That is not for me to say."

He didn't elaborate, and she wondered if that was all he was going to tell her. She moved to the next section of the fence, and he glanced up, caught her gaze.

"Caleb saved my life, so I owe my life to him. I will stay as long as he does." He chuckled. "But if you hear him tell it, I saved his life, so he owes his life to me. Truth be told, we are not sure who owes who, but it seems to be in our best interests to remain together for the time being."

"So you aren't —" Alanah paused — "Caleb's slave?"

"I am a warrior." He looked at her. "But if your people think Caleb is my master, then so be it. It is of no consequence." He flipped the ax, held it out butt first. "Your goats should not roam freely now."

"Thank you. They've been giving us fits for months."

He looked around, and Alanah had no illusions about what he saw. "You have no man to make repairs."

It wasn't a question.

Alanah followed his gaze, seeing her home through his eyes: the weather-beaten cabin, the barn in danger of collapsing with the next high wind, the rickety chicken coop, and the goat pen that Tiberius had shored up for the moment. "My uncle is oftentimes away."

Tiberius's gaze shifted toward the cabin, and Alanah turned, saw Lydia standing on the porch, her arms crossed as she stared at Tiberius. He backed away, gave a slight bow. "I should go. I must return to camp."

"Yes, of course. Thank you for fixing the goat pen."

He nodded, then turned and walked away.

Alanah glanced at the porch, where Lydia stood, her gaze never wavering until the woods swallowed him up.

The moment they entered the dining room, Caleb knew something was wrong. Isabella's ready smile looked strained, and there was no mistaking the thundercloud on Connor's face.

William stood next to an elder gentleman with patchy, puckered skin. Caleb's attention slid across the man's features, but he didn't stare. He'd seen his share of disfigurements in his travels. Some self-inflicted, others not. And he'd seen enough burn victims to recognize the aftereffects.

Connor motioned to the gentleman. "Caleb, this is my father-in-law, Matthew Bartholomew."

"Sir." Caleb gave a slight bow.

"Caleb." The older man inclined his head. "Welcome to my home."

"Thank you, sir."

Patrick slid out a chair. "Sit here, Caleb."

Connor cleared his throat. "Ladies first, Patrick."

"Oh yeah. Sorry, Isabella."

Connor seated Isabella; then they all took their places. Rory motioned to three empty place settings. "Should we wait for Quinn, Kiera, and Megan?"

"Kiera sends their regrets." Isabella held

up a folded piece of paper. "Quinn couldn't get away this afternoon. Maybe another time."

"Can't get away t' see his own brother?" Connor growled.

"Connor, please." Isabella put a hand on his arm. "Let's not spoil dinner."

Connor gave her a tight smile, then shifted his attention to Caleb, the pained look on his face making Caleb wonder if there was more to Quinn's absence than just avoiding him. Before Connor could say anything else, two servants brought in dinner. Isabella whispered to one of them, and she removed the extra place settings.

When everyone was served, Isabella glanced around the table. "So have you made it to the river yet?"

The question put the dinner guests back in good humor. Connor nodded. "Aye, we picked a spot just yesterday. A high bluff overlooking the river."

"I'd prefer a bigger sandbar." William dipped into his soup.

"It's sufficient."

As Connor and William debated the merits of the site they'd chosen, Caleb dug into the best meal he'd had in . . . well, in his whole life.

"Have you encountered any trouble?" Isabella asked during the first lull in the conversation. Silence met her question, and her attention shifted to each of them in turn, stopping with William. She cleared her throat and slowly, with care, put down her fork. "I can tell by the look on William's face that there's been trouble. You might as well tell me what happened."

"Me?" William looked shocked. "What did I say?"

"You don't have to say anything, dear William. I can read you like a book."

"It was nothing." Connor glared at William as if it were his fault that his unguarded expression had revealed so much so easily. "We were scouting out a permanent site for the logging camp close to the river, and Frank Abbott and Mr. Horne were attacked —"

"Attacked? Are they okay? Have you told Mary?"

"Mr. Horne is fine. Frank was shot, but he's recovering at Reverend Browning's, so there's nothing to worry about."

"There's a community there? And a preacher no less?" Isabella's eyebrows rose.

"Aye. There's a little river community called Cypress Creek. There's a saddler, a tavern, a couple o' other businesses. And Reverend Browning's slave is skilled in the healing arts."

"I didn't get the impression that Lydia was a slave." William glanced at Caleb. "Did you, Caleb?"

"I do no' think so." Caleb tried to recall what he knew of Lydia. "Alanah said she was her mentor, teaching her the medicinal herbs and cures and such. And she's of mixed race o' some sort."

William nodded. "She did look to be of Natchez or Choctaw descent."

"Who is Alanah?" Isabella's gaze caught and held Caleb's.

His face heated. "Reverend Browning's niece."

Isabella's lips twitched. "Is she pretty?"

"Well . . ."

"Pretty?" Connor chuckled. "Hard to tell under all that filth. Maybe she'd look all right with a bath, her hair combed, and some decent clothes, but if she's as crazy as Gimpy said, then I doubt anybody will ever find out."

Caleb tamped down his ire at the dismissive way Connor spoke of Alanah. If his brother only knew. "Pretty or no', the two o' them saved Frank's life."

"Aye, they did at that."

Isabella's gaze caught Caleb's. Looking amused, she picked up her fork. "Somehow

I get the feeling she's a lot prettier than you're letting on."

Caleb felt the tips of his ears redden, hoping his sister-in-law didn't press him further.

But Isabella just smiled, then turned her attention to William. "How are Leah and little Jon?"

"They are doing well. Or at least they were when I left." William sighed. "I've been gone well over a month, and I promised Leah I'd return for her birthday."

"I made her a present. So don't leave without it."

"Of course. I wouldn't dream of it."

Mr. Bartholomew dabbed his lips with a napkin. "You're going back to Wainwright Hall?"

"Just for a few days. A week or two at most."

"Who's going to manage the books at the logging camp while you're gone?"

Connor shrugged. "They'll keep."

"Paperwork never keeps." Mr. Bartholomew's misshapen features and gravelly voice sounded at odds with his amiable words. "You must have an accurate accounting of your inventory and labor. Otherwise, you'll have no way of knowing if the venture is profitable."

"I can manage the books." Isabella looked

at William, eyebrow arched. "Don't you agree, William?"

William nodded. "Absolutely, dear Isabella. Absolutely."

"From the logging camp?" Connor sounded as if he was choking.

"Of course, darling. Where else would I do it?"

"No." Connor glared at both of them. "It's too dangerous."

"You just told me that it's perfectly safe and that there's a small town. And a girl named Alanah and her mentor friend, Lydia." She grinned. "Oh, and a preacher."

"Take me, too, Connor," Patrick pleaded.

Connor ignored Patrick and focused on his wife. "You're no' going to the lumber camp, and that's final. Your father needs you here."

"Do not worry about Breeze Hill. I can run Breeze Hill quite well, my boy. If my daughter wants to manage the affairs at the lumber camp for the next few weeks, I see no harm in it. As William said, she's quite capable, and forgive me for saying so, but do you have anyone else who can keep the books with William gone?"

"No, sir." Connor scowled at the entire table, only Caleb and Rory escaping his displeasure.

"It's settled, then." Isabella smiled.

But from the look on Connor's face, Caleb had the impression the conversation between him and his wife was far from settled.

Three days of rain had turned the jail into a quagmire of mud.

After coughing continuously for two days, Kemper had faded to an occasional moan earlier in the day, then stopped completely late in the afternoon. When several hours of quiet had passed, Micaiah figured the man was dead, but he didn't bother to check. Morrill had developed the same cough that had plagued Kemper and grew weaker by the day. Micaiah hunkered down in his corner, elevated a bit out of the worst of the mud, wondering if he'd succumb to the sickness that had taken the other prisoners before the day of his hanging.

The guard brought their corn mush, the first they'd had since noon the day before. Morrill reached through the pole bars. "Please, mister, get us out of here."

"No place t' take ye, and besides, ye're gonna hang soon. Dying here or at the end of a rope shouldn't matter none." He tossed the trencher in, and it landed in the mud. Morrill grabbed for it, but Micaiah shoved him away, and the other man fell facedown in the mire.

Micaiah ate, the bit of cold mush doing little to satisfy his empty stomach. He retreated to his corner of the cell, feeling like a caged animal.

He *was* a caged animal, and there was no way to escape. His eyes darted toward the guards' lodgings built on pilings above the muck and mire, light spilling out the window, the porch a cool, dry place to sit while watching the rain fall. The guards ate well, drank their ale, and took turns sleeping in comfort, while the prisoners got one or two meals every few days.

Combined, they wouldn't keep a cat alive.

When daylight came, it was still raining, and Morrill was dead. Micaiah didn't know if the man had died instantly or passed out and suffocated in the mud, and he didn't care.

He heard the door to the cabin on the hill open, heard one of the guards clomp across the porch, heading toward the jail with the morning slop.

What if . . . ?

Dropping to the muck, Micaiah tucked his face into the crook of his arm, burrowed down, and lay still.

The scrape of the trencher across the threshold almost made him jump up and grab it for the little nourishment his empty stomach craved. But he remained still.

"Morrill? Jones? Kemper?"

Patience. Patience.

The guard peered through the narrow slots in the door, then swore. "Grandle, you'd better get down here!"

"What's going on?" the other man called from the porch.

"They're all dead."

"Dead?"

"Looks like they drowned."

"Drowned? Are ya sure?" Grandle's voice drew closer.

"Aye. See that Jones feller over there? Well, he makes sure he gets more than his fair share of every meal, and he ain't moved an inch."

Keys rattled, the door swung open, and the guards waded into the muck, grabbed Morrill by the arms, and pulled him out.

"Poor soul. Looks like he suffocated in the mud."

"Poor soul? They were thievin' murderers. Saves us from having to hang 'em."

As they dragged Kemper out, Micaiah's heart pounded.

Patience. Patience.

156

They grabbed Micaiah by the feet and pulled, and his face plowed through the mud. Outside, they dropped his body and left him lying there, facedown.

"Might as well go get the cart and bury them."

"Nah. Let's wait until after breakfast. They're not going anywhere."

"Aye. Good idea. Maybe it'll stop raining. No sense in getting wet digging three graves."

Through slitted eyes, Micaiah saw Grandle lean over Morrill. "Better make sure they're all dead. We don't want anybody playing possum."

The jig was up. The other guard reached down, touched a hand to Micaiah's throat. Seeing his chance, Micaiah grabbed the man's knife and plunged it into him. He barely let out a groan, but it was enough to alert Grandle. He whirled, his own knife at the ready. Shoving the dead man off him, Micaiah jumped up, eyeing his opponent.

Only one man would survive this fight, and Micaiah intended to be that man.

The sun was barely up when Caleb joined the others, and they headed toward the logging camp, Isabella and Patrick in tow.

William rode with them the short distance

from Breeze Hill to the trace, where he turned north, risking the ride to his home in the early hours of morning, when highwaymen were least likely to be out and about.

Caleb and Rory rode astride. Connor drove the wagon, his wife seated next to him, and Patrick sat on top of the supplies in the back. From their presence, it was obvious who'd won the argument for Isabella to go to the logging camp.

Truthfully, Connor didn't look too put out about having his wife along. Isabella sat close on the seat, her arm linked through his.

The morning passed peacefully along the newly cut logging road, and they arrived at the logging camp just after noon. The broad, flat plain atop the bluff had been transformed in a matter of days.

The cookhouse had been completed. An expansive porch ran the entire length of the building, and the men had already cobbled together tables and benches. They weren't taking any chances on not keeping Gimpy happy.

They hadn't had time to add a fireplace, but the cook had a pot of something simmering over an open fire when the wagons rolled to a stop. Strips of venison hung over a separate banked fire, and the aroma of roasting meat teased Caleb's stomach. Someone had bagged a deer while they'd been gone.

Gimpy dried his hands and squinted up at Connor. "Did you bring the flour?"

"Aye."

"Molasses?"

Connor chuckled. "It's all here, Gimpy."

The cook grinned. "Backstrap, biscuits, and gravy. Ain't nothing better."

Connor helped Isabella down from the wagon. "Rory, you and Patrick help Gimpy unload the wagon, you hear? And, Patrick, your job is t' be Gimpy's toady."

"But, Connor —"

"No buts. When you're older, you can help with the logs, but no' yet."

"Yes, sir." Patrick ducked his head and trudged toward the back of the wagon.

Connor pointed Isabella toward the tent he'd shared with William. "Well, Wife, there's your home for the next few weeks. Are you still glad you came?"

"Of course." Isabella grinned at him. "I've slept in worse accommodations."

The look that passed between them made Caleb wonder what she was talking about, but when Connor's face turned all sappy and sweet, he wasn't sure he wanted to know.

"Well, do no' get too comfortable. The men will have a cabin with office space and sleeping quarters finished in a day or so." Connor glanced over his shoulder. "Speaking of the men, I need to —"

"Don't mind me." Isabella lifted her skirts and headed toward the tent. "I'm sure I'll have plenty to do organizing William's papers. You know how messy he is."

"For sure." Connor grinned and slapped Caleb on the back. "Now to get started on building our first timber raft."

CHAPTER 11

Alanah foraged in the predawn hours, overturning logs, looking for leeches, moss, mushrooms — anything and everything she could use for cures of all sorts.

She moved on, harvesting some slippery elm and tucking it in her tote. As dawn broke, she spied a patch of half-dried leaves growing close to the ground. She moved closer to get a better look.

Bloodroot.

Giddy with the discovery, she fell to her knees and used a spade to dig up several roots, careful to leave plenty for later. She wrapped the poisonous roots carefully to keep them separate from the other herbs.

She sat back on her heels and surveyed the quiet glen. If she was careful and culti-vated the herb — and the deer didn't eat it all — she could supply Mr. Weaver with as much bloodroot as he needed, maybe even keep some to make red dye. Lydia would be pleased with the discovery. She'd been bemoaning the fact that she hadn't been able to make her baskets as pretty as the ones her Choctaw grandmother had made in years past.

Hefting her tote, Alanah continued to forage. When she'd get the chance to take her findings to Natchez was anybody's guess, but at least she'd have plenty to satisfy the apothecary and support her family. And for that, she had Lydia to thank.

When Aunt Rachel had taken sick almost four years ago, Uncle Jude had brought Lydia home to care for her. In spite of the fact that Lydia hadn't been able to save her aunt's life, Alanah became fascinated with the healing woman's knowledge of the forest and its medicinal herbs.

With every foray into the forest and every trip to the apothecary, she'd learned more and more, her mind soaking up knowledge like moss soaked up blood from a wound.

Her tote bulging with her early morning finds, she came to the road that led to Cypress Creek.

She stopped, looking both ways. The road was clear as far as she could see. She should turn back. She had no business anywhere near the cutthroats who hung out in Cypress Creek. But . . .

Her attention strayed across the road in the direction of the logging camp, wondering how Frank fared. He'd left with Tiberius almost a week ago, in anticipation of the O'Sheas' return, while she'd been out foraging. In spite of Lydia's objections, he'd decided he was well enough to go back to work and that was that.

The logger hadn't been a talkative man, and his presence had added to their workload, but at least it had broken the monotony of everyday life. And she missed Tiberius dropping by with fresh game or just to check on them, as well as the tidbits he shared about Caleb and life at sea.

She bit her lip. Truth be told, she was curious about the logging camp. From what Tiberius had said, she suspected the bluff they'd chosen overlooked the sandbar where she harvested squawroot. She crossed the road and hurried through the forest, hoping the men hadn't picked the one spot where she'd found the herb.

As she neared the bluff — her bluff and her sandbar — her heart sank.

Sure enough, the rising sun revealed the silhouettes of several sturdy cabins on the knoll, along with the tents she'd seen when she and Betsy had stumbled into their temporary camp weeks ago. The scent of frying meat wafted toward her as the cook prepared breakfast for the loggers.

Giving the camp a wide berth, she made her way toward the steep slope that led to the water's edge. But instead of the faint game trail she was used to traversing, she found a smooth road wide enough to accommodate a wagon. She lifted her skirts and made her way down the newly constructed road. A half-dozen logs lay scattered on the sandbar where they'd been pushed off the bluff to land in a haphazard heap at the bottom.

The sun had yet to ban the shadows at the base of the bluff, and squinting against the faint light, she skirted the pile of logs lying willy-nilly on top of each other like giant kindling, her footfalls muffled by the sandy shore along the river's edge.

Had the loggers already destroyed the squawroot?

Surely not.

The next thing she knew, she was jerked against the solid bulk of a man's chest, a knife at her throat.

"Who are ya, and what are ya doing skulking around here?"

Even as the words hissed through Caleb's clenched teeth, the shock of the soft fullness of a woman in his arms registered in his brain.

A flash of golden hair shot with red caught his eye.

"Alanah?" He let her go so fast that she stumbled back. She regained her footing, clutched one hand to her throat, and watched him, tawny eyes wide with fear.

Of him.

He held out a hand, and when she backed away, he realized he still gripped the long, wicked knife. He sheathed the weapon. "Sorry I am, lass. I did no' know it was you. Are you hurt?"

She fingered her throat. "No. I'm fine."

"What are you doing here?" Caleb gritted out, choosing to concentrate on his indignation at finding her at the base of the bluff rather than the fact that he'd almost slit her throat.

"Foraging."

"Foraging? In the middle o' the night?"

"It's not the middle of the night. It's morning."

"Barely."

And to emphasize her point, the sound of Gimpy's gong reverberated throughout the camp at that moment, calling the loggers to breakfast.

"But that still does no' explain why you're

165

here, in this spot." He motioned toward the logs. "What if the men roll another log down the bluff?" The thought of Alanah being crushed by the heavy logs made him weak-kneed.

"Well, as you said, it's barely daylight, and no one was stirring." She lifted her tattered skirts, turned away from the road, and headed toward a gully far back at the edge of the bluff.

"Where are you going?" Caleb followed, grabbing her arm. "Let's get out o' here before the men finish breakfast and start rolling logs down on top o' the both o' us."

"Not yet. I need to check on my squaw-root."

"Your what?" Caleb glared at her. "What are you talking about? I told you —"

"I know what you said, but I need this herb. And if you've destroyed it, so help me . . ."

"What's so special about an herb that you'd risk your life for it?"

"It's used to make tinctures for headaches, bleeding, and, um —" her face flamed, and she looked away — "other things. This is the only place I've found it. Well, there is one other place. But it's a day's journey from here."

"A day?" That meant two days to get this

precious herb she so desperately needed. Caleb didn't pretend to understand what it was, but he realized that the medicinal herb was used for healing, not just to add a bit of flavor to the stewpot. That made it important. He flung his hand toward the cliff. "Well, let's find this root of yours, and be quick about it, so you can be on your way."

He followed her to the farthest corner of the bluff, a steep, jagged tear in the earth filled with roots and trailing vines. A large oak clung to the top of the fissure, and Caleb wondered how long before the giant toppled into the gulch. He just hoped Alanah wouldn't be here digging for roots when that happened.

"Hold this." She handed him a large tote filled with her morning's work, tucked a small pouch in her waistband, and without hesitation, started climbing up the steep embankment.

Caleb hauled her back, growled in her ear. "Just show me what you need, and I'll get it."

She shook her head and smiled. "You wouldn't recognize it."

Caleb cut his gaze toward the deep, dark gash in the earth, the tangle of roots and vines masking a myriad of dangers.

"Don't worry." She patted his hand, then

shook off his hold. "I know what I'm doing."

Caleb watched as she scaled the cliff, clinging to roots and vines as she went. The sounds of the camp waking reached him, men calling out to each other, chains rattling, horses and mules balking at the work that lay ahead.

Caleb clenched his jaw as she climbed higher. "Alanah . . ."

"Almost there." Her muttered answer floated down to him.

She stopped, reached for something in the shadowy recesses of the vines. A snip and she tucked it in the pouch. Another snip, then another. Caleb crossed his arms, waiting for her to finish harvesting every blasted piece of the elusive root or herb or whatever it was that she found so important.

Alanah climbed down, the pouch bulging with squawroot.

Caleb stood at the base of the cliff, scowl firmly in place. "Are ya done, lass?"

"Not quite. Open that tote bag, and I'll pour these in, then —"

"I think you have enough."

"But —"

"Listen."

She stilled. Sure enough, she could hear

the rattling of chains and the rumble of logs being pulled across the ground. She stuffed the small bag into the large tote. "All right. I'll come back later."

They retraced their steps and headed toward the jumble of logs on the sandbar. A shower of rocks and debris rained down the cliff in front of them. Caleb pushed her behind him and planted his body firmly between her and the danger. She craned her neck to see around him. "What is it? What are they doing?"

"They're dragging logs into place t' roll off the cliff. Wait here." Caleb stepped away from her, cupped his hands together, and yelled at the loggers atop the bluff.

When the noise continued, he turned back to her. "It's no use. They canna hear me."

The sound of the harnesses, the yells of the men, and the logs grating across the ground drew closer. When the first of the logs tumbled over the cliff, Caleb and Alanah retreated toward the crevice where the squawroot grew.

A narrow sandbar curved around the bend, and he motioned her toward it. "We'll go this way. It's a steep climb, but we can make it. Connor's planning t' put another road here at some point."

"He can't do that. What about my squaw-root?"

Caleb shrugged. "You'll have t' take that up with me brother, lass."

"Very well." Alanah's lips thinned into a determined line. "I just might do that."

They maneuvered along the sandbar, the band of sand growing smaller with each passing step. Finally, with nowhere else to go, Alanah started climbing, Caleb right behind her.

Suddenly the vines she held on to gave way and she slipped. She yelped and slid down the steep incline toward Caleb. Clinging to an exposed root with one hand, his boots wedged against the side of the bluff, he caught her around the waist and wedged her body between his and the loamy-smelling earth. A smile kicked up one corner of his mouth.

"Whoa, lass."

Alanah tried not to stare at his mouth, just inches from hers. She looked away, her gaze colliding with his dark eyes, pools of black that flickered across her face to land on her lips.

His head lowered and —

A creak sounded, and suddenly the root cracked, and they jerked downward. Alanah's eyes widened. "Caleb!"

"They put the word out that they were looking for raftsmen." Elias whittled a piece of oak, his razor-sharp knife slicing through the wood as if it were no more than soft butter. "Now, Reverend, all you have to do is recommend these men for the job."

Jude eyed the three men standing behind Elias. "There's no reason Mr. Wainwright and Mr. O'Shea should take a recommendation from me."

"You had one of their men at your house."

"They brought him to us because of Lydia."

"They trust you well enough."

"The man had been shot." Jude glared at Elias. "He was in no shape to be moved, and Scripture tells us to love our neighbor."

"They probably paid you —"

"Only for his upkeep." Jude bristled.

Elias chuckled. "Rabbit stew and goat milk don't cost anything, not when your niece and that half-breed tend to things around here."

Jude kept silent. It was true that he'd left Alanah and Lydia alone more of late, but —

"Yes, you're just the man we need. After all, it was your idea for some of those good-for-nothing idlers hanging around Cypress Creek to go to work."

"I think it's time you left."

"All in good time." Elias peeled off another sliver of wood. Curling, the pale shaving fluttered to the ground. He shook his knife at Jude. "How's Betsy? You know, Betsy being Micaiah's girl, and you being her uncle, some would say we're practically kin." Elias laughed, and Jude wanted to wipe the smirk off his face, but he kept his mouth shut. Elias could turn in a moment, and Jude would be on the receiving end of his knife with one wrong word.

"And that other girl. What's her name? Alanah. Addled Alanah. Is she really as addled as they say? I doubt it. I mean, Betsy wasn't crazy." He cackled. "At least she wasn't much until Micaiah got ahold of her."

"You leave my nieces alone," Jude growled.

Quick as lightning, Elias flicked his knife, and it flew through the air to stab into the dirt between Jude's boots.

"You do as I say, old man, and I'll think about it."

Jude eyed the knife quivering between his feet, less than an inch from his right foot.

He swallowed the bile that rose in his throat.
Had Elias missed intentionally?

CHAPTER 12

The root snapped under their combined weight, and Caleb wrapped both arms around Alanah as they tumbled down the steep incline.

He grunted when he landed on his back on the narrow stretch of sand that sloped toward the river. But the momentum of the fall kept them going. They hit the water with a splash, and he tightened his hold on Alanah as the water closed over their heads.

When they surfaced, Alanah sputtered and flailed her arms, her heavy skirts making it difficult for her to stay afloat. Keeping a hold on her, Caleb scrabbled for a foothold on the sloping riverbed and headed for the bank. Thankfully, the current was slow enough that they weren't in any danger of being swept away, just soaked from a thorough dunking.

When they reached shore, Caleb climbed out, grasped Alanah's hand, and hauled her up beside him. They lay on the bank for a moment, breathing heavily. Caleb propped his head up on his hand, taking in the bedraggled waif beside him. "Are you all right, lass?"

"Yes, I'm fine." She pushed the hair out of her eyes, then blew out a breath.

The sun peeked over the bluff, pushing the remaining shadows away and bathing her with a golden glow. Yes, the patched and torn dress she insisted on wearing was covered in sand and dirt from where they'd climbed up the bank, but the river had washed the soot from her face and her hair, turning her golden mane into dark taffy that spread across her shoulders.

She looked like a sea nymph from one of the many seaman's tales he'd heard over the years.

Her lashes, spiked with river water, swept up. Caleb could only stare, remembering the way she'd looked the first day he'd seen her in Natchez.

"You have grass in your hair." He plucked a twig from the damp strands, flicked it away, then reached for another.

She lowered her eyes even as her cheeks turned crimson.

"And dirt on your face." He rested his hand on her jaw, using his thumb to wipe a smudge away. Only to make it worse. But even the smudge captivated him. As did the rest of her. His thumb inched downward, grazed her lips.

At his touch, she drew in a shuddering breath. "I — I need to go."

"Aye." Caleb stood, then held out his hand. She hesitated just a moment before allowing him to pull her up. And that's when he realized all was quiet. No chains rattled. No logs plummeted over the cliff —

"Are you sure he came this way?"

Alanah gasped as Connor's voice floated to them from around the bend. She grabbed the soggy tote and clutched it to her. Caleb stepped in front of her. "It's all right. You've done nothing wrong, lass."

"I'm sure." Isabella's voice sounded frantic. "But the next thing I knew, the men were shoving logs over the cliff. And then —"

Her voice broke off as she rounded the bend. Mouth formed in a perfect O, she glanced from Caleb to Alanah, taking in their disheveled state, clothes dripping and caked in mud. Her surprise quickly turned to amusement, and she arched a brow.

Connor's reaction was the exact opposite of his wife's. "What is going on down here?" His angry glare swung from Caleb to Alanah and back again.

"It was my fault." Alanah lifted her chin. "I came to harvest some squawroot."

"Some *what*?" Connor all but shouted. "Are ya daft?"

"Squawroot." Caleb crossed his arms. "It's good for what ails ya. Perhaps you should try some, Brother."

"I know what it is." Connor waved a hand at the two of them, soaking wet. "I meant this. The two of you."

"I'm sure it was an accident, Connor." Isabella stepped forward, her attention on Alanah. "I don't believe we've met. I'm Isabella O'Shea, Caleb's sister-in-law."

"Alanah Adams, ma'am." Alanah curtsied, looking like a half-drowned lion cub and just as cute.

"I suspected as much." A slight smile turned up the corners of Isabella's mouth. "Caleb and Connor told me about you. It's so nice to finally meet you."

"Likewise, Mistress O'Shea." Alanah glanced at Caleb, her tawny eyes narrowing as if she wondered exactly what he'd said about her.

"Please, call me Isabella." Isabella removed her wrap and draped it around Alanah's shoulders. "Now, if you gentlemen will excuse us, I'm sure Alanah would like to get into some dry clothes before she catches a chill."

"Please, you don't have to —"

"I insist. And besides, you don't want to walk through camp looking like that. We'll get you set to rights in no time."

Alanah threw Caleb a helpless look as Isabella led her away.

"There's no need, Mistress O'Shea." Hands clasped in front of her, Alanah faced Isabella, aware of the spectacle she presented.

Wrinkling her nose, she plucked a decaying leaf from her skirt, but one withered leaf wouldn't do much to improve her appearance. Her tattered dress stuck to her, the muggy air making the damp dress even more uncomfortable. She wiggled her toes inside her moccasins, feeling them squish against the damp leather and knowing they probably looked like half-dried persimmons by now. She should have gone barefoot today, but she hadn't anticipated falling into the river with Caleb O'Shea.

Heat rushed through her at the thought of the dark-eyed Irishman. Thankfully, Mistress O'Shea was too busy rummaging through a trunk to notice.

"I can't allow you to return home in this state. And please, Isabella will do."

"Yes, ma'am."

Alanah glanced around the newly constructed dogtrot cabin, the scent of fresh logs tickling her senses. They hadn't even hung a door yet, but a blanket covered the opening, providing a measure of privacy. There wasn't much in the room. Two trunks, a rustic table that looked to have been cobbled together out of boards from a wagon, and two stumps for chairs. A washbasin and pitcher sat on another small table by the door. No fireplace as of yet. Maybe they didn't intend to stay through the winter. A rope bed covered with a patchwork quilt took up an entire corner of the room.

"Please excuse the mess. The men just finished the cabin, and I haven't had time to sort things out." Isabella pulled out a shift, stockings, stays, tossing each piece on the bed. "But after a week of sleeping in the tent, I'm just thankful to have a roof over my head. And a bed."

She rummaged in the trunk again, then stood, hands on her hips. Pivoting, she strode to the other trunk. "I've got an extra stomacher here somewhere. It's a bit worn. I hope you don't mind."

Alanah shook her head. "I don't mind at all, Mistress —"

"Isabella." Her smile and friendly tone

convinced Alanah she meant what she said. Did the woman really want to be friends? With her?

"Isabella, then." Alanah inched for the blanket-covered doorway. "Truly, ma'am, I can wear my own clothes home."

"We've already been over this." Kneeling before the trunk, Isabella pulled out a green- and cream-colored stomacher and held it aloft. "Here it is. And now for some petticoats and a fichu, and you'll be all set. I'm sorry I don't have an extra pair of shoes."

Giving in to the inevitable, Alanah curled her toes in the damp moccasins Lydia had made for her. They were made for fording streams and would dry quickly enough. Moving to the bed, she eyed the delicate embroidery on the stomacher.

"Alanah? Is something wrong? Is the garment not to your liking?"

Face flaming, she shook her head. "No, ma'am, it's lovely. It's just that . . ."

"Ah . . . you are shy. I'll leave you alone." Isabella motioned to the washbasin. "Please, wash up then, and call me if you need assistance getting dressed. I'll be across the breezeway in the other room, organizing the office."

After she left, Alanah turned to the clean,

patch-free clothing scattered on the bed, fresh heat flushing over her body at the thought of Isabella O'Shea helping her undress, seeing that she wasn't wearing proper stays, but a strip of leather fashioned by Lydia instead. And her under petticoat? Ha!

The garment was so torn and tattered that it wasn't even a proper petticoat. It was too thin to hardly use as a sieve. But as it was one of only two she owned, she kept wearing it day in and day out. And would continue until it disintegrated, thread by thread. Then she'd use the pieces that were left to patch her other one until it too wore out.

She reached out to touch the dainty lace fichu, then jerked her hand back, curling her fingers into her palm. She daren't soil the lace with her filthy hands. But Isabella would return soon, and she expected Alanah to have bathed and changed.

The curtain over the opening swung gently in the breeze. She could leave. Just slip out. But Isabella had been so kind. Sighing, she unfastened her dress and slipped it off her shoulders. Piece by piece, she removed her tattered, torn, and patched garments, leaving them in a soggy, soiled heap on the floor.

She stalked toward the washbasin. If she

was going to wear Isabella's clothes, she'd be clean doing it.

Thirty minutes later, she ran her fingers down the dark-green skirt, the material durable and well suited for work, but still feminine and pretty. As Isabella had said, the stomacher was by no means new, but it was still the prettiest thing she'd ever donned, embroidered with burgundy flowers and green vines that matched the skirt.

Eyeing Isabella's brush, she couldn't resist unsnarling the tangles in her hair. She'd hardly made a dent when a gentle knock sounded at the doorway. "Alanah, are you decent?"

"Yes, ma'am."

Isabella entered, smiling. "You look lovely." She crossed the room and took the brush from Alanah's hands, motioning toward one of the stumps. "Sit."

Alanah did as she asked, and Isabella moved behind her and continued to brush. "Your hair is beautiful. Such an unusual color. From your mother's side of the family or your father's?"

"Both." Alanah fingered a tendril of hair. "Papa was Scottish with flaming red hair, and Mama was blonde, so I ended up with this odd coloring that defies description."

"Well, it's lovely."

"Thank you."

Isabella paused midstroke at the sound of footfalls on the porch. The blanket pushed back and Connor stood there. "Isabella —" He broke off when he spotted Alanah seated on the stump, her unbound hair fanned about her shoulders. He let the blanket fall back into place.

"Isabella." His voice floated to them through the barrier. "Where's the ledger? I have some new hires to add to the payroll."

"It's — oh, never mind. You'll never find it." Isabella handed Alanah the brush, her lips tilting into a teasing smile. "Wait until Caleb sees you in this."

Suddenly shy, Alanah stood, running her hands down the green skirt.

"Isabella?" Connor's voice boomed again. "I canna find it."

"Coming." Isabella ripped the blanket back and hurried across the breezeway, her voice floating back to Alanah. "It's right there, Husband. Plain as the nose on your face."

"Well, they all look the same to me."

The sound of boots parading into the cabin across the breezeway tied Alanah's stomach in knots, and she took her time fixing her hair, building up the courage to step through that blanket-covered doorway.

It was one thing to play dress up with the sweet and friendly Isabella. Quite another to be gawked at by Connor O'Shea, the loggers, and even worse, Caleb. Her cheeks grew warm at the thought of the kiss they'd almost shared.

But there was nothing for it. They were here, right outside, and she'd have to —

"Thank you, Reverend." Caleb's voice floated through the thin barrier. "My brother was beginning t' despair o' finding raftsmen t' run the river."

"I'm glad to be of service. Just keep your eye on them."

Alanah froze in place.

Uncle Jude?

Caleb hung back, allowing the reverend and the new hires to file inside ahead of him. Leaning against the doorway, he studied the half-dozen men lining up to make their mark. They looked hardy enough if a bit rough. Shifty even.

But that was the way of seagoing men, so he didn't really expect river raftsmen to be any different. And the reverend didn't have to tell him to be wary of such men.

Out of the corner of his eye, Caleb saw a flicker of movement. He turned, saw Alanah slip from behind the blanketed doorway across the breezeway and pad toward the rear of the cabin, the shadows masking her escape.

Escape?

Why did she feel the need to escape?

As soon as she disappeared from sight, he followed, noticing that she'd changed out of her rags and wore a voluminous green skirt instead. Something of Isabella's, no doubt. She'd gained the safety of the forest before he caught up with her.

"Alanah —"

She turned, and he sucked in a breath. Gone was the waif he'd half drowned in the river. In her place stood the woman he'd seen in Natchez. But they were one and the same, and both set his insides aflame.

"What's wrong, lass? Why are you sneaking off like a scared rabbit?"

Her attention shifted toward the cabin. "I should be getting home."

"Is it your uncle?" Caleb scowled. "Are you afraid o' him?"

"Not afraid, but . . ."

"But what?"

"He wouldn't like it if he found me here." She fingered the dress. "Or if he found me wearing this."

Caleb gaped at her. The dress was becoming and, while he wouldn't embarrass her

185

by saying so, a sight better than what she'd had on before. And her fresh-scrubbed face and golden hair pinned up in an enchanting style reminded him of the way she'd looked the first day he'd seen her on the wharf in Natchez Under-the-Hill.

"I do no' understand. Is it the charity that he would disapprove o'?"

"No, it's not that." She ducked her head. "He — he thinks that . . . that I'll be safer if I wear rags and, um . . . um, act like . . ."

"Like you're addled?"

Her lashes swept up, and her golden gaze caught his, surprise and a hint of shame written on her face. "You — you've heard the rumors?"

"About Addled Alanah and Looney Lydia?"

"Yes."

"Aye. I've heard."

"I see." She lowered her head, but not before Caleb saw the tinge of red that crept over her cheeks. "I should be going."

She froze when his hand landed on her forearm. He was so close, he could have traced the arch of her brow, the curve of her jaw, the tendril of hair she'd missed when she'd swept it into a knot at the nape of her neck. But she was poised like a gazelle about to bound away, so he simply said,

186

"You look quite fetching in your new frock, Mistress Adams."

"And that is why my uncle insists I wear something — less becoming." They both looked up when Connor, her uncle, and the others filed out of the cabin. She shook her head. "Please, don't tell him I was here."

And with that, she wrenched out of his grasp and fled.

Puzzled, Caleb watched her go, then walked back toward the cabin. Isabella stood on the porch, her brow furrowed, the blanket pushed back revealing the empty room. "Did you see Alanah?"

"She's gone."

"Gone?" Isabella toed the pile of sodden clothing. "She forgot her clothes. I'll send them home with her uncle."

Caleb shook his head. "I do no' think that's a good idea."

"Why not? He'll be going straight home, won't he?"

"She did no' want her uncle t' know she'd been here."

She'd been in such a dither, she'd forgotten her tote.

Alanah crouched in the shadows, eyeing the dogtrot cabin she'd just fled from. Should she go back for the bag that held the squawroot she'd come for as well as an entire morning's work? No, she couldn't. Not after she'd run like a scared rabbit and not as long as Uncle Jude was there.

He wouldn't be pleased that she'd disobeyed him and roamed so far from home. But how did he expect them to survive if she didn't forage? For all his itinerant preaching, he rarely brought coin or provisions home, using the excuse that the small gatherings he attended had little to spare.

Alanah didn't doubt his word. Most who lived in the small hamlets in the Natchez District were as impoverished as Alanah's own family. But she suspected the meager support from the locals had more to do with her uncle's shortage of compassion than from their lack of coin.

She loved her uncle, but his dearth of Christian charity confused her. Why couldn't he be more like her father? Papa had been a big, brawny Scotsman, loud and boisterous, but also loving and kind.

Papa loved people, and he loved telling them about Jesus. And he even loved his trips to Natchez to preach to those less fortunate.

In the end, he'd sacrificed his life for them.

Had Uncle Jude been as harsh and unbending before Papa died as he was now?

Memories of happier times surfaced, with Papa, Mama, Aunt Rachel, and the tiny babes she'd birthed.

No, Uncle Jude hadn't always been so hard and unforgiving. Unforgiving to the point that he would no longer preach to the river pirates, claiming they didn't deserve God's grace.

The sound of saws brought her back to the present. She spotted more than one draft animal pulling logs along the road to the bluff that overlooked the sandbar.

Where was her uncle?

She spotted him sitting on a stump at the cookhouse, talking to the cook. Had he hired on to help the cook? She smiled. Uncle Jude couldn't even boil water as far as she knew.

Her attention shifted to Caleb as he led the new hires toward the bluff. Her heart slammed against her rib cage as she recognized one of the men who'd been on the flatboat with Elias Jones. Then another. Narrowing her gaze, she looked closely at every one of them. All shifty characters rumored to be more thieving scoundrels than honest, hardworking men.

And all cohorts of Micaiah and Elias Jones.

True, they knew the river, and they knew

rafting, but if she didn't miss her guess, every single one of them used their skill for evil and not good. Should she tell Caleb? He needed to know . . .

She glanced back toward the cookhouse, and her uncle was nowhere to be seen. With a start, she gathered the green skirt and raced toward home.

CHAPTER 13

Head down, Jude paced, hands behind his back.

When he reached the edge of the yard, he turned, shuffled the length again, pivoted, and retraced his steps. The darkness did little to stop the unrest in his soul. If anything, it added to it.

Cry against them, for their wickedness is great.

Jude gritted his teeth. *No, Lord. I will not. These men do not deserve Your mercy or Your grace. They will not turn from their wicked ways, so why should I preach to them?*

The more he paced, the stronger God's wooing spoke to him.

Cry against them.

I recommended Massey and those cut-throats to the O'Sheas to protect my family. I could go to the O'Sheas, tell them what kind of men they're dealing with, ask for protection for myself and my nieces. The very thought

191

filled him with dread. Why should the O'Sheas help him after he'd unleashed a den of vipers in their midst?

With each step, his thoughts ricocheted from heartfelt prayer to desperation. Was he praying for the highwaymen's salvation or begging God for forgiveness for his own culpability? Shouldn't he be asking the O'Sheas for forgiveness? Shouldn't he go straight back to the logging camp and set things to rights?

He would, but for his nieces. Elias had threatened his nieces. Betsy had run off with Micaiah — or if Alanah could be believed, the fiend had stolen her away. In spite of Jude's rejection of her, even he could see that she was damaged in ways she hadn't been before. He wouldn't have his nieces' lives — or their deaths — on his head. Didn't he owe it to their parents to see them back to safety somewhere away from this vile and violent land?

"Uncle Jude?"

He stopped pacing, lifted his head, saw Alanah standing on the porch. He covered his worry with a gruff tone. "You should be in bed, girl."

"So should you." She sat on the steps, wrapping her cloak around her shoulders. "Is something bothering you, Uncle Jude?"

He searched her face, then resumed pacing. One turn, then two. Each step burying him deeper and deeper in his quandary. He would never understand why his brother-in-law had come to this backwoods place, where thieves and robbers stole and killed without compunction. Without remorse.

It was one thing for the man to come himself, but to bring his family and for Rachel to insist on coming? His Rachel. Where he'd been weak, she'd been strong, determined to face down anything to lead others to Christ.

This place, these people, had killed his Rachel, had killed their babies.

Jude paced, wanting to pray, needing to pray, but remorse smote his heart with what he'd done today. What he'd become. Halfway across the yard, he stopped, faced his niece, and rocked back on his heels. "I'm thinking of going back to Philadelphia."

"Philadelphia?" Her eyes went wide with surprise. "But, Uncle Jude, you left Philadelphia years ago."

"Yes. Fifteen to be exact."

"I don't understand." Alanah shook her head. "I thought the Lord called you to the Natchez District —"

"That was your father's calling, not mine." He thought back on the life he'd led as a young preacher in Philadelphia, following in his brother-in-law's footsteps. People had welcomed them into their homes, providing lodging and meals, but more importantly, they listened to the message of God's love. They'd *wanted* to serve God. They'd wanted to turn their backs on their wicked ways and spend their days basking in God's blessings. Not so here in Cypress Creek.

These men relished their evil ways.

"Yet you came anyway. You and Aunt Rachel."

"Yes, we came." He looked away, unwilling to let her see the indecision in his face. "But I feel led to go back."

Lord, is that the truth? Am I simply following my own will or Yours? I don't know where You want me, what You want me to do. Stay here and let men like Micaiah Jones violate my nieces? I've buried my wife, our four infant sons, and now cutthroats and river pirates are running rampant all over the countryside.

There was no answer. Jaw clenched, Jude resumed pacing.

I won't stay here and preach to men who don't deserve Your forgiveness. And I won't subject my nieces to more abuse at their hands.

■ ■ ■ ■

Alanah stared at her uncle. Had he gone daft?

"Uncle Jude, I can't go back. This is my home, the only home I've ever known. There's nothing for us back there. No family. No land. Nothing."

Bushy brows lowered, her uncle glowered at her. "You'll do as I tell you, you hear me, girl?"

"Yes, Uncle." Alanah swallowed, attempting to gather her wits, even though her uncle's sudden announcement had scattered her thoughts in a million directions. "Have you made up your mind without question?"

"Yes. We'll leave in a fortnight."

"A fortnight?" How would they make the long journey to Philadelphia with hardly the clothes on their backs? "We — we don't have any money."

"I have the coin O'Shea gave me, and we'll sell the chickens and the goats."

Those meager coins wouldn't buy food for a week, let alone the months it would take to make the long journey north.

"What about Betsy? She's not strong enough to travel that distance on foot. And what will we do when we get there? Please, Uncle Jude, this is our home. Don't —"

He whirled to face her. "What would you have me do, lass? Stay here in this hole that's being taken over by murderous thieves? We should have left when your parents died. If we had, Rachel might still be alive, and Betsy . . ."

He trailed off. Uncle Jude didn't have to say more. Alanah knew exactly what was on his mind.

"We'll head north. People will take a preacher in. They always do. We'll find a place, one filled with godly men and women. People unlike the lawless sort who've taken over Cypress Creek."

She tried one last tactic, the only thing she could think of. "It's September. Winter will be coming on. Maybe — maybe we should wait until spring."

"I dare not wait any longer." He strode past her, his steps echoing on the porch. "I'm going to Mount Locust in the morning. We'll need to join up with a party of travelers. As soon as we get our affairs in order, we'll leave."

Long after he'd gone to bed, Alanah sat on the steps, clutching her stomach, afraid if she let herself, she'd deposit her supper in the dirt at the edge of the porch.

■ ■ ■ ■

"Thank you for showing me the way, Caleb." Isabella walked alongside Caleb, Tiberius following a few steps behind.

When Alanah hadn't returned for her bag full of herbs or her clothes, Isabella had decided to go to her. She'd approached him first thing this morning asking that he accompany her to Alanah's at the end of the day.

Caleb frowned. "Connor will no' be happy."

"Let me worry about my husband."

They arrived at Alanah's, and Caleb paused at the edge of the clearing and let himself see Alanah's home through Isabella's eyes.

It was a sobering sight, even for a poor lad who'd lived in a hovel back in Ireland.

But Isabella didn't comment on the derelict cabins or the wattle fencing that needed repairs. Which didn't really surprise him. His sister-in-law didn't seem to be one fazed by difficult circumstances.

Alanah stooped over the fire under the arbor, stirring something in a pot. She'd changed out of Isabella's clothes and once again wore a hodgepodge of mismatched, patched pieces. But Caleb couldn't blame her. His own work clothes left a lot to be desired. He chuckled. Even his best left a lot to be desired. As soon as she spotted them, she quit stirring, wiped her hands on her apron, and headed toward them.

"Isabella. Caleb." Her tawny eyes met his, and her face flushed. Or was the heightened color on her cheeks simply from slaving over a steaming kettle? Her cheeks grew even redder, and she looked away, ignoring him. Caleb held back a grin. Nope. Her blush didn't have anything to do with the heat of the fire, unless it was the one he'd started when he'd almost kissed her two days ago.

"Good afternoon, Alanah." Isabella held out the bundle. "Your clothes, and Caleb has your tote."

"Thank you. You shouldn't have come all this way."

"I didn't mind. I wanted to see Cypress Creek and find out where you lived as well."

Caleb dropped the tote on the porch. "Is your uncle here?"

"He left yesterday for Mount Locust."

"He travels alone?" Isabella shook her head. "Doesn't he fear for his life with the highwaymen plying the roads?"

Alanah shrugged. "He has no coin, so they let him be."

A chopping sound came from the woods, and Alanah jerked her head up. "What's that?"

Caleb glanced around, saw that Tiberius had disappeared. "Tiberius. Sounds like he's chopping wood."

Alanah's gaze shifted to the meager pile of wood beside the cabin. "He shouldn't —"

"It's the least we can do after the care you and Lydia gave Frank." He backed away. "If you'll excuse me, I'll give him a hand."

As he walked away, he spotted Betsy watching from the shadows of the barn. He smiled and gave her a jaunty wave, but she scurried away as if he'd shouted "boo" at her. The poor girl seemed to be terrified of her own shadow.

Feeling quite shy around Isabella, Alanah moved back to the fire and stirred the pot of stew. The tantalizing aroma wafted upward. What was she supposed to do with a female guest? Other than Lydia, Betsy, and herself, there hadn't been another woman at their cabin since . . . since before her mother and Aunt Rachel had passed away.

She tried not to think how run-down everything must look to a lady like Isabella. "Could I offer you some refreshment? A bite of stew? Or —"

"No. No food, thank you." The color leached out of Isabella's cheeks, and she clutched her stomach. "Actually, if I could just sit down for a bit . . ."

Alanah rushed to Isabella's side, slid an arm around her waist, and led her to a chair on the porch. "Lydia!"

Instantly Lydia materialized out of the shadows and, without a word, pulled another chair over, lifted Isabella's feet, and propped them up.

Alanah stared at Isabella's face. "Are you all right? Should I call Caleb?"

"No." Eyes closed, Isabella wagged her head. "I'll be all right in a moment or two."

"Bring a damp cloth." As Lydia knelt by Isabella's side, Alanah ran to do her bidding.

When she returned, Lydia folded the cloth and placed it on Isabella's forehead. After a moment, Isabella sat up, the color returning to her cheeks.

Lydia stared at her. "You are in the family way."

It wasn't a question.

"How did you know?" The color deepened on Isabella's cheeks. Then she waved a hand. "Never mind. I can see you have a sixth sense about these things."

Lydia's lips twitched, and Alanah could

200

tell she was pleased that she'd been right. "How far along?"

"Two months, I think. I just began to suspect last week. This is the first time I've felt queasy, but —" a sad little smile flitted across her face, and she smoothed a hand over her flat stomach — "I was sick with my first. I lost the baby. A perfect little angel. A boy."

Alanah's heart broke at the sorrow in her voice, and she placed a hand on her arm, no longer worried about entertaining her guest, but only comforting her. "I'm sorry, Isabella. Are you sure you don't want me to get Caleb so he can take you back to the logging camp?"

"No, and I don't want you to tell him. Or anyone."

Alanah pursed her lips. "Not even your husband?"

"Especially not Connor. Not yet. He'll worry, and he'll send me back to Breeze Hill."

Lydia's gaze met Alanah's, and it was clear she didn't agree, but she said nothing. "I will make some tea. It will help with the nausea."

As Lydia disappeared inside, Alanah took the tepid cloth from Isabella and dipped it in cool water, wrung it out, and handed it back.

Isabella pressed the cloth to her forehead. Eyes closed, she asked, "Why did you leave so suddenly the other day?"

"I — I just needed to get home."

"Was it because of your uncle?"

"Why would you say that?" Alanah busied herself with the stewpot.

"Just something Caleb said." Isabella waved a hand toward the bundle. "I washed your belongings. I hope you don't mind."

Her face flamed. That meant Isabella had seen every rip, every tear, every patch. She turned toward the house. "I'll get your dress. Thank you for loaning —"

"Please, the dress is yours. It was a gift." Isabella peeked out from underneath the damp cloth. "But you have to wear it the next time you visit me at the logging camp. Promise?"

Alanah chuckled. "I promise."

"Good." Isabella removed the cloth, folded it, and gently dabbed at her cheeks. "I don't mean to pry, but how long will your uncle be gone?"

"A few days. Weeks. Months." Alanah shrugged. She hoped his declaration that they'd head north within the fortnight meant nothing. "One can never tell."

Isabella's mouth gaped. "He leaves you all alone for months? Without protection?"

"We can protect ourselves if need be." Alanah lifted her chin.

"I don't doubt that. It's just that those who intend harm are more likely to move on to easier targets if there's a man about the place."

Alanah couldn't help but agree. Would Micaiah Jones have spirited her sister away had their uncle been here to protect her? Or would he have just bashed in her uncle's head and taken Betsy anyway?

"Forgive me, Alanah. I didn't mean to disparage your uncle. It's a high calling to preach to the masses."

"Yes, sometimes I wonder if his calling would be easier on him if he didn't have us to care for." Alanah emptied her tote, spreading the herbs out on the table. She separated each, wincing that the mushrooms had already started to blacken.

"And your parents? What happened to them?"

"My mother died of swamp fever nine years ago, and my father died in Natchez Under-the-Hill not long after." She jerked her head toward the cemetery plot behind the house. "They're buried back there, along with Aunt Rachel and her four babes."

"Ah, your uncle's wife?"

"Yes."

"Poor man." Isabella gently rubbed the tips of her fingers in a circle on her stomach. "No wonder he feels lost here."

Alanah's heart squeezed, and she felt a kinship with the woman. Somehow she understood the pain of loss. The pain of looking on it every day.

"And where was your home before?"

"Philadelphia."

"That had to be a shock, coming from Philadelphia to the backwoods of the Natchez District."

"I was so young, I remember none of it."

Alanah separated the last of the blackened mushrooms from the yellow tansy and flicked them into the bushes.

"I see you know your medicinal herbs."

Alanah glanced at her. "You recognize these?"

"Some of them." Isabella pointed to a clutch of yellow tansy. "I know enough to stay away from that one."

"It has its uses." Alanah looked at her pointedly and smiled. "But you're wise to avoid it while carrying."

"You're a healer, then? Connor told me what you did for Frank."

Alanah cringed. She'd done nothing for

the injured logger except faint. "Lydia is the healer. I'm blessed to be learning from her."

"Do not let her fool you." Lydia returned, a mug of steaming tea cradled in her hands. She handed the tea to Isabella. "She has the gift."

"The gift? Of healing?"

"The gift of healing will come, I think. But she has more. She has the gift of discernment for which herbs are good for different ailments. She takes what I teach her of the woods and what Mr. Weaver —"

"Mr. Weaver? The apothecary in Natchez?"

"Yes. You know of him?"

"Who doesn't? It's fascinating that you work with Mr. Weaver. How — ?"

"I don't work with him." Alanah motioned to the herbs spread out before her. "I simply supply him with what he needs."

"She does more than that." Lydia snorted. "She listens and applies what she learns to make her own concoctions. When she can get the supplies she needs."

"You have trouble finding herbs for Mr. Weaver?"

"It's not that so much as it is getting them to Natchez." Alanah ducked her head. "Uncle Jude forbids me to go."

"But you do it anyway?"

"Sometimes it's necessary." She shrugged.

"Why not send your herbs to Mr. Weaver with Caleb." Isabella eyed her. "I'm sure he would be more than willing to help."

"Help with what?"

Startled, Alanah knocked half her squaw-root to the ground. As she bent to retrieve the roots, she peeked at Caleb, standing less than ten feet away, arms loaded with fire-wood.

CHAPTER 14

Caleb's attention swung between the two women.

"Alanah needs someone to take her herbs to Natchez." Isabella smiled, looking pleased with herself. "I thought you could do that when you go."

"Aye." Caleb stacked the firewood beside the cabin. "I would be glad t'."

"I don't want to be beholden." Alanah peeked at him from beneath lowered lashes. "But thank you just the same."

" 'Tis no' any trouble. Just let me know —"

He stopped as the thunder of hooves pounding down the overgrown lane reached him. Sounded like half a dozen horses or more. Tossing the firewood to the side, he drew his pistol and primed it. "Tiberius?"

"I am here." The Moor's voice floated to him from the shadows.

Caleb motioned to the women. "Isabella,

get inside. Alanah, Lydia, you too."

The women obeyed. Sort of. They backed into the shadows of the porch, and out of the corner of his eye, he saw Alanah nock an arrow and heard Lydia prime and cock her old flintlock.

When the riders rode into sight, Caleb breathed a sigh of relief. It was Connor, accompanied by several of the loggers. William must have returned within the last hour.

Connor threw himself off his horse, looking around. "Where's Isabella? Gimpy said she was with you."

"She's here." Caleb's relief turned to concern at the frantic look on his brother's face.

"Connor? What's wrong?" Isabella rushed down the steps. "Is it Patrick? Or Papa?"

Connor grabbed her by the shoulders. "No, they're fine. Something happened back at camp, and then Gimpy said you were gone and —"

"What happened?" Caleb interrupted.

"Jed Willis was killed today."

"Killed?" Isabella gasped. "What happened?"

"I do no' know." Connor threw a glance at Caleb, and he knew there was more to Willis's death than his brother had let on.

208

He turned back to his wife. "Isabella, promise me you won't leave camp again. When I could no' find you, I thought —"

"I'm sorry, Connor. I'll do as you say." She patted his arm. "Just let me say good-bye to Alanah and Lydia, and I'll be ready to go."

As soon as Isabella was out of earshot, Caleb moved closer to his brother. "I take it this was no' an accident?"

"No. Willis was murdered. With his own ax."

A chill settled over Caleb. "Could he have tripped and fallen? Maybe —"

Connor's face grew hard. "If you'd been there, seen . . . seen his body, you'd know somebody killed him."

"But why?"

"Do these cutthroats need a reason?"

Her good-byes said, Isabella headed back toward them. Connor glanced around, then settled his attention on Caleb. "Where are your horses?"

"We walked. It's only a couple o' miles as the crow flies."

His brother scowled. "I do no' like Isabella traipsing all over the woods with these highwaymen roaming about." Connor lifted her to his horse, then mounted behind her. He motioned to the mounted men with him. "You want to ride double back t' camp?"

"No, we'll walk. Tiberius isn't much for riding."

"All right, then." Connor nodded. "Watch yourself."

"We will."

Alanah watched his brother and the others ride out of the yard. "That man, Willis — he was murdered, wasn't he?"

Caleb sighed. There was no use in keeping the truth from her. "Aye."

Sorrow filled her eyes. "It's the way of it here in Cypress Creek."

"It should no' be." Caleb frowned, remembering the battles he'd fought on foreign soil and on ships' decks. And over what? Sometimes nothing more than the rotting hull of a sloop or a patch of parched earth. "Why can men no' live in peace?"

"Because Satan fills their hearts with wickedness and their bellies with ale, and their thoughts are on evil continually. It's been this way since Cain killed Abel."

"Aye, you're right about that, lass." Caleb rubbed a hand around the back of his neck. "Perhaps you should come to the lumber camp —"

She lifted her chin. "We will stay here. It's our home."

"Knowing there's a killer loose out there?"

She smiled, but her eyes remained as serious as his next heartbeat. "There have been killers in these parts for as long as I can remember."

"Then why do you stay?"

"Where would we go?" She sighed. "That's not true, I suppose. Uncle Jude is talking about going north, but —"

"You're leaving?"

"Perhaps." Brow knit, she shrugged. "Uncle Jude says it's the Lord's will."

"And do you agree?"

"It matters not whether I agree. I must go where Uncle Jude wishes for me to go."

A pall had fallen over the lumber camp by the time Caleb and Tiberius returned. Not even William's arrival from home with fresh butter and eggs lifted it. Everyone filed to a knoll overlooking the river, where they buried Jed Willis, his two brothers standing over his grave, hats in their hands, devastation on their bearded faces.

Horne spoke a few words over the grave, and they all tromped back to camp, a somber bunch.

Isabella pleaded a headache and retired to her cabin, and Caleb joined his brothers and William outside the office.

William leaned against a post and eyed the men as they gathered in small groups, talking of the incident. "This is unfortunate, unfortunate indeed. The last thing we need is for the men to become skittish. Do you know what happened?"

"Nay," Connor said. "Maybe he had an argument with someone at the tavern, or he ran afoul o' the highwaymen out in the woods."

"Or his killer could be one of our own." William nodded toward the men Reverend Browning had recommended. "Who are those men, and where did they come from?"

"Reverend Browning brought them over two days ago. They're riverboat men, no' loggers."

William grunted. "No wonder they're keeping apart from the others."

Caleb straightened as Jed's brothers approached the raftsmen. "Looks like that's about t' change."

The tension mounted as Sam Willis exchanged words with a sour-faced crewman who went by Whiskey Massey. The next thing Caleb knew, Massey threw a punch at Willis. Men yelled, and within seconds, the entire camp had converged around the two men, shouting encouragement. Soon, it was obvious the loggers were rooting for Sam, the river crew for Massey. As was the custom with fistfights, no one stepped in, not even William or Connor.

From his vantage point on the porch, Caleb watched the fight. Sam was a big, brawny man, muscles honed from years of swinging an ax or pulling a crosscut saw. One perfectly placed blow from a meaty fist would knock almost any man out.

Caleb's attention shifted to Massey, and he knew that even though the raftsman was smaller, more wiry and less muscled, he'd kill Willis given half the chance. And he wouldn't do it with his fists. Massey had been in camp for only three days, but his short temper and predilection for too much ale made an explosive combination. An uneasy feeling in the pit of his stomach, Caleb stepped off the porch, strode toward the ring of men, and pushed his way to the front.

The men went down in a flurry of fists, grappling to gain the upper hand on the other. Sam Willis grabbed his opponent by the throat and squeezed. Massey's eyes bugged out, and then Caleb saw him scrabble for the knife strapped to his thigh.

Caleb rushed forward and kicked the knife away before Massey had the chance to plunge the blade into Willis. Tiberius and

Willis's younger brother pulled Sam off Massey before he could choke the man to death. Connor stepped in, helped Caleb haul Massey to his feet. Both men, held at bay, growled at each other like rabid dogs.

"Let me at him. He killed my brother."

"Sam, there's no proof of that." His brother held him back.

"I asked him where he was this afternoon, and he refused to say. And that's good enough for me." Sam Willis struggled vainly against Tiberius's and his brother's hold. "He's had it in for Jed ever since that gal over at the tavern wouldn't have anything to do with him."

William stepped forward, facing Whiskey Massey. "Mr. Massey, is it?"

"Just Massey, yer lordship," Massey snarled.

William stood ramrod straight, his pale-blue eyes like ice. In spite of his dusty clothes, he still carried himself like a gentleman, his commanding presence at odds with the rough-and-tumble lumberjacks and the raftsmen. And if his cold presence wasn't enough to make the men cower, Connor's glare was.

Ice and fire. Dandy and danger. Different as night and day, but now Caleb understood the bond of friendship between the two.

"I'm not a lord, Mr. Massey. I don't hold a title of any kind. I assure you bowing and scraping is not necessary." William clasped his hands behind his back. "However, my father owns this land that we stand on, along with these trees, and up until this day, he owned the papers of one Jed Willis, deceased. And that concerns me. You've been accused of his murder —"

"I didn't kill anybody, least of all a lousy cracker." Massey glared at the Willis brothers. "But iffen he'd gotten in my way, I would have."

An angry rumble rippled through the loggers backing the Willis brothers, the tension rising again as Massey showed no remorse or compassion for the dead man.

"That's enough, sir. You'll do well to hold your tongue."

"Massey?" All eyes turned to Connor. "Would you care t' tell the Willis brothers where you were this afternoon?"

"It ain't none of their business."

"None o' their — ?" Connor glared at Massey. "Well, I suppose t' save your neck, I'll tell them. Mr. Massey did indeed spend the night and most o' the morning at the tavern but agreed to make up the time this afternoon. He was with me and Vickers working on the timber raft when word came that Jed had been found murdered."

Vickers nodded. " 'Tis true."

"I know what I know." Sam Willis stabbed a meaty finger toward Massey. "You'd best watch yer back." Sam stomped away, his younger brother following behind.

Soon the others dispersed, leaving Caleb, Connor, and William alone. Connor scraped a hand along his jaw. "There's going t' be trouble between those two."

"Aye." Caleb nodded. "The good news is that we'll be leaving for Natchez soon. Mayhap Sam will cool off while we're gone."

"What do you think?" Connor looked like the landlubber he was as he struggled to keep his balance on the logs.

"It'll do." Caleb walked the length of the eighty-foot raft. He'd put a halt to Vickers's ideas of making it bigger, wider, longer, and even more cumbersome. They had to be able to control the logs or they'd float all the way past Natchez and New Orleans into the ocean.

Vickers had proved himself to be knowledgeable about timber rafting and trustworthy to boot. And just from hearing him talk, Caleb expected he knew more about the river than the rest of them combined.

Connor stepped off the logs back onto the

sandbar. "Will it hold up t' the ravages o' the river?"

"No reason it shouldn't." Glad he'd grilled Vickers, Caleb pointed to the massive oar mounted to the front of the raft. "That's the sweep. The sweep man will make sure to keep the front of the raft away from the bank, keeping an eye out for snags and such."

"And those on the side? Does Vickers plan t' row the thing?"

"They're not for rowing. They're more for steering and shoving the raft off sandbars. And see those poles at the back? Those are snub poles. When we want to slow the raft, we drop the ends in the river and they create a drag."

"I hope this works."

Caleb slapped his brother on the back. "It'll work. Have faith."

"Easy for you t' say. I've got a crew o' loggers here itching for their wages."

"They'll have them. Vickers says we'll be back in three to four days if we don't run into any trouble."

"Closer to five. Maybe six. William plans t' buy more horses, mules, wagons, whatever he can get when he sells the logs. Locating what he needs might take time."

Thankful to hear that William would be

making the trip with them, and that they wouldn't have to walk back up the trace, Caleb hunkered down and pounded a plug through a crossbar to hold the logs in place. "Are you sure you do no' want t' go along?"

"No. We're still on edge because o' Jed Willis's death, and I won't leave Isabella and Patrick." Connor squinted at the raftsmen securing logs, Massey among them. "Even though I do no' think Massey had anything to do with Jed's death, I'd sink this whole raft on the hunch that he knows who did."

"Aye. He's a cagey one, that's for sure."

"Watch yourself. I do no' like keeping him on, but I have no reason t' let him go."

"Do no' worry, Brother. I've dealt with the likes of Whiskey Massey before."

"Whiskey?" Connor scowled. "Fittin' byname, I suppose."

"Aye." Caleb's chuckle was cut off by a shrill whistle.

"Connor!" William beckoned from the bluff overhead. "We need you up here. Björn has a problem with one of the teams."

Connor stepped off the raft and headed toward the bluff, and Caleb started making rounds on the timber raft, checking rigging, tying down their supplies, securing the three-sided lean-to in the middle of the raft.

It was rough, but plenty decent enough for a night or two on the river.

Not long after, he heard Gimpy's dinner gong sound. Massey, Vickers, and the others stopped and trooped up the steep road. Caleb finished securing the supplies, then measured the rope coiled on the raft. From what Vickers had said, they'd need eighty to one hundred feet of rope to snug up to shore if they didn't want to miss their chance of a good landing spot at night.

"Caleb?"

Heart jumping at the sound of Alanah's voice, he turned, spotted her standing on the sandbar, looking . . .

All golden and beautiful with the late-afternoon sunlight haloing around her.

Gone was the patched and worn shift she usually wore, and instead she'd donned the clothes Isabella had given her.

When he continued to stare, the expectation on her face faded, and she turned away, motioning to a packhorse loaded down with two canvas bags. "Tiberius said you were leaving in the morning, and I brought the herbs. That is — if you're still willing to deliver them to Natchez for me."

"You changed your mind, then?"

"Lydia insisted." She looked away. "We'll need every bit of coin we can scrape together if Uncle Jude is serious about heading north."

Caleb didn't stop to wonder at the knot that lodged beneath his heart at the thought of never seeing her again. "You do no' sound convinced that he'll really go."

"I'm hoping he'll change his mind because . . ."

"Because o' what?" He stepped off the raft. "Because you want t' stay?"

"Yes. I want to stay. Very much."

Caleb stared into her golden eyes and found himself agreeing with her. Very much. She looked away, and clearing his throat, he reached for the horse's lead rope, led the animal closer to the raft.

Alanah followed, her gaze taking in the logs connected to each other with poles secured by plugs. "It's huge."

"Vickers wanted t' build it even bigger."

"I can't imagine how you'll manage something this big. You must be taking half the logging crew."

"Just five or six men."

"May I ask for one more favor?" She reached into a pocket and held out a piece of paper. "Do you mind picking up these supplies from Mr. Weaver?"

"I do no' mind." He tucked the note inside his jerkin and hefted one of the heavy packs, then peered under it to catch a glimpse of her face. "Did your uncle load these packs?"

"Uncle Jude is still away." She reached for the other pack.

"I'll get that." But she paid him no heed. Caleb led the way toward the raft. "He should no' leave you women alone like that. Tiberius will check on you while I'm gone."

"That won't be necessary."

"Do no' be pigheaded. You, Lydia, and Betsy need someone to look after you, especially after what happened to Willis."

"He won't bother us." She tapped her temple with her finger. "I'm touched in the head, you know. We all are."

"Anybody in his right mind would know you're no' tetched, so that argument will no' hold water with me." He stepped onto the raft, ducked into the lean-to, and tossed the cumbersome pack toward his bedroll.

He turned, found Alanah behind him, the smaller pack cradled in her arms. A smile played across her lips. "So you weren't fooled? Not even in the beginning?"

"Especially no' in the beginning." He took the pack from her and stored it next to the other one, then moved out from under the shelter and leaned close. "I saw you first in Natchez, remember, looking like you had come from one o' those fancy mansions up on the hill."

"You're poking fun." Cheeks pinkening, she turned away.

Caleb chuckled. "Now why would I poke fun about something like that?"

She shrugged, then picked at the bark on the poles they'd used to construct their shelter. "I've seen those girls at brush arbor meetings and such, and no way would I ever be mistaken for one of them."

Caleb closed the short distance between them. Lifting her chin with his forefinger, he searched her eyes, perfectly shaped face, and golden-streaked hair that begged for his touch. Even as his gaze roamed over her face, his hand slid along her jaw, his fingers plunging into her hair at the nape of her neck.

"You're right," he whispered. "There's no way you could be mistaken for one o' them."

And as the timber raft rocked gently on the water's surface, his eyes slid shut and he dipped his head closer to hers.

Alanah froze as Caleb tugged her closer, panic warring with anticipation.

His long, dark lashes swept down over black eyes, and his lips closed over hers, soft, warm, and sweet. Her mind and Uncle

Jude's warnings told her to pull away, to run as fast as she could back to the cabin, to shuck the pretty clothes and cover the sweet-smelling jasmine that lingered on her skin with the odor and filth of dirt.

But her heart . . .

Oh, her heart said otherwise.

For just a moment, she gave in to the call of her heart. Closing her eyes, she savored the feel of Caleb's lips against hers, marveling at the way he angled her body to fit against his, one arm fitting around the curve of her waist as only he could, the other supporting her shoulders as he dipped into the kiss.

Nothing had prepared her for this gentle assault on her senses.

Her eyes jerked open when the timber raft shifted against the current. Caleb pulled back, and as if in an herb-induced stupor of her own making, she blinked to clear her head. Caleb looked as dazed as she felt. His eyes, at half-mast, flickered over her face, and her fickle heart gave a delicious shudder. The raft rocked with another surge of the current, and she clutched at his shirt. Caleb's arm tightened around her waist, his hand splayed across her back, and his lips curled into a smile.

"Do no' worry, lass. I've got you."

And so he did. Somehow she knew he wouldn't let her fall, but even if she did, he'd be there to catch her. Her heart pounded at the trust she'd just handed this man. She hadn't had that much faith in anyone, and especially a man, since her father had died. She pressed her hand against his jerkin, the feel of his chest warm beneath her palm. But still —

"Please."

Her plea snuffed the light in Caleb's eyes as surely as if she'd pinched out a candle. Just like that, it was gone. He put some distance between them but held her elbow, keeping her steady.

"Forgive me for taking liberties."

Her face flamed. "There's nothing to forgive."

"Well, that's good t' know." A grin played with his lips, the same lips that had been pressed against hers only moments before, and she —

She jerked her gaze away from his lips before he got the impression she wanted him to kiss her again. Because she didn't. Oh, but heaven help her, she did.

Before she gave in to the crazy, wild riot of feelings he'd awakened in her, she motioned to the sandbar that looked a world away. "I should go."

"Aye. You should."

And as he led her across the log raft, the surface rocking gently with the current, she realized that more than one thing had been tilted out of balance today.

CHAPTER 15

Once the timber raft got under way, it was like gliding over butter.

The heavy logs eased right out into the center of the river, and they were on their way. It wasn't long before they rounded a bend, and Cypress Creek came into view, spread out before them, the sprawling tavern that doubled as a way station for travelers perched on a hillside.

As they passed, Caleb could see why travelers liked to stop. A wide sandbar allowed flatboats to beach with ease. Someone had pounded heavy pilings into the sand to tie off boats and had taken the time to build a pier.

And Alanah lived less than half a mile beyond on the road past the landing. Suddenly he was transported to the soaring feeling of holding her close, his lips against hers. For a moment, when the raft had shifted under their feet, he'd seen complete and utter trust in her eyes, in the way she relaxed against him as if she knew he'd keep her safe no matter what.

"Stop your woolgathering, O'Shea. Pull away from the landing like this." Vickers grabbed the sweep and pushed the blade far to the right to force the raft to turn into the current. "Feel the river?"

Thankful for something tangible to distract him from his thoughts, Caleb concentrated on the long pole. "Aye."

The raft turned, but not as much as he'd hoped. The press of a hundred tons of logs drove them on a collision course toward the shore. Suddenly he realized what he was up against. The power of the river was greater than the placid waters of any ocean surface current save those driven by wind. "We're going to ram the bank."

"No, we're not. Keep sweeping." Vickers manned the pike pole on the starboard side of the next section of logs. The much smaller sweeps on the sides helped control the serpentine twisting of the raft as it plowed downriver.

Caleb kept up the motion that Vickers had shown him, his efforts seeming to do little to turn the timber raft away from the landing. Even as he watched, figures left the tavern and congregated on the knoll overlooking the river, pointing and slapping their knees. He could hear their guffaws echoing across the water. If they didn't turn it soon, they'd plow right into the landing. Frantically he glanced over his shoulder.

William and another raftsman stayed at the pike poles attached to the third and final section of the raft, but it didn't seem as if their efforts were helping to steer clear of the shore either. Teeth clenched, Caleb dug the sweep into the water. "Vickers!"

Vickers ignored Caleb's distress call but instead moved to the port side of the raft, where Massey was stationed. "Give way, Massey."

Massey waved him off. "I'll do my job, old man. You do yours."

"Well, if you were doing your job, I wouldn't have to."

Ignoring him, Massey remained at his post.

"It's not turning!" Caleb called out.

"I told you to leave off." Vickers shoved Massey out of the way. The raftsman went sprawling across the rough timbers. Vickers grabbed the oar and started sweeping the river, using a countermotion that pushed the center of the chain raft inward toward the shore each time he dug the long sweep into the water. Caleb immediately felt the front of the raft start to turn.

It was working!

Caleb put muscle behind the sweep, keeping the momentum going.

"Ease off, O'Shea. Don't overcompensate. Drive easy-like toward the center of the river." Vickers didn't sound the least bit frazzled. "We don't want to get tangled up in a knot of pinewood."

Caleb did as instructed and felt the raft pull into the current. Feeling elated, he glanced over his shoulder just in time to see Massey regain his footing and charge Vickers. "Look out!"

The wiry old river hand ducked under the handle of the sweep, jerked it down, then shoved the heavy beam forward and upward, clipping Massey under the chin as he came in swinging. Massey dropped like a rock, and Vickers went back to sweeping the water as if nothing had happened. Caleb stood frozen in shock, hardly able to believe what he'd just seen.

"Keep your mind on the task at hand, boy."

"Aye, sir." Caleb chuckled.

And just like that, the timber raft slid into the current, curled neatly around the bend, and straightened out. Caleb stopped trying to turn the raft and let it drive forward on its own. Vickers lifted the oar out of the water, strapped down the pole, then joined Caleb and William in the center of the raft.

He glanced toward Massey, still out cold, and winced. "I'm sorry about that, Mr. William. From what Massey said, I thought he could handle sweeping round a bend. But when he refused to relinquish control, I kind of lost my head."

"Nothing to be sorry about, Mr. Vickers." William shook his head. "If it hadn't been for you, we wouldn't have made it. I owe you a debt of gratitude. And an apology of my own."

"An apology, sir?"

"Yes. I underestimated your knowledge of the river. We could all use a bit of training on how to navigate the river with this much weight pushing us downriver." William looked at Caleb. "Don't you agree?"

"Aye, I agree." Caleb held out a hand. Slowly Mr. Vickers took it. "Captain Vickers."

"Captain?"

"T' the best man goes the title."

"Thank ya both, but —" Vickers twisted his hat in his hand — "if it's all the same to you, I'd planned to stay in Natchez at the end of this trip with my wife and family. I'd hoped to see Mr. Wainwright about a job at the sawmill."

"I think that could be arranged." William slapped Vickers on the back. "If you'll teach us everything you know about manning the raft during this trip."

Vickers grinned. "Be happy to. More than happy to."

Caleb grabbed a bucket, filled it with river water, and tossed the entire thing over Massey. The man groaned and sputtered, rolling on his side. Caleb hunkered down, pinning him with a look.

"Ya just bucked the captain, Massey. I'd tread lightly from now on if I were you."

A heavy fog rolled in a couple of hours before nightfall, and Vickers took down a horn, blowing it every few minutes in warning. When the fog grew so thick they could no longer see, they snugged up to the bank, secured the raft with ropes, ate supper, and were in their bedrolls by dark.

Caleb took the first watch, then woke Vickers. Seemed like he'd just dozed off when William nudged him.

"Somebody's stirring." William's voice was hardly more than a whisper accompanied by the lapping of water against the logs.

Caleb eased his pistol out. Keeping still, he primed and cocked it, the sound masked by the creaking of the logs as they shifted and rubbed against each other. From where he lay, he could see Vickers, seated in the center of the raft, his back to him.

There. He heard a faint rustle to his right, out of his line of sight. The scrape of boots along the timber raft was so quiet that if William hadn't woken him, he wouldn't have stirred from his slumber. Squinting against the darkness, Caleb spotted a figure, nothing more than a shadow.

There was no way to warn Vickers without alerting the intruder. Then he heard a second sound, one right outside the shelter. A whoosh of air and he rolled away, heard the thud of a blade as it stabbed into his bedroll.

William's pistol blasted next to his ear, and his attacker fell backward, tearing the canvas covering away. Caleb crouched, turned toward Vickers, and saw him grappling with the first man. He didn't dare shoot for fear of hitting Vickers. He rushed forward, knife in hand.

But before he reached them, Vickers fell, and the hulking form stood over him, silhouetted against the night sky, one hand gripping a wicked-looking blade. Caleb leveled his pistol and squeezed the trigger. The boom of the shot reverberated across the river, and the man stumbled backward to splash in the shallow water at the edge of the raft.

Caleb hurried toward Vickers. "Vickers, are ya — ?"

"Cut the lines."

"Cut the — ?"

"Do it. Now!"

Caleb and William rushed to do Vickers's bidding, the timber raft soon floating free. As the distance between them and the shore increased, Caleb crouched next to Vickers, eyes searching the shadowed shore.

"I'm sorry. I didn't hear them."

"They weren't making enough noise t' scare up a cat." Caleb reloaded his pistol, checked to make sure his knife was in easy reach. "I would no' have heard them if William had no' alerted me."

"Was it Massey?"

"I have no' seen him or his cohorts since the shooting began, so —"

"They're all gone. Massey, Colbert, and Wheeler," William interrupted, crouching beside them. "Are you hurt bad, Mr. Vickers?"

Vickers ignored the question. "Light a couple of lanterns in case there's any other crazy folks out on the river this night. And put up a distress flag at sunrise. You'll pass

233

a settlement about midmorning. Some . . . some good men there. You can trust . . . trust . . ."

"He's lost consciousness." William motioned toward their sleeping hut. "Let's get him inside, and I'll see to his wounds."

While William tended Vickers, Caleb hung a lantern on a pole at the front of the timber raft and one at the back, the light spilling out across the river, then joined William and Vickers.

Caleb watched William for a moment before eyeing the river. "What woke ya?"

William grinned. "Well, you probably won't believe me, but remember when I tied up the raft last night? I had about forty feet of rope left and didn't know what to do with it. So I just ran it across the logs and tossed it into the lean-to. And then, at bedtime, I unrolled my bedroll across that rope, figuring if anyone was sneaking around during the night, I'd know it."

"I canna . . ." Caleb shook his head, then chuckled. "Well, your rope trick saved our necks."

Moonlight played across the river as Micaiah shoved the wizened old Kaintuck overboard.

The frail body landed with a splash, sank

234

briefly, then bobbed back to the surface. Curiously, he watched as the body flipped straight up and the arms floated on top of the water as if the old man would swim away. Which was quite funny when he thought about it.

He wrinkled his brow as the body continued to float. Maybe he'd miscalculated the old farmer's body weight. But sometimes it took a while. He crouched on the flatboat and waited for the water to soak into the man's clothes, air pockets to dissipate, and the weight of water and the rocks tied to the old man's feet to pull him under.

The flatboat drifted downriver, leaving the old man behind, head lolling to the side, and still the body remained visible. Micaiah chuckled. The old codger should've gone straight to the bottom after all the corn whiskey he'd guzzled throughout the night. The bodies of his sons had disappeared as soon as he'd rolled them over the side.

Though Micaiah didn't really care one way or the other if the body sank, the least amount of evidence left behind, the better. The old man was being just as stubborn and hardheaded in death as he'd been in life. Long after his sons had passed out from the whiskey, their pa had still been hard at it. But finally, in the wee hours, he'd also given in to the effects of the strong brew, and Micaiah had reached for the knife tucked in his waistband.

Quietly and efficiently, he'd dispatched the boatmen from Kentucky with no more compunction than he'd feel gutting a fish.

After killing the guards and escaping from the flooded jail, he'd made his way to the Big Black River and knifed a lone traveler on a small raft, then floated downriver toward the Mississippi. When he'd spotted the larger flatboat loaded with goods headed to market, he'd cut the ropes holding the stolen raft together, letting everything float away. Except the whiskey, that was. He'd spun a sad tale about losing all his goods when his raft had slammed into a sandbar, and the old man and his sons had been more than happy to take him and the whiskey on board.

The ploy had worked more times than he could count. His men would move up the trace with a group of unsuspecting travelers, hire on as raftsmen in Nashville or some little hamlet, and then bide their time to take over the rafts. And dead men couldn't tell tales.

This time had been no different, other than the fact he'd been alone in the endeavor and had kept the old man and his sons alive until they cleared the smaller river. The four of them had floated down the Big Black for several days before he'd made his move. There hadn't been any reason to do away with them when they could man the craft until he didn't need them anymore. More than once when they'd had to dig out from a sandbar, he'd been proud of his restraint. But once they'd hit the Mississippi, he'd made his move.

As the distance between the flatboat and the body widened, the old man's hoary head finally sank beneath the smooth surface, his arms floating upward to be the last to go as if he were still grasping at life until the bitter end.

The old man and his sons forgotten, Micaiah turned away, eyed the flatboat loaded with corn, barley, wheat, and tobacco. He'd make landfall at Cypress Creek within days, bearing gifts for all.

Pleased with the turn of events, he lay down amid his newly acquired wealth and closed his eyes. With this and whatever Elias and the others had managed to take on their trip down the river, the next few weeks should be fine. Mighty fine indeed.

Caleb noticed the cabins becoming more and more frequent the farther they went downriver. "Natchez can't be too far away."

"Father's sawmill is just past the wharf at Natchez Under-the-Hill." William sighed. "We'll need to steer clear of any boats there but manage to get close enough to shore so that we can tie off. This is one stop we can't miss."

"How's Vickers?"

"He's running a fever, but at least he's alive."

They'd bypassed the settlement where Vickers had told them they could pick up an extra hand or two. They hadn't had the manpower to handle the boat and send someone to tie off the raft, and no one had been around to heed their calls. They'd just rolled on past, unable to do anything to stop their forward momentum.

When Natchez Under-the-Hill came into view, Caleb's heart sank. Several ships were anchored offshore, some tied up to the pier, along with flatboats tucked in here and there. The Natchez side of the river was a hub of activity.

"Stay t' the middle o' the river till we clear the landing."

William nodded, taking his position on the opposite side of the timber raft. As soon as they passed the congested area around the wharf, they started pulling hard on the sweeps, trying to nudge the raft toward the sawmill. Their efforts seemed to be in vain. Caleb spotted the landing in the distance, half a mile away, but —

"The horn, Caleb," Vickers called out from where he lay under the lean-to, his voice weak. "Blow the horn."

The horn. He'd forgotten the horn.

Caleb grabbed the bullock horn and gave it three long blasts, then three more for good measure. Dropping the horn to dangle around his neck, he dug the sweep into the river, pushing against the current to turn the hundred-ton raft toward the shore.

"We're not going to make it. We're still eighty yards out." William's voice sounded strained. "Blow the horn again."

Blast after blast echoed across the river, and to his relief men spilled down the bluff. They shoved off from the shore and rowed their rafts out to meet them, towing ropes they'd hitched around pilings driven into the banks.

Soon, the men met them, tossed loops over posts on the raft. Then one of the men waved his hat high and yelled toward the shore. "Reel her in."

And that's just what they did. The men onshore started taking in hitches around the sturdy posts, and the distance between the timber raft and the bank narrowed slowly but surely. When the edge of the raft stopped with a jolt against the bank, the men cheered.

Caleb accepted the congratulatory slaps on his back as he made his way toward the shelter where Vickers lay. "We're here, Vickers. We'll get you to a doctor."

"Just get me home to my wife."

"Aye." Caleb laid a hand on the man's shoulder. "You're going to be fine."

"We need some help over here." William motioned to several of the men, and they gathered around, lifted Vickers, and carried him off the raft.

William's father stood on the landing, watching them disembark. He called for a wagon, and they loaded Vickers in the back, instructing the driver to take him home and call a doctor.

With Vickers taken care of, Mr. Wainwright eyed Caleb and William. "From the looks of you two and Vickers there, I take it the trip was . . . trying."

"You don't know the half of it." William clasped his father's hand. "The rest of the crew jumped us in the night. We managed to fight them off and cut the ropes, leaving them behind. Vickers was injured and was in no shape to help. That left Caleb and me to manage the raft alone. And we had hardly a clue what we were doing."

"But you made it. And just in time, too. The crews just finished digging the saw pits, so we can start sawing logs right away. I've already signed agreements with two contractors." Mr. Wainwright slapped his son on the shoulder. "You should both be proud."

"If it had no' been for Mr. Vickers, we would no' have made it." Caleb shrugged off Mr. Wainwright's praise. "He's the one who knows how t' navigate the river."

"He'll be rewarded for his service." Mr. Wainwright studied the logs. "How quickly can you deliver more?"

"I daresay Connor and the loggers will have this many or more ready to go by the time we get back to camp." William looked at Caleb. "What do you think? Another week, maybe?"

"Aye. I do no' see why no'."

"Good. More than good. It's wonderful." Mr. Wainwright rocked back on his heels. "There are no less than five mansions being built on the bluff as we speak, and word has it that plans for more are being drawn up. I can sell everything you deliver and more."

"There's just one problem, sir." Caleb cleared his throat. "We need a trustworthy crew."

"Bloomfield should be able to help with that. And what about supplies?"

"I have a list." William handed over a sheaf of papers. "We need more loggers, more draft horses, saws, iron. It's all here."

Mr. Wainwright studied the list, then folded it and stuck it in his inside pocket. "Very well. Grab your bedrolls, and we'll head to Wainwright House. I'm sure you both would like a bath and some of Mrs. Butler's home cooking."

When Caleb dropped his gear, along with Alanah's two large packs, in the sand at the edge of the raft, Mr. Wainwright shot him a quizzical look.

William laughed. "That's not all bedding and clothes, Father. Caleb promised a certain young lady that he'd deliver a bunch of medicinal herbs to Mr. Weaver."

"The apothecary?"

"Aye, sir." Caleb hefted one of the packs and slung it over his shoulder. "If I could borrow a horse or a mule, I would be indebted."

"I'll do better than that. We'll take one of the wagons." Mr. Wainwright picked up the other pack. "Weaver's shop is not far from Bloomfield's office. William and I can stop by there while you take care of your business."

CHAPTER 16

When Mr. Wainwright pulled to a stop outside the apothecary's, Caleb jumped down and grabbed Alanah's packs from the back of the wagon.

He stepped inside the shop, dropped the packs, and looked around. Every surface was covered with bottles, jars, clay pots. Clumps of dried herbs hung from the ceiling, and a sickly sweet odor wafted from somewhere in the dark recesses of the building. Whatever the apothecary was brewing, it certainly didn't smell like supper.

The curtain in the back parted, and a wizened man with spectacles shuffled out, a cloud of steam following in his wake. He wiped his hands on a stained apron, then inclined his head in greeting. "Good day, sir. Weaver at your service. How may I help you?"

Caleb motioned to the packs. "Miss Adams sent these for you."

A smile bloomed on the old man's wrinkled face. "Miss Adams, eh? How fares she?"

"Very well. She sends her regards."

With a murmur that might have meant agreement, the apothecary cleared a spot on the cluttered countertop, then motioned for one of the bundles. Caleb obliged, untying the drawstring. One after another, the man pulled out the contents, sniffing each small bundle or jar in turn. With the hundreds of scents swirling around them, Caleb wondered how he had a clue what each contained. But apparently he had a nose for such things.

"Tansy. Slippery elm. Pokeweed. Cypress oil. Yes. Hmmm." He pulled out a good-size packet, sniffed, then shook it in Caleb's face. "Aha! Bloodroot. Do you realize how hard this is to find? That dark-haired miss must have inherited her acumen from her Choctaw relatives."

"You must be referring t' Lydia." Caleb crossed his arms, the movement stretching the leather jerkin over his shoulders. "Mistress Adams's hair is no' dark. 'Tis like honey, it is, shot through with gold."

"Gold and honey?"

Heat flushed up Caleb's face, and it wasn't from the close quarters. "If ya do

244

no' want t' buy the herbs, say so directly, and I'll be on me way."

"Don't go off half-cocked." The old man cackled. "I just wanted to be sure you hadn't filched these herbs from the miss, tried to sell them to line yer own pockets."

Caleb glared at the crusty old man, then relaxed. The apothecary was only watching out for Alanah. With that in mind, he kept silent, watching as Weaver finished his inspection of the bulkier but much lighter bundle, containing what looked to be little more than weeds and vines.

"What?" He riffled through the packs strewn across the counter. "No turkey tails?"

"I would no' be knowin', sir."

"I know it's a harrowing journey, but you tell Miss Adams I'll make it worth her while if she'll send me some mushrooms post-haste."

"Aye. I'll be sure t' relay the message."

The apothecary finished his inspection of the contents of the packs, then removed his spectacles, cleaned them with his apron, and squinted at Caleb. "I shouldn't give you the coin for Miss Adams's herbs, but —"

"Maybe this will convince you that Alanah sent me." Caleb held out a piece of paper. "She asked for these supplies."

With another suspicious grunt, the apothecary hooked his spectacles over his ears and took the note. He held it close, read it, then nodded. "It's her handwriting all right."

"Aye. I'll see that she gets the supplies and the coin."

"See that you do." As he gathered the supplies, Weaver's rheumy eyes caught and held Caleb's. "I don't believe I caught your name, young man."

"Caleb O'Shea."

"If I may be so bold, Mr. O'Shea, as to ask how you know Miss Adams?"

Caleb pinned him with a piercing look. "I do no' think that's any o' your concern."

The apothecary sighed. "Forgive me. I shouldn't have asked, but I was hoping you might have plans to marry the girl —"

"Take her t' wife?" A flush crept up his neck. What did Mr. Weaver know of what had happened back at the logging camp? Was he a soothsayer as well as an apothecary? "I hardly know the lass."

You know her well enough to kiss her.

"I shouldn't have said anything." Mr. Weaver shook his head. "It's just that I worry about her, what with that uncle of hers leaving her alone for weeks at a time, especially after what happened to her sister."

"Betsy?" What had happened to Betsy?

246

He'd just assumed she was a simple, shy woman-child who had a way with animals.

"Yes. That's the one."

"What happened t' her sister?"

Mr. Weaver consulted the list again, then uncorked another bottle. A foul-smelling odor assaulted Caleb's nostrils, bringing tears to his eyes. The apothecary didn't seem to notice as he tipped a small portion into a smaller vial. "You haven't been here long, have you?"

"A few weeks."

"Ah." The apothecary looked askance at him. "Ever heard of Micaiah Jones?"

"The name is no' familiar."

"Micaiah Jones is a thief, a cutthroat, and a river pirate. He and his outlaw bunch landed in Natchez a few times, and they always strike fear into the hearts of everyone they encounter. Young Betsy is the latest in a string of girls those brutes have kidnapped over the years." Weaver's reedy voice vibrated with indignation. "They take them as their women — if they don't murder them outright."

Caleb's stomach turned at what Mr. Weaver had told him. But surely he was wrong about Betsy. "I saw her — the one they call Betsy. She's home with her sister."

Mr. Weaver glanced up. "Is she now? And

how does she fare?"

"She seems . . . disturbed." Caleb lifted a shoulder. "But I did no' know her before."

"A sunnier, friendlier young lady you couldn't have found." The apothecary shook his head. "Those cutthroats. They should be hanged for what they've done."

Memories of the raid on a village on a small island in the Atlantic swamped Caleb: the fierce battle, the thunderous roar when the soldiers of fortune were victorious over their adversaries. And then . . .

Fortified with the flush of victory and the abundance of strong drink, he and his fellow soldiers set about celebrating, drinking and dancing with the grateful islanders. Hours later, after consuming more ale than should have been humanly possible, Caleb found himself squared off against one of his compatriots, a sharp, curved blade pointed at his stomach.

And a tavern wench at the heart of the squabble.

He couldn't say how he'd gotten to the point of fighting over an island girl whose name he didn't even know. But as the others gathered round and goaded his opponent to defend the girl's honor, it was too late for either of them to back down.

Even to this day, he could still see the

other man's blue eyes staring at him with the same dazed and confused look that must have mirrored his own. Both had been young. Both *eejits.* Both determined to show the hardened mercenaries they had what it took to stay the course, and that killing — even over the smallest slight — meant nothing to them.

Wielding his knife, the other man had lunged, lost his footing, and ripped open Caleb's thigh. They fell to the ground, and Caleb's own knife tore through the man's torso. And just like that, the drunken revelers cheered, their disregard for human life evident in the fact they didn't care one way or the other if either man lived or died.

His blood seeping into the sands of an island he couldn't name for a cause he didn't believe in, Caleb had lain there, his eyes glued to the man he'd just gutted. And for what?

Nothing, save the approval of men who'd sunk to the very bottom of all that was holy and decent.

Unable to look away, he watched as the life in the man's eyes faded and they became set, staring into nothing but the finality of death. Filled with horror, shame, and disgust at what he'd done, Caleb vowed to do better.

And by the grace of God and the steadying hand of Tiberius, he had.

"Mr. O'Shea?"

Caleb blinked, returning to the present. The apothecary held out the last vial, carefully wrapped to survive the journey home. "That's everything. See that you handle these with care, and tell Miss Adams that I am pleased her sister has returned safe and sound. If I were you, I'd keep an eye out for Micaiah Jones. He's not one to give up a girl as pretty as Betsy without a fight."

Caleb left the shop, Alanah's packs no longer weighing him down. Unlike the heavy burdens he carried from his past and the worry that plagued him over what Mr. Weaver had told him of Alanah and Betsy.

The afternoon was far gone when Lydia snorted. "It's that man again."

Since Lydia didn't sound overly concerned — just irritated — Alanah didn't reach for her bow. She looked around but saw no one. "Who?"

"Tiberius." Jaw clenched tight, Lydia jerked her chin toward the tree line. "There. He just stepped out of the shadows."

Alanah spotted him then. He stood at the edge of the clearing, his ebony skin glistening, sunlight glinting off the gold hoop in his ear. She cast a sly grin toward Lydia. "Aren't you going to welcome him?"

Lydia pummeled the kernels of corn with her mallet with more force than necessary. "I do not trust him."

"You don't trust anybody." Alanah chuckled. "Methinks you like him more than you let on."

"You think wrong. That one is up to no good."

"He seems nice enough. And look how polite he is. Waiting for an invitation to join us." Alanah dusted her hands on her apron and turned toward where Tiberius waited patiently for permission to come near the house. "Tiberius. Welcome."

"Miss Alanah." He moved out of the shadows, something tucked into the crook of his arm.

"How's Mr. Abbott?"

"Not happy to be doing odd chores around the camp, but he is mending. He sends his regards."

"What brings you out today?"

He threw a quick glance in Lydia's direction, then just as quickly returned his attention to Alanah. He opened his coat and a tiny black-and-white masked face peeked out. Then another.

"Oh, Tiberius. Baby raccoons." Alanah

moved forward, taking one of the tiny kits from him. "What happened?"

"Moses and I found them in a tree yesterday."

"The mother?"

"We saw none. Moses said to leave them, and the mother would return." He shrugged. "But this morning they were still there, crying. And this afternoon, still no mother."

Alanah knew the loggers cut trees and moved on. Tiberius must have gone out of his way to check on the kits this morning, then to return to see about their welfare again this afternoon.

His dark eyes rose to meet hers. "I didn't know what else to do with them."

"You did the right thing." She turned, spotted Betsy peeking out the open doorway. "Betsy, come. Look what Tiberius found."

Unable to resist the furry babies, Betsy inched outside, her attention shifting from the large man to the tiny kit nestled in Alanah's arms. Soon her desire to hold the raccoon overrode her fear of Tiberius and she took another step, meeting Alanah at the edge of the porch. She smiled as Alanah handed her the cuddly animal. Carefully, she wrapped the tiny raccoon in a piece of her tattered skirt and snuggled it close, crooning softly.

Tiberius stood uncertainly, the other kits still nestled under his coat. Lydia pounded corn, her disapproval of the turn of events evident in every loud thwack of her mallet against the wooden bowl.

Alanah found a basket, lined it with some moss before grabbing one of Uncle Jude's undershirts off the line.

"Don't use that," Lydia barked, looking disgruntled.

Alanah frowned, holding up the garment. "But it's already threadbare."

"It's serviceable. There's an old apron in the cupboard inside. Use it instead." Lydia jerked her head toward the cabin. "They're likely hungry as well. Betsy, fetch the last of the goat milk cooling in the creek."

Grinning, Alanah rushed to do Lydia's bidding. The woman had a soft heart underneath all that bluster. Betsy returned with the milk, and Alanah poured a bit of it into a bowl. It wouldn't take much to satisfy the kitten-like creatures. She placed the bowl on the ground, and Betsy lowered the one kit to the bowl, then crouched, watching. She turned worried eyes on Alanah. "It's not eating."

"It will. Give it time."

Tiberius hunkered down, pulled raccoons from his coat until a total of six kits tottered around on the ground. After sniffing at the milk, one brave babe poked his nose in, jerked back, and shook his head, blowing milk out his tiny nose. Betsy giggled.

Tiberius dipped his finger in the bowl, then held it out to one of the kits. The babe wrapped its paws around his finger and suckled. One by one, he coaxed each of the tiny animals to the bowl, helping them learn how to drink. Soon they dove in, each scrambling for its share.

Leaving Tiberius and Betsy hunched over the raccoons, Alanah joined Lydia. Lydia had stopped grinding the kernels as if she needed to beat them to a fine powder.

One of the kits pushed its way forward until half its body was immersed in the bowl, hogging the milk. Tiberius fished the raccoon out of the bowl and held it fast to keep it from diving back in. The feisty kit scrabbled on all fours, pushing against his hold. Betsy's laugh mingled with Tiberius's deep chuckle, and Alanah caught a smile pulling at Lydia's lips.

Tears sprang to her eyes, and she turned away lest Lydia see and ask what ailed her. Nothing ailed her. It was pure happiness that welled up from inside, clamoring to be free.

It was the first time Lydia had smiled today and the first time she'd heard her sister laugh since she'd returned home.

Wainwright's housekeeper shooed Mr. Wainwright and William off to get washed up for dinner.

"And be quick about it." She motioned for Caleb to follow her. "Right this way, Mr. O'Shea."

She showed him to a room, then begged his pardon to go put the finishing touches on the meal.

His thoughts still on what the apothecary had shared about Alanah and her sister, Caleb washed up before following the sound of voices. He walked into the Wainwrights' dining room and came face-to-face with his brother Quinn. William and Mr. Wainwright stood on the opposite side of the table.

Quinn's ice-blue eyes met his, as cold as the Irish Sea in the dead of winter. His brother blinked, glanced at their hosts, and when his gaze once again met Caleb's, the ice had melted somewhat.

"Caleb. 'Tis good to see ya looking well . . ." Quinn paused and cleared his throat. "Mr. Wainwright told me how you and your friends made sure that Reggie Caruthers made it safely back t' Natchez. Me wife's sister married Reggie's brother, and we're beholden."

Caleb inclined his head. "It was a matter o' honor."

Silence followed, and when Caleb didn't elaborate, Mr. Wainwright motioned to the table. "Please, both of you, sit. Mrs. Butler has prepared an excellent supper. William, please let her know we're all here."

"No need, Mr. Wainwright." The portly housekeeper bustled in, carrying a tureen of soup.

"Allow me." William rounded the table, took the heavy dish from her, and placed it in the middle of the table. Leaning down, he kissed the elderly woman's cheek. "It's good to see you, Nanny."

She batted him away, looking flustered. "Go on with you, Master William. I've not been your nanny for these many years."

"You'll always be Nanny to me."

"I'd rather be Nanny to that sweet little Jon boy of yours." She plopped her hands on her ample hips. "When are you going to bring him to Natchez?"

"Next month for sure, and you can rock him all you want. If you can catch him, that is. At thirteen months, he's quite a handful."

Mrs. Butler beamed, then glanced over the table. "Oh, mercy me, I left the ham and the biscuits on the sideboard."

Within minutes, she'd finished serving the meal and left them, in spite of Mr. Wainwright's insistence that she stay. William's father unfolded his napkin. "Mrs. Butler will never change. She insists it's unseemly for her to dine with the family."

Caleb gripped his fork and fixed his brother with a look that he hoped wasn't as dark as it felt. "So what brings you t' Natchez, Brother?"

You could travel twenty miles to the city when you couldn't travel three to welcome me back into the fold?

"Delivering cotton for Breeze Hill."

"What of Magnolia Glen? How is the harvest there?" William asked.

His brother flushed. "The fields were no' properly laid by, and the yield has been poor. Mews assures me that we'll have a few bales o' cotton t' show for our efforts, though."

"With proper care, next year will be much better." William motioned between Caleb and Quinn with his fork. "I find it interesting that Quinn brought a shipment of cotton down the trace at the same time Caleb and I drove logs downriver. Father, have

257

you considered hauling cotton down on the timber rafts? You know, kill two birds with one stone and all that."

For a moment, Mr. Wainwright looked dazed, but a grin quickly spread over his features. "That's a splendid idea, Son. We wouldn't need as many men —"

"Or horses. Mules. Wagons."

"Quinn, what do you think?"

"I think Connor will have something t' say about it."

"Yes, of course." William grinned. "I can't imagine he'd be opposed to the idea, though. It's brilliant."

"Well, I wouldn't go that far, Son, but still . . ."

Caleb listened as Quinn and the Wainwrights discussed the benefits of loading their cotton on the timber rafts and floating them downriver as opposed to using horses and wagons and traveling on the trace. They debated the merits of time gained and time lost, the risk of river pirates versus highwaymen, and the possible loss of an entire crop on a capsized raft.

And all the time, Caleb wondered how he'd come full circle with his feet under the same table as the brother who'd stolen his one chance to make something of himself back home in Ireland.

Suddenly he wished he'd given in to the urge to leave Natchez, because nothing good would come of spending time with Quinn.

CHAPTER 17

Alanah froze when the nanny goat lifted her head from the feedbox and stared toward the woods beyond the clearing. It was all she could do to keep milking and pretend nothing was wrong, but the goat's curiosity with whatever moved in the woods couldn't be ignored.

Something or someone was out there in the early morning shadows.

Foolishly, she'd left her bow and arrows inside, not thinking that any highwaymen would be out and about so early. Her hand on the knife at her waist, she stood.

"Alanah?"

The tension drained out of her when she heard Caleb's voice. He stepped out of the shadows, a small tote slung over his shoulder. He joined her in the goat pen, dropped the tote beside her, and reached for a pouch tucked inside his shirt. "Your supplies and coin from Mr. Weaver, madam."

Her fingers curled around the pouch, still warm from his body heat. "Thank you, sir."

"You're welcome, ya are. And before I forget, Mr. Weaver said he needs more turkey tail mushrooms. Said he'd make it worth your while. What did he mean?"

"Nothing." She tucked the money pouch in the pocket sewn into her skirt.

"I did no' get the impression he would have said such a thing if it meant nothing."

She sighed. "It's a day's journey to get the most potent ones he favors."

"A day's journey, as in one day or two?"

"Two days. I haven't been in a long time. I have to go by Breeze Hill and then past the ruins of what used to be Braxton Hall. I didn't go last year, when the highwaymen got to be so bad. I was afraid to risk it."

"But you're surrounded by highwaymen." Caleb frowned. "I would no' think you'd be put off by a few more."

"Better to be wary of the dangers you don't know than those you do." She shrugged and coaxed another goat onto the milking stand, then sat on the low stool, her tattered skirt pooling around her.

"Dangers like Micaiah Jones?"

Her hand slipped, and she almost knocked the bucket over. "What do you know of Micaiah Jones?"

"Only what Mr. Weaver said." Caleb crouched, eye level with her.

"Micaiah Jones was a river pirate who cared for nothing except robbing and killing." With quick, practiced movements, she stripped milk from the goat's teats. "He took what he wanted, when he wanted it, without —"

She broke off, unable to continue.

"And what did he take from you?" Caleb's voice had turned to ice.

"My sister, Betsy. He was to be hanged for murder in French Camp. He's —" She sucked in a steadying breath. "He's probably dead by now."

"Ya do no' seem pleased by the thought."

"I'm . . ." Alanah kept up the rhythm of milking, trying to verbalize how she felt about Micaiah and what he'd done to Betsy. Uncle Jude preached an eye for an eye, but her father had preached grace and forgiveness. Sometimes it was hard for Alanah to reconcile the two.

"Relieved." She cleared her throat and changed the subject. "How was the trip? All went well, I take it?"

"Aye, all went well." Caleb's lips twisted in a bit of a smile, and he picked up a piece of straw and slid it through his fingers.

"Don't tell me the raftsmen Uncle Jude

recommended made the journey without incident."

"No." He chuckled, the sound of his deep laugh warming her insides. "Massey and two others tried to dry-gulch the rest o' us in the middle o' the night."

Alanah's blood ran cold, and she jerked her attention to him. "You are well?"

"Aye." He smiled, gave her a wink, and her stomach did a slow whirl. "I am well."

Hoping he didn't notice the flush that rolled up her neck and over her face, Alanah concentrated on her milking, afraid if she looked at him, he'd see how relieved she was that he'd returned whole. Somehow she hadn't let herself think that he might not return —

"But there was an injury. One o' the men, a Mr. Vickers, was stabbed."

Thank You, Lord, that it wasn't Caleb. Remorse smote her that the welfare of the poor injured man wasn't her first thought. Chagrined, she bit her lip. "And Mr. Vickers, will he live?"

"He'll live."

"A blessing indeed." Alanah turned back to the task at hand. "Will you make the trip again?"

"Aye. We have t' finish another raft, and the Wainwrights are talking about shipping cotton bales down the river." He eyed her. "Will you be wantin' t' send more herbs t' the apothecary?"

"Yes, please. If it's not too much trouble."

"It is no trouble."

Alanah finished milking, and Caleb removed the bucket while she released the nanny. She reached for the pail, but he held fast to the handle, sliding his hand to cover hers. "Promise me you will no' go after the mushrooms on your own."

He moved closer. With his warm fingers covering hers, and his dark eyes searching hers, she found it hard to think, let alone answer him. "I . . ."

"Promise me."

"I — I promise." She lifted her chin. "But I would ask a promise of you as well. Don't hire more men from Cypress Creek. They're all part of Micaiah and Elias Jones's gang of cutthroats. I'm afraid —"

Caleb reached out, shushed her words with the pressure of his thumb against her lips. "Do no' worry, lass. William hired another crew in Natchez."

She breathed a sigh of relief, the feel of his thumb sliding across her lips doing funny things to her insides. "All is well, then."

"All is well." His gaze dipped, slid across

her face to her lips. Time stood still, the quiet of the early morning broken only by the goats jostling for the last bit of grain left in the trough. Then, a furrow between his brows, Caleb let go of the bucket. "I should go. Good day, Alanah."

With one last swipe of his thumb, he turned and walked away.

The sun was up by the time Caleb made it back to camp. He made a detour by the cookhouse. "Gimpy, me stomach's glued t' me backbone. Do you have a wee bit o' breakfast left for a starvin' man?"

The cook lifted the lid off a skillet. "A couple of half-burned flapjacks and a few pieces of ham."

"A feast fit for a king." Caleb grabbed the flapjacks, wrapped them around the ham, and headed toward the landing, eating as he went.

Halfway down the steep road that led to the sandbar, he slowed. Quinn and Connor stood off to the side in heated discussion. He and Quinn had hardly spoken two words to each other on the trip out from Natchez. Whether by design or by accident, he didn't know. But the anger of past hurts simmered just below the surface, so it was better that they kept their distance from each other.

Connor glanced up, spotted him, and stopped mid-sentence. Quinn looked over his shoulder, then faced him. "Where have ya been? The mornin's half-gone already."

Caleb ignored his brother, rolled up his sleeves, and picked up a long-handled grapple. He moved toward a log.

"I asked ya a question, Brother."

Caleb hooked and rolled the log. "And I did no' see the need t' give an answer."

Quinn placed his boot on the log, stopping its forward motion. "Ye'll answer or —"

"Enough." Connor stepped between them. "What's gotten into you, Quinn?"

Caleb waited. Would Quinn tell all, or would his brother skew things in his favor as he'd done when they were kids?

"He canna be depended on, and ya want t' entrust our livelihood and that o' our families t' him?" Quinn jabbed a finger in Caleb's direction. "What if he gets t' Natchez, sells the timber and the cotton, and takes off again?"

"I would no' do that, Quinn, and you know it." Caleb straightened, determined not to throw the first punch, but if Quinn goaded him much more, he'd —

"I know no such thing." Quinn leaned forward, blue eyes flashing, jaw clenched.

266

"Do ya no' remember the day ya left home without a word t' a livin' soul? The day after our fight? I came home from the smithy and —"

"Aye. I left, and I would —"

"Stop. Now. The both o' ye!" Connor bellowed. "Or so help me . . ."

The sound of labored breathing from all three of them filled the heavy silence. Caleb slowed his breathing and glared at Quinn. He hadn't started this fight, not now and not three years ago. And he wouldn't finish it.

"The two o' ya had a fight, and ya left home, left Ireland, over it?" Connor looked at Caleb as if he'd lost his senses. "What did ya fight about that was so bad ya'd leave home without so much as a good-bye?"

"Ye're a fine one t' be calling the kettle black." Quinn raised a brow. Caleb suppressed a chuckle. Finally one thing he and Quinn agreed on.

Connor scowled. "My sudden departure from Ireland was no' me fault, and I've explained it all away. Caleb, what do ya have t' say for yerself?"

Quinn smirked. "Aye, but our dear little brother has no' explained a thing."

Caleb slapped the grapple against the log and faced Quinn, ready for the brawl that

267

was sure to follow. "You really do no' remember what we fought about?"

Quinn's gaze narrowed, and his eyes took on a distant look as if he was trying to recall the events three years past. "I do no' remember. Ya'd gotten sick — injured or something. And the mine boss gave ya the rest o' the day off. And then, at the end o' my shift, he called me up from the mines and offered me a job with Seamus." Quinn smiled. "I remember thinking how excited ya and the lads would be that I'd be working for the blacksmith. I could no' wait to tell ya. But when I got home, ya lit into me like a banshee, and the next thing I remember, one o' us threw a punch. After the fight, ya stormed out o' the house, and by morning ya were gone." A hardness flattened his features. "Patrick cried for a month, and I had no answers for the lad."

Caleb searched his brother's face but saw nothing but sincerity. He turned away, ran one hand around his neck. Could Quinn be telling the truth? After all these years? Had he truly *not* known?

He looked up at the sky, blew out a breath. "It was me ankle. I twisted it at the end o' me shift. Being a careless *eejit,* I was, but truth be told, I was in a hurry t' get home and share me news with me brothers."

"What news?" Connor all but shouted.

"The mine boss had just offered *me* the job with Seamus. Me ticket out o' the mines." He looked at Quinn. "Only t' have me own brother steal it out from under me nose."

"I see." Connor's calm voice, devoid of his usual roar and sounding so much like *Da*'s, transported Caleb back to his childhood.

Quinn gaped at him. "I did no' know. Seamus, the mine boss, neither o' them ever mentioned it." He took a deep breath, then jutted out his chin. "It's no' in me t' say I'm sorry, but if ya want t' take a swing at me, I'll stand here and take it like a man."

Caleb snorted. Quinn's acceptance of his part in the debacle made him feel like he was still a wee lad. But hadn't squabbles with Quinn always ended with him feeling like that?

Like he was the younger brother playing second fiddle to his elders?

He'd looked up to Connor, idolized him; then in the blink of an eye, he was gone. After *Da* passed, Quinn had taken over, bossing him around. Quinn hadn't ever asked for his opinion on anything. He'd just given orders and expected them to be obeyed.

"I will no' hit ya, Quinn. If it was as you say, it's best left in the past."

The three of them stood, facing each other, and Caleb hardly knew what to do now that taking a swing at Quinn wasn't an option.

Connor stepped between them, shoulders slumped as if the weight of every past mistake and misunderstanding rested with him. "We left a lot o' problems back in Ireland, and I blame myself for most o' them. If I'd been there, things would have been easier for both o' ya. The truth is that God brought us out o' poverty and gave us all a future here. More o' a future than we could ever have had back home. The Wainwrights have put a lot o' trust in me t' see that this logging operation is a success. I need ya both — here in the logging camp, at Breeze Hill, and at Magnolia Glen, but . . ." Connor paused, his furrowed brow giving credence to the battle he fought within. "But if the two o' ya can't get along, then I do no' need either o' ya."

"You'll hear no more from me on the matter." Caleb tried not to glare at Quinn, but years of bitterness were hard to erase in a moment's time.

Connor looked at Quinn. "Quinn?"

"Nor me."

"Now that everything's settled," Connor growled, sounding a lot like *Da* when he was about to issue an order, "then there's no reason the two o' you can't make the trip with me to Breeze Hill and Magnolia Glen next week to haul back the cotton."

Dawn had yet to break when the sound of horses coming down the lane reached Alanah. She plucked the last egg from the nest and hurried toward the cabin, where she met Lydia, flintlock in hand, a determined glint in her eyes.

Alanah shoved the basket of eggs at Betsy. "Get out of sight."

Her sister didn't have to be told twice. Alanah grabbed her bow and faced whatever danger was coming their way. A mounted rider came into view, leading a saddled, riderless horse.

"It's Caleb." Alanah slung her bow across her back and stepped out of the shadows. She eyed the empty saddle, a sense of foreboding chilling her bones. "Is something wrong?"

"No, nothing's wrong." He pushed his hat back and leaned on the saddle horn. "Connor's sending wagons t' Breeze Hill and

Magnolia Glen t' get some cotton. Do you want t' come along and harvest those mushrooms you're so keen on?"

Alanah frowned. It was unseemly for her to travel such a distance with the loggers. But it was even more unseemly — and dangerous — for her to make the trip alone. And that's why she'd only chanced it twice in the last three years. "Thank you, but I shouldn't —"

"If it's propriety you're concerned about, do no' worry. My brother's wife will be at Magnolia Glen, and you'll be safe. We'll return on the morrow with the wagons."

She glanced at Lydia and Betsy, who'd ventured out on the porch when she'd realized it was someone she knew and trusted.

"Are you coming, lass? If no', I must be getting back."

"It is good that you have an escort to get the mushrooms that Mr. Weaver needs." Lydia lifted her chin, her stance brooking no argument.

Torn, Alanah shifted her attention from Lydia to Betsy, hovering in the shadows. She hated to leave them overnight, but who knew when she'd get another chance to harvest turkey tails from the nutrient-rich swampland.

"We will be fine. You go."

"Of course you're right." Alanah turned back to Caleb. "I'll get my things."

She rushed inside, grabbed a tote and a basket so the mushrooms wouldn't be crushed. Thinking quickly, she pivoted, lifted the lid on a trunk, and pulled out her heavy cloak. Even in September, the nights could turn chilly, and it would suffice as a blanket if they became stranded on the trail. She eyed the green skirt and lacy fichu Isabella had given her. Before she could change her mind, she stuffed the clean clothes in with her cloak.

Once outside, Caleb helped her mount, then led the way back to the logging camp. They cut through the woods following a game trail, crossed the road that led to Cypress Creek.

The camp was practically deserted with all the men working in the woods or down on the sandbar. Which suited her just fine. Several wagons were hitched and ready to roll out.

Caleb dismounted, then reached to help her down. The sandy-haired man who'd been with Caleb and the others the day they'd brought Mr. Abbott to her house doffed his hat. "Good day, miss."

"Good day, Mr. —" She broke off, at a loss to recall his name.

"Horne, ma'am. The name's Horne."

"Mr. Horne."

A young boy — the spitting image of Caleb's brother, Connor — watched them from the bed of the wagon. Another man propped his arm on the wagon, eyeing their approach.

Caleb motioned toward them. "My brothers. Quinn and Patrick. This is Alanah. She's —"

"Ye're going home t' Breeze Hill, and that's final." Connor's unmistakable growl rolled out of the dogtrot cabin.

"Now, Connor, we agreed . . ." Isabella's voice trailed off.

Caleb jerked his head toward the cabin. "What's going on?"

"Connor wants Isabella t' go home, but she insists on staying here until William returns. They've been at it all morning."

Just then Connor stormed out of the cabin, his gaze raking the wagons and the horses, to settle on the boy. "Patrick, get down from there and find Rory. Tell him I need him to make the trip to Breeze Hill in my place."

"Can I go — ?"

"Yes! Yes! You can go." Connor threw his arms out, shooing the boy away. "Now go get Rory before I change my mind."

274

The boy took off, and Alanah caught the smirk on Quinn's face before he wiped it off and faced Connor. "Ye're no' going?"

"It appears not. It seems me dear, sweet wife thinks I canna run a logging camp on me own and insists on staying." He raked a hand through his hair. "Me wife won't leave and Patrick is determined t' go. The two o' them are going t' be the death o' me."

"Ah, never mind Patrick. He thinks o' the trip as one big adventure." Quinn slapped him on the back. "I'll see after the lad."

Connor spotted Alanah. There was no place to go, so she just stood there, hoping he wouldn't take his ire out on her. Not that she was afraid of the man, but she didn't want to be ordered home like a whipped dog with her tail tucked between her legs.

"Good day, Miss Adams." He offered her a curt nod.

She gave a small curtsy, knees quaking. "Sir."

His attention shifted from her to her pack to Caleb. "May I have a word with you, Caleb?"

They walked away, and Alanah busied herself scratching one of the horses behind the ear, her hand shaking.

Well, maybe she was a wee bit afraid of Caleb's oldest brother.

CHAPTER 18

As the wagons jostled along the logging road toward Breeze Hill, Caleb glanced at Alanah. She sat quietly, bottom lip pulled between her teeth, looking worried.

"What's wrong?"

She glanced at him. "What did Connor say?"

" 'Bout what?"

"About me going along. That's what he wanted to talk to you about, wasn't it?"

"Aye. But do no' worry. He was fine when he found out why you needed t' go."

Looking relieved, she motioned toward Rory and Patrick in the wagon ahead of them. "Just how many brothers do you have? It seems that every time I see you, I meet a new brother."

He chuckled. "I have four, so you've met them all now."

"No sisters?"

"No."

She was quiet, and he slapped the reins against the horses' backs, urging them to pick up the pace. He jostled her shoulder. "What? No more questions?"

She shrugged. "It's not polite to ask too many questions."

"So you do have them."

A blush rolled over her cheeks, but she shook her head and pressed her lips together.

"Let's see. We hail from Ireland, but I suppose you figured that out already. Connor immigrated t' the colonies almost ten years ago, and Quinn, Rory, and Patrick came earlier this year. I arrived the day we met in Natchez."

Her tawny eyes flickered toward him, a frown wrinkling her brow. "You don't sound like you're fresh off the boat from Ireland."

"Now how would ya be knowing that, lassie?" Caleb deliberately deepened his brogue.

"I don't know." She fluttered her hands. "It's just that your brogue isn't as pronounced as . . . well, even as much as Quinn's and Patrick's, and they've been here longer than you have."

"That's because I left Ireland three years ago and have traveled the world, earning my keep as a merchant seaman, a vagabond, and a soldier."

"Then you found out your family was here, and you came to find them?" She was looking at him as if she thought the decision was the sweetest thing he'd ever done.

"No' exactly. The ship I was on docked in Natchez, and I discovered by accident they were here. The plan was t' see for myself, then head back t' sea."

She blinked. "You're leaving?"

"Aye." He winked at her. "And why no'? Now that me favorite lass is planning t' head north, there's no reason t' stay, is there?"

The look she threw his way said she didn't believe a word of his blather, so he just laughed and turned his attention to keeping the horses moving forward. But the truth was he would miss her when she was gone.

The rest of the trip was quiet enough and they arrived at Breeze Hill by a little after noon.

Caleb pulled to a stop just in time to hear Quinn's instructions. "Mr. Horne, you and the others stay here and load the wagons. Caleb and I will go on to Magnolia Glen. We'll be back bright and early in the morning."

"Yes, sir."

Without further ado, Quinn urged his horses on down the road, and Caleb's team fell in behind them. When they'd gone another mile, he noticed some clouds forming in the west.

"Are ya familiar with this road?"

"I've passed this way a few times."

"How much farther is it, then?"

"Not long. An hour at most."

"If Quinn hopes to get an early start in the morning, we'll need t' gather your mushrooms tonight."

"You don't have to go with me. I can —"

"I'm no' about t' let you go off on your own, so you can get that thought right out o' your head."

An amused smile twisted her lips, but she didn't argue. They traveled in silence for a while, then came to a swath of destruction where the trees had been sheared off ten to fifteen feet aboveground. The dead sentinels marched along both sides of the road, silent testimony to the devastation that had ripped through. The road had been cleared, but twisted, broken trees lingered as far as he could see.

"What happened here?"

"A hurricane came inland, spawning several tornadoes." Alanah's quiet voice bled through the desolation around them. "It was a little over a year ago. You could tell there was a storm brewing off the coast, but we never dreamed it would come so far inland. The tornado touched down a few miles from Cypress Creek, then jumped over the trace and cut a path through here. We heard later that Braxton Hall was completely destroyed and Nolan Braxton was killed. But he wasn't really a Braxton. He was an impostor . . . and the leader of the highwaymen."

"And now my brother owns his land. Hard t' believe."

Alanah glanced at him, surprise on her face. "Don't tell me that the O'Sheas were the real owners of Braxton Hall?"

"No." Caleb chuckled. "It would no' be that simple. All I know is that the governor awarded the land t' Connor after Braxton died. Something about saving his wife from highwaymen."

"Yes, I think I heard about that. It would be like Governor Gayoso to do that."

They left the devastation and dipped into a long, narrow valley, the road lined with magnolia trees that had been spared even if the plantation home had not. Caleb could see why his brother had renamed the acreage Magnolia Glen. At the end of the valley, massive columns marked the spot where Braxton Hall had once stood.

Quinn drove past the windswept foundation of the destroyed home, circled behind a barn, and pulled to a stop in front of a row of cabins. A woman and a young girl, both with wheat-colored hair, rushed from one of the cabins.

His brother jumped down from the wagon, kissed the woman, and gave the girl a hug. Caleb set the brake, climbed down, and reached for Alanah. When her feet touched down, he let her go, only to reach out and grab her when she stumbled on the uneven ground. When he snagged her against his side, her golden eyes went wide.

"You all right?"

"I'm fine."

She pushed away. Eyebrow raised, Quinn stood watching the two of them. The blonde, an amused look on her face, nudged his brother with her elbow. Quinn cleared his throat. "Kiera, this is me brother Caleb and Alanah Adams from Cypress Creek. My wife, Kiera, and her sister Megan."

His sister-in-law hurried forward, hand outstretched. Caleb took it in greeting. Quinn's wife was the exact opposite of Connor's. Pale and blonde where Isabella was dark and exotic.

"Pleased to meet you, Caleb. I've heard lots of good things about you." A hint of old country brogue mixed with highbrow

British could be heard in her tones.

"You're Irish?" With a name like Kiera, he couldn't imagine her being anything else.

"A bit o' Irish when I choose t' be. And —" she grinned, the brogue falling away at her command — "at other times, I'm a proper English miss transported to the colonies." She patted Quinn's jerkin. "Much to my husband's chagrin."

"Ya might have been born with a bit o' blue blood in yer veins, Wife, but ye're Irish through and through now, and do no' be forgetting it."

"For sure, Husband." Kiera turned her smile on Alanah. "Miss Adams, welcome to Magnolia Glen, such as it is. I imagine you'd like to freshen up."

"That'll have t' wait, if you don't mind." Caleb lifted the empty totes out of the wagon. "Alanah needs to gather some mushrooms before dark. She's an herbalist."

"This afternoon?" Kiera's brows rose. "But —"

"Quinn wants to get an early start in the morning." Caleb glanced at the darkening sky. "And besides, it looks like we're in for a bit o' rain, so we'd better go."

"Take some horses." Quinn jerked his head toward the stables. "No need in walking with the threat o' rain on the horizon."

Thankful for the use of the horses, Alanah led the way deeper into the wilderness. They hadn't gone far when a light mist began to fall. She grabbed her cloak, tossed it around her shoulders, and pulled the hood over her hair. Twenty minutes later, she dismounted at the edge of the swamp and slung the basket over her arm. "We walk from here."

"You did no' say these mushrooms were in a swamp."

"You didn't ask."

Growling low in his throat, Caleb dismounted and tied the horses to a low-hanging branch. "Lead on, then."

Alanah zigzagged across the wetlands, keeping to the highest ridges. There was a high point where the ground was usually fairly dry, but there had been a lot of rain lately. She paused, searching for the three large oaks on the other side of the bog. If she didn't get her bearings, they'd never be able to cross the slough. There. She spotted the trees a hundred yards or so across a quagmire of black, gooey mud, the dry ridges barely visible.

There was nothing for it but to head across. She gripped her skirt in one hand, the basket held tight in the other.

"Alanah, this is no' a good idea. Piling off into the middle o' a swamp with night coming on."

She glanced over her shoulder, saw Caleb dogging her steps. "Don't worry. I know where I'm going. This ridge should be firm enough to get us across. Just follow me and head straight toward the oaks and you'll be fine."

Even as she slogged forward, feeling the spongy earth beneath the soles of her moccasins, the brackish water rose, covering her feet, then her ankles, on up to her calves. Had she gone the wrong way?

Suddenly she felt the ground firm up beneath her moccasins as the land sloped upward. "We made it."

"Well, no time t' gloat about it. Let's find those mushrooms and get out o' here before the bottom falls out."

Eyeing the sky, which was growing darker with purple rain-soaked clouds, she couldn't help but agree. But climbing the hillside was not an easy task. She pulled her way along by grasping the root system, slick to the touch.

"Here, let me." Caleb climbed past her, then reached for her.

Alanah gripped his hand, the tips of her fingers engulfed within the warm strength of his callused palm. He pulled her up level with him, dark eyes narrowed in suspicion. "Tell me you've never come t' this place alone?"

She swallowed, lowered her gaze. "I have. Once."

"*Eejit* woman," he growled. "You could have died and no one would've been the wiser."

In that instant, the root he'd anchored himself to gave way.

Alanah screamed.

Caleb threw himself sideways to keep from crushing her in the fall. He slid, then groaned as his back slammed against a tree. He looked up, saw Alanah tumbling toward him, her cloak twisting around her in a billowing cloud of black cloth.

Bracing himself, he caught her against him, halting her descent toward the marshy bog. As they lay against the rain-soaked hillside, both breathing heavily, the heavens opened and poured more rain down on them.

As the rain drenched his face, Caleb blinked away the moisture, trying to come to grips with the fact that he could scale the rigging on a ship and hang on in the middle of the worst gale, but for some reason he couldn't manage to scale a slippery slope while holding on to one tiny slip of a woman.

"Are ya all right, lass?"

"I'm fine." She shoved the hood off her head, tried to straighten the cloak twisted around her body, but the cloth, covered in mud and becoming heavy with rain, wasn't being very cooperative.

And all that squirming wasn't doing anything to help him keep his grip. He cleared his throat. "Well, let's try again. Heave ho."

They made it to the top of the incline, where the ground leveled off somewhat. Caleb let Alanah go, and she led the way forward. Suddenly she flung out both arms. "Stop."

Without thought, Caleb palmed his knife, ready to slaughter whatever threat she'd spotted. He went to push by her. "What? What is it?"

"No, don't step there. You'll step on them."

"Step on what?"

She sank to her knees. "The mushrooms."

"I wouldna want t' do that, now would I?" He eyed the riot of multicolored mushrooms growing on the log at his feet.

She handed him the basket. "Hold this."

Alanah took a small, curved blade and started snipping mushrooms. Caleb hunkered down, holding out the basket. "Do you need some help?"

"I'll do it. I have to be gentle. I don't want them bruised."

"I can be gentle."

Alanah glanced at him, eyebrow raised, lips pursed. "All right, then."

He watched her for a moment, then mimicked her movements, carefully cutting the mushrooms and placing them in the basket. The log stripped clean, Alanah moved on, leading him farther along the secluded knoll surrounded by swamp waters. In moments, she'd found another log covered in mushrooms, the colors even more vibrant than the ones before. The clouds rolled in, obscuring any light from the sun, and the rain grew heavier. They worked in silence save for the plop of fat raindrops slapping against the canopy of leaves overhead.

Alanah showed no signs of stopping, and after she'd harvested mushrooms from a third, then a fourth log, Caleb cleared his throat. "We need t' head back. It'll be dark soon."

"Yes, of course." She gave him an apologetic smile. "I tend to get carried away when I'm foraging."

She deposited the rest of the mushrooms in the basket, dusted the earth from her hands, and to his relief, headed back the way they'd come. Suddenly she stopped and pointed toward a cluster of blue flowers. "Look. Irises."

"Alanah —"

"It will only take a moment. I promise."

She hurried forward, then dropped to her knees. But instead of picking the flowers, she pulled a small spade out of her waistband and dug in the dirt. She dug up half the roots, then gently smoothed the soil, patting it in place. Clutching the roots in her hand, she turned, her face glistening with happiness, health, and the gentle spray of rain.

"I'm ready now."

Caleb swallowed. In spite of the smudge of dirt on her cheek, the mud-stained and wilted cloak that hung about her, she was the most beautiful thing he'd ever seen.

Her smile faltered. "What is it?"

"Nothing." The rain fell harder, and he reached for her arm. "Let's go."

CHAPTER 19

The saturated ground squished beneath Alanah's moccasins, but she ignored the sensation and set her sights on the higher ground on the other side of the bog, squinting through the deluge of rain and the gathering gloom. She headed across, Caleb on her heels. The farther she went, the deeper the quagmire.

"Alanah, do no' stop now, but . . ." The tenseness in Caleb's voice had her searching the swampy ground around her feet, the deluge making it hard to see.

"What is it?" A shiver of apprehension slithered down her spine, and she reached for her knife.

"Alligator. To your right. Just keep going."

Alligator?

She'd never seen an alligator here before. But the swamp waters had never been this high. Working to control the shudder that crawled across her skin, she tried to walk a straight line while searching frantically to locate the predator.

Another involuntary shiver racked her body.

They were almost across when a splash and a hiss sent her scrambling for the bank. She slipped and, with a squeak, fell broadside into the slough. Her hood slid over her face, but she could hear the animal coming, the splash of water, and —

The next thing she knew, Caleb was pulling her to her feet. He shoved her ahead of him toward higher ground, and she gained her footing even as she saw the behemoth surging toward him. Without thought, she reached for an arrow, nocked it, and let it fly. Then another and another. The arrows glanced off the animal's tough hide, and it kept coming.

Heavenly Father, please help us.

Caleb gained solid ground and turned, facing the animal, a deadly-looking blade in his grip that would be little defense against the beast's powerful jaws. Now that they were out of immediate danger, Alanah could see that the brute was small, maybe three feet long, but that didn't make it any less dangerous.

As they backed away, the alligator halted its advance and slowly eased down into the swampy abyss. A firm grip on her arm, Caleb didn't relax his guard until they were a good thirty feet away. Then he turned, took her by the shoulders, and searched her face. "Are ya hurt?"

Alanah shoved her hair out of her eyes. "No. Just scared out of my wits. I've never seen an alligator that close before."

"You are no' t' come here again." Rain sluiced over his face, dripping off his chin. "Is that understood?"

Alanah lifted her chin. "But —"

"Do no' argue." His hands tightened on her shoulders. "Promise me, lass."

"I can't promise that. Gathering herbs is how I make my living."

"You are one stubborn woman." Eyes flashing, he jerked his head toward the swamp. "What would you have done had I no' been there? Could you have gotten out o' there before that beast attacked you and pulled you into the swamp?"

Alanah blanched. "I . . ."

The anger — or maybe terror — on his face shifted, softened, and growling low in his throat, he hauled her to him, his lips crushing hers. But just as quickly, his lips gentled, his arm around her waist lifting her to her toes as he deepened the kiss. He groaned as if their near-death experience had unleashed a primal longing that he could no longer hold in check. Thunder rolled overhead, and uncaring of the rain that soaked them both, Alanah wrapped her arms around his neck and kissed him back.

Long minutes later, Caleb drew back, his chest heaving. He touched his forehead to hers.

"I should no' have done that, lass, but you make me forget reason, forget logic, forget everything but . . ."

His dark eyes searched hers; then he lifted one hand, cupped her jaw, and drew her close again, his lips covering hers. Alanah didn't go weak-kneed over much of anything, except the sight of blood and now . . . Caleb's kiss.

She wanted his kiss, wanted —

Her heart pounded. What was wrong with her? This was the very thing her uncle had warned her against.

She wrenched out of Caleb's grasp and rushed for her horse, jerked the slipknot free, and mounted.

"Alanah? Wait!"

Ignoring Caleb's call, she kicked her horse into motion, headed back toward Magnolia Glen. Behind her, she could hear pounding hooves as he urged his mount to catch up.

Grabbing her reins, he hauled her mount

to a stop. "Alanah, lass, look at me. I'm —"

"There's no need to apologize." She cut him off before he could make a false declaration of undying love — or worse, say he should never have kissed her.

Caleb gaped at her. "It was just a kiss, lass."

Embarrassed and terrified at the same time, Alanah dropped her gaze and toyed with her horse's mane. "And if I had not run, would it have ended there? With . . . with just a kiss?"

When he didn't respond, she peeked at him. The warmth in his dark eyes had disappeared at her words.

"I'm no' Micaiah Jones." His voice came out hard. "I would no' force myself on a woman, and if you think that o' me, then you do no' know me at all."

The patrons at Cypress Creek Tavern were in high spirits, celebrating Micaiah's return with gusto.

Micaiah grinned. Against all odds, he'd thwarted the authorities and escaped from their clutches. Not only had he returned, he'd brought gifts. Corn, wheat, tobacco, and ale, appeasing the tavern owner, the tavern wenches, and his men. As soon as it stopped raining, he'd take the rest of the supplies to Cottonmouth Island, a safe and secure location on the Louisiana side of the river. Ale flowed freely as the river pirates told him of the new developments in Cypress Creek.

"A logging camp?" Micaiah lifted his tankard of ale. "I suspect they're ripe for the picking."

His cousin Elias bellowed with laughter, reached out a meaty hand, and closed it tight into a fist, his bloodshot eyes glowing with greed. "Easier than plucking a low-hanging plum. Some of the men hired on as raftsmen."

"Raftsmen?"

"They're supplying logs for a new sawmill in Natchez, floating timber rafts downriver instead of hauling them down the trace. It was the reverend who gave me the idea to have my men right in the thick of things."

Micaiah's gaze narrowed at Elias's choice of words.

His men?

Since when had Elias started thinking of their motley crew of thieves and cutthroats as his own? Probably since they'd left Micaiah to rot in that hole in French Camp. Elias might be his own kin, but he hadn't spent one minute worrying over Micaiah's fate. And Micaiah didn't expect him to. Life was cheap on the river. They both knew that. He'd cheated death. He wouldn't be cheated out of his rightful place as leader of their small band.

But he would have to act swiftly if he was to wrest power back. "That was wise. Tell me, other than the men who hired on with the logging crew, have you had much success these last weeks?"

Too drunk to know that Micaiah was needling him, Elias scowled. "None. We attacked a group of travelers. They should have been an easy target, but someone warned them. And instead of staying with the wagons, they swarmed the woods and fought back. Those milksop farmers never tried such a thing."

"Well, that shouldn't have been a problem. You should've killed them all and let them lie."

"We saw no one, Cousin." Elias shook his head, eyes wide. "There was this terrible screech; then we heard a scream. One after another, our men were being slaughtered by a ghost flitting through the forest."

"A ghost?" Micaiah snorted. "There is no such thing as ghosts."

"Believe what you will, but Tremain died within twenty feet of me, a knife to his heart, and I saw nothing. There were men from the logging party with them. Men armed to the teeth. Men who didn't look or act like farmers or loggers."

"A knife-wielding ghost?" Micaiah chuckled. "So that's all you've been up to. One botched raid, eh?"

Elias tipped up his tankard of ale and took a gulp. "I brought your woman home to Cypress Creek like you asked. That should count for something."

Ah, the fair Betsy. He'd have to visit her soon, but she could wait. No need in raising the ire of the few morally upright men in the territory as of yet. No, he'd figure the lay of the land, the best way to profit from the loggers who dared to venture into his territory, and then he'd take her back when it suited him.

Or not.

She wasn't the only fair wench to be found in the hills and hollows between here and Natchez.

"And I'll tell you something else. I'm not so sure that sister of hers is quite as addled as she makes out. I saw her the other day with one of them loggers, all cleaned up, looking pretty as a picture." Elias winked and wagged a finger at Micaiah. "I think I'll just take that one for my own woman."

"And what of Reverend Browning?"

"Posh on Reverend Browning. He didn't care what happened to Betsy, did he? Why would he care about the other one?"

Micaiah grunted. For once Elias was right. Somewhere in the dark recesses of his mind, he remembered another time, another place. An old man with a long beard who talked of God and blessings on the Lord's Day, but then beat the living daylights out of him and his ma the other six.

Micaiah had snapped the day the old man went too far. He'd left them both where they lay in the blood-soaked cabin and never looked back. Hers was the only death he'd been blamed for that he hadn't committed.

There was a time and a place for Christianity, he supposed, but if his old man and Reverend Browning were the example, Micaiah wanted no part of it.

"Interesting." Micaiah slid his mug back and forth across the table. Maybe Elias had managed to do more in his absence than he'd thought. "When will they make the first trip?"

"Already gone." Elias took another gulp of ale, looking quite pleased with himself. "Left over a week ago."

"A week?" Micaiah's gaze shot to Elias's. "And you haven't heard from them? Who are these men?"

"Massey, Colbert, and Wheeler."

"Whiskey Massey?" Micaiah gaped at his cousin, then threw back his head and roared with laughter. "No wonder you haven't heard from them. Massey's probably long gone by now, whatever he could get from the sale of the logs lining his own pocket."

Elias frowned, the ale he'd consumed dulling his thinking. He lurched to his feet and stumbled out of the tavern.

Micaiah sat back, took a sip of ale, and thought of all he'd learned. The fate of Massey and the timber was of no consequence. Elias should've known better than to trust the man. But it was an interesting turn of events that the loggers had men who were as skilled at fighting as they were at felling trees. Most of the settlers were too lily-livered to put up much of a fight.

His gaze roamed over the men in the tavern. It was obvious in the way they'd satiated themselves with the food and drink he'd pilfered from the Kaintucks that the recent weeks hadn't been kind to them. From the looks of things, it would be easy to turn their loyalty back to him.

All he had to do was provide them with the promise of an easy target, and the logging camp seemed the place to start.

■ ■ ■ ■

By the time Alanah made it back to Magnolia Glen, she was drenched from head to toe.

Kiera waited on the porch of one of the cabins, light spilling out of the doorway. Before she could dismount, Caleb was at her side. Rain splattered against his upturned face, mingled with the shadow on his jaw, and ran down his throat to soak into his shirt.

He lifted her down from the horse, holding her a moment longer than was necessary, a frown knitting his forehead, his gaze searching hers. Alanah resisted the urge to apologize, to tell him she hadn't meant to offend, but the feelings he stirred in her scared her senseless —

"Get inside, lass, before you catch a chill." He stepped away and pushed her toward the porch, then took up the reins and led the horses away. She had no choice but to join Kiera.

"I was worried." Kiera followed her inside. "I thought you'd be back before now."

"It took a little longer than expected with the rain." Alanah removed her drenched cloak, hung it up to dry, and shivering, moved toward the fire. The days of September were still comfortably warm, and even the nights were not overly cool, but the temperature had dropped with the sudden rainstorm.

"I was afraid of that. We've eaten, but I kept some stew warm for you. I'll get it while you change." She motioned to a nightgown and wrap laid out on the bed. "I didn't know if you brought nightclothes, so I took the liberty of bringing something. I hope you don't mind."

"Thank you."

While Kiera was gone, Alanah stripped out of her wet clothes and sponged the mud and muck off. Hands shaking, she dressed in Kiera's nightclothes, wrapped her arms around her waist, and stood in front of the fireplace, the blaze doing little to drive the chill away. A chill brought on not only by the rain, but by Caleb's kiss.

No, not by his kiss, but by her reaction.

What was she going to do?

The tears she'd held at bay on the long ride back from the swamp spilled over. And for just a moment, she allowed them to fall.

"Alanah?" Kiera stood in the doorway. She crossed the room, set the bowl of stew on a table, and turned to Alanah. "What's wrong?"

"Nothing." Alana swiped at the tears, sniffed, and shook her head. "I'm . . . just tired. And cold."

"That's not enough to set you to crying." Kiera searched her face; then her brows dove downward over clear blue eyes. "It's Caleb, isn't it? What did — ?"

"He didn't do anything."

Kiera crossed her arms and raised a pale brow. "Then why are you turning three shades of red?"

"It's the fire." Alanah moved away. "I got overheated, that's all."

"Please, be honest with me. I — I don't know anything about your circumstances, other than what Quinn has told me — and that was precious little — but I know the desperate circumstances a woman can get caught in. I have been there. If Caleb did something to offend —"

"He kissed me." Alanah lowered her gaze.

"He forced himself on you?"

Alanah shook her head. "It . . . it wasn't like that."

"I see." Kiera reached for the coverlet, wrapped it around Alanah's shoulders before giving her a gentle push toward the table. "A kiss is nothing to be ashamed of."

Stomach rumbling in spite of her worries, Alanah picked up the spoon, dipped it into the stew. "It is where I come from."

A smile played over Kiera's lips. "I wouldn't be too concerned over propriety, Alanah. If Caleb is anything like his brothers, I doubt your family has anything to worry about."

"You don't understand." She put the spoon to the side, her appetite gone. "You see, where I come from, when a man shows an interest in a woman, he's just as likely to take her for his own, whether she's willing or not."

She didn't know what she expected . . . Kiera to swoon or gasp in surprise, perhaps, but her steady, clear regard didn't waver.

"And you think Caleb is that kind of man?"

"I —" Her stomach churned. She'd been around Caleb enough to believe he'd never mistreat a woman. "No, but what if I entice him, and he loses his head? It's better to stay away from him completely than to risk . . ."

"To risk being attacked? Raped?" Kiera reached across the table and clasped Alanah's hands. "Alanah, have you ever done anything to entice a man?"

"No." Aghast, Alanah shook her head. "I would never —"

But she'd wantonly kissed Caleb. She had

enticed him.

"Listen to me." Kiera's hold on Alanah's hands tightened. "There are two types of men in this world: men who have no qualms about crossing the line between common decency and doing unspeakable acts of evil, and those who fight for what's good and right."

"But couldn't a man lose that common decency if he's immersed in sin and debauchery?"

"I don't know, but the fact that you were willing to make this trip with Caleb says something of his character, doesn't it?"

"Yes."

"Alanah, listen to me." Kiera's voice turned serious, her eyes searching Alanah's. "I don't know Caleb, but I'd like to believe that he's cut from the same cloth as his brothers. I pray that Quinn, Caleb, and even my bear of a brother-in-law, Connor, show you what a morally upright and godly man looks like."

Alanah's lips twitched. "You're afraid of Connor too?"

"Oh, you don't know the half of it."

CHAPTER 20

The next morning dawned hot and muggy, the sudden thunderstorm having blown itself out overnight. Caleb joined Quinn and the other men in front of the barn, where they hoisted bales of cotton onto the wagons.

Soon, Alanah and Kiera emerged from the cabin, Kiera helping Alanah carry her belongings. Alanah wore the green dress Isabella had given her. He wanted to tell her how pretty she looked but, after last night, decided the best course of action would be to keep his mouth shut.

"Oh, I forgot my cloak." Alanah lifted her skirt. "I'll be right back."

Caleb climbed up and made room for the totes between the bales of cotton and the sides of the wagon. His sister-in-law handed him each tote.

"Quinn told me of Reggie Caruthers's safe return and of your part in it."

"Aye." Caleb searched his memory, trying to piece together Reggie's connection to Quinn's wife.

"I can see you're confused." Kiera smiled. "My sister is married to Reggie's younger brother."

"Ah, I remember now." Caleb stored another pack in a corner of the wagon. "Reggie was a bit concerned to learn that his baby brother was a married man."

"Yes, they were young, but —" she spread her hands — "once they were wed, there was nothing to be done about it. It's good to know that Reggie is alive and well. The family has had more than enough tragedy of late."

Caleb jumped down and reached for a small satchel on the ground. Kiera waved him away. "That's mine. Since Quinn is going to be at the logging camp for the next few weeks, Megan and I have decided to go back to Breeze Hill. Put it in Quinn's wagon."

Alanah returned, her cloak over her arm. She didn't look at him, not even when he helped her into the wagon. As they got under way, Caleb's frustration grew with each passing mile. What did she expect of him? He'd apologized. Or at least he'd tried to.

"If —"

"I'm —"

They broke the silence at the same time. Caleb clamped his mouth shut, and after a long moment, Alanah blew out a slow breath.

"I'm sorry I got so upset last night. It wasn't you. It was me. And Betsy." She twisted her hands in her lap. "The men who frequent Cypress Creek aren't known for respecting women. They . . . they take what they want, and if it's not freely given, they take it anyway. A man's life means nothing to most of them, and a woman's life — or her virtue — even less. They're evil, just plain and simple."

Jaw clenched tight, Caleb gripped the reins, his eyes focused on the lead draft horse, his attention on Alanah's strained voice.

"Micaiah saw Betsy, and he wanted her. So he took her. I didn't see her for six months until Elias brought her back. I thought . . . I thought she was dead."

"It does no' matter." Caleb wasn't sure he wanted to hear any more.

"It does matter." Her head jerked up, her golden eyes flashing fire. "Betsy matters."

"That's no' what I meant, lass. I meant that you do no' need t' explain yourself."

306

"My apologies. I misunderstood your intent. But don't you see? What happened to Betsy is part and parcel of who I am too." She looked at him, pain in her searching glance. "Betsy didn't deserve to be treated like a piece of trash."

"No one tried t' get her back? No' even your uncle?"

"Uncle Jude blamed Betsy." Caleb barely heard the words, Alanah's voice was so quiet. "Said she'd made her bed and could lie in it."

Caleb tightened his grip on the reins, wondering what kind of man would leave his niece to suffer that kind of fate. "He blamed her?"

"Yes." She pinched the folds of her skirt between her thumb and forefinger, pleating the material. "Do you know why I'm called Addled Alanah, why Betsy and I wear rags?"

"No, it's beyond my ken."

"Because Uncle Jude thought it would keep the likes of Micaiah Jones away." She fisted the green material in her hands, her knuckles white. "But Betsy grew tired of looking like a wretch. We found a trunk of dresses, and she started wearing them when our uncle was away. She liked feeling pretty. Micaiah saw her, and the next thing I knew, he'd taken her."

307

"All men are no' cast from the same mold," Caleb said. "And neither are all women. Wearing rags and heaping ashes on your head would no' stop someone like Jones from following through on evil intentions. But neither would wearing something decent."

"All men are not cast from the same mold."
Alanah stared at her hands gripping the pretty green material of her skirt. Very carefully, very slowly, she relaxed her grip, bringing herself back to the present.

"And why is that?" she asked, not really expecting an answer. "What causes one man to respect a woman and another to have no more concern over her than if she were a dog?"

Caleb shifted, and she glanced at him, saw the frown that pulled his brows down.

"I'm sorry. I didn't mean to be offensive."

"You did no' offend. I was just trying t' think o' an answer that made sense."

"I'm not sure there are any answers that make sense."

"Aye. You may be right. But if it's any consolation, I've known many men who would've defended your sister against Jones."

Alanah smiled. Kiera had said much the

308

same. Bless them both for saying such, but she wondered if there was any truth to their words. Having lived amongst the lowest of the low hadn't given Alanah any reason to believe otherwise.

And you, Caleb O'Shea? Would you have defended her? Or me, for that matter, if the need arose?

She clamped her lips shut, unwilling to press the issue. Caleb owed her and her sister nothing. Not his protection, his loyalty, or his life should it come to that. And going up against the river pirates could very well mean losing one's life.

They rounded a bend, and the lane took them between fields white with cotton. Laborers, already hard at work, waved as they passed by. Breeze Hill and the outbuildings lay on the other side of the fields beyond a grove of shade trees. The wagons clattered along until the buildings came into sight, then skirted around the back of the plantation home and headed toward the smithy and a building that looked like two cabins had been combined into one.

A hand-lettered sign declared the establishment as the Breeze Hill Inn. A group of men exited, walked toward a cluster of wagons already lined up and ready to go. Before Quinn and Caleb pulled their wagons to a halt in front of the inn, the travelers were heading out.

The other wagons from the logging camp were loaded with cotton, and a passel of children with straight black hair surrounded the third with various baskets, bundles, and sacks. A dark-skinned woman with braids stood nearby, and Mr. Horne knelt in the wagon, looking a bit overwhelmed. A little red-haired girl in the midst of all the dark-haired children stuck out like a sore thumb.

Quinn set the brake. "How goes it, Horne?"

"We'll be ready shortly. We're just loading the last of these supplies."

Caleb jumped down, then held out his arms for Alanah while Quinn did the same for Kiera. Megan hopped down from the wagon without assistance and ran toward the children.

Alanah joined Kiera, and they walked toward the inn. "Megan looks happy to see her friends."

"She gets so lonely at Magnolia Glen. That's one reason I decided to stay here until Quinn returns from the logging camp." She motioned toward the Natchez woman, heavy with child. "And I daresay Mrs. Horne can use my help running the inn, given the fact that she's expecting her eleventh child any day now."

Caleb and Quinn joined the other men sorting and packing, being careful to use every spare inch of space for the supplies Gimpy had asked for. Finally they were done, and after strapping a piece of canvas over the supplies, they jumped to the ground.

Mrs. Horne sidled up to her husband and murmured a few inaudible words. Then she turned and waddled toward the cabin. Just before she went inside, she paused beside Kiera. Patting Kiera's cheek, she smiled. "It is good to have you home, child."

Kiera hugged the woman. "It's good to be back, Mary."

An elderly man approached from the big house on the hill, and it was all Alanah could do not to stare. His face was pulled and puckered, his hands drawn into claws.

"That's Mr. Bartholomew, Isabella's father. He was severely burned when Breeze Hill caught fire two years ago."

Mr. Bartholomew nodded a greeting, then turned to the men. "Quinn. Caleb. I have news from Reggie Caruthers that he wanted me to pass on to you."

"He's well?" Caleb asked.

"He is. He sends his regards." A frown knit the man's brow. "But there was some-

311

thing in his letter that concerns me."

Quinn straightened. "What is it, sir?"

"A river pirate who was tried for murder escaped from the stockade at French Camp. Reggie warns us to be on our guard as the man has ties to this area, especially Cypress Creek."

Caleb speared Alanah with a look. "Did he provide a name?"

"Micaiah Jones."

"When?"

"Almost three weeks ago."

Alanah's heart thudded against her rib cage. Micaiah was alive and —

And her sister was almost a day's journey away, unprotected.

The trip back to the logging camp went slower with the wagons groaning under the weight of the cotton. Alanah willed the horses to go faster, but there was nothing Caleb nor any of the drivers could do.

The day passed slower than sap rising, but finally the wagons rolled into the logging camp just as the sun dipped in the west. Even before Caleb had set the brake, Alanah hiked her skirts and jumped to the ground.

She slung her bow and arrows over her shoulder, then absently motioned toward her totes. "I'll come back for these later. I must get home."

"Alanah, wait —"

But she didn't linger. She hurried away, her only thought to get to her sister. Had Micaiah made it to Cypress Creek? Had he taken her sister once again?

Please, Lord, let Betsy be there.

She glanced back, saw Caleb gaining on her. He caught up and, without a word, joined her.

"You — you don't have to go with me."

"I do." His dark eyes met and held hers. "You do no' know what you'll find, lass."

Tears pricked her eyes, and she turned away lest he see her weakness.

Her feet flew through the forest, the trip home seeming to take longer than ever. But soon she stepped into the clearing surrounding her home. All was quiet. Lydia had banked the fire beneath the arbor that they used throughout the summer and fall to keep down the sweltering heat in the cabin. The goats bleated a greeting, and the chickens scratched in the yard. Feeble light spilled from inside the cabin. Nothing seemed amiss. Nothing at all.

"Lydia? Betsy?"

Betsy came flying out of the cabin, ran straight to her, and threw her arms around her. The baby raccoons tumbled down the steps chasing her like rambunctious puppies. "Alanah, you're home."

Alanah hugged her sister tight, overwhelmed with gratitude to find her safe. "Yes, I'm home."

One of the raccoons started climbing up Alanah's skirt. Laughing, she reached down and plucked the little animal off. Cuddling it close, she nuzzled it. "You are spoiled."

Betsy picked up another of the babies, then stiffened as she spotted Caleb standing a few feet away. Alanah patted her arm. "It's all right, Betsy. Don't be afraid. Caleb is a friend."

"Tiberius is my friend." Betsy shrank against her side, her whisper barely audible.

"Yes. And Caleb is Tiberius's friend as well."

Caleb's compassionate gaze caught and held hers before he hunkered down, held out his hand, and made a clucking sound by pulling air through his teeth. One of the raccoons ambled over, sniffed his fingers, and Caleb ruffled a hand across the animal's fur before flipping the baby raccoon on its back. The kit kneaded its paws against his palm and nibbled on the tips of his fingers with his tiny teeth. Caleb laughed, then palmed the baby raccoon and picked it up.

Nestling the tiny masked animal against his chest, he scratched the soft spot behind the raccoon's ear. The kit let out a contented chatter-purr.

And in that moment, Alanah knew she was falling in love.

Caleb looked over their progress. He and Quinn had managed to work together without an argument for three whole days.

It had to be a record.

They'd made the trip to Magnolia Glen and back without arguing, but Alanah had been along, as well as Mr. Horne and Rory and Patrick. And they'd been in separate wagons, so that could have accounted for the amicable trip. But the close proximity on the sandbar —

"I do no' think this is going to work." Quinn scowled as he drilled a hole in a log.

So much for burying the hatchet. Caleb stabbed the tip of the curved roller into the log at his feet and pulled it toward him. "Why no'? We've already made one successful run. No need t' think we canna make another."

Quinn walked out onto the log raft, his unsteady gait showing he was not used to the rolling deck of a ship. He paused, bent his knees, and bounced on the balls of his feet. The raft rocked, barely. Quinn scowled. "We could lose thousands o' dollars of cotton if this thing capsizes. The whole venture is too risky."

"Why don't you let William and Connor be the judge o' what's risky or no'?" Caleb squinted at his brother. "It's not like you have any cotton o' your own."

"That's no' exactly true." Quinn jerked a thumb toward the cotton stored under a tarpaulin. "I've got one bale t' claim as me own."

"A whole bale o' cotton? Why, that's —" Caleb bit off his sarcastic retort about the small amount of proceeds from one measly bale of cotton when he saw the look of pride on his brother's face. "That's mighty fine."

" 'Tis no' much, but 'tis a start. Next year will be much better. Connor gave me a tenant's share on every bale produced at Magnolia Glen. We've harvested ten bales this year. With hard work, we can double that next year. And then . . ."

"And then what?"

"And then I'm going t' build me wife a house." A flush rolled up his brother's cheeks. "Connor says that Magnolia Glen belongs t' me as much as it does t' him. 'Tis me job t' make sure it prospers."

Caleb took a deep breath, hooked the

other end of the log, and together they rolled it across the sand toward the timber raft.

Had he heard right? Connor had given part of Magnolia Glen to Quinn?

And why shouldn't he? While Caleb had taken off for parts unknown and wasted his youth, Quinn had sacrificed his to stay in Ireland. He'd made sure Rory and Patrick had food to eat, peat for the fire, and clothes on their backs. Quinn deserved to reap the rewards that came from being loyal to the family.

And what did Caleb deserve? Nothing. Not even the food he ate at the cookhouse up on the bluff. He should leave, catch the next boat out of Natchez —

"Quinn." Patrick raced down the incline toward them, his voice strident with fear. "Something's wrong with Isabella."

CHAPTER 21

"Betsy and I are going to gather *pacanes.*" Lydia stepped off the porch, a large basket under her arm. "Will you go?"

"Not today. I need to finish this tincture." Alanah waved them away. "I have a lot to do if I'm going to have everything Mr. Weaver needs before Caleb heads back to Natchez."

"Do you need my help?"

"No. I can do it. And the pecans won't wait. It will be nice to have roasted pecans this winter."

"Good, then. We will not be long." Lydia turned toward the barn. "Betsy, are you ready?"

"Coming." Betsy came running, the baby raccoons chasing after her. Alanah watched her, her heart full. Her sister was slowly returning to normal. Would she ever be her old self? Alanah didn't know, but she'd take every laugh, every smile, and every day with

318

gratitude and a thankful heart.

"Put those animals in the barn."

"Can I put them in the house?"

"No. They will destroy everything." Lydia pointed to the barn. "Put them in the crate Tiberius made for them."

Betsy led the way back toward the barn, the raccoons following like puppies.

Lydia frowned. "You know we're never going to be able to eat those raccoons."

"Probably not. But the joy they bring her is worth having them around."

"That man." Lydia scowled. "He should have left them in the woods, where they belonged."

"They wouldn't have survived."

"They're not going to survive here if they get in my pantry again."

Alanah chuckled, then turned serious. "I've been meaning to talk to you about something. Uncle Jude wants to go north. Back to Pennsylvania."

"I see." Lydia stared at her. "How soon will you leave?"

As was Lydia's way, she didn't ask questions, just accepted the inevitable.

"I don't know. I told him I didn't want to go, but when he insisted, I asked him to wait until spring." Alanah shrugged. "But now . . ."

"You are worried about Betsy. Micaiah."

"Yes." She lifted her gaze. "Maybe Micaiah won't come here at all."

"Are you willing to take that risk?"

"No," Alanah whispered. "If moving to Pennsylvania would keep Betsy safe, I'll do it gladly. But —" tears burned her eyes — "I'd never see you again."

"It's one thing to never see someone again because they are no more, but another to know they are alive and well. So do not feel sorrow if leaving keeps you and Betsy safe." Lydia searched her face. "Is there another reason you do not want to go?"

"What do you mean?"

"You would never see Caleb O'Shea again either."

Alanah stared at Lydia. "I —"

"I'm ready." Betsy tugged the barn door shut. With a meaningful glance in Alanah's direction, Lydia allowed Betsy to lead her away.

As soon as they were out of sight, Alanah ducked into the arbor and stirred the mushroom tincture, thinking on the question Lydia had left hanging.

Did it have to be one or the other? She picked up a knife, tossed a handful of squawroot on the scarred table, and chopped, the knife flashing as rapidly as the thoughts churning in her head. She didn't even know if Caleb cared for her. As far as she knew, he might kiss every girl he saw — even those dressed in rags with a rat's nest for hair. There was no reason to think she meant anything at all to him.

Her sister or Caleb? Her sister or Caleb? Her sister — ?

As much as it pained her, there was no question what she needed to do. As soon as Uncle Jude returned, she'd tell him she was ready to leave. The sooner the better. If he hesitated, she'd tell him about Micaiah —

A rustling in the woods wiped every thought from her head, except for focusing on the noise she'd heard. Without looking around, she picked up the kettle, walked to the porch, and set it down. With one practiced movement, she snatched up her bow, nocked an arrow, and turned.

And saw Caleb break into the clearing, hatless and disheveled. She lowered her bow. From the look on his face, something was horribly wrong.

"Where's Lydia?"

"She's not here. What's happened?"

"It's Isabella. She's sick. She wouldn't tell me what was wrong. Just said to get Lydia."

The babe.

"I'll do what I can. Let me get my pack."

■ ■ ■ ■

"Let me pass."

Sweat-stained and wild-eyed with worry, Connor had a growl that would strike fear into any man, but Caleb blocked the entrance, thankful for the heavy door Connor had finally managed to hang just last week. "Alanah said to no' let anyone in."

"I do no' care what she said." Connor raked a hand through his hair. "I want t' see me wife. They've been in there for hours."

That was stretching it. As soon as Caleb had returned with Alanah, Isabella had sent Quinn into the woods to bring her husband back. If she'd told Quinn what was wrong, he hadn't breathed a word to Connor.

"No' until Alanah says —"

The door behind him opened, and Alanah stood there. "It's all right. He can come in now."

At her words, Connor stopped pacing. He didn't move even when Caleb stepped aside. It was as if Alanah's quiet words had rooted him to the spot. Finally he glanced at Caleb, the terror on his face hollowing Caleb's own stomach. Connor took one step forward, then another, and disappeared inside.

Alanah slipped out and quietly pulled the door shut.

Caleb searched her gaze. "What's wrong?"

"It's not for me to say. But she's all right. For now."

"For now? What's that supposed t' mean? Either she's sick, or she isn't —"

"With child?" Connor's roar drowned out what he'd been about to say. "Dear saints above, woman, ya are with child and ya let me drag ya out here t' a logging camp, with no modern conveniences, no midwife —"

"Connor, darling, you didn't drag me."

"But the babe." The anguish in Connor's voice leaked through the closed door. "I do no' want t' lose ya, lass."

"Shh, darling. Do not worry so. I'm fine. The babe is fine . . ."

Alanah moved away from the room, and Caleb followed, glancing over his shoulder at the door. "Is she really going t' be all right?"

"Time will tell."

Caleb frowned at the closed door, hoping she was right.

Alanah jumped when Connor jerked open the door and barked out her name. "Isabella is asking for you."

He stepped aside and let her enter the

cabin. Then he stood waiting, arms crossed.

Alanah rested a hand on Isabella's stomach, waiting to see if her muscles contracted. "How are you feeling?"

Isabella gave her an encouraging smile. "Much better."

"Did you finish your tea?"

"Every drop."

"I think you'll be fine if you take it easy for a few days."

"I promise to stay abed until you tell me otherwise."

"I'll leave some squawroot, and if you start cramping, Connor or Gimpy can brew you some more tea. Lydia and I will come back and check on you tomorrow."

Connor straightened from his slouched position against the doorframe. "Ya — you canna go. What if I do no' make the tea strong enough? Or — or too strong?"

"I cannot stay." Alanah shook her head. "Lydia and my sister will be worried."

Connor looked like a caged lion. "I can send someone to tell her where you are."

"Tiberius will go." Caleb stood in the doorway. "And he'll keep watch over them until you return."

"See there. Your family will be safe, and they shan't worry over you." Connor's gaze flickered to his wife, then back to her.

"Please, miss."

The three of them stared at her as if she had the power to keep Isabella alive and save her babe. Only God could do that, but she'd do what she could to help. Knowing they'd already lost one child in the early stages of pregnancy sealed her own fate for the night.

She nodded. "I'll stay if that is your wish."

"Thank you, miss." Looking like the weight of the world had lifted off his shoulders, Connor started issuing orders. He motioned to the room across the dogtrot. "You'll need supper and some bedding. The office is close by if Isabella needs you."

"Connor, she can't sleep on the floor —"

"It'll be fine, mistress, thank you."

"I'll see that she's comfortable." Caleb held out a hand. "Let's get you something to eat, and I'll have Rory and Patrick gather some bedding for you."

Caleb led the way toward the cookhouse, where the loggers were eating their evening meal. When several of the men glanced their way, Alanah paused.

"What's wrong?"

"I'm really not that hungry."

Caleb's attention shifted toward the gawking men, and changing course, he propelled her away from the cookhouse. "Is it the men?"

"Yes. Could I just eat back at the cabin?"

He led her to a stump at the edge of the bluff, where the evening breeze blew in from the river. "Wait here."

"Caleb —"

But he was already gone. Instead of sitting, she walked to the edge of the bluff that looked over the river. The sloping hill was bare of scrub brushes and grass where the logs had rolled down to land in piles at the bottom.

She shaded her eyes against the sun as it sank in the west and looked toward the side channel where a second timber raft was taking shape. She'd thought the first raft had been huge, but this one was three times as big. And not only that, but true to their word, Caleb and the others had loaded it with bale after bale of cotton.

"What do you think?" Caleb stood beside her, two bowls of stew in hand.

"It's impressive." Accepting one of the bowls from him, she sat down on the stump. "When do you plan to leave?"

"Tomorrow or the next day at the latest." He hunkered down next to her. "I'll take your herbs to Weaver if you like."

Alanah bit her lip. She needed to go back

home and pack everything that she planned to send to Natchez. But tomorrow would be soon enough, if Isabella didn't develop any complications during the night. "Thank you. I was preparing a batch of mushroom tincture when you came this afternoon."

"Will it be all right overnight?"

"It's covered and should be fine."

They ate in silence, until she motioned to the sandbar. "I wonder if the recent rains exposed more squawroot?"

"You need more?" Caleb arched a brow.

Alanah pointed to the pile of logs at the base of the cliff. "It's much like your logs there. One can never have too much of what provides their living."

"You have a point. I'll be right back." He took both bowls to the cookhouse, then returned with a bag. "Let's go before it gets dark."

They walked to the road that sloped down the bluff to the sandbar and skirted around the pile of logs waiting to be lashed together. The timber raft bobbing in the water was even bigger than it had looked from above.

They reached the jagged edge of the bluff where rains had washed away more dirt. Alanah was pleased to see more pods of squawroot clinging to the roots.

She moved toward the cleft, but Caleb

waved her away. "I'll do the climbing this time, lass."

He handed her the bag and climbed up, then cut the pinecone-shaped roots away from the root system they'd attached themselves to. One by one, he tossed the roots down, and Alanah stuffed them in the bag. Finally, the bag overflowing, she called out, "That's enough."

"What, ya canna keep up?"

"The bag's full, and it's almost dark."

"Just one more." He leaned farther out, stretching for a cluster of roots almost out of his reach. Suddenly the root he clung to broke and he came crashing down.

Alanah dropped the bag and rushed to him, falling to her knees. "Caleb? Are you all right?"

He opened one eye, squinted up at her, then held out a piece of squawroot. "I think I broke your herb, lass."

Alanah laughed. "It has to be chopped or pulverized into a powder anyway. So I don't think breaking it is going to hurt it any."

She started to stand.

"Alanah —"

She froze. The teasing tone of his voice was gone. He lifted his hand, ran the tips of his fingers along her jaw. Alanah shivered at his touch; then, panic winding through her, she inched back.

He dropped his hand. "I would never hurt you, lass."

"Would you — ?" Alanah broke off as heat rushed to her face.

"Would I what?"

"Would you kiss me if you thought I was willing?" she whispered.

"If you have t' ask that, then —" He chuckled, sounding a bit strangled. He stood, reached for her hand. "We'd better head back before one o' us does something we regret."

As his hand closed over hers and he pulled her to her feet, Alanah reached up and pressed her lips against his.

Immobile for the space of a heartbeat, he didn't respond. Feeling foolish, Alanah broke contact, but before she could move away, he swept an arm around her waist and pulled her to him, deepening the kiss. Heart soaring, Alanah savored the touch of his lips on hers. It was just as magical as the first time.

Slowly he lifted his head, giving her the opportunity to stay — or flee.

Time stood still, save for the gentle flow of the river and the sun sinking below the horizon in the west. Caleb's breath feathered across her cheek, and the longing that spiraled through her stomach reminded Alanah that she shouldn't linger, no matter how much she trusted Caleb to honor his promise.

She touched the tips of her fingers to his lips, then turned and fled.

CHAPTER 22

When word came that the loggers were almost done with the timber raft, Micaiah decided it was time to act.

While it would seem best to attack at night, he'd decided that daytime suited him better.

The sawyers would be out in the woods, others would be spread along the logging trails snaking logs toward the bluff, and the raftsmen would be on the sandbar preparing to leave for Natchez.

If all went well, they could dispatch the loggers, gather the spoils, and float them downriver themselves. They'd pass Natchez by and sell the goods in New Orleans, where no one would be the wiser. But first he had to gather his men and relay his plan. He looked around the tavern for his cousin, didn't see him, then caught the tavern owner's eye. "Where's Elias?"

"He said something about paying a visit

to Addled Alanah. Didn't seem to be sick or nothing." The man shrugged. "Don't know why else he'd head over there as late as it is. Looney Lydia's liable to shoot him."

Micaiah scowled. Would his cousin's hankering for Betsy's sister put a kink in his plans? Now that he noticed, several men loyal to Elias were also gone.

Slamming his tankard down on the table, he lurched to his feet. Tonight was not the night to put the locals on guard, not when he'd just decided on a plan of action to purge Cypress Creek of the interlopers in their midst. He snapped his fingers and five of his men stood and followed him into the night.

When they were within a hundred yards of the preacher's cabin, Micaiah motioned the men to a halt. Through the trees, he could see the cabin, dark and silent. There wasn't anything unusual about that. Darkness had fallen hours ago, and there was no reason for the women to burn candles needlessly.

But something was wrong. He could feel it. He could smell it. What — ?

Then it hit him. It was the metallic scent of warm blood wafting on the night air. His hackles rose. "Look lively. Something's amiss."

They inched forward; then Finley hissed, "Look here."

There on the ground lay a body. One of Elias's trusted compatriots. By the light of the moon, they could see that he'd been knifed, mercilessly so.

Finley backed away. "That's Looney Lydia's doings."

"Don't be a fool, man," Micaiah growled. "This is no woman's handiwork."

A slight rustling sounded off to their right, followed by silence. Finley crouched low, the whites of his eyes shining.

"Spread out," Micaiah ordered. The men melted into the darkness, and Micaiah pressed his back against a tree. For a long time, he heard nothing, not even the peeps and calls of the night creatures, the goings-on in the woods having disturbed their nocturnal habits.

Micaiah trilled the call of the whip-poor-will, waited a heartbeat, then followed with the deep-throated call of a bullfrog, ending with three more birdcalls.

If Elias was out there, his cousin would know the signal.

There. At the edge of the clearing, close to the cabin. The sounds were faint, but it was the right sequence of calls.

Micaiah circled the clearing, drawing

closer to the source of the calls. A coldness settled over him, and he debated whether to give the signal to fall back or to rush the cabin. The signal came again, so feeble that Micaiah wondered if he'd imagined the whip-poor-will's call and the bullfrog's croak that didn't sound like Elias at all, but more like somebody strangling.

He eased around a tall oak, then peered through the darkness. A faint gleam caught his eye. Something red and wet and the unmistakable stench of blood and entrails. Next came a low moan and a soft rustle as the dying man moved.

Micaiah gave a call, so low that only the figure ten feet away would hear it. The prone form stilled.

"Micaiah —"

The voice was Elias's.

Micaiah inched forward, knife in his clutches. He stopped beside his cousin, saw there was no hope for him. Elias's heavy-lidded gaze met his. "I'm done for, Cousin."

"Who did this? Jude?" But Micaiah couldn't see the lily-livered reverend having the guts or the skill to knife two men in the dead of night. Two men who'd done their own share of killing and relished the doing.

"Big man. Ebony-skinned. Gold . . . gold hoop in ear. Knife . . ." Elias's hands fluttered. "This long. Cut me open like a fish . . . left to die."

Micaiah had seen the man working as a sawyer with another man of similar size and strength.

"How many men came with you?"

"Two." Elias chuckled. "To handle Looney Lydia, you know?"

"And the women?" Micaiah asked. "Betsy?"

"I don't know."

Elias moaned, then lay still. Micaiah moved away, intent on finding this ebony-skinned man before the man found him.

"Micaiah, don't leave."

"There's nothing to be done for you. You'll be dead within the hour."

Elias cursed him, the words barely audible. Without a backward glance or another thought for his cousin, Micaiah eased silently through the underbrush toward the cabin in the clearing. He had five men with him. Surely they could take out one lone man. And they'd start by taking the women. He gave the signal to rush the house.

Within minutes, he and his men had surrounded the cabin, rushed up the steps, and slammed through the doors into the two rooms flanking the dogtrot. Only to find them empty. What had happened to Betsy,

Looney Lydia, and Addled Alanah? Had they run away? Or had the black-skinned man butchered them as he'd butchered Elias and the other one?

Rage boiled up and over, and growling low in his throat, Micaiah stomped out of the room to the porch. "Betsy, girl, where are ya? Come to Micaiah, girl, if you know what's good for you."

His answer was a scream, then a crash in the underbrush, followed by silence.

His men bounded off the porch into the woods toward the sound. An hour later, they returned to the cabin, having found neither hide nor hair of the African or the women. But it didn't matter. Micaiah knew where the man had taken them.

And he'd pay. They'd all pay.

Starting now.

He grabbed a firebrand from the fire pit and set the buildings blazing one by one.

Alanah lay on the pallet across the way from Connor and Isabella's room, thinking about the kiss she and Caleb had shared. She'd invited that kiss.

Nay — she'd *initiated* that kiss.

She groaned. How could she have been so brazen?

She was no better than the harlots who

worked at the tavern in Cypress Creek. She'd enticed him, just as Uncle Jude accused Betsy of enticing Micaiah Jones.

And look at what had happened to her sister.

She was stolen, raped, abused.

But by the grace of God not murdered.

Was Uncle Jude right? When did one cross the threshold from courtship to lust to outright wanton behavior? She curled into a ball, thoughts whirling. Would one kiss lead her down the same path of destruction?

Would Caleb take advantage of her weakness? She couldn't believe it of him. He wasn't like Micaiah Jones and men of that ilk. He was kind and good and honorable. Like his brothers. Both were upstanding men. They owned land. Property. They had wives. Women who loved them and whom they loved in return.

By Kiera's own admission, his brothers cherished their women, their families, and protected them. That was the kind of man Caleb O'Shea was.

Wasn't he?

She wouldn't — couldn't — believe that he'd take liberties just because she'd kissed him and let him kiss her in return.

But where did a few kisses leave them? She couldn't have it both ways, Caleb's kisses without thought of what would happen tomorrow or the next day or the next.

Her face flamed.

Nothing had been said about love or marriage or any kind of future between them.

Even when she'd told Caleb that they were heading north, the news hadn't fazed him. He'd just winked and made some remark about heading back to sea. She clutched the thin blanket to her, not that she needed it for warmth, but for something to hold on to.

With Caleb gone, the only real reason to stay would be for Lydia's sake.

A commotion outside halted her thoughts. Tensing, she listened as the sound of men's voices drew closer, then boots pounded along the porch. Throwing back the covers, she grabbed her bow and had just nocked an arrow when someone rapped at her door.

"Alanah, are ya awake, lass?" Her heart did a little jig when she heard Caleb's voice.

"Yes."

"Unbar the door."

She put her bow to the side and obliged, met his troubled gaze. "What's wrong? Is it Isabella?"

"Isabella is fine." Connor stood framed in the door across the breezeway. "Caleb, what's the meaning o' —"

"Alanah?"

Her heart hitched when she heard Betsy's voice.

She looked past Caleb, saw Betsy, Lydia, and Tiberius just behind them. Betsy rushed toward her. As she folded her sister into her embrace, her questioning gaze sought out Lydia. "What happened?"

"Elias Jones came to the house looking for you. He was drunk. When he didn't find you, he went after Betsy."

Her arms tightened around her sister. *No.*

"He didn't touch her." Lydia jerked her chin toward Tiberius. "And he will not bother you or Betsy again. Tiberius has taken care of that."

Alanah's attention shifted between Lydia and Tiberius. "He's — he's dead?"

"He is dead. Along with two more."

"Who's Elias?" Caleb asked.

"Micaiah's cousin."

Fear grabbed hold of Alanah's insides. With Elias dead, would the other river pirates leave them alone or — ?

"There's more." Lydia glanced at Betsy. "Micaiah was there. I heard him call out."

"Micaiah?" Betsy looked at her, her eyes filled with tears. "Don't let him kill the babies, Alanah."

Alanah folded her broken sister in her

arms. "I won't, Betsy. I won't."

"What babies?" Connor straightened, and Alanah could feel the fury rolling off him. "Were there children left behind?"

"No. She's talking about the baby goats and raccoons back at their place. Betsy's very protective of the wee animals."

"I see." Compassion swamped Connor's face. Blowing out a breath, he raked a hand through his hair. "Well, there's nothing else we can do tonight other than double the watch."

"Caleb?"

Caleb woke instantly when Patrick called his name. "Aye, lad, I'm here."

"Connor's asking for ya."

"Tell him I'll be right there." Stumbling out of his tent, he splashed cold water on his face and eyed the faint light of dawn cresting the horizon. He'd taken the first watch with Tiberius, and it seemed as if he'd just fallen into bed a short while ago.

He joined the group congregated around the cookhouse. Tiberius stood nearby, looking on. Connor paced and William leaned against a post, arms crossed. Connor pivoted. "I do no' think it's a good idea to send the logs and the cotton downriver right now."

Caleb eyed his brother. "Why no'?"

"Those cutthroats out there. They might be planning to attack us. We'll need every man t' defend the camp."

"We can't just hunker down and let them pick us off one by one. We should take the fight t' them." Caleb made a chopping motion with the heel of his hand. "Flush 'em out and be done with it."

"That's what a man does when he has no wife, no children, no home or property t' defend." Quinn scowled. "I suppose ya think we can all just run off after them and leave the women and the camp unattended. Ya know nothing o' the matter."

"I know that if you sit back and let a bunch o' thieves 'n' murderers overrun you, then ye'll have nothin' in the end t' show for it. No' your land, no' your goods, no' your wives."

"Enough. Sit down, the both o' ya." Connor waited until they complied. "You're both right. We have t' protect what's ours, but we canna wait them out. We have t' come up with a plan."

"Maybe they'll leave us alone." William shrugged. "They haven't attacked us yet. Why now?"

"I do no' know why they haven't attacked before now." Caleb stared at him. "But

341

we're going to have a fight on our hands now. Men have died, and from what little I know of Micaiah Jones, he won't stand for it."

He could all but feel the anger bouncing off Tiberius. His friend hadn't said a word, but his country had been torn apart by rogue bands of men no different from the ones who roamed the Natchez District. Men who raped and pillaged and took what they wanted, leaving the land and the people with nothing. No livelihood, no hope, and no future.

And but for a sword of vengeance and the grace of God, Caleb would have ended up just like them, a man with no conscience and only shame to his name.

" 'Tis true, I'm afraid." Connor scraped a hand over his jaw, his attention on the cabin that housed the women. Isabella on one side of the dogtrot, Alanah, her sister, and Lydia on the other. "And me wife needs to be back at Breeze Hill. I should never have allowed her t' come here. She's a distraction I canna afford."

Caleb's gaze followed his brother's. Aye, Connor was right. Women had no business being in the thick of things. They distracted a man and kept him from doing what needed to be done.

William took three steps away, rubbed the back of his neck, then turned back. "We'll figure out a way to get the women away, but in the meantime, we need to keep the men close to camp today and fortify ourselves as best we can."

Caleb blocked thoughts of Alanah from his mind and focused on the task at hand. "Well, if you're determined to fortify the camp, I have some ideas."

Jaw rigid, Connor folded his arms and nodded. "Say on. We're listening."

Jude walked toward home, making plans.

He'd heard that Micaiah had escaped from French Camp, and it would only be a matter of time before he and the other river pirates started killing and stealing, just as they'd done in the past. At least with Elias, Jude could sometimes sway him to his way of thinking, but Micaiah would not be swayed.

In spite of Alanah's pleadings to stay until spring, they'd leave as soon as his nieces could gather their meager belongings.

He refused to preach to people who would not listen. He would wipe the dust of this place off his feet and take what was left of his family and go back to Pennsylvania. He was tired of trying to turn cutthroats into

Christians, bring robbers to repentance, and instill thankfulness in thieves.

The men who roamed these woods and frequented that den of iniquity called Natchez Under-the-Hill didn't deserve to be saved. They lived by the sword and they would die by the sword, and in all his years in this wilderness, he had not seen a one of them turn from their wicked ways.

And he was tired of fighting God's urging. The farther away he could get from this place, the better off he'd be. They could be gone within the week. Sooner —

A flash of color caught his eye. Light-brown hair, a slim figure. Skirts swishing along the faint trail. *Rachel?*

Chin quivering, he watched as she meandered through the forest, stopping to pick a handful of flowers. She held them to her face, then moved on. Humming came to him, an old hymn they'd sung in church back in Pennsylvania.

She turned, and he caught a glimpse of her face. He blinked.

Not Rachel. But his niece Betsy. So much like her aunt Rachel. Such an innocent, sweet child, until . . .

He frowned.

What was she doing out in the woods, tempting fate once again?

He hurried forward. "Betsy!"

Startled, she turned, a look of fear on her face. Then she saw it was him. She smiled, then just as quickly lowered her face, looking at her feet.

"Uncle Jude," she whispered.

His heart smote him. He'd done that to her with his gruffness. But it had been for her own good. He clasped his hands behind his back. "What are you doing so far from home, young lady?"

"I . . ."

"Speak up, girl."

She backed away. "We spent the night at the logging camp, and I — I came home to check on the kits."

"The logging camp? What were you doing at the logging camp?"

"I —" Confusion clouded her features at his sharp tone. "Micaiah —"

"Micaiah?" Jude's heart slammed against his rib cage. He gentled his tone, knowing that anger and bluster would get nothing out of Betsy. "What about Micaiah?"

"Don't be angry." Her big brown eyes pleaded with him. "Elias came and Tiberius helped me and Lydia, but then . . ." She shook her head. "I don't remember."

"Has Micaiah been here? Answer me, girl."

"I — I don't know . . ." She trailed off, dropped her head, and stood silent, the sweet, sunny girl who'd been humming and picking flowers moments ago gone. "The kits will be hungry. And the goats need to be milked."

She sounded so desolate, so lost, that he felt a prick of conscience. "Never mind, then. Let's go home, and you can see to the animals."

Maybe Alanah could make sense of the tale. He reached for her arm, then felt the hair rise on the back of his head as five men stepped out of the woods.

"Well, if it isn't the esteemed Reverend Browning."

Jude recognized one of the regulars who spent most of his time at the tavern. "Let us pass, Finley."

Finley's gaze landed on Betsy. Smirking, he stepped aside, swept his hat off his head, and bowed low. "Of course, sir. You may go. But Micaiah requested this little morsel be served up on his plate, so we'll be taking her with us. With your permission, of course."

Sweat broke out on Jude's scalp and poured down his face to mingle with his beard. Betsy didn't utter a sound. She didn't scream. She didn't cower. She just stood there, head down, looking like the broken woman-child she was.

Lord Jesus, help me.

But he was unable to move. Unable to tell them no. Unable to save his niece for the second time.

Finley chuckled, and the vile men who cared nothing for life walked by him, so close that they could stab him and not even turn aside for the effort. The smallest of movements from Betsy caught his attention, and then she was looking at him, the pain and fear in her eyes reaching out to him, begging him to be the protector that he'd promised her father he'd be.

The short period of lucidity vanished, and she lowered her gaze.

"No."

"What did you say?" Finley whirled, his eyes flashing with anger.

"I said no. You are not taking my niece again." Jude tossed his heavy pack on the ground in front of him. "Take the supplies I bought at Mount Locust. I have a bit of coin as well. But leave the girl alone."

An evil grin formed on Finley's face. "How generous, Reverend Browning, but I'm afraid it's not enough. Kill him."

His gaze met Betsy's. "Run, girl!"

To his surprise, his niece took off.

And just like that, they turned on him, ravenous dogs devouring everything in their path. He saw the flash of a blade, felt the white-hot pain as the steel ripped through his flesh. The next thing he knew, he was falling, rolling down an incline. Tumbling, twisting, briars tearing at his clothes, shredding his flesh.

Pain exploded when his head slammed against a tree.

Then everything faded to black.

Chapter 23

Two bowls of Gimpy's stew in hand, one for Betsy and one for herself, Alanah pushed open the cabin door with her elbow. "Betsy, I brought you some stew."

But the cabin was empty. Alanah dropped the stew onto the table and rushed out on the breezeway, her gaze sweeping the camp. The sound of saws and shouts rang out as the loggers worked to secure the camp against attack. Her sister was nowhere to be seen.

With so many men around, she'd never dreamed that Betsy would venture out of the dogtrot cabin. But her sister had disappeared in the time it had taken for Alanah to fetch a bit of nourishment for the noonday meal.

"Betsy!" she called.

Lydia came out of Isabella's room, a washbasin in her hands.

"Betsy's gone."

"Gone? You don't think Micaiah —"

"No. I don't think he snuck into camp and spirited her away. But I wouldn't be surprised if she went home. You know how worried she was about the baby raccoons."

"And the goats."

"I'm going to look for her."

"I'll go with you."

"No, stay here with Isabella. I'll be fine."

"Now, Alanah, you can't do that." Lydia's dark eyes flashed. "With Elias dead, there's no telling what Micaiah will do."

"That's why I have to go. If he finds her first, he'll —"

"Find Tiberius. Take him with you."

"He's busy. And besides, I'll be back before anyone knows I'm gone."

"All the more reason I should go with you." Lydia tossed the dirty water over the porch railing. "Isabella is resting. She'll be all right for a while."

"Please, Lydia. Connor will be livid if we leave Isabella unattended. Just stay here. I'll find Betsy, and we'll be back as fast as we can."

"I don't like it." Lydia frowned.

"Trust me."

Alanah left the camp, hurried through the woods, keeping to the shadows and hoping she didn't run into Micaiah or any of his men. She crossed the road, and as she neared home, the scent of smoke wafted on the breeze. Smoke? Had they left the fire burning? Even if they had, she'd never smelled smoke this far from home.

The scent grew stronger, and a haze hung low over the trees. She reached a ridge with a clear view of home and spotted tendrils of smoke curling skyward.

No. Lord Jesus, no.

A sob caught in her throat, and then she was running toward home. Running to what? She didn't know. Running to save Betsy, running to save the goats, her herbs, their precious few belongings, and the tiny raccoons Betsy was so fond of. All of it.

She halted in the middle of the barren yard and stared at what used to be her home, the barn, the arbor where she prepared her tinctures, the wattle fencing, crushed and broken and scattered on the ground.

All gone.

Except for the goats. They'd escaped the carnage and roamed freely, sniffing curiously at the charred remains.

Her gaze shot to the hillside that rose upward behind the barn. The root cellar? Could Betsy have possibly sought shelter there?

She rushed forward, stumbled once, then regained her footing. She reached the hillside, wrenched open the cellar door, and peered inside the darkened hole. Empty. She shut the door and slumped to the ground, drained and in shock. Micaiah and his men had burned them out, stolen their provisions, and —

Eyeing the devastation around her, she tried to make sense of everything. The fire had been set hours ago. But Betsy hadn't disappeared until today. Had she come here or gone to Cypress Creek?

Where was her sister?

She took a deep breath and stood. She'd return to the logging camp and ask Caleb for help, something she should have done the minute she'd found Betsy missing. But she'd never dreamed —

Halfway across the yard, she heard the chatter of the kits. In spite of the bands of fear around her heart, she smiled and dropped to her knees as they ran to her, searching for a morsel of food.

The noon hour had come and gone by the time the men cleared all the trees, creating an open space around the camp a good three hundred yards in every direction. Next they snaked logs around the perimeter. Unless Micaiah Jones and his men had draft horses of their own, they'd be hard-pressed to move the massive logs or to get over or around them.

Quinn stood, hands on his hips, surveying the scene. "What do ya hope t' gain from this?"

"We need to defend the camp as best we can. It won't stop them, but at least we'll see them coming." Caleb crossed his arms. "If we had time, we'd clear the land all the way to Cypress Creek."

"To what purpose?" William pursed his lips.

"These men thrive on using the woods as cover. The open land would force them to take to the river."

"Or they'd become so enraged, they'd attack."

"Aye." Caleb shrugged.

Quinn stared at him, a look of consternation on his face. "Ya act like ya want to fight these river pirates."

"If it becomes necessary." Caleb squared up to him. "Tell me, Brother, if you had the choice between fighting them yourself and having someone who's trained t' do the fighting in your stead, what would you choose?"

"The trained fighter."

"Then I'm your man, and the sooner we get this camp protected, the sooner I'll be off t' fight them."

"Ye're no' serious, are ya?"

"Why would I no' be?"

"Caleb!"

He glanced up to see Connor headed their way, his long strides eating up the distance.

"That fool girl has run off again."

"Betsy?"

"Well, her too. Lydia said Betsy was nowhere to be found, and Alanah went home t' fetch her back." Connor shoved a hand through his hair. "*Eejit* women. The two of them are going t' get themselves killed over a couple o' baby raccoons —"

But Caleb was no longer listening to his brother. He hurried away, determined to find Alanah and Betsy before Micaiah did.

Alanah found a basket and tucked the baby raccoons inside. She trudged to the edge of the forest, then turned back, looking at the charred remains of her home.

It hadn't been much, but it had been hers. She should have begged Uncle Jude to head north the day he'd first mentioned it. They would have been long gone by now. And now everything was lost. Even Betsy.

A sudden thrashing in the woods had her

melting into the underbrush beneath a towering pine. The basket bumped the tree and the kits whimpered. She draped her cloak over the basket and whispered a soothing "Shh."

Three goats came rushing past, over the ridge, back to the smoldering remains of their home. Something had disturbed them. She waited, tuning out the minute scratching of a bird searching for bugs, the squirrel chattering in the tree thirty feet to her right, the soft breeze rustling the leaves overhead. All common, normal sounds that wouldn't faze the goats in the least.

Instead she listened for the uncommon.

Gradually she picked up the slow, consistent crunch of leaves, the shuffle of feet as someone made their way through the forest.

Crunch. Crunch. Crunch.

The sound of footsteps and the unmistakable swish of clothing.

Crunch, crunch. Crunch, crunch, crunch, crunch, crunch.

A whimper.

She reached to quiet the baby raccoons but froze before her hand touched the basket.

Betsy.

The whimper had come from her sister, being hauled through the forest by a man

Alanah knew only as Finley. A vicious man that Lydia had stitched up more than once. Finley jerked her sister forward, uncaring when she fell at his feet. With hardly a pause, Betsy's captor yanked her up and marched on.

Alanah reached for an arrow, nocked it, then went still when four more men materialized out of the shadows.

Her hand shook as her gaze shifted to the man who held her sister captive. The arrow was centered on his back, an inch to the left of his spine, below the shoulder blade. A shot to the heart. He'd be dead before he hit the ground.

But so would Betsy. So would she.

After these men had their way with them.

"Do no' do it, lass."

She almost let the arrow fly when Caleb's whisper floated to her from inches away. Her hand shook. The slightest tremble.

As the distance between her and her sister grew, so did her despair of rescuing Betsy from her captors.

She lowered the bow as a silent tear slid down her cheek.

"Those men are taking her to Micaiah." Alanah shoved the hood back, climbed out of the underbrush, and glared at him. "We have to get her back —"

"I will get her back." Caleb wrapped his fingers around her wrist to keep her from taking off after the cutthroats and getting herself killed. "You will go back t' camp."

"I'm going after my sister." Her golden eyes, dark with determination, rose to meet his. "If we don't go now, they'll cross the river, and we'll never catch them."

He heard a whimper and palmed his knife. "What was that?"

"The kits." Alanah picked up the basket, lifted the lid, and a baby raccoon poked its head out. "The reason Betsy went back home."

He hunkered down, ran the tip of his finger over the head of the tiny animal. "She'd want you t' take 'em to safety."

"She would, but I know where they're taking her. You don't."

"What do you mean?" He jerked his attention to her face.

"I know where their hiding place is. Cottonmouth Island, on the other side of the river."

"A large, long stretch of land about three miles downriver?"

"Yes. How did you know?"

"I saw it when we took the timber downriver."

Alanah started walking.

"Where are you going?"

"Home."

He wondered at the catch in her voice but followed her anyway. Moments later, he saw the devastation.

"They burned us out." Her voice sounded so small. So lost. "Everything's gone."

"I'm sorry, lass."

"I am too." She tucked the basket under the corner of the barn that remained. The kits tumbled out, raised themselves on their hind legs, and chattered at her. Reaching into her pocket, she dropped a handful of corn on the ground. The kits grabbed the kernels and started chewing. "Let's go."

Caleb followed in her wake. "Would they no' cross the river at Cypress Creek?"

"No one keeps a boat at the landing. They keep it hidden if they want it to be there when they come back."

"And you know where Micaiah's men keep theirs?" Caleb scowled at her back.

"I know. But we'd better hope there is more than one."

They were too late.

Alanah stood on the shore and watched two flatboats angling across the river, the late-afternoon sun blinding her to who manned the oars. But she had no doubt that Betsy was in one of those vessels.

As the boats disappeared downriver, her heart went with them. She turned away from the river. "Come on. I have a small raft. We'll —"

"Alanah." Caleb grabbed her arm. "We canna storm the island alone."

Alanah stood, her arms clutched against her midsection, battling with the logic of his statement and the stark fear of losing her sister for good this time. "That's what I did when Betsy disappeared the first time. I waited for Uncle Jude, and when he didn't come, I went there alone. But they — they were gone. They'd taken Betsy and abandoned the island."

She and Caleb would have to return to the logging camp, and by then . . .

Her stomach churned, and she pressed harder lest she be sick. She didn't want to think about what Betsy might be going through at this very minute, but she couldn't *not* think about it. Her sister had already endured more than was humanly possible for a girl who had become a woman barely three years ago.

Dear, sweet Betsy. She'd been an outgoing, bubbly child who'd never known a care in the world save her parents' deaths, and she'd been too young to remember them. When Aunt Rachel had died, Lydia had taken over the role of mother for the then-thirteen-year-old.

And then she'd blossomed from a beautiful, carefree child into an even more beautiful young woman, and Micaiah Jones had taken notice.

Oh, Betsy, I failed you once again. My poor, sweet Betsy. Dear God in heaven, please protect my sister. Please don't let her suffer more at the hands of that monster. Instead, allow her a quick and painless —

Horror filled Alanah at the thought that ricocheted through her brain. *Had she actually just prayed that her sister would die at the hands of Micaiah Jones?*

Lord Jesus, please no . . .

Unable to stop nature itself, she fell to her knees in the sand and retched.

As the contents of her stomach soaked into the sands along the Mississippi River, Caleb dipped his neckerchief in the river, then dabbed her forehead with the cool cloth.

"We'll get her back, we will, lass." But even as he lifted her to her feet, wrapped one arm around her waist, and led her away from the river, from her sister, back toward

Cypress Creek and the logging camp, she knew.

There was nothing anyone could or would do to save one poor girl from the likes of Micaiah Jones.

Hadn't her own uncle proven that all those months ago?

CHAPTER 24

"Look what we found."

Micaiah lifted his head, saw Betsy hunched into herself. He shifted his attention to the men fanned out behind her, grinning like fools.

Finley pushed her toward Micaiah, and she stumbled, lost her balance, then scrabbled inside the dilapidated cabin to the back corner, the same place she'd hidden and trembled months before.

He chuckled, remembering how she'd fought him tooth and nail when he'd first brought her to Cottonmouth Island. But this time she was silent as a tomb. He took a gulp of ale, not sure if he wanted any part of her now. Who wanted someone who couldn't be bothered to fight back?

Besides, he had more important things to handle right now.

He turned toward the man cowering before him. "Where's Massey?"

Colbert swallowed, his Adam's apple bobbing like a cork. "Dead. So's Wheeler."

"What happened?"

"Elias told us to go downriver with the timber raft, to watch and listen and report back. But Massey and Wheeler decided to kill the others and take the timber for themselves. Only it didn't work out the way they planned. Wainwright and that O'Shea feller got the upper hand and killed them."

"But you got away and made your way back to here."

"To tell Elias what had happened —"

"And the horse?" Micaiah glanced at the sleek black animal Colbert had ridden across the shallows to the island. "Where did you get the horse?"

"I stole it. From travelers on the west side of the river. That's the truth of it."

River pirates sat on stumps, lounged on bedrolls, or just stood around watching. Brows lowered, Micaiah stalked toward the horse. He ran his hand down the powerful neck, along its sleek back to the rounded hips and fingered the brand on the horse's haunch.

"Now, tell me again. Where did you get the horse?" He knew, but he wanted Colbert to tell him.

Before he killed him.

"I told —"

"You told me nothing!" The horse jerked away, startled by the roar of his voice. He soothed the animal with a gentle pat, then reached the idiot who'd dared to defy him in three long strides. The man cowered before him, which served only to enrage him.

"That horse belongs to Monsieur Boucher. You knew not to touch anything this side of the river. Not the horses, the plantations, the women, nothing. Now you're going to bring the wrath of the French down on our heads. Cottonmouth Island was the one place we had no fear of repercussions."

Eyes gleaming, Finley fingered his knife. "What are you going to do with him?"

"Get him out of my sight. And at first light, take him and the horse to Boucher and beg his forgiveness."

"Beg his forgiveness?" Finley spat in the dirt. "Ye're growing soft, Micaiah."

Micaiah's knife flashed, the tip pressed against Finley's throat before the man could move. "Does this look soft to you?"

Finley raised his hands. "No."

Micaiah glared at the men scattered around. "Nothing has changed. We leave the plantations and the settlers on this side of the river alone, and we are left alone in return. Is that understood?"

The men murmured agreement. They knew when they had a good thing. Situated downriver from Cypress Creek in a sharp bend in the river where most heavily laden flatboats ended up grounded on the hidden sandbars, Cottonmouth Island was ideal for waylaying unsuspecting travelers.

Or it had been before that logging crew had moved in.

There'd always been a lookout on the bluff where the loggers had made camp. Travelers would stop at Cypress Creek to trade, to gather news, and to ask about hidden dangers along the river moving forward. Since they valued their lives, the inhabitants of the small burg kept their mouths shut.

By the time a flatboat left Cypress Creek, Micaiah knew how many men were on board, how well armed they were, and what they were carrying to market. Some flatboat crews were allowed to go on unharmed. Sometimes the risk was too great, the paltry rewards too few.

But then there were the crews who'd grown complacent with their journey, those who'd overly enjoyed a night of revelry at the tavern, those who had horses on board, guns and shot, ale and coin.

A flotilla of armed men ahead, a flotilla behind, a prearranged schedule of waiting one day or two before attacking; then they'd close the gap and tighten the noose. None of them ever had a chance, and none ever escaped to tell the tale of what had happened to them.

The only tales they told were to the fishes that swam the river.

But now that the loggers were clearing more land, Micaiah could see the writing on the shifting sands of the Mississippi. As more travelers came down the river, some would decide to make their homes here. While some of his men thought that gave them more opportunity to kill and steal, Micaiah knew better. He and his kind couldn't live in harmony with the morally upstanding sort that would start flooding Cypress Creek. They would be driven out as soon as the settlers outnumbered the river pirates.

Which brought him back to the loggers who had encroached on his territory.

It was time to wrest control of Cypress Creek back.

Clutching his blood-soaked side, Jude staggered another ten feet, then collapsed against a pine, the bark scraping his cheek.

Don't stop now. Home is just over the next ridge.

Summoning strength he didn't know he possessed, he let go of the tree and forced himself to put one foot in front of the other, his attention focused on home.

Alanah and Lydia would see to his wounds. Everything would be fine.

But he'd have to tell Alanah that Finley had taken Betsy. He'd tried to save her, but he'd failed. Even in his moment of glory, of trying to do the right thing, he'd failed.

The next thing he knew, he was in the clearing, just standing there, weaving on his feet, breathing heavily. For a moment, he thought he'd misjudged, that the destruction laid out before him was someone else's homestead, someone else's charred remains.

But the goats roaming the yard were his. The bit of wattle fencing, the position of the barn all too familiar.

Where . . . ?

What had happened here? The two cabins he and his brother-in-law had built for their families, nothing more than charred logs. The barn gone, save a rear corner that had survived the fire.

"Alanah?" His niece's name was hardly more than a croak through parched lips. He swallowed, licked his lips, and called her name again, but there was no answer.

Where was Alanah? Lydia?

The root cellar.

He staggered across the yard toward the cave he and his brother-in-law had dug out of the bluff the first summer they'd arrived. If Alanah was alive, she'd be in the cellar. Falling to his knees, he clawed at the door, pulled it open.

The cellar was empty. No food, no supplies, no Alanah, and no Lydia.

What had Betsy said? Something about spending the night at the logging camp. He prayed his niece and Lydia were there.

His wound burning with fire and fever, Jude crawled inside the dark, dank hole in the ground and curled into a ball on the dirt floor.

Caleb helped Alanah down an embankment.

Night had fallen by the time they cleared the dense forest and came to the footpath the loggers had worn between the logging camp and Cypress Creek.

"We're almost there, lass. Can you make it?"

Her glassy eyes rose, met his, and he had the feeling her thoughts had been far, far away from him and the path they were on.

She blinked. "Yes, of course."

Then she promptly stumbled and would have fallen at his feet if he hadn't had hold of her arm. Without further ado, he swept her into his arms.

"No." She struggled with about as much strength as those wee kits she'd been bound and determined to save. "Put me down. I can walk."

"When was the last time you ate, lass?"

"I'm not sure. Last night. No, a biscuit this morning."

Ah, Gimpy's stew. More broth than meat most of the time. And one measly biscuit to break her fast today. It hadn't helped that she'd left whatever nourishment both provided on the riverbank. "You're weak as a cat, and I do no' want ya keeling over on me."

Surprisingly, she didn't resist but rested her head against his shoulder. "As you wish. But just for a moment."

"Just for a moment."

Her eyes slid shut, and soon she was breathing the even cadence of exhausted slumber. He cradled her slight form close to his chest, his heart swelling with the need to protect her, to make things right for her and her wee sister. What if Jones had gotten his hands on Alanah? What if . . . ?

He would have moved heaven and earth to get to her, to tear Jones apart, limb by limb. He couldn't bear the thought of Alanah being violated. His arms tightened like a vise around her, and she let out a low moan. Loosening his hold, he tried to breathe.

And what of Betsy?

Jaw clenched, he marched forward, thoughts spinning. Betsy deserved no less protection than Alanah or Isabella or Kiera. He'd find a way to rescue her or die trying.

Alanah roused as Caleb lowered her to the pallet in the cabin back at the logging camp. Jerking awake, she searched his face in the dim light cast by a single candle. Compassion filled his dark eyes, and pain pierced her heart as everything came rushing back.

Betsy.

He lifted her hand to his lips, kissed her knuckles, and in one fluid movement, stepped back. The candlelight wavered; then Lydia was there, kneeling on the pallet beside her, arms open.

As Lydia enfolded her in her embrace, Caleb slipped out the door.

"She's gone," Alanah whispered. "Micaiah's men took her to Cottonmouth Island. I have to go after —" Her words broke on a sob.

"You must not make yourself sick with worry," Lydia crooned, pressing a bowl into her hands. "Now eat."

"How can I?"

The thought of food made her want to throw up again. She looked around the dim cabin, the rough-hewn desk pushed to the side, allowing room for the three of them to have pallets. She shuddered, the thought of a safe place to lay her own head making her heart pound afresh, when Betsy —

"If you do not eat, I will feed you myself." Lydia dipped the spoon into the bowl.

Reluctantly Alanah took the bowl and, under Lydia's watchful gaze, forced herself to eat every bite. She'd just finished when she heard a light knock on the door. It opened and Isabella stood there.

Lydia frowned. "Miss Isabella, you should not be out of bed."

"I'm feeling much better." Isabella crossed to the pallet, took her hand, and squeezed. "Connor told me about Betsy. I'm so sorry. Connor, Caleb, and the others will get her back."

"I want to believe that, but if Uncle Jude didn't care enough to go after her before, why would they?"

Isabella's expression became guarded.

"Betsy was kidnapped before?"

"Yes. Micaiah Jones took her away last spring. He used her. He . . ."

"I — I think I need to sit after all." Isabella's face had gone pale.

Lydia reached for a chair and Isabella sank down, the compassion on her face palpable. "I'm sorry, Alanah. I didn't know. I just thought . . ." She shrugged.

"You thought Betsy was dull-witted?"

"Yes." Isabella's face went from pale to scarlet. "Please forgive me."

"There's nothing to forgive." Alanah held out the rags she wore, a glimmer of humor twisting her lips. "Half the locals around here think I'm addled, but the ruse did nothing to stop Micaiah. I thought when he'd been captured and was to be tried for murder, Betsy would be safe from then on. I was glad he was to be hanged, if not for what he'd done to my sister, but for murder. The end result would be the same, would it not? But then he came back, and I'm afraid nothing will save her this time."

Isabella took her by the hand and tugged her to the seat next to her. "Nothing is too big for God if we pray and believe."

"Uncle Jude has prayed. He prayed for Betsy's soul and for destruction to fall on Micaiah —"

"Destruction?" Isabella frowned. "Forgive me once again, but it seems that your uncle is more concerned with passing judgment than saving souls."

Lydia grunted, and Alanah knew she agreed with Isabella's assessment. "He can be harsh, but I believe his heart is in the right place."

"That may be, but he needs to examine it more closely if he believes leaving Betsy to her fate is God's will. Perhaps an earnest prayer that woos God's favor is more effective than calling down fire and brimstone." Isabella looked at Lydia. "Will you join us?"

Lydia scowled and crossed her arms, refusing to sit.

Isabella arched a brow at her. "Lydia, you don't believe that God can help in this situation?"

"No offense to your God, Miss Isabella, but if anybody's going to save Betsy, it'll be Tiberius, Caleb, and your man."

Isabella's lips twitched. "Have you considered that my God sent Tiberius and Caleb for such a time as this?"

Lydia's gaze narrowed, but still she didn't join them. Instead, she grabbed one of the chairs and scooted it across the floor to the corner, then sat, the shadows engulfing her. "Go ahead and pray. I suppose it will not hurt."

"Thank you, Lydia." Isabella took Alanah's hands in hers, closed her eyes, and started praying, her voice barely above a whisper. "Our heavenly Father, we beg of You . . ."

Focusing on Isabella's voice, Alanah searched for God in the darkness. She'd tried not to become jaded by Uncle Jude's harsh view of the world around them, but the light in her life had grown dimmer and dimmer with each blow — the deaths of her parents, who'd taught her to trust God, to depend on Him, to lean on Him. Then Aunt Rachel had died, and Uncle Jude's rigid view had become even narrower. Her faith had almost been snuffed out completely when Betsy had disappeared. Oh, she'd prayed to God. She'd grasped at her feeble faith, at the hope that Betsy was still alive, but had she really, truly believed that God would save Betsy?

In spite of all the hurts and abuse her sister had gone through, Betsy had survived. She'd come home. And — tears pricked Alanah's eyes as remorse smote her —

And she hadn't even thanked God for her sister's safe return.

Not once.

The hot tears spilled over, ran down her

face, and dripped onto her hands, still clasped tightly in Isabella's.

I'm sorry, God. I'm sorry. You saved Betsy's life, brought her back to me, and I didn't even acknowledge that the only reason she survived those months with Micaiah was because You willed it. Did my ungratefulness lead to Betsy being taken again? Perhaps not, but I can't stand the thought of being the cause of more hurt for her. God, help me to be strong, help me to believe in You, and . . . and help me to believe in the help You've sent to us. She took a shuddering breath. *But in all things, Your will be done, Lord.*

Isabella's quiet voice seeped into her consciousness. She opened her eyes, blinked, and the first thing she saw was Lydia seated in the corner. As stoic as ever, at first glance she seemed unmoved, but the moisture glistening on her cheeks told a different story.

Alanah's heart did a joy-jig, and she shifted her attention to Isabella's downcast head, her lips still moving in prayer. She didn't even know what Isabella had prayed, didn't know what she'd petitioned God for, but something — her words, her faith, the groanings of her spirit, or just the wooing of God's still, small voice — had touched Lydia.

Just as it had touched Alanah.

The heavy cloak of fear and uncertainty that had blanketed her lifted, and for the first time in a long while, Alanah felt at peace.

CHAPTER 25

"Tiberius and I will go after Betsy."

"The two o' you can't go up against them alone. You would be slaughtered." Connor hunkered down. "Now show me where they are, and we'll figure out what t' do and how many men t' send."

"They're on a small island about three miles downriver, closer to the Louisiana side." As best as he could, Caleb described the island he'd seen on his trip to Natchez. "We could be there in an hour or so. Attack in the middle o' the night."

"Our first priority is t' this logging camp," Quinn gritted out.

Caleb stared him down. "*My* priority is t' rescue that girl."

Some of the men were asleep, rolled in blankets scattered around the camp where they could catch a bit of night breeze. But several had joined Caleb and his brothers around the fire pit in front of the cookhouse.

"Do ya no' have a brain in that thick head o' yours? That's just what that madman wants." Quinn flung his arms out. "He wants us t' run off all over the place looking for a half-wit girl who does no' have the sense t' get out o' the rain, while he attacks the logging camp, left undefended."

"You are right, Brother, about him attacking us, but you are wrong about Betsy. She did no' ask t' be taken by Micaiah Jones. She's just a wee lass who canna defend herself against a bunch o' murderous dogs who would use and abuse her for their own pleasure."

Connor stepped between them, rested his hand on Quinn's shoulder. "Caleb is right."

"And what about Isabella?" Quinn stabbed a finger toward the cabin where Isabella, Alanah, and Lydia were. "Will ya risk yer own wife and child by engaging these cutthroats?"

"I do no' have a choice." Looking torn, Connor glanced toward the dogtrot. "I know you mean well, Quinn, but that lass needs help. Just as much as Isabella needed me, and Kiera and her sisters needed you. More so, I think." He shook his head. "If you'd seen her that first day when she tried t' steal the bacon from Gimpy. She was like a dog that had been kicked and cowed until she had no more fight left. I thought she was just addled in some way, and I suppose she was, but it wasn't because she was born that way. It was from the abuse heaped upon her after months in captivity." Connor glared at the loggers standing around. "Nobody deserves t' be treated like that. Especially no' a wee lass."

A rumble of assent passed through the men.

"All right. I give in." Quinn ran a hand through his hair. "But how — ?"

A commotion at the edge of camp halted his question. The men parted, and Tiberius led a bedraggled man forward and tossed him on the ground at Caleb's feet.

"I found this one watching from the bluff." Tiberius's voice rumbled like angry thunder.

"One of Jones's men?"

"He will tell you all you need to know." Tiberius slid his scimitar out of its scabbard, the grate of iron against the leather ominous. He took a step forward, and the man scrabbled backward. "If he wishes to live."

"I won't go."

The peace Alanah felt less than an hour ago had vanished, to be replaced by the familiar fear that had dogged her these many months. Arms crossed, she faced Caleb, candlelight flickering across his shadowed face.

"It's the only way. And we do no' have much time. You, Lydia, Isabella, and Patrick need t' leave for Breeze Hill now, while we know that Micaiah and all his men are across the river."

"Isabella can't travel."

"She'll make it. She must. It's the only way t' get all o' you out o' harm's way so that we can rescue Betsy." Caleb clasped her arms, forcing her to look at him. "Please, Alanah. It's for your own good."

"If I can't go with you, I'll stay here." She waved a hand toward the door. "I'm just as good with a bow — better — than any of the men out there. They know how to wield an ax, nothing else."

"Their axes are sharper than any two-edged sword and just as deadly. Besides, it will be close fighting, at night. Your bow would be useless."

She sighed. Inside the cabin, all was quiet. Lydia had gone across the dogtrot to gather a few belongings and bedding to ease Isabella's journey. And even beyond the walls, there was controlled chaos as the men prepared the surprise attack on Micaiah and his men.

She searched Caleb's gaze. "Why are you doing this?"

"Because . . ." His eyebrows pulled down into a deep V as if he hadn't really thought it through. " 'Tis the right thing t' do."

"For a girl you don't even know?" Her lips twisted as she recalled Uncle Jude's accusations. "A used one at that?"

"What makes Betsy less valuable than me — or you, for that matter? Only a savage would knowingly leave her t' such a fate."

"Uncle Jude did."

"I canna be knowing what yer uncle was thinking. He didna have the know-how to rescue her, and he didna have the men. We have both." Caleb rubbed his hands up and down her arms, his eyes troubled. "Alanah, sending you and Isabella t' Breeze Hill is the only way I can be assured o' your safety. Please, do as I say."

Alanah closed her eyes, weary of fighting. Weary of trying to nearly single-handedly carry the burden of keeping her sister safe. Maybe he was right, but how could she be sure?

"Trust me, Alanah. I'll bring your wee sister back unharmed."

She looked into his eyes and pressed her palm against his jerkin, the tips of her fingers resting on his thin shirt, the warmth of his skin branding her fingertips. "Not just my sister, Caleb O'Shea. I would that you return unharmed as well."

His dark gaze raked her face, seeking, searching, asking for permission that she'd already given with her words. She leaned closer . . .

Then she was in his arms, his lips crushing hers, the tips of her toes the only thing anchoring her to the floor. And unlike the last time he'd kissed her, she didn't pull away. Instead, she wrapped her arms around him and held on tight.

All too soon the kiss ended. Caleb lifted his head, his eyes glittering in the flickering light of the candle. One thumb slid across her lips, and a smile tilted up one corner of his mouth. "We'll have t' continue this conversation when I return, lass."

And then he was gone.

They'd learned everything they needed to know and then some from the pirate Tiberius had captured. The Moor had a way of striking fear into the hearts of all he met. But even now, as the men worked to finish loading the raft, Quinn still wasn't convinced.

"So let me get this straight. These pirates

lie in wait for flatboats t' come down the river; then they kill everybody on board, dump their bodies overboard, and take the goods on t' Natchez or New Orleans?" Quinn scowled. "And we're going t' go ahead with our harebrained scheme and attack the murderous thieves?"

"You forgot the part about rescuing Betsy."

"I did no' forget. Rescuing the girl is the least o' our worries. Even if we succeed in retrieving the girl, somehow we've got t' get back here t' protect the camp and the women. And if we fail, then —"

"We do no' need to protect the women. They will no' be here."

"What do ya mean?"

"The minute we leave, Connor, Horne, and the rest o' the men are taking the women, the draft horses, the mules, and the rest o' the supplies and heading t' Breeze Hill. If we fail, the only thing left here will be a handful o' cabins." He shrugged. "If Jones torches them, it'll be a small price t' pay."

"And what about the timber raft and the cotton? What's going t' happen t' that when we storm the island?"

"William and the raftsmen from Natchez will continue downriver, so your precious cotton will be safe."

"Ya've forgotten one thing."

Caleb squinted at his brother. "What might that be?"

"What t' do with Jones and his men after we defeat them."

"You assume there will be survivors."

"I'm assuming we will be victorious, and I'm assuming we are no' butchers."

Alanah stood on the bluff overlooking the sandbar. The men scurried to and fro re-arranging the bales of cotton. From her vantage point, she could see that the cotton was placed to form a block around the perimeter of the timber raft, leaving space for the men to hide inside.

When they'd finished, they covered the bales of cotton with canvas. Bible in hand, Mr. Horne motioned for the men to gather around. Both crews — loggers and raftsmen — stood with bowed heads as he lifted his hands toward heaven and beseeched God for favor for their mission. After the last *amen,* the men filed inside under cover of darkness, moonlight glinting off flintlocks, axes, and any other weapon that came to hand.

Quiet descended, and two men untied the ropes holding the timber raft in place. The raftsmen took up positions, using poles to push the unwieldy raft toward the center of the channel.

The logs floated free, caught by the current, and headed toward the massive river.

And Alanah's heart went with them. Not just with Caleb, but with all of them. They were risking their lives to get her sister back. Oh, she had no illusion that was the only reason. After all, it was in their best interests to rid Cypress Creek of the river pirates terrorizing the area.

The sooner Micaiah and his men were gone, the sooner the logging camp and Cypress Creek could flourish. Families would come. The men would take wives. Some whose talents lay more to farming would take William Wainwright up on his offer to cultivate the freshly deforested land. And others would continue to work in the logging camp.

But what of her and Betsy? Her livelihood was slowly being destroyed by the very men who were bringing peace and safety to the settlement. Would Uncle Jude see that things were changing? In spite of the fact that their home was gone, would the elimination of the river pirates change his mind about heading north? She prayed it was so.

Because she didn't want to leave Cypress

Creek, and she didn't want to leave Caleb O'Shea.

She watched the timber raft drift out of sight, then whispered, "Godspeed, my heart."

"Alanah, we must go." Lydia stood nearby.

"I'm ready."

She turned her back on the river, on Caleb, and on her sister and followed Lydia toward the waiting wagons. With each step, she felt she was abandoning her sister, just as Uncle Jude had abandoned her months ago. And even now he was off somewhere in the Natchez District and Betsy needed him again.

But Caleb was going after her.

He'd bring Betsy back, safe if not completely sound.

But what if he didn't?

What if . . . ?

She stopped, grabbed Lydia's arm. "I — I can't go."

Lydia stared at her. "Why not?"

"I have to go after them. What if the loggers fail in their task? They aren't skilled in fighting, not like Micaiah's men, who kill for the sheer meanness of it. If —" her voice broke — "if Caleb and the others fail in their task, Betsy will be lost forever."

"You have so little faith in Caleb and Tiberius?"

"It's not that. But I can't leave my sister. I just can't." She searched Lydia's gaze, her thoughts touching on everything that could go wrong during the rescue. "Betsy's liable to take off running or end up in the thick of things. If I get there in time, I can locate her and spirit her away the minute the fighting starts."

"You cannot do this thing. You promised Caleb you would go to Breeze Hill —"

"I never said I was going to Breeze Hill."

"I will no' allow it." The nearest horses jumped at the sound of Connor's bellow. He jabbed a finger at the wagon where Isabella reclined, every blanket and pillow they could find cushioning her journey back to Breeze Hill. "Ya will both get in that wagon with me wife, and we will be on our way."

Lydia crossed her arms and glared at him. Feeling less confident, Alanah squatted next to the fire pit, the ashes long cold. She dug her hands in the ashes and rubbed soot and dirt on her face and hair, darkening her skin and dulling the golden glint of her hair.

Satisfied that she was sufficiently covered, she faced Caleb's brother. "Thank you for your kindness and your offer of protection, sir, but my sister needs me, and nothing will keep me from her."

Hands on his hips, he advanced toward her, and she realized in that instant how much he and Caleb were alike. Not in looks so much, but in their overbearing, demanding ways. She lifted her chin. Nothing short of trussing her up like a chicken would get her in that wagon.

"Connor." Isabella's voice halted him.

He pivoted and in an instant was at his wife's side. "Are ya in pain? Is it the babe?"

"No, love. The babe is fine. I'm fine." Isabella took his hand and held it fast. "Alanah is right. She needs to go after her sister. She needs to see that she's safe."

"But —" Connor threw a glance over his shoulder, his glare encompassing both Alanah and Lydia — "I promised Caleb I'd see them safely t' Breeze Hill."

"You can't force them to go if they don't want to."

"Caleb's going t' have me head over this, he is." He let go of his wife's hand and stomped to where Patrick held the reins, muttering his displeasure the whole time. "Fool women going on an *eejit*'s errand."

Alanah rushed to the wagon, grabbed her pack of medical supplies, rummaged through it, and found the packet of dried

388

tea leaves. She handed the pouch to Isabella, then took her hand. "Rest easy, and don't forget to drink your tea as soon as you get to Breeze Hill."

"I will. Martha will take good care of me." Isabella squeezed her hand. "I will be praying. Be careful."

Connor released the brake on the wagon but didn't urge the horses forward. He glanced at them, his brow furrowed. "Watch out for me brothers and for William. Any time there's a scrape, William tends to come out the worst for it."

And with that, he slapped the reins against the horses' backs and the wagon jolted forward, leaving Alanah and Lydia alone in the deserted logging camp.

CHAPTER 26

The pounding of a horse's hooves approaching camp jerked Micaiah awake, and he grabbed his pistol. All around him, his men did the same, most of them melting into the thick underbrush.

At least they were alert enough to react quickly. He'd forbidden the consumption of ale hours before so that they'd be sober enough to attack the logging camp on the morrow. Knowing the loggers would expect it of him, he'd decided not to wait until the timber raft and the cotton headed downriver.

No, they'd attack this day, late in the afternoon, when the men were exhausted from a hard day's labor. They'd ride upriver past the logging camp and find a flatboat. There was always a farmer willing to trade a rickety skiff for a horse or two. And if not, they'd just take what they wanted. They'd put in on the west side of the river, cross over, dig in, and lie in wait for the loggers. Once they'd eliminated the threat in the woods, they'd take care of those in the camp.

With them gone, Cypress Creek and the surrounding area would be cowed as they had been in the past.

The horse and rider came barreling into camp.

Simpson.

Micaiah stuck his pistol in his waistband, strode forward, and grabbed the reins. "What are you doing here? You're supposed to be upriver, keeping watch."

"I was, but not fifteen minutes ago I caught sight of a flatboat floating down-river."

"You fool. I told you not to worry about the flatboats. My concern is the loggers."

"But that's just it. It looks like the timber raft the loggers were building, and it's loaded to the gills with cotton bales."

Micaiah stared at Simpson. "The timber raft and the cotton, you say?"

"Aye."

Micaiah scratched his jaw, then turned away, thinking. The loggers were trying to outwit him by sending the cotton downriver under cover of darkness, hoping maybe it would slip through undetected. He chuckled. They thought they were being smart, but they'd just played right into his hands. He'd kill the boatmen and take the timber and the cotton as well.

Then, tomorrow after he'd rid himself of the rest of the loggers back in Cypress Creek, he might just take a trip downriver to Natchez or New Orleans. A load of cotton would bring a pretty penny there.

Perhaps he'd take young Betsy with him. And if she was good, he might change his mind and keep her.

"Man the boats. There's a load of cotton floating down the river, and it's ripe for the harvest."

The men whooped and hollered, brandishing their weapons.

There was no sound except the quiet splash of sweeps as the experienced raftsmen navigated the river. With nothing to do until they neared Cottonmouth Island, Caleb hunkered down next to a bale of cotton and squinted at the distant riverbank barely visible in the light of the moon and with the mist that rose over the water.

Quinn joined him. "See anything?"

"Nothing. If memory serves, we should be getting close."

From inside the fort-like enclosure made

of cotton bales, someone let out a snore, quickly followed by a grunt. Someone hissed, "Quiet, you fool. Do you want to alert them that we're coming?"

Quinn chuckled. "Can't imagine anyone sleeping right now."

"Whoever it is, he's either too cocky or too much of an *eejit* t' realize what he's about t' get into."

"The closer we get, the more o' an *eejit* we all are."

"You should have gone with Connor if you're that worried."

"And let ya have all the fun?"

Caleb was barely able to make out his brother's features in the shadows cast by the bales of cotton silhouetted against the night sky. "Watching a man die by your hand is no' fun."

"Aye, I'll grant ya that." Quinn nodded. They sat in silence for a long stretch, before Quinn spoke again. "Caleb, why are ya doing this?"

"Doing what?" Caleb shifted the pressure off his left leg and rested his back more comfortably against the bale of cotton.

"Riding down this river, possibly t' yer death." Quinn turned to face him. "For some o' us, it's t' wrest control of Cypress Creek and the logging camp from a bunch o' cutthroats and thieves, t' carve out a safe and profitable life for our families. But ya? Ya've never said ya planned t' stay, t' make a life here. And ya do no' have a wife or land."

Caleb eyed the river, undulating with the tiniest of ripples. "Maybe I'm doing it for my brothers. T' make up for the past."

And not just for what he'd done to his brothers, but for others he'd wronged.

"Ya do no' have t' make up for the past." Quinn's voice sounded strained.

"Do no' tell me that you do no' hate me for leaving you t' raise the little ones all by yourself?"

Quinn was silent for so long, Caleb didn't think he was going to answer. Finally he sighed. "Aye. I hated ya. But ya were in the right t' hate me in return. I took yer one chance t' get out o' the mines. But I did no' know . . ."

"It's all right, Brother. I believe you." Caleb held out his hand. "Truce?"

Quinn hesitated; then a grin flashed across his face. He grabbed Caleb's hand and gave it a hearty shake. "Truce."

The raft floated along, slowly, leaving them all plenty of time to think. And apparently Quinn was in a thinking frame of mind. "So if it's no' for the logging camp or yer brothers, it must be for the girl."

"O' course it's for the girl. I told you that. She's just a wee lass and —"

Quinn chuckled. "I'm not talking about that girl. I'm talking about the other one — Alanah. I did the same thing for Kiera and her sisters. Love makes a man do some mighty strange things."

"Love?" Caleb was glad for the shadows that hid the flush creeping over his face. "I do no' —"

He stopped, squinted, saw the outline of the island in the distance. He motioned for Quinn to get out of sight. "There it is. Pass the word."

Quinn disappeared among the bales of cotton, passing the word to the men to keep quiet.

Caleb stood. As they closed the distance between the raft and the island, he spotted a sandbar. He hissed and pointed. The boat-men nodded. They'd seen the sandbar already. Probably even before he had. Without making so much as a ripple on the river, they used the sweeps to maneuver toward the island.

The closer they got, the harder his heart pumped. They'd land and the men who'd volunteered to flush out the cutthroats would disembark, and they'd push the timber raft off to float downriver to safety. They'd search out the pirates' hiding place and —

His blood ran cold at a flicker of movement on the water. Squinting, he stared at the spot. A boat materialized out of the mist, then another and another, until the horizon was broken by half a dozen boats of various sizes converging from all sides, closing in and cutting off the path downriver.

The tables had been turned and their surprise attack had turned into a counterattack.

"Quinn?" Caleb uttered the one word, quiet-like.

"Aye. I see," Quinn muttered from just inside the square of cotton bales.

"Stand down, lads," Caleb ordered the raftsmen. "Let 'em come t' us."

Caleb counted maybe twenty to thirty river pirates standing on the boats, ghostly-looking in the foggy night shadows. The timber raft jolted from the impact as the first of their crafts rammed into them. The pirates tossed grappling irons, crisscrossing from vessel to vessel, ensnaring the timber raft loaded with cotton — and loggers — until they were all bound together like one of his *mam*'s patchwork quilts.

He stood his ground, anticipating the

pirates' surprise when the loggers swarmed out of the hidden space in the center of the raft.

One man stepped forward, long hair hanging past his shoulders and a heavy brow that gave him a menacing look without even trying. His gaze swept the river, the timber raft, before settling on Caleb. "Strange time to be traveling."

"Aye." Caleb inclined his head. "Hoping t' beat the heat o' the day."

"And who might you be?" The stranger spat a chew of tobacco, splattering the timbers and the toe of Caleb's boot. Caleb paid the diversion no mind.

"Caleb O'Shea. And you, sir?" It grated to call the cutthroat *sir*, but he'd have his day soon. Very, very soon.

"Micaiah Jones."

"Jones, eh?" Caleb leaned forward. "My apologies if I do no' recognize the name. T' what do I owe this unannounced social call?"

A thundercloud rolled over Jones's features. "Make light if you will, O'Shea, but as you can see, my men and I have the upper hand, and you and your companions will float with the fishes this night."

"I think not."

"You think —" Jones chuckled, then

snapped his fingers. With a roar of sadistic glee, the river pirates surged forward.

They were met with an equal sound of rage as Quinn, Tiberius, William, and dozens of loggers spilled out from hiding and met force with force.

But Caleb had eyes only for Micaiah Jones. He pulled his pistol, took aim, and fired.

Heart lurching, Alanah drew in a ragged breath as the first yell, followed by shouts, shots, and iron striking iron, rang out from around the next bend in the river.

How had Caleb and the others found the river pirates so quickly? She'd hoped to make landfall and be on their heels when they attacked the camp, but now —

"Hurry, Lydia."

Paddling the small flatboat they'd unearthed did little to hasten their progress, but finally they rounded the bend, and she gawked at the sight laid out before her.

A whorl of flatboats and rafts all tethered together rocked and bucked as men stumbled for footing on the uneven surfaces. Sparks flew from the clash of weapons, and the grunts and groans of those fighting mixed with the screams of the injured. A splash resounded as someone fell into the river.

She tried to make sense of what was happening.

"It is as I feared," Lydia whispered. "Micaiah is no fool. He would have had lookouts posted, watching the river. Our men had little chance of succeeding."

Horrified at the scene before her, all Alanah could do was stand and stare. At the forefront of the timber raft, Caleb would have been the first to encounter the pirates. Alanah's lips moved, but no sound came out.

Please, Lord, no. Not Caleb. Don't let him be dead. I can't bear —

"Get down." Lydia jerked her down to lie flat on their raft. "We cannot be seen. There's Betsy to think of."

Coming out of her stupor, Alanah grabbed one of the sweeps and helped Lydia steer the small flatboat into the side channel. Lydia was right. They'd come to get Betsy, and she couldn't let the fighting on this side of the island deter her from that goal.

"She will be in camp," she whispered. "We'll ease into the channel and pray no one notices us."

Hugging the shadows along the shoreline, they let their raft drift between Cottonmouth Island and the mainland. The water here was shallow, but their raft had little draft to it. They skimmed along the surface easy as could be.

The towering trees and low-lying fog blocked much of the light from the moon, and Alanah squinted as they floated silently along, the sounds of fighting growing fainter. The narrow channel widened, the ebb and flow of the current cutting into the outer bank on the Louisiana side of the river, the inside curve leaving an exposed sandbar on the island side. A hodgepodge of dilapidated flatboats lay beached, half in the water, half out. But no one guarded the boats. And why should they post a watch here?

There was no need to suspect anyone would dare be caught in the very mouth of the pirates' lair.

Their raft slid past the makeshift landing, and Alanah didn't turn in until they'd gone another hundred yards, where the bank rose up out of the water and the underbrush hung low. Without discussion, she and Lydia snugged the small craft close to land and tied it off.

They climbed the bank, then crouched, getting their bearings. Before the river pirates had discovered the island and claimed it for their own, she and Lydia had harvested medicinal herbs from the island, always watchful of the cottonmouths sunning on the sandbars.

But tonight was not the night to be squeamish of snakes.

Other than to search for Betsy, she hadn't returned, but there was only one place with elevation high enough that anybody with any sense would set up a permanent camp. Micaiah was a lot of things, but dull-witted wasn't one of them.

She touched Lydia's arm, then set off toward the highest point on the island.

Jude woke to pitch-darkness, his mouth tasting like cotton, his insides on fire.

He lay there, trying to get his bearings. What had happened and where was he?

He moved his hand, felt the cold, hard-packed earth beneath his fingertips.

The cellar.

The dank earth closed in around him, and like Jonah, he was in the pit of despair. He heard the drip of water, and he groaned with longing. Just one drop of the water that trickled along the back wall of the cellar would slake his thirst, but he lacked the strength to crawl to the seep.

After drifting in and out of consciousness

for . . . he knew not how long — he'd resigned himself to the fact that no one was coming. Perhaps his nieces were dead or captives of the murderous swine that roamed the land.

He'd preached to those men, told them of the wrath of God to come, but what had happened? Nothing. They'd continued to flourish as they wallowed in their sin, and he and his were left to die in their piety.

"What do You want from me, God?" His voice was hardly more than a croak.

Cry against the wicked.

"To what end? So that the inhabitants of Natchez Under-the-Hill can gut me as they gutted my brother-in-law? So that as I lay dying, praying for their souls, like my brother-in-law, they can strip me of anything with the least amount of value? Better that they are destroyed, as you destroyed those wicked cities in the days of Lot."

Cry against the wicked.

"I cannot. I will not." Jude's anger was kindled anew, and like the men of old, he would have smitten his breast, had he the strength to do so. "My wife, my children, my nieces, all gone, taken from me by this savage land and the vile men who inhabit it. All that is left is my life, and that as good as dead."

The silence surrounding him was broken only by the incessant drip in the far reaches of the earthen hole.

His meager strength spent arguing with God, Jude fought to remain conscious. Why, he didn't know. Wouldn't it be better to quit fighting, give in to the darkness, and simply pass into eternity?

As he hovered between wakefulness and oblivion, he was transported back to his youth, to the brush arbor meeting where a fire-and-brimstone preacher had talked of far-distant lands and the dark and lonely souls who begged for salvation. The man had talked of the lost sheep, the lost coin, the Prodigal Son. If but one repented, he said, all toil and tribulation would be worth it. And Jude remembered the vows he'd made that night. Vows to go wherever God sent him, to pull one lost soul from the very pits of hell.

Would he have made such a vow if he'd known what God would ask of him? Nay! Where was the one soul he'd vowed to save? Had there been one? *Who, Lord?*

If but one . . .

"Who, Lord?" he croaked. "Who?"

CHAPTER 27

Caleb's shot had missed its mark when the rafts shifted.

And when he looked again, Micaiah Jones was gone. But he couldn't be worried over the pirate leader at the moment. He had more pressing matters to attend to.

As the battle raged around him, he squared off with a cutthroat crouched before him, a wicked-looking blade in the man's hand. Caleb had fought his share of violent men intent on taking his life, and this one would be no different. One of them would come out victorious; the other would die. It was the way of the underworld of cutthroats and highwaymen, rogues and pirates.

Either kill or be killed.

As they circled, his opponent's eyes shifted left, then right. What had drawn his attention? Caleb had learned to ignore the sounds of battle around him, but he snapped out of the single-minded focus that had kept him alive all these years.

Tiberius, knife drawn, and Moses, wielding a bloody ax, flanked him.

They'd come to his aid, and Caleb realized the clash of blades and the reverberations of shots being fired had become sporadic. He glanced around and spotted the loggers rounding up their captives.

A surge of relief, not pleasure — he found no pleasure in killing — swept over him. It seemed the loggers had gained the upper hand. Perhaps the element of surprise or their sheer numbers had swayed the fight in their favor. Or possibly Mr. Horne's prayers. Regardless . . .

"Do you surrender?"

With one glance at Moses's ax, the man tossed his knife away, the blade clattering against the timber raft. Moses grabbed the river pirate and led him away. Tiberius sheathed his long, curved knife and followed, taking account of their losses.

Stomach churning, Caleb surveyed the carnage. After more battles than he could count, he never got used to it. He took a deep breath. With the river pirates subdued, the inhabitants of Cypress Creek and the surrounding areas would be safe. There would be less bloodshed, more families.

And . . . he wanted to be part of one of those families. With a home of his own, a wife, children. With tawny eyes and golden hair. Even if Jude went north, there was no need in Alanah going, not if she were married to him.

Suddenly he couldn't wait to find her sister, get back to camp, and —

"Caleb, I need ya."

He pivoted, saw Quinn bending over William, ripping away the man's blood-soaked breeches. Caleb crouched next to them. "How bad is it?"

"I'll live. I always do."

Caleb arched a brow. "Sounds as if ya've been wounded before."

"Every time I meet up with one of you O'Sheas, it's inevitable that I get shot or stabbed." William winced when Quinn probed his leg. He tapped his stomach. "First, I got stabbed here at Brice's Tavern with Connor. Then shot in the head when highwaymen kidnapped Isabella —"

"Shot in the head? And you survived?" Caleb couldn't keep the shock from his voice.

"He's got a hard head, he has."

"The bullet just grazed me." William rubbed the side of his head. "I was beaten to a pulp just before the tornado ripped

Braxton Hall apart and —" William squinted at Quinn — "beaten again trying to help Quinn rescue Kiera from Le Bonne."

"Le Bonne?"

As Quinn scowled at the name, William waved a hand in dismissal. "It's a long story. Anyway, I should have known better than to think I could just float on down the river with my cotton and the timber unscathed if an O'Shea was within a hundred miles of me."

"Ya do seem prone t' getting into scrapes, William. Ya should stick closer t' home."

"Yes, that is my plan from now on. Close to home and as far away from you O'Sheas as humanly possible."

Quinn chuckled, and Caleb had the feeling his brother didn't believe a word of it.

A shadow fell over them. Tiberius with his report. The Moor spoke, his voice devoid of emotion. "We lost five men. Many injured. Two unaccounted for."

Caleb eyed the murky water. Bodies that would probably never be found. *God rest their souls.*

"And the pirates?"

"Eleven dead, seven captured, two who will not live to see another day. There is no accounting for how many fell overboard, either dead or alive."

"And what o' Micaiah Jones?"

"He is not among the dead or the living." Tiberius's black eyes scanned the river. "Perhaps he fell in the river."

"Perhaps." But Caleb's instincts told him otherwise. "Divide the men. Half keep watch and half bury the dead. Then cast off and head for Natchez."

"Cast off?" William struggled to sit up. "What of the girl?"

"I'll see t' the girl." Caleb motioned to the flatboats abandoned on the sandbar. "There are plenty o' boats here for the taking. We'll catch up."

A commotion onshore had Caleb drawing his pistol, the other survivors crouching as they palmed their weapons. Were they to be attacked yet again?

Skirts billowing behind her, a tall, robust woman burst from the tree line, half-carrying, half-dragging another female. The women staggered toward the jumble of rafts grounded on the sandbar.

Lydia? And Betsy?

Caleb jumped off the raft, Tiberius not far behind. They rushed forward, and Caleb took Betsy as Tiberius lifted Lydia as if she weighed no more than a feather.

Lydia's gaze met his, the fear in the dark depths piercing his soul.

"Alanah. Micaiah is after Alanah."

Keep coming, Micaiah. Keep coming.

Alanah broke from cover and raced away, making enough noise that Micaiah was sure to follow. She heard him crashing through the forest, chasing her like a deranged bear. She zigzagged down a bank, ran along a sandy beach, and dove into the forest again. Leading him farther away from the direction Lydia and Betsy had gone.

Ten minutes later, she hunkered down in the shadows beneath a massive oak and deliberately slowed her breathing. Not a sound disturbed the predawn hours, save the nocturnal creatures that went about their business. Crickets chirped, a whip-poor-will called, and the occasional splash resounded. Whether the sounds came from a fish jumping, a snake capturing a frog, or nothing more than a dead limb falling into the river, she couldn't tell.

But one thing was for sure. She'd managed to lose Micaiah in the darkness.

And that was the last thing she wanted.

Had he given up the chase? Alanah's heart thudded as another thought ricocheted through her brain. Or had he figured out that he'd been hoodwinked and gone after Lydia and Betsy instead?

On her own, Lydia might be able to avoid detection, but not with Betsy in tow.

Betsy had been practically comatose when they found her. Not injured, just not all there. After a cursory examination, Lydia had assured Alanah that she'd be fine with time. Alanah prayed it was so. They were still inside the cabin when Micaiah returned, yelling for Betsy to get out there.

Alanah had done the only thing she knew to do. She'd darted out of the cabin, and as expected, Micaiah had taken up the chase, bellowing with rage.

She eased out of her hiding place and retraced her steps, determined to keep him occupied as long as it took. She wouldn't take chances, but she'd use herself as bait if it meant Betsy would be free. She'd never dreamed she'd be stalking Micaiah Jones when she'd made the decision to rescue Betsy. All she could think of at the time was that Caleb and the other men would have too much on their minds to worry about her sister.

Moving stealthily through the forest, focusing on the sights and sounds around her, she prayed that Lydia and Betsy had made it to safety. But was there safety on the other side of the island? Surely if Micaiah's men had been successful in routing

410

Caleb and the others, all of them would have returned to their camp flush with victory. Instead, she'd seen only one man — Micaiah.

Did that mean he'd abandoned the others in the heat of battle?

If it came to it, he would. She swallowed the disgusted snort that threatened to erupt. Micaiah looked out for himself, and if that meant saving his skin over anybody else's, there was no question what he'd do.

Without encountering a soul, she retraced her steps, skirted the ramshackle huts, and made her way to the highest point on the island. Crouching, she could see snatches of the moonlit river through the trees. By her calculations, the northern tip, where the fighting had taken place, was about a mile upstream, the abandoned camp a half mile behind her. There had been plenty of time for Lydia and Betsy to make it by now.

But what of Micaiah? Had he completely abandoned the search and escaped by raft or gone across the channel to lose himself in the wilds of Louisiana? Was he even yet still on the island? As terrible as it would be to have him return someday to exact his revenge, she prayed he'd taken the coward's way out and fled.

She tried not to think about whether Ca-

411

leb, Quinn, Tiberius, and the others had survived the fight, but their fate — along with Betsy and Lydia's — lay heavy on her mind.

When Micaiah held Betsy captive, she hoped and prayed that her sister would return, but as time passed, she'd held out little faith she'd ever see Betsy again or even that she might still be alive. And while she didn't wish her uncle ill, she knew she couldn't depend on him to be around to help in an emergency. Her life consisted of keeping herself and Lydia alive in a place that had become a den of cutthroats. Her goal had been to simply survive day by day, keep body and soul together, nothing more, nothing less.

But then Caleb had shown up. Caleb, with the same rough edges as the river pirates, but an honor that defied their fiendish cruelty. And as Kiera had assured her, Caleb was a man who had shown that he would risk life and limb for her and her sister.

Tears pricked her eyes, and she suddenly wanted to be safe on the timber raft with the loggers, with Betsy and Lydia and with Caleb.

She started to ease out of her hiding place, then froze as movement on the river caught her eye. Slowly, like sap rising, the massive timber raft loaded with bales of cotton glided around the bend. Four smaller flatboats followed close behind, like sentinels keeping watch.

Her thoughts collided and fought for attention even as her heart turned to lead inside her chest.

Who was manning the rafts, and were Lydia and Betsy on board?

As soon as the flatboats disappeared around the bend, Caleb gathered his weapons and slipped into the trees. Lydia had told him to head for the highest point on the island, and he couldn't miss Micaiah's lair. As he climbed, he caught glimpses of the timber raft through the gaps in the trees, flanked by the flatboats they'd confiscated from the pirates, the entire flotilla meandering peacefully toward the middle of the river as if there hadn't just been a bloodbath on Cottonmouth Island.

Betsy and Lydia were on one of those boats, with Tiberius and the crew charged with seeing them safely back to camp along with William and the other injured. They'd angle across the river, make landfall a half mile or so downstream, then hike back up.

Quinn had insisted on going downriver

with the logs, the cotton, and the captured river pirates.

His brother, the landlubber, in charge of a flotilla of flatboats, logs, cotton, and prisoners. But the raftsmen they'd hired in Natchez knew the river, and they'd proven their loyalty this night. By God's grace and mercy, they'd make it to Natchez without further incident.

Caleb had his own duty to fulfill. He turned away, followed the faint smell of woodsmoke wafting through the underbrush, and soon crouched on the outskirts of the camp. Empty, save for a couple of chickens pecking at the ground and the remains of a fire that had almost burned itself out.

Had Micaiah taken Alanah and made a run for it?

He eased back into the shadows, hunkered down next to a massive tree. It would be daylight soon, and he had no hope of finding Alanah now, unless —

His next thought turned his stomach. He'd seen what Micaiah had done to Betsy — the shell of a woman-child left behind. Would he take Alanah on the spot, kill her, and leave her body on this island for the scavengers to find? Or spirit her away to some place where Caleb would never find her?

Either way, the woman he loved would be lost to him.

Love?

Quinn's assumption punched him in the gut, and in that instant, Caleb's heart exploded with a feeling so big, so all-encompassing, so overwhelming that he thought he'd shatter into a thousand tiny pieces. He finally understood what his brother had been talking about.

He loved Alanah Adams. With all his being.

And it had taken losing her to a madman to pull back the fog so he could see.

Pain clutched his chest as if he'd been running full speed and lost every wisp of breath in his lungs. Nostrils flaring, he sucked in a deep, life-giving breath, gritted his teeth, and pressed hard against the tree trunk, feeling the grind of the rough bark against the back of his head.

No, he could not — *would not* — accept that she was gone.

He shoved the fear, the worry, the very thought of losing her forever, deep down inside and covered all those weak emotions with anger, sheer force of will, and determination to find her, no matter what it took.

A faint sliver of light spilled over the horizon to the east and the sky faded from black to the first blue of dawn. Jaw clenched, he stood and melted into the forest. He'd search every inch of this island until he found her.

And if that murderous dog had violated her, Caleb would make him pay with his life.

"Lord, please . . ."

As dawn broke, Alanah peered toward the river, trying to see who was manning the sweeps on the rafts. All she needed was to recognize one man.

The mist made it hard to distinguish their features, but one of the men lifted his face toward the island and stared. Was that Quinn on the timber raft? And . . . yes, Tiberius on one of the flatboats. His tall, broad-shouldered form was hard to miss.

Thank You, Jesus.

Her heart leapt with joy. God had given the loggers victory over the river pirates.

She wanted to believe that Lydia and Betsy were on one of those rafts, that Lydia had reached help. Surely Tiberius wouldn't leave Lydia. Her heart slammed against her rib cage. He would if they hadn't made it to the raft, because the men didn't even know she and Lydia had followed them.

What if their sole purpose for attacking and defeating the river pirates was to open the waterway for safe transport of the logs and the crops gleaned from the plantations?

No, Caleb had promised he'd find Betsy. *He'd promised.*

But the evidence was before her. The loggers were leaving. She continued to search the rafts, the forms growing smaller and smaller. At this distance, she wouldn't recognize Caleb. Had he left Betsy to her fate? Had he left *her* to hers?

Even as she berated herself for doubting, she couldn't help but worry. She'd depended on no one but herself for so long it was hard to accept Caleb would keep his word. The very thought that he might have abandoned them hurt worse than anything. Worse than her parents' and Aunt Rachel's deaths. Worse than Uncle Jude's disapproval and renunciation of Betsy's plight.

Her parents and Aunt Rachel hadn't wanted to die, but it was their time, and they couldn't be faulted for leaving this earth. From an early age, she'd stood in awe of Uncle Jude and his steadfast determination to live a spotless, blameless life. His disdain for those who failed to live up to his expectations.

She remembered her father's gentle admonition that they should love the unlovable, and Uncle Jude arguing that the unlovable needed to face the wrath of God. And after her father had died in Natchez Under-the-Hill, her uncle refused to set one foot in the den of iniquity and forbade her to go as well. But God forgive her, she'd disobeyed him more than once, not because she wanted to defy his authority, but because —

A rustling sounded off to her right. She shrank back against a pine, her patched dress blending with the rough bark at her back.

A deer feeding at dawn? Or Micaiah?

Willing her pounding heart to slow, she nocked an arrow, then remained motionless. Through the trees, she caught a glimpse of something moving stealthily along a game trail. Too tall to be a deer or any other four-legged animal, the figure could only be human.

If it was Micaiah or one of the river pirates . . .

Alanah eased from her hiding place, being careful not to make a sound. She inched along and then crouched behind an embankment. Hidden from view, she ran a hundred yards, searching for concealment that gave her a view of where her prey would emerge.

Prey?

She slid into position behind a large oak. When had she started to think of the man she stalked as prey? The only prey she'd ever killed had been animals for food and hides for her use.

But if Betsy was still on the island, she had to protect her sister. Could she kill a man to save her life? Or Betsy's? If attacked, she could defend herself, surely, but —

Eyes darting back and forth, she scanned the area and saw nothing. Had her quarry led her into a trap?

Where was he?

CHAPTER 28

Caleb stepped into the open.

As soon as he saw the arrow pointed at his chest, the terror in Alanah's wide and frightened eyes, he regretted his decision to show himself. He should have called out to her first.

Slowly the bowstring became lax, and the bow lowered. Her lips trembled.

"Caleb."

And then she dropped the bow and ran toward him. She threw her arms around his neck, and he caught her in a tight embrace.

"Shh, lass." He backed into a thicket, the feel of her safe and sound in his arms warring against the threat of a killer stalking them both.

"I was afraid you'd left with the others."

"I would no' leave ya, lass." Caleb held her away from him, cradling her face in his palms. "What are you doing here? You and Lydia are supposed t' be on your way t'

420

Breeze Hill."

"I couldn't leave Betsy." She shook her head, tears shimmering in her eyes. "I'm sorry."

Unable to stop himself, he lowered his mouth to hers, covering her trembling lips with his, tasting the salt of her tears and the sweetness of her mouth. It was a heady combination, and he groaned, swept her closer, and deepened the kiss.

Her kiss washed away his fear of having lost her, and all he could think about was that he'd found her, he had her in his arms, and nothing and nobody was going to take her away from him ever again.

She pushed away, worry clouding her gaze. "I saw the timber raft and the flatboats leaving. Betsy? And Lydia?"

"Safe and sound. The loggers were going t' cross the river and head back t' camp."

Her sigh of relief was palpable, and she wilted against him again. "Thank You, Lord."

They stood like that, him holding her close, just breathing. Just living.

Finally she whispered, "Micaiah got away. Like the coward he is, he left his men to die."

"Aye. Lydia told me."

They stepped from the safety of the

thicket, and Alanah retrieved her bow. As she slung it over her back, she lifted her gaze to his, looking troubled. "I don't know if I could've killed him."

"Micaiah?"

"Yes. I've — I've never used my bow on a human being." She shook her head. "I don't think I could."

"Sometimes you're no' given a choice." He held out a hand, and without hesitation, she took it. "Come on, let's get off this island."

"What about Micaiah?"

"I have a feeling he's gone already. And if he hasn't, he's watching the flatboats beached on the sandbar. He knows we'll need one o' those t' cross the river." Caleb frowned. There was no guarantee they'd be able to get to the boats without being spotted.

"I have a better idea." Alanah turned and led him in the opposite direction, away from the sands where the flatboats were.

He pulled her to a halt. "Where are we going?"

She gave him a saucy look. "You want to get off the island, do you not?"

"Aye, but —"

"Then we shall. Let's go."

Alanah skirted around the outlaw camp

and led the way toward the opposite side of the island. She ducked into the thick underbrush and slid down an embankment. Caleb followed, trusting that she knew what she was doing.

And there, hidden beneath the overhanging branches of a weeping willow, lay a small raft.

She grinned. "Impressed?"

"Aye."

He didn't have to ask where it had come from or how she knew it was here. For the space of a heartbeat, he considered waiting until nightfall to cross the river, but the idea of lying in wait until Micaiah found them wasn't appealing. They'd take their chances on the river.

Alanah boarded. Caleb untied the ropes and used a pole to push the small craft into the current. "Keep a sharp eye out. We're easy pickings out here."

Within minutes, they cleared the channel and floated free into the immense river. But Caleb didn't feel at ease until they were well out of range of a musket ball.

Even then, he couldn't shake the feeling that someone was staring a hole in his back.

The trip across the river was uneventful.

"There's a good place to make land just

around the next bend." Alanah manned one of the sweeps, nodding toward the shore. "We need to get closer."

Caleb dipped his oar into the water. "And how would you be knowin' that? You've traveled the river quite a bit, have you?"

"Not recently. But Lydia and I foraged on Cottonmouth Island, before Micaiah and his gang of outlaws started using it to waylay unsuspecting travelers."

"You weren't afraid o' the cottonmouths?"

"Not as much as the two-legged ones who came after." She shrugged. "Besides, there weren't that many snakes on the island. No more than anywhere else around here."

The sandbar came into view and Alanah was relieved to see two flatboats bobbing in the shallows, tied up to a sturdy tree. She'd hoped the loggers had made landfall here. Lydia, for one, knew about the spot even if none of the others did. She pointed. "There."

They slid their raft in next to the larger boats and tied it off. From the looks of the landing and the beaten path leading away from the bank, it was obvious travelers from both sides of the river used the sandbar quite often. They left the rafts where they lay. Someone would probably come along and take them, but that was the way of the river.

There was plenty of evidence that Tiberius and the loggers had come this way. They'd cut poles to make litters to haul the wounded, and they made no effort to hide their trail.

Caleb started down the trail. "It shouldn't take us long t' overtake them, not with them carrying the wounded."

Even as tired as she was, Alanah didn't mind the pace Caleb set. Every so often, he glanced back, making sure she was keeping up, and when they came to an embankment, he braced himself, held out a hand, and handed her down to even ground. While she didn't need assistance, it was nice to know that he *wanted* to take care of her.

They'd traveled less than half the distance when they heard the shuffling of feet along the forest floor, the grunts and groans of the injured, and the murmur of voices.

Caleb stopped, held up a hand for her to keep quiet before giving a series of calls that didn't sound like any bird she'd ever heard. Instantly the noise up ahead ceased. Presently the same calls floated back to them. Caleb nodded and motioned her forward. "Go on, lass. Tiberius is expecting us."

Pushing past him, she barreled along the

trail, rounded a bend, and spotted Lydia standing there, arms around Betsy. An explosion of joy burst inside her, and she ran forward, throwing her arms around her sister. Her gaze met Lydia's, and she reached out, took her hand, and squeezed. She didn't ask if Betsy was all right. Just seeing her clutching a handful of wildflowers, safe and alive, was enough for now.

She linked an arm through Betsy's, and they fell into step behind the loggers carrying the litters. Half the burly men stood by the wayside, letting them pass, before falling in behind to bring up the rear, putting Betsy, Lydia, and herself in the middle of the party.

Keeping them safe.

The trek upriver was slow and tedious as the men took turns carrying the injured. When they drew near home, Alanah caught Lydia's attention and shook her head. Better not to mention home at all. Hopefully, Betsy wouldn't think of the kits or the goats, and they could avoid an outburst. There would be time enough to round up the animals later.

Everyone had grown silent except for the occasional groan from the injured. They crossed the road and one by one hoisted the litters up an embankment. Suddenly one of the loggers lost his footing on the uneven ground. As he fell, the litter tipped sideways. Shouting and cursing, the loggers grabbed for the litter, but it was too late. The injured man slammed into a tree. Screaming in agony, he curled into a ball.

Lydia rushed to his side, Alanah close behind. Gently they rolled him to his back. His face was wreathed in sweat and his jaw clenched as he fought against the pain. Someone handed Alanah a moistened cloth, and she blotted his face while Lydia checked his bandages.

The logger batted her hands away and jutted out his chin. "Put me back on the litter." Then he glared at the man who'd dropped him. "And, Corrigan, if ya drop me again, so help me, I'm going to bust your noggin, ya ken?"

Twisting his hat in his hands, Corrigan nodded. "And I'll let ya do it, too."

Lydia pressed him down. "I don't think —"

"Load me up, and let's be on our way."

The men looked to Lydia for permission. "Do as he says."

After securing the man on the litter, the men eased up the incline, being more careful this time.

"What happened to that man?"

Startled, Alanah glanced at Betsy. They were the first words her sister had spoken all day. She weighed her answer, erring on the side of caution. The less said about the river pirates, and Micaiah specifically, the better. "He was stabbed."

"Finley stabbed Uncle Jude."

"Why would you say that? Uncle Jude left days ago to collect supplies."

"No." Betsy's lips flattened into a firm line. "Finley stabbed him. I was there."

Caleb's gaze met Alanah's; then he bent so that he could look into Betsy's eyes. "When did this happen?"

"I —" Betsy looked away, shifting closer to Alanah. "I don't remember."

"It's all right, Betsy." Alanah put her arm around her sister. "You can tell us. When did Finley stab Uncle Jude?"

"Finley grabbed me by the hair, and he was hurting me, and Uncle Jude tried to stop him. Then they —" She stopped, a frown on her face. "Alanah, where are the babies? Uncle Jude was going home with me to milk the goats and feed the babies. But Finley . . ."

She trailed off, turned, and followed meekly along behind the convoy. Caleb fell into step beside Alanah, his attention on the troubled girl shuffling along in front of them.

"Do you think there's some truth t' what she says?"

"I don't know."

"Is she prone t' weaving tall tales?"

"No. She says very little, but what she does say is usually truth. And Finley *was* the man I saw dragging her through the woods." Alanah reached for him, her nails digging into his forearm. "Do you suppose it really happened? That Uncle Jude came upon them and they — they killed him?"

"There's only one way t' know for sure." Caleb pulled her out of the procession, motioning to Tiberius and Lydia to stop. Quickly he told them what Betsy had said. "I'm going t' scout around between the logging camp and Alanah's home place. If Jude *was* there when Finley took Betsy, he might still be alive."

"I'm going with you." Alanah's voice was firm.

"No —"

"You can't stop me. This is my uncle we're talking about." She left the trail and dove into the woods.

Tossing Tiberius and Lydia a glance, Caleb took off after her, grabbed her arm, and spun her around. "I do no' know what I'll find, lass."

Face pale, eyes large, she nodded. "I know, but if he's alive, you'll need me."

"You faint at the sight o' blood."

She blanched but lifted her chin. "If — if I do, just throw a bucket of water on me."

He searched her gaze, then nodded. "All right. Let's go."

Alanah wove a zigzag path through the woods, and ten minutes later, they came to the spot where they'd seen the cutthroats hauling Betsy away.

She pointed northward. "They came from that way."

Caleb followed the direction of her outstretched arm. "A fairly straight shot t' the logging camp, aye?"

"And it makes sense because I was pretty sure Betsy was headed home that morning, and she said as much to me when she said Uncle Jude was here with her."

"Or she'd already been home and was heading back t' the logging camp."

"No." A frown pulled Alanah's brows together as she put the pieces together. "She wouldn't have left the kits behind."

They split up and began sweeping the area back toward the logging camp. They'd gone half a mile not seeing anything, when Alanah rushed forward. "Caleb, look."

He hurried toward her. "What is it?"

She fingered a ripped piece of cloth caught on a tangle of thorns. "This could be a piece of Uncle Jude's shirt."

"Aye. Or anybody's for that matter."

Caleb scrutinized the ground, searching for something that might tell him if anything of import had happened here. He stepped to the side of the path, looked down a steep embankment. The broken tangle of vines and briars looked as if something had slid or rolled down the incline. He stair-stepped down the embankment.

What he saw chilled his blood.

Alanah joined him, stared at the strands of bloodstained gray hair caught on the bark of a tree. "Uncle Jude," she whispered. "He was here."

"Aye." Caleb didn't try to tell her any differently. "The good news is he is no' here now, so he might still be alive." He studied the scuffed leaves and crushed vines. "He went that way."

The trail was faint, but it clearly led toward home.

Alanah stopped at the edge of the yard, Caleb close on her heels. For the second time, the total devastation almost took her breath away.

"Do no' worry, lass. You can rebuild."

"There's no need, not if Uncle Jude still plans —"

She broke off. If her uncle was dead, they wouldn't have to go north. But would she want to stay here? She shook her head to clear it. She couldn't even think about any of that now. Her uncle's fate first, then she'd think about the future.

"Uncle Jude?" she called out. No answer.

They separated, Caleb searching around the cabin, down by the creek. Alanah headed toward the barn. Had her uncle become disoriented and wandered off the trail to die cold and alone in the woods?

Please, Lord, help us find him.

"Uncle Jude, where are you? Can you hear me?"

She walked between the charred remains of the cabin and the barn, saw the bluff at the rear rising upward. Her gaze landed on the root cellar, half-hidden in the underbrush, the door ajar.

Ajar? She didn't remember leaving the door open.

Praying she'd find her uncle inside and alive, she hurried up the path toward the cellar.

Just before she reached the cave-like hole, a blur of movement cut her off, and a band of steel clamped around her waist. Another hand covered her mouth, the rough fingers digging into her face so hard she thought her jaw would break.

She clawed for the knife at her side, but her captor slammed her against a tree and shoved a wicked-looking knife against her throat. "You so much as whimper, and I'll slit yer throat."

Micaiah.

Alanah didn't utter a sound. If she'd learned anything in the time she'd known Micaiah Jones, it was that he meant every word he said.

And killing her wouldn't bother him any more than squashing a bug.

CHAPTER 29

"I did no' find anything —"

Caleb rounded the corner of the burned-out barn and stopped dead in his tracks.

Micaiah Jones held Alanah in front of him, a knife at her throat.

Caleb's attention shifted to Alanah's face, then focused on her eyes, wide and terrified, pleading.

He attempted to convey the way he felt about her in that one look, trying to somehow stop time. Would this be the last time he looked into her eyes before Micaiah snuffed the life out of her forever? The few seconds he held her gaze unveiled a lifetime of painful longings that would never be.

"So we meet again."

Micaiah's gravelly voice shattered the ache into a million pieces.

Turning as cold as a winter storm blowing across the ocean and just as deadly, Caleb shifted his attention to the cowardly cur who held Alanah captive. For the first time, he got a good look at the man. Long, stringy hair hung past his shoulders, the color indistinguishable in its filth. A scraggly beard covered a square jaw, and heavy brows jutted over eyes filled with emptiness, save the intent to do evil at every turn.

"Aye, we meet again." Caleb crossed his arms, then jerked his head toward Alanah. "But I see you're hiding behind a skirt this time instead o' a sniveling bunch o' scum. What happened? Did the vermin run out on you, back t' the holes they came from?"

"Nobody runs out on me." Micaiah sneered. "They go when and where I tell them to."

"Ah, forgive me." Caleb laughed. "So you sent them all t' Natchez, then? What, pray tell, will they do there? Plan your escape out o' Governor Gayoso's Spanish prison?"

"I won't be going to prison."

Alanah whimpered as he pressed the knife against her throat. Caleb's mind raced. Was it a good idea to goad the man? Would he grow so angry, he'd do something foolish and give Caleb an opportunity to kill him? Or would he slit Alanah's throat first before coming after Caleb?

The cold that had taken over his brain swooshed down and spread to the rest of his body, like ice shattering from head to toe. Just one chance at Micaiah. That was all he needed. Just one —

Suddenly a yipping sounded off to his left, and half a dozen streaks of black-and-white fur bounded out of the one corner of the barn still standing. Making a beeline, they tumbled over themselves to get to Alanah. Micaiah's eyes widened as one of the baby raccoons slammed into his leg and started climbing.

Cursing, he tried to shake the kit off, but to no avail. With a howl of rage, he slashed downward with a vicious swipe, but before the blade made contact with the wee animal, Alanah twisted out of his grasp. It was the only chance Caleb would have.

"Alanah. Run." He rushed forward, slammed into Micaiah, knocking him over. Slung free, the frightened kits yelped and ran back to safety beneath the charred remains of the barn.

Alanah scrambled to her feet.

Breaking apart, Caleb and Micaiah circled, looking for a chance to rush in for the kill.

Her stomach twisted. While she'd lived in the wilds as far back as she could remember and had heard tales of the vicious end many men met at the hands of another, she'd never actually witnessed two men facing each other, knives at the ready, intent on killing the other.

Dear heavenly Father, please don't let it be Caleb. Please, Lord, help him. Please.

Repeating her pleas under her breath, she fumbled for the knife tucked in her belt, then let it lie. She'd just be putting Caleb and herself in danger if she rushed in wielding the puny blade.

Her bow.

Her cheeks wet with tears, she reached for her bow with trembling hands. Nocking an arrow, she backed away. Caleb had told her to run, but how could she? She couldn't leave him here to fight Micaiah alone. But if — heaven forbid — Micaiah knifed Caleb, she'd put an arrow in his heart before he could reach her.

She had no choice if she wanted to survive.

Micaiah swung at Caleb, the tip of his knife missing by inches. With a clear shot at Micaiah, she took a steadying breath, but Caleb stepped into her line of sight before she could let her arrow fly. Hands shaking, she realized that she'd come within a hairbreadth of shooting Caleb.

God, give me strength.

The men crouched, each waiting for an opening in order to gut the other.

She prayed for one shot. Just one.

They continued to circle, and Caleb's gaze flickered toward her, widened. The distraction was all Micaiah needed to make his move. He jumped forward, swiping at Caleb with his blade. Caleb's own knife went flying, and he fell back, rolling away before Micaiah could stab him again. Micaiah kicked out, the blow catching Caleb under the chin. He lurched toward Caleb, and Alanah let the arrow fly.

It ripped through Micaiah's bicep to land with a thwack in a nearby tree. He roared, sounding like a wounded bear. Switching the knife to his left hand, he turned on her. She backed away, reaching for another arrow. She tried to nock it, but her hands were shaking so much, she couldn't —

Beyond Micaiah she could see Caleb struggling to stand. *Please, Caleb. Please don't die. Please. I love you. I love you. Please.*

Ten feet away, Micaiah stopped, gaping at her as if he were looking at the very dead.

Except he wasn't staring at her, but at —

"Micaiah Jones, you have been weighed in the balances and found wanting."

Alanah turned, saw her uncle, and gasped.

Dried blood covered his head, his gaunt face, and a filthy, bloodstained bandage was wrapped around his middle. She started to rush to his aid, but he held her at bay with a trembling hand, rust-stained with blood and dirt. He walked past her, straight toward Micaiah, never wavering, never hesitating, not even seeming to notice the knife in Micaiah's hand tipped with Caleb's blood.

"Micaiah Jones, you have terrorized this country for too long." His voice was hardly more than a raspy whisper but somehow carried more weight than if he'd bellowed the pronouncement from the bluffs overhead. "Mark my words, God will punish you for your evil deeds. The souls from their watery graves have called out against you."

Caleb struggled to his feet. Alanah turned toward him, but he shook his head, the small movement meant to keep her from doing anything foolish. She blinked her understanding and remained rooted to the spot. Uncle Jude was closest to Micaiah now. If either of them moved, he would be the one to die.

With each pronouncement of Micaiah's fate, her uncle moved closer. "No matter where you run or where you hide, you cannot escape God's presence. Even when you lie down to sleep, He knows the deepest, darkest parts of your soul. He calls you to repentance for every evil deed you've done."

"Shut up, old man." Micaiah hefted his knife but didn't rush her uncle. He backed away so that he had the three of them in his sights. "You're as good as dead, and I've lived this long without dreaming of what I've done or fearing death. Why should I fear it now?"

Her uncle kept moving toward Micaiah in a shuffling, unsteady gait. Finally he stopped, smiled as if he were having a friendly conversation over tea. "Micaiah, no matter what happens today, you need to know that God loves you, that He stands ready to forgive you. Of everything. Of every man, woman, and child whose life you took, of every woman you violated, of everything you stole, and every vile and evil thought you've ever had. Even if you take my life today, He will forgive you if you but ask. Why? And how? He died a cruel death on the cross, more cruel than even you can imagine, and overcame your sin so that you might live with Him in eternity."

"I don't know what you're up to, old man, but whatever it is, I want no part of it." Micaiah crouched, blade held at the ready. "Come any closer, and I'll cut you open and leave you to die right here."

"I'm not afraid to die." Her uncle spread his hands in a gesture of total surrender. "I've been at the point of death for these many hours, and I'm more alive than I've ever been. You hold no power over me. If I die and leave this sinful world, I'll wake up in heaven with my Lord and Savior." Uncle Jude paused, and sadness crept into his voice. "But you, my son — you will awake in a lake of fire and brimstone where there is no escape. Unless you accept that Jesus died on the cross to take your sins away. He did, you know. All you have to do is say that you believe."

Micaiah glared at her uncle, and Alanah knew he wasn't convinced. How could a man who'd lived a life as vile and vicious as Micaiah be forgiven so easily? Yes, the Bible said all who sinned would be forgiven if they repented. But did that truly include Micaiah Jones?

Then again, if Jesus had forgiven the thief on the cross . . .

Uncle Jude took another step, held out a trembling hand, and clutched Micaiah's jerkin. Micaiah stood frozen, looking as if a viper had attached itself to his vest.

"Know this, Micaiah Jones: God forgives you, and I do, too."

And with that, Uncle Jude tipped forward. Micaiah's eyes widened, and instinctively he caught her uncle in his arms, staggered, and fell backward, her uncle's deadweight on top of him.

Alanah screamed, rushed toward them, and out of the corner of her eye, saw Caleb doing the same. Whatever compassion or remorse — or even surprise — had caused Micaiah to hesitate vanished in an instant, and he shoved her uncle off of him, raised his knife —

But before he could plunge the blade into her uncle, he was surrounded.

Tiberius. Moses. Caleb. Others from the logging camp.

Caleb kicked the knife from Micaiah's hand, and Tiberius stood over him, his long, wicked scimitar pressed against Micaiah's throat.

Alanah ignored them all and turned to her uncle.

"Uncle Jude? Can — can you hear me?"

With Micaiah subdued, Caleb knelt at Alanah's side.

Her uncle's eyelids fluttered, and he licked his cracked and bleeding lips. "Water."

"He's alive." Tears tracking down her cheeks, Alanah's gaze jerked to Caleb's.

Someone handed Caleb a flask, and he passed it on to Alanah. As she dribbled water into her uncle's mouth, Tiberius strode across the yard and handed her a tote. "Lydia said you would need this to tend your uncle."

"How did she know we'd find him alive?"

"She didn't."

Alanah stared at the bag and nodded. "I'm going to need a fire."

An hour later, the fire going strong, Alanah soaked her uncle's makeshift bandages, stiff and sticky with dried blood, and peeled them off. With Caleb's and Tiberius's help, she flushed the angry red cut on his abdomen, applied a poultice, and bound him once again.

After washing all the blood from his face and hair, she gently kneaded his scalp, then sat back. "There's a gash on his head, but nothing that needs stitches."

"Perhaps from when he hit his head on the tree."

"Perhaps." Alanah rummaged in the tote, pulled out a pouch. She opened it and smiled. "Bless you, Lydia." She held out a piece of dried meat. "Lydia sent pemmican."

"She really did think o' everything, did she no'?" Caleb took it and ripped off a chunk. As he chewed, he watched Alanah fuss over her uncle. "You need t' eat, too, lass. You haven't eaten since early morn."

"I will." She shrugged. "I must see to Uncle Jude first. He needs nourishment."

Caleb leaned over, eyes level with hers, and shoved a piece of the meat in her hand. "Eat. I'll scare up some broth for your uncle."

Eyes flashing golden fire, she ripped a tiny piece off with her teeth and chewed. Satisfied that she'd finish what he handed her, Caleb searched through the ruins until he found a small cast-iron pot that had survived the fire. Shredding pemmican into it, he added water and let it boil. Using cheesecloth, he strained the broth into a chipped bowl and added a bit of water to cool it.

He hunkered down next to Alanah, held out the bowl. "Here. 'Tis no' much, but it'll do."

"Thank you." Tears shimmered in her eyes.

Alanah spooned the broth into Jude's mouth. He never roused but continued to swallow until every drop was gone.

"That's all you can do for him here. But we need t' get him t' the logging camp." He reached for the tote.

Alanah clasped his arm. "Caleb, you're hurt."

"It's nothing." Caleb shrugged.

"Please, Caleb." She moved closer. "Let me see."

" 'Tis no' as bad as it looks."

Alanah reached for his sleeve, began rolling it up, revealing the jagged gash on his forearm, inch by inch.

"Oh, Caleb," she breathed. "Why didn't you say something?"

Tsking and muttering, Alanah washed the blood off his arm, then applied a thick layer of salve. She rummaged through the tote, found a bundle of needles, and threaded one. Her gaze met his. "This is going to hurt."

"Aye. I figured as much." He nodded at the needle. "Just get on with it, lass."

Caleb gritted his teeth and ignored the tug of her needle. Instead, he watched Alanah as she worked, her golden hair tickling his forearm, her bottom lip caught between her teeth as she concentrated on making neat, even stitches. When she was done, she sat back. "There. That should do it."

"Aye. A mighty fine job." Caleb eyed his stitches. "And you did no' even faint. No' once."

Alanah blinked, then grinned. "I didn't, did I?"

CHAPTER 30

The next few days were a blur as Alanah helped Lydia care for Uncle Jude and the other wounded. Unfortunately, Alanah's squeamishness returned the minute she arrived back at camp, but she knew that in a pinch, when those she loved needed her, she could stay the course.

Uncle Jude was the sickest of the lot, and Alanah was astounded that he'd survived. They took turns sponging him, trying to get his fever down. After three days — weeks, it seemed — Lydia finally convinced her to rest. It felt as if she'd just closed her eyes when Lydia woke her, shadows dancing from the single lantern she held aloft.

"Your uncle's fever broke. He's asking for you."

Alanah jumped up from her pallet and rushed to his side. His tired eyes met and held hers in the flickering light of a single candle. "Lydia said you were unharmed, but

I wanted to see for myself. Your sister?"

"She is well. Nary a scratch." The loggers had fetched their animals and built a pen for the goats in the clearing behind the cabin. With the animals to care for, her sister hadn't ventured far, which was a good thing.

"And what of Micaiah?"

"Don't worry. Micaiah is long gone." She patted his arm. "He won't hurt us again."

"He's dead?" He shook his head, a frown pulling his bushy brows together. "He can't be dead —"

"No, not dead. Caleb and Tiberius took him to Natchez, to Governor Gayoso's prison."

"Prison? But — but they'll hang him." Her uncle tried to sit up, but groaning, he slumped back, his eyes searching the ceiling. "I must go to Natchez posthaste. I've got to —"

"Please, Uncle Jude." Alanah's heart ripped with worry. "You're in no shape to travel, and the authorities will take care of Micaiah."

"No, they won't." A tear seeped out of the corner of his eye. "They'll hang him before he repents. If but one . . ."

His voice trailed off, and worried, Alanah clasped his hands. "Don't distress yourself.

All is well. As soon as you're recovered, we'll head north, just as you wanted. You, me, and Betsy."

"Is that what you want, Niece? To go north?"

She thought of Betsy. Wouldn't things be better now that the highwaymen were gone? Even now, a group of travelers — families, men, women, and children — were camped out at Cypress Creek, some considering staying, farming the freshly cleared land.

"I will do as you say, Uncle." She lowered her gaze.

"What of the young man, Caleb O'Shea? Have you not thought of him?"

Please don't ask me this, Uncle. Not yet.

"Alanah?"

"He has not returned from Natchez. And — and he made no promises."

"I see." Her uncle rested his head against the pillow, eyes closed. "It is no longer my wish to go north. And I know it's not God's will. I've known all along. When I was at death's door, I realized I'd been running from God all this time. I was running back to the safety and security of my childhood in Pennsylvania, when God wanted me to run toward Cypress Creek and Natchez Under-the-Hill." He opened his eyes, pinned her with a look. "And when I refused to go where He wanted me to go, He sent Micaiah and the others here, to Cypress Creek."

"God wouldn't do that." Alanah stared at her uncle in horror, thinking of all that Betsy had been through, the evil the high-waymen had perpetrated on innocent travel-ers in and around Cypress Creek and the river.

"Would He not?" Her uncle sighed. "I've been a fool, turning my back on the wicked that God sent me to save, including Mi-caiah. As soon as I am able, I must go to Natchez."

"To see Micaiah?" Her heart slammed against her rib cage. "To what end?"

"To do all I can to save his soul from eternal damnation."

Caleb jerked awake to the sound of Gimpy's breakfast gong.

Heart pounding, he blinked at the top of the tent he shared with Tiberius, the first light of dawn spilling over the horizon, bath-ing the logging camp in a golden glow. They'd returned from Natchez late last night after everyone had long gone to bed. And as much as he'd wanted to go to Ala-nah, sneak off somewhere quiet, and con-tinue the conversation they'd started four days ago, the middle of the night was not the time for such goings-on.

His grogginess vanished as anticipation of what the day would bring flooded him. He rolled to his feet, washed away the grime of travel, and quickly dressed.

Tiberius's bed was empty, the Moor having no doubt gone in search of Lydia. How long it would take for his friend to soften that woman's resistance was beyond Caleb's ken. But the process sure was interesting to watch.

The camp buzzed with activity as men gulped down breakfast in preparation for the hard workday ahead. In spite of the clash with the river pirates, the logging operation must go on. They had contracts to fulfill in Natchez.

Connor and Quinn stood on the bluff overlooking the sandbar, deep in conversation. Quinn looked to be about to explode. Caleb pivoted and headed in the opposite direction. An altercation with his brothers was the last thing he wanted right now. Would Alanah be stirring? Surely so. She was an early riser. He'd search her out, make his intentions —

"Caleb." Connor's voice pulled him up short. "Could I have a word with you?"

Blowing out a breath of frustration, Caleb

changed course and headed toward his brothers. Connor would want a report of everything that had gone on in Natchez. Best to get it over with. William Wainwright joined him, and he slowed his pace to accommodate the man's limp.

"Should ya be up on that leg?" Connor scowled at William.

"I'm fine." William turned to Quinn. "How did the trip downriver go?"

"We made it without issue. The raftsmen knew their business, and both the cotton and the timber were delivered safely." Quinn chuckled. "We caused quite a stir in Natchez, we did."

"And the captives? Did they give any trouble?"

"We did no' give them the chance."

William shifted his attention to Caleb. "And you delivered Micaiah to the palisade as well?"

"Aye. He is locked up, and I do no' think he'll escape that jail as easily as he did the one in French Camp."

"Good. Maybe things can get back to normal around here, and we can concentrate on the business at hand instead of fighting highwaymen and river pirates." William settled himself on a stump. "I for one am ready to go home to my wife without worry over the state of affairs here. Connor, what say you?"

"Aye. I'm in agreement." Connor turned to Caleb. "Which brings me to the reason we wanted to talk to you, Caleb."

Caleb's attention shifted from Connor to Quinn to William. Each man watched him carefully, a different look on his face.

Connor's furrowed brow made Caleb wonder exactly what the three of them had been up to. Quinn's folded arms and stormy countenance convinced him he didn't really want to know, but William's grin gave him the impression that whatever it was, it shouldn't end in blows, regardless of Quinn's glower.

He supposed he could be thankful for that. He took a deep breath. Might as well get it over with. "I'm listening, I am."

Connor nodded at William. "Tell him."

"Very well." William cleared his throat. "Caleb, it's imperative that I spend more time at Wainwright Hall. I have a wife and responsibilities there that need my attention. Connor and Quinn are in similar predicaments. Connor is needed at Breeze Hill, and Quinn at Magnolia Glen. We find ourselves in a quandary, as none of us have time to oversee the logging camp as well as meet our other obligations at home."

"So after routing the river pirates, ye're just going t' scuttle the logging camp, eh?" Caleb glared at the three of them.

Quinn stared at him as if he'd gone crazy. "Whatever gave ya that idea, ya blockhead?"

"Ya heard what he said, did ya no'?" Caleb flung an arm at William. "He's shutting down the logging camp so that the three o' ye can run home t' yer wives."

Connor slapped a hand on William's shoulder. "Well, you botched that, did you no', Master William?"

"It appears I left something out. That powder Lydia gave me for pain must have muddled my thinking." William rubbed his temple, then gave Connor a slight bow. "I give you leave to explain it all in due fashion, sir."

Still chuckling, Connor turned to Caleb. "You're right about going home t' our wives, Caleb. All o' us couched that desire beneath talk of responsibilities, plantations to run, cotton to harvest, laborers to oversee, but the truth is that a man should be with his wife, his children, his family. But we're no' about t' abandon the logging camp. It has proven too valuable a resource for that."

"What he's trying t' say is that they want t' turn the whole thing over t' ya t' oversee, lock, stock, and barrel." Quinn scowled at them all. "I do no' think it's a good idea, but I do no' seem t' have any say in the matter."

"Well, there you go, Wainwright." Connor tossed his arm around William's shoulder. "With that rousing endorsement from Quinn, I have no doubt Caleb will take on the job or die trying."

Caleb stared at the three of them. "No, I canna accept."

Quinn snorted. "I told ya he wouldna be interested. He's still got the wanderlust, as always."

" 'Tis no' that." Caleb looked at the dirt at his feet. "I do no' — I do no' deserve what ye're offering. I abandoned Quinn and the lads back in Ireland, without a backward glance. And . . . if you knew the things I'd done, you'd —"

"Caleb, there's no' a man among us who has no' done something we're no' proud of." Connor clasped his arm, forcing him to look him in the eye. "The difference is we've asked God's forgiveness for those sins. That's the important thing. Will you stay?"

Alanah slipped into the forest, barely heeding the dew that dampened the hem of her skirt. She needed to think and to pray.

Uncle Jude's decision to follow God's will and go to Natchez Under-the-Hill and preach left Betsy and her with an uncertain future.

She wandered aimlessly, her thoughts ricocheting between what her heart told her to do and what God's will might be. She didn't want to make the same mistakes her uncle had confessed to. Out of habit, she dug roots, picked berries, made note of every medicinal vine and herb that she could use.

God, is it Your will for us to go to Natchez with Uncle Jude? Please, Lord, I cannot . . .

The thought of exposing her sister to Natchez Under-the-Hill filled her with terror, but if Uncle Jude went, wouldn't they be expected to go as well?

Perhaps they could rebuild here in Cypress Creek, but with what resources and to what end? The locals would frown on the women living alone, even though they'd been alone most of the time as it was. The only reason no one ever said anything was because Uncle Jude came home often enough that it gave the appearance he was the master of the house. Tears pricked her eyes.

Lord, show me Your will . . .

Time passed as she prayed and wandered the cut-over forest she'd thought would be destroyed by the loggers. She found clumps of catnip growing in the newly exposed undergrowth, a meadow dotted with red clover. Her gaze landed on a decaying log, the riot of multicolored mushrooms exploding over the log making her smile. She dropped to her knees, fingered the mushrooms, then spotted more on the stumps close by. Bright reds, blues, greens, creams, and vibrant yellows. She'd never seen such colors this close to home. How . . . ?

Had the loggers brought more than desolation to the forest? Had they also brought new life in ways she hadn't thought of? Warmth spread through her and she realized that this was where her heart was. The forests, the swamps, the bluffs. Foraging was her home, not Natchez. But was it where God wanted her to be?

She leaned against the base of a tree overlooking the meadow filled with clover, then rested her head against the bark at her back. It was easy to feel at peace sitting beneath a tree in the forest she'd called home for as far back as she could remember.

Lord, show me Your will . . .

"Alanah?" The quiet was broken by Caleb's voice calling her name.

Her heart gave a little joy-jig inside her chest. *Caleb.*

She stood, saw him across the field walking toward her, his eyes trained on her face. She'd feared he wouldn't return now that the threat from the river pirates was eliminated, that he and Tiberius would go to sea again, but here he was, in the flesh.

Unable to contain her joy, she hastened toward him. But suddenly shy, she stopped short of throwing herself into his arms. He seemed not to have any qualms about marching right up to her.

She sucked in a breath as he stopped inches away, his dark eyes catching, holding hers. Without a word, he reached up a hand, cupped her jaw, the tips of his fingers warm against her skin. His thumb nudged her chin up, and in an exquisitely slow movement, he closed the distance between them.

As their lips touched, Alanah sighed.

This was home. The forest and streams, the herbs, the roots, the flowers, and Caleb.

He broke off the kiss, rested his forehead against hers. "I missed ya, lass."

"I missed you, too."

He ran both hands down her arms, took her hands, and laced his fingers through hers. Resting their entwined fingers against his chest, he smiled into her eyes. "I have something t' tell you."

"And I you." Her insides turned to mush.

Would he confess his love for her? He hadn't said anything about love, just that he'd missed her.

One side of his mouth quirked up. "A lass always has the first say."

I love you. Her stomach gave a slow roll of panic as the words tumbled over each other in her mind. Should she . . . ?

"Uncle Jude has decided not to go north after all," she blurted out. "He's going to Natchez Under-the-Hill to preach."

Did the warmth in Caleb's eyes fade at the news or was it a trick of the light? "And what o' you and your sister? Will you go as well?"

"I don't know." She shrugged, looking around at the sun-kissed meadow. "That's what I was doing out here. Asking God to show me His will."

"And did He?"

"I . . ." Tears misted in her eyes, and she blinked them back.

"What's this? Tears?" Caleb let go of her hands and swiped at the tears with his thumbs. "No tears, lass. Surely 'tis no' as bad as all that."

"No, I suppose not. If God wills it, I don't want to go to Natchez. My heart is here." She lifted her gaze to his, her voice lowering to a whisper. "With you."

A slow smile pulled at the corners of his mouth, and for a long moment, he didn't say anything. Then his arms were around her, and he lifted her off her feet and twirled her around, his laughter filling the meadow with joyous sound. When he stilled, he let her slide back to the ground, his dark eyes shining. "As is mine."

"Truly?"

"Aye. I love ya, lass, and I want t' spend the rest o' my life with you as me bride." His attention shifted, swept the meadow dotted with clover, then swooped back to her face. "Here, at Cypress Creek, managing the logging camp for the Wainwrights with me brothers and friends nearby. Does that suit your fancy, lass?"

What he'd said about running the logging camp vaguely registered, but there would be time enough later for her to find out exactly what that meant. For now, only one thing mattered, and it didn't have a thing to do with logging.

"It suits me just fine." Alanah searched his face, saw the love shining out of his eyes.

He lowered his head to kiss her again, but Alanah pressed the tips of her fingers to his lips, holding him back. He eyed her with curiosity in his expression. Smiling, she wrapped her arms around his neck, her fingers tangling in his hair, and whispered, "I love you, too, Caleb O'Shea."

Then, without reservation or fear, she pulled him close and kissed him.

EPILOGUE

Breeze Hill Plantation
One year later

Connor O'Shea stood on the balcony over-looking the lane that led to the trace. One by one his family gathered, but not for a happy occasion.

No, the circumstances were far from pleasant, but not totally unexpected.

The man who'd inadvertently seen that Connor's and his brothers' futures were secure now reposed in his sitting room, his wasted, scarred body prepared for burial. The curtains were closed, mirrors covered, and Martha and Susan spoke in whispers as they prepared food for the mourners.

In the distance, the fields were white with cotton ready for harvest, but no one worked the fields. The sawmill was silent, the blacksmith's hammer did not ring, and a black banner over the sign at the end of the lane alerted strangers to pass on by: the inn at Breeze Hill was closed for mourning.

Quinn and Kiera had arrived from Magnolia Glen late yesterday. They'd taken up residence in the wing he'd built for Leah and little Jon before she'd married William and moved to Wainwright Hall. In spite of the sadness of the occasion, a chuckle of humor rumbled from his chest. His brother's three-month-old twins would certainly put the wing with its sitting room and nursery to good use.

The sound of jingling harnesses and the clop of hooves reached him from somewhere down the lane. Could it be Caleb and Alanah? He'd sent word to Cypress Creek and to the Wainwrights yesterday, knowing the journey would take time.

Finally a wagon rolled into view, then another and another. Caleb and Alanah, followed by most of the logging crew. Caleb had more than proven his worth at Cypress Creek. The river landing flourished with new families excited about harvesting their first crops in the fertile soil along the river. The logging crews had become expert at cutting logs, lashing them together, and sending them downstream to meet Natchez's ever-growing demand for lumber.

Tiberius and Lydia rode in the back of the wagon, along with Alanah's sister, Betsy.

The girl had recovered from much of the trauma of her ordeal, but who knew what demons she battled in the dark of night? Tiberius had finally broken down Lydia's defenses, and she'd agreed to marry him. They'd jumped the broom and spoken their vows before Reverend Browning six months ago.

As the wagons drew nearer, Connor searched the group and wasn't surprised to see that the reverend wasn't with them. True to his word a year ago, the reverend had made haste to Natchez as soon as he was able. As if to make up for lost time, he continually preached repentance to all who would listen in Natchez Under-the-Hill and begged for entrance into Gayoso's prisons. He'd finally been granted leave to preach to the prisoners, to do his best to save their souls even if he couldn't save them from whatever earthly punishment they faced.

And Micaiah Jones? He'd hanged for his crimes, but not until he'd spent hours with the reverend. Had he repented of his sins and asked God to forgive him before his day of reckoning? Only God, and possibly Jude Browning, knew.

"I heard wagons coming down the lane. Is it Caleb and Alanah?"

He turned, saw Isabella walking across the

464

balcony toward him, little Matthew asleep on her shoulder. "Aye."

She reached his side, and his heart twisted at the dark circles under her eyes. He took his son, hoisted him to his shoulder, and felt a tug on his heartstrings as Matthew's pudgy hand fisted in his shirt. Without so much as opening his eyes, the baby's bow lips pursed; then he snuggled up under Connor's chin and relaxed again.

"It's good to see them, but not under these circumstances." Isabella's voice broke, and he had no words to comfort her.

Instead, he wrapped his arm around her and tucked her against his side. She rested her head against his chest, and he dropped a kiss on her temple, feeling the soft brush of her hair along his jaw.

She reached up, enclosed their son's tiny fist inside her hand, and whispered, "He would've wanted it this way, don't you think? To go . . . to go quickly . . ."

"Aye." Tears stung Connor's eyes, but he blinked them away. "He would no' have wanted it any other way."

ACKNOWLEDGMENTS

We've come to the last of the Natchez Trace Novels. It's been fun to write this series. I learned so much about life in the eighteenth century and hope I conveyed to my readers a bit of what the time period was like.

As always, the entire Tyndale team has been amazing to work with: my editors, graphic design, publicity and marketing, sales, and everyone in between. It's a joy to work with you all, and I'm honored to have the opportunity.

I appreciate my husband for never ever complaining if the house isn't spotless or the laundry isn't done or if supper isn't on the table . . . or even on the horizon! So glad you love fruit, peanut butter, and cereal.

And last, but certainly not least, thank you, dear reader, for going on this journey with me.

DISCUSSION QUESTIONS

1. At the beginning of *The Crossing at Cypress Creek,* Caleb O'Shea and Alanah Adams are each facing significant issues from their pasts and in their present lives. How do they cope with these problems? When you hit a roadblock or come to a crossroads in life, how do you decide what step to take next?

2. Both Caleb and Alanah's uncle Jude note that the hearts of men all around the world contain evil. Do you agree with that assessment? How do their opinions change, if at all, throughout the story? Read Romans 7:14-25. What does the apostle Paul say about doing right and wrong?

3. Caleb is reluctant to face his family after so many years away. How does Connor welcome him? What does Quinn do?

Consider the Prodigal Son story (Luke 15:11-32). What other parallels or similarities can you draw between the biblical account and this novel?

4. After the deaths of their parents and aunt, Alanah and her sister are left under their uncle's thumb. Are Jude's demands and concern for his nieces valid? How should a guardian balance the cost of living in a dangerous place with the calling to preach the Word of God? If you were counseling Jude, what advice would you give him about caring for his charges?

5. Having fulfilled his obligation to see a fellow crewman safely home, why does Caleb stay in the Natchez District?

6. Alanah admits that her uncle's "eye for an eye" style is different from her father's message of grace and forgiveness, and it's hard for her to reconcile the two. Is one idea better or more biblical than the other, or are there times when both are justified? When you feel you've been wronged, which side do you tend to land on?

7. When Caleb meets William Wainwright, he makes an observation about wealthy

men who "made their livings on the backs of others, and no matter where he went, he didn't expect that to change." Is Caleb being fair to label William in this way? Does his opinion of William change as they work together? When you consider the history of the United States, in what ways does this statement ring true across the decades? Is it still true today?

8. As the loggers continue chopping down trees around Cypress Creek, Alanah worries that she'll lose her livelihood. What does she come to realize by the end of the story? What things in your life might need to be destroyed in order to make way for new growth?

9. Even after repenting of past mistakes, Caleb feels undeserving of any good things in his life. Why do you think he feels that way? What does God promise He will do when a person seeks Him and turns his or her life around?

10. Jude struggles with the calling God has given him, frustrated by the lack of results from his preaching. What did you think of Jude at first? Why isn't he being more effective in reaching the lost souls around

Cypress Creek? Did your opinion of him change over the course of the story? What biblical character does he remind you of?

11. As Alanah and Caleb grow closer to each other, she wonders, "When did one cross the threshold from courtship to lust to outright wanton behavior?" Is she right to believe that Caleb is trustworthy and will honor her with integrity? Whose responsibility is it to maintain safe boundaries in relationships outside of marriage? How would you answer her question?

12. What encouragement does Isabella offer to Alanah when they discover Betsy missing? Where do you turn when you face troubles in your life?

13. What events from Micaiah Jones's childhood shaped him into the man he's become? What would it take for a vicious man like this to be forgiven by God? By Alanah? By you? How might Micaiah's life have been different if someone had shown him grace and mercy? What do you think becomes of Micaiah ultimately?

14. Jude suggests that when he refused to go where God was leading him, God

brought people to the reverend's door, even if that meant innocent lives were put in danger. Do you agree with his assessment? Does God cause or allow difficulties to come into a person's life for a greater purpose?

15. As the family gathers at Breeze Hill, how do you imagine their stories continuing to play out?

ABOUT THE AUTHOR

Christian Booksellers Association bestselling author **Pam Hillman** writes inspirational historical romance. Her novels have won or been finalists in the Inspirational Reader's Choice, the EPIC eBook Awards, and the International Digital Awards.

Pam was born and raised on a dairy farm in Mississippi and spent her teenage years perched on the seat of a tractor raking hay. In those days, her daddy couldn't afford two cab tractors with air-conditioning and a radio, so Pam drove an old model B Allis Chalmers. Even when her daddy asked her if she wanted to bale hay, she told him she didn't mind raking. Raking hay doesn't take much thought, so Pam spent her time working on her tan and making up stories in her head. Now that's the kind of life every girl should dream of.

Visit her website at www.pamhillman.com.

The employees of Thorndike Press hope you have enjoyed this Large Print book. All our Thorndike, Wheeler, and Kennebec Large Print titles are designed for easy reading, and all our books are made to last. Other Thorndike Press Large Print books are available at your library, through selected bookstores, or directly from us.

For information about titles, please call:
(800) 223-1244

or visit our website at:
gale.com/thorndike

To share your comments, please write:
Publisher
Thorndike Press
10 Water St., Suite 310
Waterville, ME 04901